An *Atlanta Journal-Constitution*
Best Book of the Year

"Positively breathtaking."
—*Booklist* (starred review)

"Dark and comedic."
—*Redbook*

"[Rose Mae's] journey pulses
with fierce determination."
—*People* (a "Great Escapes" pick)

"Powerful."
—*Washington Post*

"Fast-paced and darkly funny."
—*Cleveland Plain Dealer*

"Riveting."
—*Publishers Weekly*

"A rollicking good time."
—*Kirkus Reviews*

Praise for

Backseat Saints

"[A] cleverly twisted mix of comedy, mystery, and new Southern Gothic . . . practically dares you to stop reading from the very first sentence."
—*Atlanta Magazine*

"The work of Joshilyn Jackson is genius and she proves it again with BACKSEAT SAINTS . . . she uses the finely honed sense of irony and the absurd that characterize the best Southern novelists to not only give faces to a very important issue, but to do it in a most entertaining way . . . Although not reading Jackson's earlier works would in no way diminish a reading of BACKSEAT SAINTS, it's something I heartily recommend."
—*Las Vegas Review Journal*

"[It] soars . . . magical . . . the work of a first-rate writer."
—*BookPage*

"Builds to a nail-biting 'Who's at the door?!' climax."
—*Minneapolis Star Tribune*

"Jackson wraps these frequently examined themes in quirky humor and refreshing twists. Flannery O'Connor meets Dave Barry."
—*Newark Star-Ledger*

"A book full of her trademark sly wit, endearingly off-kilter characters, and utterly riveting plot twists."
—*Sacramento Bee*

"Witty, moving . . . a 'Hot Read.'"
—*New Orleans Times-Picayune*

"Jackson writes real, raw, and emotional stories about flawed women and the powers of faith. The strength of her characters lie in their ability to overcome obstacles, rise above difficulties and hardship, and stay true to themselves. Her novels are riveting, emotional, and passionate and this one is not to be missed."

—BookFinds.com

"Absorbing and rewarding . . . Jackson peels back Rose's hard edges and resignation to reveal a smart, earnest, brave, and surprisingly hopeful young woman who yearns to make a better life for herself."

—*Booklist* (starred review)

"An unputdownable story about love, survival, and shedding the past. Rose Mae Lolly is tough, passionate, funny, and fierce, one hell of a heroine to guide us through one hell of an adventure. Any time Joshilyn Jackson is in the driver's seat, I'm along for the ride."

—Michelle Richmond, author of *The Year of Fog* and *No One You Know*

"A riveting read. Rose Mae is strong and determined and you will cheer for her until the dramatic conclusion. This is Jackson at her best."

—BookLoons.com

"Readers everywhere will rejoice to be back in the land of *gods in Alabama*. BACKSEAT SAINTS is a heart-thrilling, can't-stop-reading book about the unique and unforgettable Rose Mae Lolley. Loved this novel."

—Michael Lee West, author of *Mermaids in the Basement*

"Inspiring . . . A wonderfully written story and a great read . . . The book left me breathless. I actually realized I was holding my breath because I was so addicted and involved in Ro's journey."

—ReaderViews.com

Also by Joshilyn Jackson

gods in Alabama
Between, Georgia
The Girl Who Stopped Swimming

Backseat Saints

JOSHILYN JACKSON

GRAND CENTRAL
PUBLISHING

NEW YORK   BOSTON

For Lydia of Netzer, the patron saint of never being wrong.

Copyright © 2010 by Joshilyn Jackson
Reading Group Guide Copyright © 2011 by Hachette Book Group
"Rose Mae Rambles" Copyright © 2011 by Joshilyn Jackson
"Rose Mae's Reading List" Copyright © 2011 by Joshilyn Jackson

Grand Central Publishing
Hachette Book Group
237 Park Avenue
New York, NY 10017

www.HachetteBookGroup.com

Printed in the United States of America

Originally published in hardcover by Grand Central Publishing.

First Trade Edition: May 2011
10 9 8 7 6 5 4 3 2 1

Grand Central Publishing is a division of Hachette Book Group, Inc.
The Grand Central Publishing name and logo is a trademark of Hachette Book Group, Inc.

The publisher is not responsible for websites (or their content) that are not owned by the publisher.

The Library of Congress has cataloged the hardcover edition as follows:

Jackson, Joshilyn
  Backseat saints / Joshilyn Jackson. — 1st ed.
  p. cm.
  ISBN 978-0-446-58234-6
  1. Abused women—Fiction. 2. Abusive men—Fiction. 3. Spousal abuse—
Fiction. 4. Family secrets—Fiction. 5. Domestic fiction. I. Title.
  PS3610.A3525B33 2010
  813'.6—dc22
                                                    2009032518

ISBN 978-0-446-58237-7 (pbk.)

Book design by Charles Sutherland

ACKNOWLEDGMENTS

I'm so ridiculously over-blessed.

This is my fourth book with Caryn Karmatz Rudy, and she is like editorial heroin. I'm addicted to her keen insight and insatiable love of getting the words right, and so she is hereby forbidden from moving to France to be a perfumier and/or running in front of a taxi. Jacques de Spoelberch has been my agent and good friend ever since I pulled his name out of a book and he pulled my letter out of his slush pile. I cannot do without either of them.

I'm privileged to have a mighty army of friends and advocates at my publishing house who fight with flaming swords to help my work find its readership: Jamie Raab, Martha Otis, Karen Torres, Chris Barba, Emily Griffin, Amanda Englander, Harvey-Jane Kowal, Evan Boorstyn, Elly Weisenberg, Miriam Parker, Nancy Wiese, Nicole Bond, Peggy Boelke, Anne Twomey, Liz Connor, Thom Whatley, Toni Marotta, Les Pockell, and Cheryl Rozier.

The above list hardly covers it. I have endless thanks for everyone at Grand Central Publishing; they gave me my dream job. And thanks to the host of righteous handsellers in bookstores of every stripe who have allowed me to keep it. I am hugely indebted to all of them, from Jake Reiss and the Alabama Booksmith Gang who were kind enough to read my first book in MS form, to the bookseller halfway across the country that I have never met who just put a copy of *Backseat Saints* in the hands of a reader and said, "Oh, you have to try this one!"

I misplace modifiers as if they were my keys, and sometimes I think I am on a mission to let no comma pass unspliced. It is terrifying to think I once taught English to America's youth. God bless copyeditors in general and Sona Vogel in particular. STET!

Big thanks and night whispers to the community of writers and readers and friends who give me their time, support, patience, and martini recipes: Lydia Netzer, Karen Potsie Abbott, Sara Fonzie Gruen (Wait, did I just by the process of elimination make myself Ralph Malph?), Anna Schachner, Julie Oestreich, Mir Kamin, my Best Beloveds at Faster Than Kudzu, and the crew of foul reprobates who WoW around with me in BoB. Lok'tar Ogar!

Jill James put me up for weeks so I could learn firsthand how a small-town southern girl would see the gorgeous, eclectic, and endlessly fascinating Bay Area, and she went with me to have our cards read and our auras cleansed. (They were filthy.) Tarot maven Deb Richardson read for Rose.

Boundless thanks to the quiet heroes of Building Futures with Women and Children (especially Dr. Liz Nickels) in San Leandro, California. They are working tirelessly to end violence against women, and their input was invaluable.

My family (Scott, Sam, Maisy Jane, Bob, Betty, Bobby, Julie, Daniel, Erin Virginia, Jane, Allison) and my extended family (Macland Presbyterian Church, especially the very Slanted Sidewalk-ers and smallgroup) are my living home. Thanks for reminding me daily that Love wins.

Most of all, I thank you for reading.

PART I:

∽

A MARRIAGE MADE
OF SWORDS

Amarillo, Texas, 1997

CHAPTER

∽

1

IT WAS AN AIRPORT gypsy who told me that I had to kill my husband. She may have been the first to say the words out loud, but she was only giving voice to a thing I'd been trying not to know for a long, long time. When she said that it was him or me, the words rang out like church bells, shuddering through my bones. For two days, they sat in the pit of my belly, making me sick. I had no reason to trust her, and I'd as soon take life advice from a Chinese take-out fortune cookie as believe in tarot cards, but I'd lived with Thom Grandee long enough to recognize the truth, no matter how it came to me.

So on Thursday morning, I got my Pawpy's old gun, and I lay for my husband near Wildcat Bluff. Thom liked to run a trail out there. It was too far from the picnic grounds to attract most day-trippers, and he got his miles in early, when he could trust it would be his alone. That day he had me for secret company.

Not two hours ago, I'd gotten up before the sun to make him real biscuits. I'd cut Crisco into flour until it felt soft, like powdered velvet. I'd mixed the dough and rolled it and pressed out circles with the top of a juice glass. I'd fried bacon and then cooked two eggs sunny-side up in the grease. I had loaded his grits with salt and cheese and put thick pats of butter to melt on everything that looked like it could hold butter. There must have been a thousand calories in fat alone floating on that plate.

I'd often made him devil-breakfasts like this after fights, so I hadn't thought of it as a last meal. It was more of an absurd apology. Like me saying, "Baby, I'm scared I might blow holes in you later, but look, I made you the naughty eggs." Last night I'd made sex for him, too, in the same way, buttery slick and fat with all the things he liked best.

An hour before the sex, he'd held my head sideways in his big hand, my other cheek pressed into the cool plaster of the wall. I'd been pinned, limbs flailing helpless sideways, while he ran four fast punches down one side of my back. Then he'd let me go and I'd slid down the wall into a heap and he'd said, "Lord, Ro, why do you push me like that?"

I didn't say a word. He knew the answer. We both knew; I was a good wife most times, but I was made like nesting dolls. I had something bad, some other girl, buried way down in the meat of me. That inside girl was the thing that needed to be hit, that deserved it, and I called it to her. Last night, I'd lay coiled on the floor at Thom's feet, wondering why a big man like him couldn't hit through, could never hit me hard enough to reach her.

On Tuesday morning, I'd driven my elderly neighbor, Mrs. Fancy, to the airport. She'd come over the week before with a plate of her hot cheese cornbread and asked me if I would drive her. She was on a fixed income, and I knew four days of airport parking would be a trial for her, so I'd lied and said I'd love to spend a solid hour fighting highway traffic. I owed her more than a ride to the airport, as good as she had been to me.

"We can take my Honda," Mrs. Fancy had said, smiling her thanks at me with her brown eyes squirrel bright. "You're saving me the parking, Ro. At least let me save you the gas."

Since my ancient Buick got about twelve miles a gallon with the wind behind me, I was happy enough to take her in the Civic. That would have been the end of it, if I hadn't helped Mrs. Fancy tote in all her luggage. The gypsy was standing near the airport's little coffee shop like she'd been waiting for me. Like she'd known that I was coming.

That gypsy looked at me and knew me. She saw me whole, inside and out, as if my skin was made of glass. She laid her tarot cards for me, and that reading . . . it was like she took my life and ran it through a Cuisinart. She told me it was Thom or me, and God help me, I believed her. As I drove home after, I was shaking so hard I like to run off the road. I pulled onto the shoulder and sat, trying to remember how to make my lungs work right. My hands gripped the steering wheel so tight, the knuckles had gone bloodless. As I looked at them, a chill, small voice rose up inside of me, not shaking at all. It said, clear and cold, *What we got here is an almost anonymous car for three days. That could be right useful.*

So instead of taking the Honda back to Mrs. Fancy's garage, I'd parked it on a busy street a few blocks over. The hours until Mrs. Fancy's return began ticking backwards in my head, like a countdown. I was set to pick her up come Friday, so this muggy Thursday morning was my last chance. As I'd made Thom's final, butter-logged breakfast, my eat-in kitchen had looked as fake as a movie set, the sunflowers nodding cheerful on the wallpaper, the mellow old linoleum gleaming under its fresh coat of Mop & Glo. I'd whisked about, wiping down the countertop and washing the cook pans like I was an alive cartoon, hand drawn into a sunshiny kitchen.

"You trying to kill me, woman?" Thom had said when I'd set the plate in front of him. My mouth had gone slack, and he'd grinned up at me. He'd tucked into the bacon, eyes closing as he chewed. "I can feel my arteries hardening, but my tongue don't much care." I'd managed to get my lips to close before drool fell out. He'd broken the yolk with one of the biscuits and said, "You're gonna get me as fat as your damn dog."

Gretel had thumped her tail on the floor in honor of the word *dog*, or maybe the word *fat*. She knew both words meant her. Gretel was mine. She was a khaki-colored mutt, mostly hound dog, but

Thom always said at least one of her ancestors must have been a piece of carpet, as much time as she spent sprawled out snoozing on the floor. I'd listened to the real sound of her tail on the linoleum and thought to myself, *This is how to kill a man. I keep myself believing I won't, but I keep going, until I am there and already doing it.*

It was a trick I was playing on myself, and it worked even though I knew I was playing it.

Thom left early. Before his run, he had to drop Fat Gretel off to get her shots, then go by his daddy's main store and put an antique Winchester in the safe. He practically had to drag poor Gretel; she knew a car ride alone with Thom meant the vet. Thirty seconds after the front door shut, I was butt-up under the kitchen sink, digging my Pawpy's old .45 revolver out from the stack of rags behind my cleaning products. We had another .45 and a .38 at the house, both automatics, but they were registered. Not even Thom knew I had Pawpy's. A gun this old and unused was off the books even before I stole it out of a shoebox in my daddy's closet and carted it halfway across America. It's the kind of gun a certain type of cop would like to have on hand. A "drop weapon," they call it, because they can lay it down by the body of a bad man and say that he pulled first.

The pin had broken off years ago, and since revolvers don't have safeties, I took the barrel out to travel it. Until I put the barrel back in and latched it, it was only two lumps of inert metal. I dropped both pieces in a Target bag. Then I ran back to our room to grab a handful of bullets out of the gun safe. While I was there, I changed into baggy, dark jeans and a floppy T-shirt, tucking my long dark hair under a baseball cap. Short as I was, in these clothes I looked like a kid. No neighbor, catching a glimpse of me trit-trotting down the street near school bus time, could possibly think of pretty, feminine Ro Grandee.

I jogged to Mrs. Fancy's car and got in. I shoved my gun under the passenger seat, then I started up the car and headed out to Wildcat Bluff. On the flat land behind me, Amarillo stuck up like an ugly thumb, and I was glad when the rare hills near the bluff began to hide it. I parked in a pull-in lot that bellied up to the woods, a mile and change past the lot Thom favored.

Counting the time it would take for him to finish his errands, I was a good half hour ahead of him, but I found myself running down the trail like he was fast after me. The Target bag banged against my leg, the loose bullets jangling. I made myself slow to a measured jog and breathe deep, scanning the woods for the right spot every time the trail took a sharp turn. *Ready, Teddy, hands rock steady*, as Daddy used to say when he was teaching me to shoot. He'd started me on .22s when I was so small that the knock back from a .38 would have pitched me over.

At a hairpin curve near the middle of Thom's route, my gaze caught on an underdark beneath the waxy leaves of a thicket of ground ivy. I paused. Peering down, I could just make out the lip of a long ditch, running like a crossbar to the point of the trail, about a yard past the first row of trees. Perfect.

I slid myself into the woods, easing between the questing offshoots of a honeysuckle vine. I curved my spine to limbo under branches. I slipped each foot between the high fronds of ground fern to the dirt underneath, precise, like I was stepping into strappy shoes. Once off the trail, I looked back the way I came and saw every leaf unbent, every twig unbroken. Even Davy Crockett wouldn't think so much as a rabbit had passed. Some days it's good to be slight.

Some days it's not; I could feel the bruises running in a chain down my back, left of my spine, four in a vertical row. The purple black bloom in the center of each was the size of Thom Grandee's fist, and the yellow and pale green mottling was different around each, like the off-sparks from a firework caught in a picture on my skin. They ached me something fierce as I squatted to check the trail's visibility through the green haze of leaves.

Down in the ditch, I'd have a clear view up the slope. I would see him coming. He'd be at the top of the gentle hill, the rising sun's light in his face. I'd wait to shoot till I could see the whites of his eyes. Better yet, I'd watch his Roman profile pass, his short forehead leading directly into his long, straight nose, his wide mouth set in a line as he pushed himself. His blond hair would be darkened down by sweat. I knew every line of his face; I loved them all. The beauty of my laying at the hairpin was that I would see him going, too. His familiar face might stay my wifely hand as he passed, but I could bury two bullets in the anonymous back of his head.

As I lowered myself down into the ditch, motion caught my eye. At the other end, perched on a branch, a long-legged burrowing owl was swiveling his head around in a perfect half circle to face me. He'd been sitting still, and his mottled feathers blended with the shadows, so that he'd been invisible until he moved. He was perched on a root, head poked up over the lip. He was unconcerned, sure that he was not what I was hunting. Still, his round eyes, gold and blank, looked mildly affronted by my intrusion.

"Leave if you don't like it. I have business here," I told him, but I didn't sound like myself. The words came out pure Alabama, neglected consonants, long vowels.

If the owl had had shoulders, he would have shrugged. He was a witness, not a judge. I kneeled down in my half of the ditch, and he stayed in his.

I said, "Lord, I am talking to owls. I might well be crazy enough to shoot my husband." Now I could hear the sharp, small twang Texas had given me. Half a dozen years here, and my voice had grown corners.

The owl fluffed himself. He didn't like me breaking the quiet morning. I shouldn't be making noise anyway.

I scrabbled in the Target bag, finding the loose barrel by feel and then picking out six bullets. I palmed five and slotted the last one into an empty chamber. It made a snicking sound, then the whispery rub of metal on metal as it slid home. And there I stuck, one bullet loaded, as if I were undecided.

"Nothin' left to decide," I whispered. Pure Alabama again. I didn't sound like Mrs. Ro Grandee, Thom's cool-mouthed wife whose tongue would not melt butter. I sounded like Rose Mae Lolley, a girl I'd buried years ago, when I was eight, the year my mother disappeared. She left her rosary and took her flowered shoes, the ones she seldom wore because the toes were stuffed with money.

Thom knew Rose Mae was there, though. He'd known she was in me from the very night we met. Sometimes I wondered if that bad girl hidden in the deeps of me was the thing he really loved.

Seven years ago, at three A.M. on a warm spring morning, he'd come into the diner where Rose Mae Lolley was working. She was wearing the mask—warm smile, light step—of the fake girl she'd grown over herself. Rose Mae had worn that face over hers all the time, every waking minute for almost two years now, since the moment she'd figured she'd taken enough beatings for her long-gone mother and lit out from her daddy's house. She'd waitressed her way west down the coast, every few months trading one small town with a bad job and a worse boyfriend for another, much the same.

She'd yet to find a town or job or man that made her feel safe enough to take that face off. At work, her sweet exterior upped her tips, and her most recent home was a cheap furnished room with kitchen privileges and no privacy. Her landlady, Kim, claimed to be a lesbian, but Rose guessed she had given up women in favor of Captain Morgan. Kim would barrel into Rose's room at all hours, demanding to know where the salt had gotten to or asking if Rose had taken any messages. She never knocked or apologized, even the time she burst in on a freshly showered Rose wearing nothing but a sheer white bra.

"You ain't got drugs in here, do ya?" Kim'd said that time.

"Of course not," said Rose in her best pep-squad girl voice, picking up her towel. She was trying not to glance at her bed. A pair of red fuzzy dice was lying beside Rose's uniform. The dice were Kim's, and Rose had stolen them out of the coat closet. She planned to take them to work and sneak to hang them in the short-order cook's car. He seemed like he was a single pair of fuzzy dice away from lighting out for Vegas, and since he couldn't keep his hands off her ass, Rose Mae wanted to give him a nudge.

Kim didn't notice the dice. She didn't seem to notice Rose's state of undress, either, even though Rose Mae Lolley laid bare was worth seeing: long waist, tightly curved hips, creamy skin. Kim turned laboriously and began her drunken shuffle out. *Some lesbian*, thought Rose, tossing the towel over the dice in case Kim looked back.

"I don't do drugs," Rose called after her, still working the perky, and Kim grunted in a way that could have meant satisfied or disappointed.

With no safe space, Rose kept her smiling shell on all the time, but some days it felt as thin as the candy pink cotton of her retro fifties waitress uniform. The uniform had a white Peter Pan collar and a miniature apron. It was cut to fit and the skirt was short, and when Thom Grandee came in on a double date that first evening, his girl didn't like that uniform one bit.

The sign by the door said, "Seat Yourself," so Thom did, sliding into one side of a four-top booth. His date followed, and the other couple sat down across. Rose was the only waitress on at this hour. She could tell by looking they were from the A&M Kingsville campus. She'd pegged them as sports boys, taking their dates for eggs after the victory party.

And it had been a victory. Rose Mae could smell it on the boys as she came around the counter bringing the coffeepot and four plastic-coated menus, a mix of pheromones and beer and fresh male sweat. The smell of win.

They were both good-looking boys, but her eye went right to Thom. He was six feet tall with a thick, meaty build that said football to her, and she liked the Roman nose. She also liked the way he eyed her as she swayed toward them. To the other couple she was a vague pink waitress shape, bringing menus. Thom looked.

Thom's date had a high ponytail that was beginning to unravel into fronds onto her pretty neck. She had a mound of bangs, flat on the back side, teased into a rigid foam of curls that humped over her forehead. This late, her Breck was beginning to fail her, and the bang puff was listing to starboard.

When Thom spent too long looking at Rose's face before the inevitable stealthy eye slide down her body, Rose could feel the girl bristle up. Rose was only twenty-one, but this girl looked young even to her. A freshman with a glamour shot fake ID. The girl narrowed her eyes, venomous, telling Rose plain that she wasn't used to chapped-lipped waitrons with no tan stealing her male gazes. She'd no doubt been the prettiest girl in her high school, but Rose was willing to bet that it had been a small school.

"Good morning!" Rose gave them her best three A.M. cheerful, passing out the menus. "Welcome to Duff's. I'm Ro. I'll be taking care of you this morning."

They all had flipped their mugs right-side up, so Rose leaned across to pour coffee, first for the dark-haired boy, then for his date.

"Morning," Thom said back.

He was the only one who spoke to her. She turned to pour his coffee. And then, because he was looking at her face again, not her tits and not his date, looking at her like she was a person, she found herself saying, "So, what position do you play?"

"Outfield," he said. "Sometimes third base."

She shook her head. "I asked what position you played, mister. I didn't ask what you did in spring to stay in shape."

He grinned then, giving her an assessing nod, like he was adding smart and sly to the pretty. "Strong-side safety."

"Oh. Fast boy," she said, and started filling his date's cup.

"What the hell are you doing?" his date demanded, bangs atremble.

Rose stopped and tipped the pot upright, smile fading. "I'm sorry?"

"Did I order coffee?" Bangs asked.

Rose said, "I'm sorry. You turned your cup over."

"Yeah. Because I want hot cocoa."

"Sure thing," said Rose. "I'll get that while y'all look over the menu."

"What can I get for you today?" the girl said to her friend across the table. "What would you like to drink? Would you care for a beverage? You'd think you'd get those lines on, like, the very first day of waitress school."

Rose felt the fever of a blush rising in her cheeks, and she knew it was painfully visible on her pale skin. Dropping her eyelids, she focused on her feet so that none of them could see the furious deeps in her eyes. She held her hand very still to keep from pouring scalding coffee over that bang puff. She could practically smell the ashy scent the girl's hair products would release, could hear her surprised cry as the hot liquid seared her scalp and ran down to blister that smug face. While the girl was screaming and clawing at herself, Rose would say, calmly, "You turn your cup over in a diner, it means you want coffee." Then she'd call an ambulance.

"I apologize," Rose said. Her voice was trembling with the effort that it took to stay her hand. She picked up the cup with the small splash of black liquid in the bottom. Made herself pivot. Forced herself to walk away.

Duff's was quiet. She heard her every footfall on the floor. There were the two obligatory old drunk guys silently nursing coffee at the counter, yellow-skinned because they had maybe half a working liver left between them. They hadn't asked out loud for their coffee, just flipped their mugs over and waited to be served. A couple in the back had cuddled up on the same side of their booth, whispering to each other. No one was feeding the juke. She could hear Bangs saying something low and giggly. She caught the word *Casper*.

Her blush was traveling, flushing the backs of her pale, bare legs. The girl's friend was laughing with her now in a high-pitched trill that sounded to Rose like a mean pig squealing.

Back behind the counter, Rose dumped a packet of Swiss Miss with minimallows into a clean mug. That girl, Bangs, was wearing a sundress, crisp green and new. She had a sheer white sweater thrown around her shoulders. It was a frivolous sweater, the kind a doting mother would buy along with new bedding and a tiny dorm refrigerator. Rose would bet her week's tips that that same mother kept Bangs's girlhood room intact, waiting for Christmas and spring break.

And meanwhile here was Rose, prettier and smarter and nicer in public, drifting motherless from town to town. Rose lived alone in her dank room with no lock on the door. Even Kim's damn cat, Boo, could open Rose's door. He'd stand on the back of the couch and bang the knob with his scabby paw. He was all over scabs. A flea allergy, Kim said, but she never took him to the vet. He'd creep into Rose's room when she was sleeping and slide under her blankets to press against her side, desperate and moist. Rose was allergic to cats, but she dry-swallowed Benadryl and let Boo press and press against her, because she was that desperate right back.

She acted like a girl in hiding, but her father was too busy, what with his part-time construction work and his full-time drinking, to ever come looking. No one else came, either. She daydreamed her long-gone mother would burst in, crying, "I'm so sorry! This time I'll take you with me!" or that her high school boyfriend, Jim Beverly, would reappear to shoo the foul cat away and say, "Here you are! Thank God, I finally found you!" They never came. The room, the cat, the diner, the chafing mask of a happier girl, they were her whole real life, and she was living it.

It should be me in that booth, Rose thought, a college girl like Bangs, smart and busy and worthy, going places with a sharp-looking sports boy watching. For half a minute, bantering about football, the smiling girl with the sass and the bouncy step hadn't been a skin. Rose had really been her, and it had felt like coming home to someplace new and clean.

Bangs could have spared her that thirty seconds, because Bangs had all night. Hell, Bangs had all year, and more years coming.

Rose poured hot water and watched the cocoa foam to life. All Rose had was prettiness, a spoon, and the right to stir the cocoa of bitches until it was smooth. It was too much to swallow, and Rose found she had literally built up a fine and bitter coat of spit inside her mouth.

She couldn't help it. She had nothing, and her thirty seconds had been ruined. She crouched down, her sweet second skin finally off, disappearing behind the counter. She pursed her mouth into a kiss and bent her head over the mug. The long wad of spit drooled down into the cocoa. Rose stirred it in. She was smiling now, a genuine and ugly thing, so wide that it showed her back teeth.

When she looked up, Thom Grandee was leaning over the counter. She froze, more naked in that moment than she had been the day Kim came barreling into her room. He saw her. He saw the real Rose Mae Lolley, no longer hidden by Ro-the-perky-waitress. His face wasn't readable.

She stood up, slow, holding the mug, trying to call back her sugary smile.

He said, "I came to get change," and his smile was plain and open.

She blinked stupidly at the dollar he held out, uncertain. Maybe he had only just poked his big head over the counter when she looked up?

"For the jukebox?" he said.

"It takes dollars," Rose said, her voice rusty. "It's one song for a quarter, but if you put in the dollar, you get five."

"That's cool," he said, retracting the money.

The closest drunk said, "Refill?" It seemed he was blessed with the power of speech after all. The red vinyl on his stool creaked as he shifted his butt, backing away from the surprise of his own voice.

Thom said, "Want me to tote her cocoa back to the table for ya?"

He couldn't hold the plain face he was making anymore. His

eyebrow quirked and his bland blue eyes changed. They filled up with enough devil to match her. He had seen.

She felt another blush coming. "I'll make her a new one."

She pulled the spoon out, but he was already reaching for the mug.

"I'm Thom Grandee," he said.

"Ro," she said. She let him take the mug.

"I saw that," he said, and for a second she thought he meant the spit. Then he gestured with his free hand to the gold name tag pinned north of her left breast. "Rose Mae," he read. "Go ahead and get that guy his coffee. No worries. I'll take this over."

She went to pour for the drunk, peeking out from under her lashes as Thom Grandee walked back to the table with the cocoa. He handed it to Bangs.

The second drunk was pointing at the doughnuts in the cake stand. Rose got him one and then picked up her pad, prepping to check on the couple in the back booth and then go take Thom Grandee's order. All the while, she watched him watching Bangs sip spit.

As she came across to their booth, Thom pried the mug from Bangs's fingers. All four were laughing and talking now. As she came toward them, Thom was saying to Bangs, "Didn't you go to kindergarten? Didn't you learn to share?" and as Rose came close he lifted the cup and drank, and his eyes met hers over the rim. He was drinking in her spit, greedy, taking all of it, though the cocoa was still so hot that it must have been scalding him. He opened his throat and drank it down and didn't for one second look away from Rose.

"Oh, my God! You hog!" Bangs said, laughy-teasy. "Now you have to buy me another."

"What can I get y'all to eat?" Rose asked cautiously.

They ordered their breakfasts, and at the end Thom Grandee said, "And Caroline wants another cocoa." He grinned at Rose. "Exactly like the first."

She recognized him then. He was every boy that had ever belonged to her, from her daddy on down. He'd recognized her, too, when he'd peered over the counter and seen what was under the sweet waitress. He liked the whole package. He would be back. Rose smiled and walked away.

She'd been the prettiest girl in her high school, too. Maybe she didn't get her diploma, but she'd damn well learned how boys worked. He'd come back to the diner alone, soon, hoping to follow the blush he'd seen on the backs of her legs all the way up, as far as she would let him. Tomorrow, maybe the next day, she would see him coming toward her through the big front window, moving fast in his swingy athlete's gait. She would have to stay ahead of him and keep him coming toward her, fast and sometimes angry. She'd stay in sight but out of reach. If she kept him on the far side of that window glass long enough, she could keep him always coming toward her.

He was coming toward her now.

I could hear him, his big feet pounding up the trail.

My lips were moving soundlessly, but I recognized the shape of the words. *Hail Mary, full of grace. The Lord is with thee.* My mouth was getting a jump start on the thousand rosaries I'd have to say to get clean after killing him.

I felt the vibrations of his pounding run, heard his sure and steady gait. I socketed the barrel into the well-oiled cradle of the gun. I felt more than heard it slide home while my lips shaped, *Blessed art thou among women and blessed is the fruit of thy womb, Jesus.*

I saw the top of his head clear the gentle upslope of the trail. I pulled the hammer back, waiting for the cool metal to shift in my hands and come alive. This gun, put together, was stronger than the sum of the lumps that had bounced around in the bottom of the bag. I'd brought it with me all the way from Alabama, an object stolen directly from my childhood. It belonged to Rose Mae Lolley, not to me. Rose Mae had held this gun a thousand times, and each time, it had felt as if her blood was circulating through it. It had always done her will as surely as her own hands did.

But not today. Pawpy's revolver was a dead bird cradled in my fingers. No heartbeat.

I could feel the air Thom Grandee pushed ahead of him wafting past me, bringing me his scent. I looked down the barrel and saw that it was shaking. I was Ro Grandee, righteous in my bruises, shaking my hands to save my husband from myself. I tried to steady them, breathing in so deep it felt like I pulled the air past my lungs into my stomach, swallowing the next words. *Pray for us sinners, now, and the hour of our deaths.*

As the prayer ended, I thought to myself, *Put the gun down. These days even Catholics get divorced.* But if I left or started up with lawyers, he would kill me. The airport gypsy had told me so, and I'd believed her to the marrows of my ill-mended bones. God help me, I believed her still.

Thom Grandee himself had told me he would end me, many times: Across the table during breakfast. With his big hands wrapped around my throat, flexing to close me at his will, then granting me the barest sip of air. When he moved inside me like a savage and I wept with it, it felt so good. Those times it sounded like the sweetest promise ever made. *Don't you ever leave me, Ro. I'll see you dead before I'll let you leave me.* I'd long known I couldn't simply pack a bag and call a lawyer.

But the gypsy had told me he'd also kill me if I stayed. I hadn't ever allowed myself to think that. When she said it out loud, I heard it ring in the deeps of me, true as gospel. One day, and soon, I'd push him so far he couldn't come back. He would put all of his big weight behind his fists and break me and be sorry later. Shooting him was only jump-starting some self-defense. Yet my weak hands shook, and my fingers felt rigid, unable to squeeze, and my mouth was shaping out another silent plea to Mary.

He was rising over the slope like the sun. Two more of his huffing steps and I could see his shoulders. Two more brought me a view of his trim waist, and it was then I realized that he sounded wrong. Thom kept fit, so why that huffing breath? Was it my breath? Was I so loud? His footfalls had a shuffling echo.

I had no time to be distracted by his noises. I sighted him down the length of my trembling barrel, and my vision blurred. I might have been crying. It seemed to me that he left a thin red wake, like he was trailing a single, mournful streamer. I let him be blurry, let the gun come into sharp focus. When I was little, before he even let me shoot a pellet gun, Daddy had shown me this very revolver in two pieces, innocuous. He let me look down the hole and put my finger in it.

"Rose Mae, this is the only safety lesson you will ever need," Daddy said. "But I'm going to tell you ever' time you shoot. Until you know it in your guts. You see down that hole? You must never, never point that hole at anything, at anything, ever, unless you want to see it utterly destroyed." He said it with no irony, while he and I together looked down that very hole, its dark eye looking back at me, the barrel cradled in my daddy's hands.

Now I was sighted on the center of Thom's chest, where I had so many times pressed my ear to hear the boom of his large, red heart. He was ten feet away. I was stiff, half-blind with tears, and I knew then that I would let him pass, unharmed. I was spineless enough to let him kill me, when it came to that. My eyes closed, the gun pointing at air or the owl or Thom or nothing.

I could see my own death, accept it, see his hands close around my throat too hard, too long. But I could not see Thom. At once my hands were loose and easy and my own, and I could squeeze the trigger. So I did.

It seemed only half a second passed between aiming and my eyes closing, between looking at the backs of my eyelids and my hands easing enough to let me pull. I was squeezing even before I felt the scalding tears that were pushed out of my closing eyes on my cheeks. The suddenly living gun contracted in my hands, once, twice, spitting bullets that I felt leave me before I heard the fierce crack of splitting air. Eyes still closed, tears dripping off my jaw now to spatter down my shirt, I heard a terrible, hupping yelp, surprised and not quite human.

A great calm took me, and the gun became so massive and heavy that my hands dropped. The hole pointed into the earth.

I opened my eyes. For a minute I could not understand what I was seeing. Thom was standing, jaw unhinged, still trailing his thin red streamer. He was whole and unshot, upright on the trail. The noise grew, became a howling, and as Thom yelled, "Hold your fire! Hold your fire!" I saw the streamer was my old red leash, saw the tan, crumpled body behind him, at the very apex of the slope. I had missed him, missed him entirely. I had shot my dog.

The noise was Fat Gretel's noise, and I had shot my good, good dog. Time stuttered and slowed so abruptly that the next eight seconds was a series of Polaroid pictures. The first one was Gretel, kicking on the ground, and I understood that Thom had brought my dog with him, running. Gretel had been that huffing echo, and now she was the wretched howling, and all at once I was so angry that the tears stopped.

He was supposed to drop her at the vet, but he must have waited there until she had her shots and then brought her along to make her run. He was always wanting me to run the fat off her, even though I said to leave her be. I got Gret from the pound soon after we married, and she'd lived a sinless life with me for five years now. I didn't often cry, but when I did, she padded around and around me in worried circles, making houndy sorrow-groans in her throat, keeping vigil till I stopped. She had earned the right to spread out happy on the floor and be as fat as she wanted.

We moved forward, all of us, one frame. The owl burst upwards in a panicked ball of feathers, like a flare marking my spot. Gretel howled. Thom, spooked by the owl, yelled, "You fucking moron, hold your fire. We are here!" My mouth gaped open and nothing came out but a thin whine of released air.

He couldn't possibly have heard my breath, but Thom started

toward me. Gretel's howl broke and wavered, becoming a long, betrayed yodel. This lower sound went on and on, as if she would never inhale again. I squatted in the ditch, inert.

He reached the hairpin in two elongated lopes that ate up the ground between us. He was coming to drag me out and kill me. Now. For one frame, I was helpless skin half-filled with air, floppy and useless. In the next frame, I was Rose Mae again. The separation I'd felt earlier ended, and there was no girl inside a girl. I was Rose and here was Thom, coming toward me like always, this time to kill me. There was my dog, hurt on the ground, needing my help, and Thom stood between us. My hands lifted the gun, rock steady, one eye squinched shut, and I went for the head shot. Twice. I had no time for true aim; my bullets whined past his left ear. They came so close that he must have felt the heat of their whistling trail.

Thom guttered to a halt, and I watched him understand that this was not someone shooting. This was someone shooting *at*. He wasn't heading toward a stranger's dumb mistake. He was heading into bullets, purposeful and aimed. He dove sideways as I tried to get a bead on him, his body an indignant line that disappeared into the trees on the left side of the trail.

Gretel stopped yodeling. I listened hard, terrified she was gone, and then caught the sound of her ragged breathing. I could feel a scream building up inside me, swelling, pushing up into my throat. I turned the gun sideways and banged myself in the head with the flat side, hard enough to daze myself and stop it.

Two bullets past Thom's ear. Two in my dog. I had two left. I crouched low in the ditch, gun pointing at the lip. I listened for his creeping sounds to come at me from one side or another. Thom was smart. He would choose a route and come as quiet as he could to the spot the owl had marked. When he looked down into the ditch and saw that the face of the shooter was his Ro's face, maybe there would be a pause in him, a small window where I could finish this. That close, I wouldn't miss. I would have to shoot him if I wanted to live long enough to save Gretel.

Fat Gretel moaned. I heard her feet scuffling against the dirt. I poked my head up just over the lip, alligator style, and there was Thom. He was back on the trail. Bent over her. My hands were steady. My eyes were clear. I lifted Pawpy's gun and lined him up, tracking him. My finger tightened. Two bullets left, and I could feel how perfect the shots were, one in the spine as he bent over, one in the head.

Then he scooped up Gretel. My breath caught and my mouth rounded into a surprised O. He was not creeping through the trees, seeking out the shooter. He was not turning tail and sprinting away as fast as his strong legs could carry him. He was risking himself to rescue my dog. The skin on his back shuddered like a horse's skin, and I knew he felt my sights creeping across him like flies.

He lifted fifty pounds of dog like she was nothing, adrenaline assisting the hours he'd spent lifting weights and running this trail. He started loping away, slow, hampered by my crying dog. He ran serpentine, trying not to be an easy target, but Gretel ruined his balance and his speed, so he was. I could have shot him with no effort. I tracked him, but my finger remained slack against the trigger. His courage and his weighed-down grace knocked me breathless. I watched him risk his hide for a dog he'd never had much use for, saving her because she was mine, because I loved her so. He zigzagged away as fast as he could, all the while feeling the black gaze of the gun on his back.

It was the most romantic thing that I had ever seen.

I'd stopped the Hail Mary a while back, I realized. Now a rhyme was running in my head, from the Grimm's fairy-tale book my mother used to read me when I was too small to shoot anything but a BB gun. *Oh Snowy-white, Oh Rosy-red, Will you beat your lover dead?* It was a poem from a prince, trapped in bear form. He slept on Snow White's hearth, and she and her sister, Rose Red, would beat the snow out of his fur and roll him back and forth between them with their naked feet. He'd say the rhyme to make those rowdy girls be gentle with him.

The bear's poem looped around and around, catching and matching the weaving bob of Thom's head as he ran serpentine away down the trail, ungainly but whole.

My finger stayed lax. Only that morning, I'd lifted my face, open like a posy, for him to lean down and kiss. Only that morning, I'd gotten up early to fix his eggs. Then I'd come out here ahead of him to drop the body I had fed, leave it to keep the ants company in these green woods. Thom's blond head set behind the slope. He was gone. I pulled the gun back into two pieces and dropped them in the bag.

I leaned forward in the ditch and put my face into the earth. I felt roots poking me. I'd starting crying again without noticing. I was crying for Gretel and for my own spineless love. I wept until my bones went liquid, and then I wept them out. I lay against the ditch like a tired piece of rag.

An idle part of me began to wonder where Thom was. I felt like I'd been lying in the dirt and crying for hours, but when I looked at my watch, I saw less than ten minutes had passed. There was a Shell gas not two miles away, and they'd have a pay phone. I wanted to call Thom and ask how Gretel was, where he was taking her, if she was still breathing, but I didn't know where to reach him. Thom's skinflint daddy had yet to join the rest of the world and replace Thom's pager with a mobile phone.

He'd take Gretel to the vet, I thought, and then what? Home? The police station? I sat up straight, pulled up in the sudden understanding that I didn't have to track him down. He would be tracking me, and soon. Men who got shot at called their wives, the very first minute they could.

I scrambled up out of the ditch, clutching my bag. I could not have Thom wondering where his wife had been. Not today, of all days. When his call came, Ro Grandee had to be at home in a daisy yellow skirt and ballet flats, tenderly hand-washing the sticky yolk off Thom's breakfast dishes. I took off for the car at a dead run.

CHAPTER

❦

2

I BLAMED THAT AIRPORT gypsy. I tried to kill Thom Grandee because she'd told me it was him or me. She'd urged me to choose him. I don't know how long she'd been lurking around in Amarillo; I caught her just as she was leaving. If Mrs. Fancy hadn't asked me to drive her to the airport, the gypsy would have left town without me ever knowing she was here, alive and chock-full of dire pronouncements. The airport trip was like that nail that dropped the shoe that lamed the horse that lost the battle. If I hadn't taken Mrs. Fancy, I never would have been laying for my husband in the woods.

Mrs. Fancy was my next-door neighbor, and her baking pans had been on a mission to make me go up a dress size since the day Thom and I had moved into the house. She'd come by with a muffin basket, and when she'd handed it to me, she'd taken aholt of a piece of my arm and breathed up in my face, saying, "It's so nice to see young folks moving back into the neighborhood!" She had puppy breath and a pincery grip. Thom had gotten rid of her as fast as possible, and then I'd leaned against our closed front door, laughing while Thom pretended to nail it shut.

But that didn't stop her from tottering back across the narrow strip of lawn, bringing me baked goods and small talk. She showed me how to feed my sick forsythia bush, and it came back the next spring blooming brighter than ever. She seemed to understand immediately that she shouldn't come by when Thom was home. The first time she saw my arm in a sling, she asked, but only the first time. She accepted my explanation that I'd tripped in the dark with a long blink and a tutting noise. Then she'd made the chewy brownies she'd discovered were my favorite, and she never asked again. Before we'd lived there a year, I'd grown a taste for both her pastries and her undemanding friendship. I found myself crossing that strip of lawn almost as often as she did, carrying homemade lemonade or a pot of flavored coffee. She was my little secret.

Last week she'd come to my porch with a covered plate in one powder-dry paw, asking for a lift to the airport so she could go see her new grandbaby. "My last grandbaby," she called him. She'd smiled at me, and the skin around her eyes had looked like ancient paper, so folded and creased that it might have been used to make a hundred different origami cranes.

"I'd love to drive you," I'd said, and she'd smoothed a strand of hair out of my eyes and gone home, leaving me with five thousand pepper-jacked calories and a Tuesday so overbooked that I was going to have to hire a neighborhood girl to go pee for me.

My plan was to go on my run, grab Mrs. Fancy, drive like a cocaine-addled hell bat to the airport, hurl her and her bags out as I slowed down in the drop-off lane, then do an Olympic-speed grocery store sprint and get a dinner going in the Crock-Pot before I jumped in the shower and headed in to work a shift for Thom's daddy. I ran the cash register at his main store most weekday afternoons, while Joe Grandee sat on his stool by the door to the offices and watched me with his gaze set low, a smolder on my hips.

Last week he'd said to me, "It wouldn't hurt business any if you took that blouse down a button, sugar," just as if my husband wasn't on the phone with a vendor not five feet away.

Even when Thom came over, Joe didn't stop looking at me like I was hot cornbread, buttered up and dripping honey. He elbowed

Thom and said, "Knowing guns like she does, I bet your wife could outsell my best floor man if she got out from behind the counter in that tight blue skirt."

A muscle jumped in Thom's cheek, but Joe was too busy ogling me to notice. He lumbered off to the back to get a Coke. I smiled at Thom and said, "Sales out the ass, he means," to lighten up the mood.

Thom only grunted and said, "Watch your mouth." He didn't have much of a sense of humor when it came to his daddy.

Tuesday morning, I ended my run at Mrs. Fancy's house and rang her doorbell, panting like an animal, my hair scraped back in a sweat-slick tail. She was packed up and ready to go, with three enormous suitcases waiting by her front door. I dragged one in each hand out to the car while Mrs. Fancy followed, carrying the third bag. As I stuffed my two in her Honda's trunk, she set the last bag flat in the driveway and popped it open to show me.

That suitcase paused me. I stared down into a swamp of rabbit-covered receiving blankets and stuffed animals and those weird onesie T-shirts with the snaps in the crotch and a whole stack of blue and yellow baby gowns, the kind that look like pastel lunch bags with drawstrings at the feet.

My gut went soft as taffy. Mrs. Fancy was a widow lady on a fixed income, and she'd bought a whole suitcase full of presents for this grandbaby, even though it was her ninth. She would have to lay out plenty more to take the extra bag on the plane. She could probably have sent the presents FedEx for cheaper, but I could see how it was. She wanted to be there when her daughter opened up that bag. I bent my head and picked up a floppy giraffe doll so she wouldn't see my eyes had glistened up. As soon as I could blink myself back right, I helped her tuck all the gifts back in and loaded that last case.

Digging through those presents cost me time I didn't have to spare. I wove us in and out of traffic in a way that irked the hell out of me when other people did it. Mrs. Fancy sat in the passenger seat, too excited to notice her sweet friend was driving like the very devil. She smiled at me as I got on the highway, and I glimpsed a streak of hot pink lipstick on her teeth.

"Janine only just got married last year," she said, turning to face forward again. She wasn't watching the road, though. Her eyes focused on the horizon like she was already airborne. "She's forty-two. The babiest of all my babies, in her forties. Can you imagine?" I nodded and slipped in between two enormous trucks like one of those crazy little remora fish that lives its whole life darting from shark to shark. "I never thought she'd have children."

Mrs. Fancy had raised her voice to talk over the enraged blast of honking from the trucker I'd cut off, but there was something in her tone that made my ears prick up. She sounded sly, and sly wasn't like her. "A long time ago, she got herself married to a very bad man. Never even finished high school. When she finally got shut of him, she was done with men and all drove to get careered. Never thought this day would come." Mrs. Fancy started rooting in her bag, trying to look anything but crafty, but I could smell crafty coming off her in waves.

"Don't," I said, but she ignored me, or maybe she thought I was talking to the guy in a red Nissan who was trying to slip into my lane.

"She traded that bad husband in for a spine and started her own business. Spring Cleaners, it's called, and she had to hire her own ladies to scrub out her toilet. She got so busy getting other people's houses clean that hers was about to get carried off by the bugs. Seemed to me like she hardly noticed she was getting older, but I kept thinking about this *Newsweek* article I read, something about how a woman her age was more likely to get shot by a terrorist than get a husband.

"Then last year, every time she got on the phone, the name Charles would find itself in my ear. Charles this and Charles that and Charles says. I kept casual because I liked the sound of this Charles. I didn't want to spook her. He seemed like a door opener, you know? The kind who helps you on with your jacket. Sure enough, now my Janine's married, living regular and peaceful, with a sweet little baby. That's all I ever wanted for any of my kids." She was still rooting around in her bag, being careful not to look at me, because her story damn well did have a point, and she was poking Rose Mae's craw with it. "Oh dear, I hope I have my ticket with me. Did you see me get my ticket?"

I glanced down, and I could see that ticket right in the middle. She was digging all around it, though it was one of the three biggest things in her jam-packed handbag. I reached over and jerked it out of her bag and threw it into her lap. I toted her big trash can down to the curb every Tuesday. I fed her cat when she was out of town. In return, she talked to me about her knitting club and her reader's circle at her church, and she made it a point to never ask me why I wore long sleeves all summer. She was deal breaking, I felt like. She was ruining something.

"Thanks, honey," she said, so warm, showing me her lipstick teeth again. I looked at her frail shoulders, her soft lady belly setting on her lap, and mad as I was, I knew I had to help my friend. There was no way she could manage those three suitcases alone, even across Amarillo's teeny airport.

I could feel my tightly scheduled Tuesday start to pull ahead and leave me behind, and that made me madder. I put my blinker on and swapped lanes again, taking the fork that led to hourly parking.

"I'll walk you in," I said, snappish.

"Oh, no, honey. You can just drop me," she said.

"I want to take you in. Really. I like airports," I said, like I'd been born stupid. No one likes airports.

But she brightened and said, "I like them, too! I love to see folks so busy and going places."

I parked and got the trunk unloaded in one-sided silence while Mrs. Fancy hummed and peered about, blind to the smoke leaking out of my ears. I got a cart and trundled all her luggage in. Once inside, she stood blinking, round-eyed as an owl, then started digging in her bag for her ticket again.

"You need to be in this line," I said, impatient. I'd already given up groceries. I could feel dinner and the shower escaping, and I wondered if Joe would still think I could outsell his best floor man if I smelled like a walking armpit. On the other hand, it might get me out of doing the damn shift. "Come with me."

I got her into the right line, but then she couldn't find her ID. I decided I better stay and make sure she got properly checked in. I dug her wallet out from under her travel-size tissue and a herd of Trident gum packs and handed it to her.

She took it absently, peering all around her, and then she poked me with her elbow and whispered, "Look, that's me! That's me at thirty!" She nodded sideways at a slinky brunette who was standing two lines over.

I looked at the brunette, mystified, and then back to Mrs. Fancy.

She said, "It's a game, silly. Mr. Fancy and I used to play it all the time, in airports. We would try to find us, how we would be in twenty years, or thirty, and maybe eavesdrop and see if we were going anyplace interesting. He liked to tease me with his picks! He'd find old crabby couples bickering, and he'd say, 'There we are in fifty years!' Or he'd play sweet, and find the prettiest girl you ever saw and say, 'Now that one is almost you, only not so cute, not so cute.' These days I don't travel much, but when I do, I try to find me when I was a young mother or a newly married lady. I can't hope to find me older, unless someone is being flown home in a box!"

She laughed, but I shifted my feet, uncomfortable. I said, "You have plenty of kick left in you, Mrs. Fancy."

She waved that away. "Only thing older than me in this airport is God," she said. "But I'm telling you, I looked a lot like her when I was thirty."

She nodded her head at the dark-haired lady, a leggy object with a hint of a cleavage and a saucy way of standing. Mrs. Fancy's pow-dered cheeks hung down off her face in ladylike jowls. She wore walking shoes with high-waisted polyester slacks and a blouse in a fussy floral print, but under, I could see good bones and the ruins of a tight and curvy figure.

I sized up the brunette and said, "Welp, you at thirty is . . ." I paused. I couldn't quite bring myself to say "dead sexy" to some-one who smelled so strongly of talcum powder, so I ended with, "a looker."

"I turned some heads," she said, matter-of-fact, and then peeped at me through her lashes, like she knew I'd been thinking dead sexy. Then she spun in a slow circle, peering around until some-thing stopped her.

"I found little you, I think." She tilted her head over to the water fountain where a black-haired girl was standing with her parents. The child was about nine, wearing a stiff, frilled dress that told me there was someone to impress waiting at the other end of the flight. The dad looked relaxed, slouching beside the bags in chinos, but the mother was gussied up in a full face of makeup, and she had teased and sprayed her hair into a shining hump. My guess was she was flying toward in-laws. The mother kept sending one nervous hand down to smooth her girl's pigtail, but it was more like a love pet than grooming.

I looked away. The mother's hair would fall on the plane, and the child's girly dress would be a mass of crumples and likely stained with juice by the time they arrived.

I said, "That's me all right," tight, still too annoyed to play with her. In truth, she'd got me all wrong. At that age I had a long rat of unbrushed hair and hand-me-down clothes from the church box. I spent all my free time with a book, up trees or under the crawl space, reading and hiding from all the chores my mother wasn't there to do.

"Let's find you older," Mrs. Fancy said. "Let's find you, say, twenty years from now."

She rocked faintly up onto the balls of her feet, lifting herself, having a fun time playing line games like she was no older than that starchy little girl.

She couldn't find an older me, and I didn't look, just stood by her as we wound our way slow to the head of the line. The man in front of us had been called to check in when I saw Mrs. Fancy wasn't looking anymore either. She was staring straight at the me I was right then, and her eyes had gone dangerously soft. It was a look so close to pity that I could feel my mad cresting again even before she spoke.

"Maybe there's a reason we don't see you older, Ro," she said.

"Don't. I told you," I said, but her eyes stayed all melty chocolate colored. I blinked hard and said in a fierce whisper, "Don't say things. You'll wreck it. You can't wreck it. You're my only friend."

She darted out her hand and put it on my cheek. I could feel her age in the folds and creases of her palm. She said, "Then I'll only say, I pray better things for you, like I used to do for Janine."

An airline girl called, "Next," right then, so I didn't have to decide if I was going to yank her hand away so hard that the hollow bird bone in her wrist would snap, or drop my head down on her shoulder and bawl like a toddler. I bent down and jerked up her luggage, practically hurling it onto the scale, piece by piece. The girl checked it, and I watched it roll away down the conveyor.

Mrs. Fancy said, "I land at eleven o'clock on Friday."

"Fine," I said. Three days, and by then I would have put this conversation away. I could be Ro Grandee next time she was in my kitchen, helping her get enough cans for her church's food drive with my skirt swirling around my knees and my happy smile tucked firm into place. "That's fine."

I turned to go, but she said, "Wait, Ro! There you are, at last! The face is you in twenty years to a dime, although I can't imagine you would ever wear those clothes."

I was already walking back toward my life, ready to pick it up and keep living it as if Mrs. Fancy hadn't spoken, but I couldn't help but glance the way she was pointing.

That's when I saw the gypsy, and the gypsy was me.

Me in twenty years, exactly as Mrs. Fancy had said. She stood across the small expanse of the airport by a coffee stand, a slight figure in her forties with long dark hair. At first glance, I thought I'd turned out to be homeless, because the woman was wearing so many layers that she looked like she'd wound everything she owned around her. All her layers were clean and well tended, though, and her face was clean, too. She had a long red paisley print skirt tied up in a knot to show a yellow flowered skirt under. She wore a simple purple top, but at least three shawls were layered over it: a blue one slung around her waist and tied, a green one, and then another, in an entirely different green, knotted haphazardly around her shoulders. She had a suitcase and a huge cloth handbag with bamboo handles, the kind of thing a different sort of woman might keep her knitting in. Both bags sat at her feet, and her hands were busy shuffling through a deck of outsize cards, as if she was setting up a magic trick.

She must have felt my stare because her hands stilled, and she looked up, straight back at me. Her eyes were so black that I could see their darkness from halfway across the airport. They were magic eyes, nothing like the lavender-blues I'd gotten off my daddy. Even so, her gaze left me poleaxed with all my breath pressed out.

Her mouth dropped open when she saw me staring so intently, and she fumbled her cards. They went sliding in a fall to scatter at her feet.

Mrs. Fancy had her back to me, checking in. I said a vague good-bye, and I started to walk toward the gypsy. My feet went toward her like called dogs. She dropped into a crouch and scrambled to gather up her cards, breaking eye contact, scooping up the deck as fast as she could.

As I got closer, I saw her quick hands pause over one card. Most of the deck had landed facedown, but the card that paused her had flipped over as it fell. It lay faceup, directly between her feet.

She stared from the card to me as I approached her, then back to the card. She picked it up last, tucking it into the deck, her movements slower, more deliberate now. She seemed somehow reconciled, waiting for me to reach her. Her hands busied themselves straightening her deck back into a neat packet.

I found myself slowing down, too. All at once I was at a creep, like the air around me had turned thick as honey. It felt both familiar and strange to move this way, so slow. I realized I was doing a kind of float-walk I'd perfected back in high school, back in Alabama, where I'd been Rose Mae Lolley, the prettiest girl at Fruiton High.

Rose Mae had called this kind of going "walking underwater," and she had thought of it as the opposite of what Jesus could do. She would imagine herself upside down, her feet touching the surface and the whole world way above her, dizzy from having her head pointing downward into blue depths that chilled and darkened.

I wasn't that girl anymore. I was Ro Grandee. Married lady. Cashier at my in-laws' gun store. Texan. But walking this way called up that girl again. Back then, boys were always watching Rose's body, and girls had watched her face. Rose had figured out that slow, underwater movements bored the eye. Everyone turned and looked when she first came into a classroom or the cafeteria, but as long as she kept moving in a consistent, almost continental drift, people's attention would slide away. Ten minutes after she came into a place, Rose learned, was the best time to steal things.

Not to keep. It was more about moving things, getting objects to the place they most belonged. Rose had an eye, even then, for what went where.

Rose was the one who hooked Dana Ostrike's copy of *Forever* and took it to the Baskin-Robbins. With a smooth sleight of hand, she deposited it in Esther Jenkins's purse. Esther was head dog in the small pack of homeschooled Pentecostal Holiness girls that marched through Fruiton's tiny mall in formation, wearing a uniform of white Keds and long denim jumpers. The ends of their hair were ratty and fine. It was their baby hair, never once cut. They were a wedge of ignorance and virtue that pushed through the Fruiton Baptist kids in a viceless unit, except that every single one of them was addicted to orange-flavored baby aspirin. The weight of so much uncut hair gave them all near constant headaches.

Esther had a pretty face with a pointy mouse nose, and the next two times Rose saw her around town, the nose was pointed down at that book. Her gaggle of dowdy friends were crowded around her, all of them listening as she whisper-read the dirty parts to them. They probably had no more than an inkling about what might go where before that book, but lucky for them, Dana had dog-eared the sex parts.

Rose also spent a solid week hooking the wallets of every boy on the football team and removing the hopeful condom. In one fell swoop, she transferred the entire handful to Myla Richard's lunch box. She'd gotten ribbed and plain, latex and lambskin, even one exceptionally optimistic Trojan Magnum XL lifted off a jock whose ex-girlfriend had once said, in an unrelated conversation, that he emphatically did not need the accommodation. "I can tuck the whole thing in my cheek, like a Tootsie Pop drop," she'd told Rose, her tone fond. "I call it Little Turtle Head, but not out loud anymore. He gets mad."

Myla found a condom assortment in her lunch that was as plentiful and varied as the boys she took up to the old tree fort behind her house. She made a fuss when she found them, though, demanding to know who had put them in her food. Then she made a big show of dumping them out in the trash with her sandwich rind and empty fruit cup. She should have shut her pie hole and used them; by the end of the year, she'd dropped out to have a baby.

Ro Grandee had no reason in her life for Rose Mae's brand of object-shifting thievery. I'd lost the habit of moving with sleepy slowness, but as I walked toward the waiting gypsy, it came back to me. As I got close, I had time to see all the ways that we were different. Her long hair had salt white stripes running through it, and it was chocolate brown, not dark as mink. She had my small-framed, curvy kind of figure, but even with the layers I could see she was bigger on top. Her skin was olive where mine was paper white. Still, she had a tippy-tilt nose and my same kind of bowed, fat-lipped mouth. We were so alike, and even before she spoke, I believe I must have known her.

As I reached her, she gestured toward a table near the coffee stand. Her hands were bare of rings. No bracelets, and no watch, either, as if all her extra clothes had made jewelry unnecessary. I could see beads at her throat, though, peeping through the scarves. A rosary.

I nodded and she flowed past me, moving easier in her body than I ever had, and I found myself turning as smoothly as if I were on a lazy Susan, carried by her momentum. I followed her five steps to the table, still so slow that she was seated and settled two breaths before I eased myself down in the chair across from her.

"If you want coffee, you have to get it at the counter," she said. Her voice was throaty and low, like she was hoarse or a heavy smoker, but she didn't smell like ashtrays. She smelled tangy, like ginger and orange peel.

"I don't want coffee," I said.

Her lips pressed together, exasperated. "I'm not sure we can sit here if we don't get coffee."

I shrugged, my shoulders coming up slow, slow, and then I eased them down an inch at a time instead of dropping them.

"What are those cards?" I asked.

"A tarot deck," she answered. I had never seen tarot cards, but I knew what they were all right. She fanned the deck out, face-down on the table. They looked well thumbed and soft around the edges.

"One fell faceup," I said.

She nodded. "That's why I'm sitting here."

"What card was it?"

She cocked her head to one side, considering that, and then she said, "Say I told you. Say I said three of wands or nine of cups, would that mean anything to you?" I shook my head no, and she seemed to think that through. She said, "I don't think I'll tell. That card's message was for me, not you. Do you want your own reading?"

"I guess," I said.

"At home, I get fifty dollars to lay a full deck." She had a flat, plain way of talking, but I could hear an old accent under her words, something ripe that bulged out around the edges of her television vowels.

"Where's home?" I asked.

She shrugged. "I've been asking myself that question my whole life. I haven't found the answer yet."

I had to manually stop my eyes from rolling. I put my hands flat on the table, and I could feel the difference in my movements. Anger made me faster, and I had to stop myself, slide back into being slow. I moved like I was fifty fathoms down, spreading my fingers, fanning my hands out like she had fanned the cards. Hurried travelers strode past us toward security. Their passing pulled her eyes away from me for half seconds at a time. That's when I understood that I was moving like this because I was going to steal something. Had to steal something. She had some object on her, I wasn't sure what, that belonged elsewhere. Belonged to me.

My lips creaked open and I said, "I don't have fifty dollars."

Her response was prompt, like she'd loaded it in her mouth and aimed while I was thinking. "I do a half-deck read for thirty."

"Don't have thirty," I shot back.

After a brief, blank pause she said, "Why don't you have thirty dollars? Everyone should have thirty dollars. Don't you have a job?"

I thought about saying I was a wife. Or that I worked part-time in my father-in-law's shop, right under his broad thumb, and that it was plenty crowded there, since it was the same space where my husband lived crammed up most days. I thought about saying, "I've been asking myself that question," to pay her back for going all Zen-ass cryptic on me when I asked where her home was. But in the end, all I said was, "Yes. I'm pretty."

"For a living?" she said, dry, and then when I nodded she looked me up and down, as if weighing that. "Well, you're good at it. One would think it would pay more."

"One would think," I said, but I wasn't agreeing with her so much as trying to catch her inflections. She hadn't picked up that flat accent anywhere in Texas. "You don't live around here."

"No," she agreed.

She looked away, and I took the opportunity to flick my gaze down and glance into the large, open handbag that now rested beside the table. I clocked a wallet, a compass, the paper folder with her ticket in it, a can of WD-40, a jumble of pens and mints, a bottle of water, and a hardback book pressed against the side, the jacket protected by a clear plastic duster. I thought, *Ticket*, but my body, reverting to Rose Mae Lolley's old slow ways, had ideas of its own. My hands slid back down into my lap and stayed there, biding.

I said, "Why are you here?"

"Not for this," she said, flicking her hand at the table, the fan of cards, me. "I went out to Cadillac Ranch yesterday. Have you ever been?"

I shook my head.

"You should," she said. "People travel across the world to look at wonders, and here you have one in your own yard you've never seen."

"So I'll go," I said.

She flicked her eyelids in a disbelieving blink. "When?"

"Tomorrow," I said.

She made a scoffing noise and then intoned, "There's no such thing." My eyes wanted to roll again.

The coffee shop guy called from the booth then. "That table is for customers."

When she turned in her seat to face him, my fast hand darted down. I thought it would be the wallet. The wallet would have a driver's license, an address. But my hand plucked out the hardback book and then slid it into my lap, under the table.

"Then bring us coffee," she called to the guy.

"I'm not supposed to come out from the booth," the guy said. His voice had a whine in it. I looked right at him until he felt it and looked back. I smiled and warmed my eyes for him.

"Please?" I said.

"Okay," he said.

When I looked back at her, she had turned to face me again and her eyes had narrowed.

"What?" I said.

"You're very good at your job," she said. "I remember, in my twenties, especially, how I would feel a young man turn and see me. I'd watch his face become bright and greedy. Always made me feel like a naked Christmas tree, how he'd be hanging things all over me, expectations and wants. Young men, romantics, call it love at first sight, but even then I understood it was only prettiness. Young men see pretty, and they start hanging all the things they hope you'll be onto you till you're so weighed down you can't move."

She shut up as the guy came over with the coffee, and then she picked up her handbag and paid him for both. I let her pay, glad I hadn't taken her wallet. She might have missed the ticket too soon as well, but she wouldn't go rooting around for that book until she was settled on the plane headed toward her secret home.

When he was gone, she turned back to me and said in an impatient voice, "Ten dollars. For a three-card read. I'd do it for free, but then the cards wouldn't answer. Nothing is free."

"I've read that before, in fairy tales," I said. "You have to cross a gypsy's palm with silver. To make the magic work." I got very sarcastic with the word *magic*.

She shrugged. "If you like. I would say it's an energy force, but you can say magic."

"Thank you," I said, even more sarcastic. I pointed at the rosary beads peeking out between her shawls and asked, "Do you still go to mass?"

She chuckled and said, "Goodness, no!" She sent a hand searching through the shawls to touch the beads. I saw her index finger was stained metallic silver. It looked shimmery, as if she had recently been arrested and fingerprinted by fairies. "Madonna wears one of these. You think she goes to mass?"

"Madonna was raised Catholic."

"She isn't Catholic now," the woman said. "She's only using it, tapping into the whole virgin-whore archetype."

She said it like that had already been determined, as if Madonna "tapping into the whole virgin-whore archetype" was a line from a conversation she had had with a bunch of shawl-wearing gypsy friends when they were out drinking wine and being mystical and deciding things.

"People can't stop being Catholic," I said. "You're born it. You are it. I'm Catholic, and I've been to mass maybe twice in the last three years."

"If you were still Catholic, you would go to mass," she said, like it was that simple. She said it like a challenge.

"My husband's family doesn't . . . Mass upsets them. But I'm Catholic. It's a thing I am, not a thing I do. I can't stop being it."

She looked away, and just like that, snap, I was dismissed. The tension that had held her thinned like rising fog and she said, "Anyone can stop being anything at any time. All they have to do is choose to."

"You would know," I said, furious, my voice so loud that the coffee guy looked over again. My hands trembled around the book lying in my lap. I slid it between my knees and clamped my thighs on it to hold it, then leaned over and grabbed up my own purse. I scrabbled down to the very bottom of it until I found an old dime. It was dirty and tarnished. I slapped it onto the table between us. It landed tails-side up. "Silver," I said, "to cross your fucking palm."

She stared at me with eyes so calm and foreign that I felt that scalp prickle I got sometimes, going eye to eye with the unblinking green lizards in my garden. Those lizards gave off a strong sense of other. Not a mammal, not like me, I would think, and I got that same creeping, separated tingle now, from her.

She picked up the dime with a pursed mouth. "This doesn't make us even," she said.

I pursed my mouth back just the same and said, "No." I tapped her deck of cards, because I'd known her before she spoke, and I was sure now. "*This* doesn't make us even. I can't think of a single thing you could do that would."

That hit her low, and she dropped her gaze. She stared at the dime in her palm so hard that I was shocked it didn't smoke. "I read for Wayne Newton once," she said.

"I don't know who that is."

"He came all the way out to my place. He wore a slouchy hat, pulled down low, and he paid cash. He didn't give a name, but I knew it was him. No, I suspected it was him. The first two cards told me I was right. Wayne Newton came all the way over from some show he was doing in town to ask me to read his cards."

The silence got long, and at last I said, "Is he a Catholic?"

She truly laughed then. Threw back her head and let out a throbbing, hooty sound that turned heads toward us.

"All right, then," she said. She dropped the dime off the side of the table and let it clink its way down to the bottom of her purse. She extended the cards toward me. "Shuffle."

I took the deck. The cards felt worn from a lot of human touching, soft with oils. I thought of all the people who must have handled them—her kind, swathed in shawls and rattling with healing crystals—and I wanted to go wash.

While I was shuffling, she said, "Now ask."

"Ask what?" I said, pausing.

"Whatever question I can see in you, burning you up. You ask it while you shuffle, and then you stop when you feel the answer is in the cards."

I thought about it, turning the cards over and over into themselves.

I said, "Why did you—" But she held one hand up, like a stop sign, and I paused again.

"You're asking the cards, not me. I don't need to know the question."

I said, "But don't you want to know my question?"

People flowed around us, all trying to go home or to leave it. A good minute passed, and then she said, "I don't think I do. No."

So I shuffled, and I chose a different question this time. Since it was only in my head, I didn't think it in exact words, more like pictures. I thought about men, the men I chose and the men I had been given. My father flashed through my head beside Jim Beverly, my first love. I could only think of them together, like they were the two sides of the same thin dime.

I saw the lineup of Rose Mae's road men, the ones she left in a scatterpath as she waitressed her way along the coast from Alabama to Texas. Most of them had been like Daddy, hard drinkers with hard fists, with not much sweet to hold me. I'd kept moving until I came to my husband, a ball of charm and anger. He had an eager grin like Jim Beverly's and overeager fists like Daddy. Two for the price of one.

I had an uptilt of thought at the end, like a question mark. It wasn't words, just a bafflement—why these men?—and a fear; Mrs. Fancy could not find a future me because she couldn't imagine I would live to get much older. Maybe she was right.

I didn't feel anything from the cards, but I did start to feel silly, waiting for some inside yes to chime. I stopped shuffling and handed her the deck.

"The first card is your past," she said, her voice flat. She turned it, and I saw a slight widening of her eyes.

It showed a tall and spindly tower, rising to a sky that was blue on one side and black with sooty clouds on the other. A narrow bolt of lightning, sharp-tipped like a crookedy pencil, was neatly slicing the tower's top off. Bright flames licked at the edges, and people were running out the front door and away. One girl had been left behind, framed in the highest window, and she stared right out at me, peaceful, as if she didn't see the flames or the people fleeing.

"Rapunzel," I said, tapping the girl with one finger. "Now there's a chick who used a lot of hair products. Hope they weren't flammable."

"Don't be flip," said the gypsy, her voice sharp. "This is major arcana." She rapped the tower twice with her knuckle. "It can be the scariest damn card in the whole deck." Her eyes met mine directly, and now there was a glimmer of something human in them. Maybe kindness, maybe apology, maybe a trick of the light. "In your case, I suspect it means you lost someone."

"Who hasn't," I said.

"This loss haunts you," she said, and I recognized the glimmer. Pity.

I kept my face from changing, but on the inside, I was bristling. "I lost my high school boyfriend," I said. "It must mean him."

The pity hardened over and she said, "No. This would be a big loss."

"It was," I said, my lips pulled back, baring my teeth, and hoped it looked something like a smile. "Huge. He disappeared our senior year. We'd planned to marry right after graduation. He was sweet to me like no one ever had been. He loved my sorry ass. And then one day, boom, he was gone. A runaway, they said. I never saw him anymore. I felt like I'd gone missing, too. Up until then I was an honor roll kid, someone with a future. But losing him wrecked me. I never bothered to show up to take my final exams. He put me where I am right now."

"That is a big loss," she said, tight-voiced. "Perhaps it's him. But I don't think so."

"Jim Beverly," I said, firm, punching his name at her like a fist. "That's the loss. Not—"

"Fine," she said, cutting me off. "This card represents your present." She turned it. It took a second to make sense of the image. A slim woman in a blindfold stood in front of a lake. It was sunset, so the water had gone red behind her. There were twisted, mossy shapes humping out of the water. Logs, or maybe crocodiles. She held a long sword in each hand, crossed over her chest to make an X.

The gypsy put her silver-tipped finger to her bottom lip and tapped, thinking. "It can't have been that bad, losing this Jim. You married someone else, after all."

"How do you know that?" I said, spine a-tingle. She might have seen my rings. But for most of the conversation, my fingers had been hidden in my lap, touching her book. "Have you been watching me?"

She snaked one hand under the tiny round table and pushed a fist hard into my ribs, just under my left breast. I gasped, unable to help it as she pressed directly down on a fresh bruise.

"You've married," she said, as if the pain that flashed across my face confirmed it. Her hand hovered half an inch above the spine of her own book. I waited, breath held, until she leaned back. "This is the two of swords, and it stinks of violence. That's some man you picked." She put her hand back on the deck, readying to turn another card. "Want to see your future?"

"Why not?" I said, still trying to sound casual, but the way her hand had gone straight to my freshest hurt spot had gotten to me. I didn't want my question answered, did not want her to say out loud all the reasons Mrs. Fancy had not been able to imagine a future for me.

At first I thought the card was upside down, but then I realized it was the figure in the center. It was a man in a wolf's-head helmet, hanging from a grape arbor by one ankle. His feet were bare. His hands were clasped in front of him, and I thought he was praying, but then I realized they were bound by slim, thorned vines.

The wolf-head on his helmet snarled, but beneath, his human face looked perfectly calm.

I felt my eyebrows come together. "I've seen this card. It was on that mystery show with the old lady who solves crimes. She said it was a death card."

I looked up at her, and the gypsy's eyebrows mirrored mine.

"Most readers will tell you it isn't a death card," she said. "They'll say it is a card about change."

"Being dead would be a pretty big change," I said.

The gypsy's eyebrows were still pushing inward, as if they'd been exchanging letters for a long time and now they were trying to meet. "Some readers would say it only means you need to alter your perspective. Or you should do the opposite of what you would normally do, or you should make a sacrifice."

"So your stupid cards say I should, what, kill a goat?"

"Literal and flip, are those your only settings?" she asked, sharp. "I'm telling you what other readers might say. They'd say it's not a death card. He's hanging by his ankle, not his neck."

"Still," I said. "That can't be all that comfortable."

She waved a hand at me to shush me, and then she spoke again in an urgent whisper. "Most readers would say it's about change. But I'm looking at a girl with the tower in her past. I'm looking at a woman in a marriage made of swords. These cards are screaming. They are saying, Change or die. I suggest you change, and if not, then you should go see Cadillac Ranch today, because for you, there isn't a tomorrow."

I found myself leaning in to catch her words, my hands clamped down tight on the stolen book, as she went on.

"Sometimes, Mrs. Professionally Pretty, those ornaments men hang on your branches get so heavy they can crush you dead, and in this configuration, death is what I see. I'd say it's either for you or your husband." She looked up from the cards, her black eyes burning. I felt held by them, breathless, and she was a visionary in that moment. "Choose him. You live. It's the choice that I would make. If it's a death card, you choose him." She leaned back from me and said, louder and slower, "Until you do, I don't have one damn word more to say to you."

With that, she scraped up all the cards and dumped them willy-nilly down into her bag. She picked up her coffee cup and drained the last, cooling third. I didn't speak, and she stood up and said more words to me anyway. Three of them.

"You are welcome."

I hadn't thanked her, but she wasn't being sarcastic. She said it like she was opening a door, inviting me inside.

"Why are you in Amarillo?" I asked. "You didn't come here to see Cadillac Ranch."

She grabbed her purse and slung the bamboo handles over her shoulder. "It's just a stop," she said.

I shook my head. This could not be coincidence. "Did you come here to see me?"

"Everything is just a stop," she said, picking up her suitcase.

She walked away. I stared after her, sitting like roots had grown out of my hips and twined themselves around the chair legs. At the last moment, she did turn back, looking annoyed. "He's the guy that sang 'Danke Schoen.' Mr. Vegas. You would know him if you saw him."

She went through security.

I sat there, shaking, watching her disappear down the hallway.

When she was truly gone, I scooted my chair back so I could look down at the book in my lap. My hands had been wise. They had understood what the cellophane wrapper meant before my stunned brain had: This was a library book. I expected some new agey self-help thing or maybe something by Robert Penn Warren or Flannery O'Connor. But it was *The Eyes of the Dragon*, by Stephen King. Fairy tales again. She'd always been a scattershot reader.

I flipped open the front cover and saw the manila pocket. There was no card in it, of course. The card would have told me the name she was living under, but it was filed at the library. The words,

Property of the West Branch Berkeley Public Library, were stamped in black.

The words looked more serious and permanent than ink to me. They seemed carved, as if the page was made of stone. The book in my lap felt heavy enough to be solid granite.

I touched the word *Berkeley*, disbelieving.

Until half an hour ago, I hadn't seen my mother in twenty years. Now, suddenly, my mother was alive. My mother was a gypsy who lived and breathed and checked out books in California. This woman had left her child to save herself, and now she'd come back to flip the hanged man card and say I had to make a sacrifice. What did she know about sacrifice? I'd been hers.

But she had said, "Live."

She had said, "Choose him."

My mother had appeared just long enough to tell me that if I wanted to survive, I would have to kill Thom Grandee.

CHAPTER

3

I TRIED TO CHOOSE HIM, and I failed. What did that leave? That was all I could think as I tore through the woods, sprinting back to Mrs. Fancy's Honda. The next thing I knew, I was zooming east down Highway 40 toward home, praying harder than I had ever prayed in my whole life. I called every saint it seemed might do a lick of good. I called them out loud, demanding intervention with the kind of flailing desperation that can rise when even hope has left.

Francis, patron of cars and drivers, answered first. He was in the car with me. I could hear him breathing easy in the seat behind me. Then Michael took the seat beside Francis. He'd come to close the eyes of his policemen, making their radar guns heavy in their hands, sending them for coffee at any Dunkin' Donuts that took them off my path.

I should have been surprised. Hell, I should have been wetting myself. I'd been calling my saints my whole life, but I hadn't had one show before. I must have wept out Mary's name for comfort, because she was in the back as well, even though she had to squash into the narrow middle seat with her patient feet on the hump.

"I'm sorry," I told her, but if saints were answering, then the place by me was only for Saint Roch, patron of both dogs and pestilence. I needed him for Gretel and for Rose Mae Lolley, in that order. As I thought his name, before I could call, he was already obliging me. He appeared beside me with his ankles crossed, one gentle arm's length away.

I was driving fast enough to make the blowsy air outside sound like a great wind. I was sweating hard. I could feel it clotting in my hair, which was once again tucked up inside my baseball cap. I reached up to pull the cap off, but my hand U-turned on the way up, going to the dash to flip on the AC instead.

That was when the first shiver hit me: My body understood the danger long before my mind did. My hand had been right not to remove the hat. I needed it to shade my face and hide my hair.

I was driving down the very road Thom would be taking. My heart bounded up from my chest, lodging in my throat. Each beat banged against my gag reflex, choking me. I could pass him at any second. Het up as he must be right now, if he saw me tearing down the highway in a borrowed car, he'd run it off the road and yank me out of the wreckage, demanding answers. Then he'd find Pawpy's gun in the Target bag, and he'd know in two heartbeats where I'd spent my morning. I hadn't looked down into the gun's black eye since I was little and my daddy and I stared down into it together. *You must never, never point that hole at anything, at anything, ever, unless you want to see it utterly destroyed.* If Thom caught me now, I had no doubt I would be looking it in the eye again.

My foot went weightless on the gas pedal, and the car slowed. Then I stomped down again. What if I had passed him already? I could have easily slipped by in Mrs. Fancy's plain car while he was checking on Gretel, who I had to believe was absolutely still alive. Saint Roch nodded in comforting agreement.

Thom could already be behind me, or he might be two cars ahead. There was no way to know. I twisted my head this way and that, trying to see all around me, searching for his Bronco. The road got away from me, and I listed so far right that I ran up onto the bumpy shoulder. I wrestled the wheel and got mostly back in my lane. I saw the next exit, mercifully close. In two minutes, I was safe off the highway, panting as I pulled into a gas station.

I drove around to the back side of the building, letting the Honda idle by the restrooms while I tried to swallow my heart back down and breathe. Every piece of me hollered to keep moving, to run, to go far and fast. But where?

I knew three things: That I had to get home. That Thom was somewhere on the road between me and my house. That I must not be seen as I made my way. These were facts, true and unchangeable, and they bounced off each other in hopeless, tangled equations. I couldn't go home, and I couldn't be still. Maybe I should start driving and hope that the Honda and my saints would know a safe path. If Mary had her way, we'd head east, very quickly, putting state after state between us and Thom Grandee until we came home to Alabama, to hill country, with its thousand places to hide. This flat state gave me nothing.

I started praying again, calling Rita of Cascia now. She watched over shitty marriages and all things impossible. She appeared crunched up on Michael's lap, the low roof making her bend her head to a miserable angle. I still had no idea where to go, but a picture of our arrival flashed into my head. They would pile out of the tiny Civic after me, wispy saint after wispy saint, like the Honda was a mystical clown car made up special for Catholics.

I got the giggles then. My own laugh scared me, it was so high-pitched and hysterical, and I tried to make it stop. The laugh turned into hiccuping, and the lady figure on the closest bathroom door got all bendy and rubbery. My vision went gray around the edges, and it was all I could do to keep my foot pressed down onto the brake so I didn't rev slowly forward and have a five-mile-an-hour collision with the back of a Shell station. I thought, *It's bad to faint while the car is on.*

I saw my bottle of Coke resting in the driver's-side cup holder. I focused on it, and the rest of the landscape became a fuzzy backdrop that looked like it was being filmed through cheesecloth. I bought these small bottles instead of cans and allowed myself one a day; Thom, an ex-jock, liked my body tight beneath its curves. I'd grabbed it this morning on my way out the door, thinking about how the cap would pop off with a hiss of gas I would feel more than hear. I'd planned to have it when I had finished up my morning's awful business, a working-class girl's champagne. Now here it sat like a party favor left over from my real life. I picked it up. It still felt cool.

I held the bottle first to one eye, then the other, trying to clear my vision. *More than that.* It was the word version of that same impulse that had turned my hand when I went to take the hat off, but now it had a voice. I recognized Rose Mae, working to save my ass while Ro Grandee, professional nice girl and dedicated victim, hunched and writhed in a lathery panic. Rose knew to press the cool bottle to my eyes to take the swelling down and ease the red. When next I saw Thom Grandee, I could not look like I'd been crying.

As far as Thom knew, I was home right now, chirping a happy tune while I bleached his underpants back to white and waltzed the vacuum back and forth across the den. When I saw him, I couldn't even ask how Gretel was, or even if she was alive, which she absolutely had to be and was. Roch nodded his agreement. I had to be like regular until Thom told me what had happened. I'd need to listen to him say all the things I had done to him in the woods as if the story was new and strange to me. I felt my eyes widening, practicing surprise.

"Oh, my God, Thom, are you okay? Is Gretel okay?" I said. It sounded fake. I tried letting my mouth drop open. "Are you kidding me? They *shot* at you?" That sounded worse. "I am completely fucked," I said, and that, at least, rang absolutely true.

I pressed the bottle against my other eye. It felt good, that cool smoothness holding my eyelid closed. My saints rustled around me, impatient for action but low on actual suggestions. Why should they help me, anyway? What kind of a low-rent Catholic shoots at her husband because of mystical tarot cards?

Something about that pinged around in my head like a false note. Not tarot cards. One card. The last card.

But the gypsy had turned three. Past, present, future. A loss, a marriage made of swords, a choice. I'd been running for days on the steam of the third card alone. I hadn't thought about the rest of them. When a twenty-years missing mother pops up at a routine airport drop-off, a person can miss a few tricks. If the mother then drops a bomb like "Kill your husband," the rest of the conversation tends to get shit-canned in the fallout. But we hadn't started with change or death. We hadn't even started with my marriage. We'd started with a loss. The gypsy acted like she was the thing I'd lost, but the card hadn't been the four of *mothers*.

It was a tower on fire, and it could mean anything. I'd said it was Jim Beverly mostly to hurt her, but she'd insisted she was the thing I'd lost with all the things she didn't say. She'd tucked messages all sneaky under her words. Under every word. Even her pauses seemed, in my memory, to be dripping secret meanings. I could see her in my mind's eye, giving her lip a sly tap with that silver-stained finger.

Not fairy dust. Paint, I thought, and at once I understood where I had to go. My hands were still shaking, but my vision was clear. I put the Honda in reverse and pulled out, heading back to the highway.

I got back on 40, going west this time. I drove one-eyed, with only one hand on the wheel. The other hand still held my Coke bottle to my face, letting the coolness do its good work. Amarillo grew smaller again in my rearview mirror. If I'd been Lot's wife, I'd have been salt nine times over by now; I made myself quit stealing peeps at it.

I had to look sharp and purely forward and check oncoming traffic for Thom's Bronco. Nothing passed me going the other way except a jewel bright VW Beetle. Back in Kingsville, when Thom and I were first dating, I'd have said, "Punch buggy blue!" and knuckled him in the shoulder. We'd graduated to harder hitting games since those days.

When 40 ran into the remains of the old Route 66, I knew I was close. I scanned the horizon, slowing. Over the years, Thom and I had driven past Cadillac Ranch a few times on the way to other places, but its graffiti greetings were for teenagers and tourists. We had never stopped.

The land was so flat, I saw the silhouette of the cars jutting up against the horizon from a long way off. Sunlight bounced off the metal. They were in the middle of a wheat field, ten Cadillacs buried butt-up in the soil, rusting out slowly in the dry air and covered in graffiti. I pulled off the road and eased down the shoulder until I came up even with them.

I turned off the engine, and the only sounds left were the outside wind and my own heart pounding. It hammered so strong that I could feel my pulse in my hands and in my ears. It banged at my ribs from the inside. I pictured the backside of those flat bones shivering into a lacy network of cracks that matched exactly the healed ones Thom had put on the other side. My heart was the only part of me that felt like moving. My eyelids felt cold and heavy, and my worthless legs were made of slag.

"What's wrong with me?" I asked Saint Roch. He only shrugged. It was Rose Mae who knew the answer. *You're in shock, you moron. Eat some sugar.*

I popped the cap off the Coke with the opener on my key chain and drank half of it off. I usually carried a granola bar, but I'd left my purse at home. It hadn't seemed right to bring my driver's license and a lip gloss along to shoot my husband. All I had was Pawpy's gun, both pieces stuffed back inside the Target bag, and the gypsy's Stephen King book, sitting on the passenger seat.

Then I thought to look in Mrs. Fancy's glove box. She had three snack-size boxes of Sun-Maid raisins tucked away in there. I dumped one box out in my hand and started eating them, picking them up one by one with unsteady, pinching fingers, like a toddler. They had no taste, but I swallowed them dutifully, taking them like pills. When they were all gone, I got out of the car. The wind grabbed at me, stronger than it sounded from inside. There was nothing in these flat fields to slow it.

I pulled down the brim of my cap so the wind couldn't take it. I walked across the field, my saints trailing behind me in a line. The only footfalls I heard were mine, but the heavy wind was saint's breath on my neck, strong enough to move ships, yet sweet like a cow's, warm and grassy.

There were no tourists, no one at all around right now. Just me and the cars. I stepped in between two of them to get out of the wind. The closest car looked ready to crumple in on itself. The looping net of spray-painted words over words over words might have been the only thing holding the back doors on. The graffiti overlapped, letters and pictures and colors canceling each other out, layered a hundred deep. I found I still had the Coke in my hand, and I finished it off, staring at the closest car over the tilted bottle.

The gypsy had told me to come here. She'd been insistent. She hadn't wanted me to wait even an hour, and now I understood why she'd been so demanding. I knew what I would see. Somewhere on these cars, she'd left a message for me. Maybe she wasn't sure if she even wanted me to see it, so she had hinted it was here and then left it up to fate. She'd seemed like she was big on leaving things to fate.

I could imagine her with a spray can, the wind in the wheat field blowing her scarves and layered skirts around as she covered over older words with silver, the paint staining her finger, making one car's side into a blank, clear page so she could write to me. It was the safest way to tell me how to find her.

You are welcome, she had said, right at the end. Not like I had thanked her, which I most certainly had not. She'd said it like an invitation, but an empty one, to nowhere in particular. I'd been focused on stealing her book, looking for the information she'd already left here for me. It seemed so obvious now, and now was when I most needed it.

Thom was out there, so angry that he had swollen up to be miles wide, filling up all the space between me and home. The sun was rising up and making full, bright morning, and every minute that passed made it more likely he would catch me out.

I wasn't sure exactly what-all she would have written. An apology? She owed me a thousand of those. I wanted her note to say that I was a red hole dug out of the guts of her, a seeping wound that hadn't healed a lick in the twenty-odd years since she had left me. More likely it would be more crystal-fueled dumb-assery, telling me which stars were sorry. She'd left a map or an address, that I was sure of. *You are welcome*, she'd said. It was an offer. There would be a place for me to come, to hide, if I failed and had to cut and run the same way she had done.

If I was like her.

I went to the end of the row and began searching the cars, working my way down, looking only for newer messages that had silver in them. I found quite a few on the first car. *Neal + Wanda = 4ever. Tre is a manslut. Cowabunga!* Metallic paint was popular.

The second car said that gay men were for peace, and they'd drawn silver hearts and stars and peace symbols all around the words to prove it. There was a tic-tac-toe game that the cat had won. My saints trailed me, mournful, offering no guidance as I moved to the next car. I found more silver paint, spelling out *Karen has June Fever* and *Uncle Kulty was here!*

On the fourth car down, on the side that faced away from the road, I saw the rosebud. It was the wrong colors: red with a long green stem and poinks of brown paint for thorns. But a rose is a rose, and my heart stuttered at the sight of it. I quickly scanned the words around it, regardless of color. To the right, someone had written, *Sex, Drugs, Rock-n-Roll, Anna!* in thick blue paint, and on the other side, there was only *I am the Bringer of Blood* in dark red. I looked down the row and saw the next car sported a red-and-green tulip drawn by the same sure hand. I walked down a few steps, and sure enough, the next car's side had a red daisy. The rose was not for me. It was only some LSD-infested flower child in a belled ankle bracelet, getting all literal.

I went back to the fourth car. The only silver here was under the rose, and it said, *The fun's at RODEO!* That had to be the gay men for peace again; Rodeo! was Amarillo's most notorious drag bar. I saw some glints of older silver, but the newer messages were all in neons and primary colors.

I moved on to the next car, then the next, working my way down the row. I found a silver proposal, *Marry me, Lia!* and pictures of musical notes, boobs, and a pair of running horses that looked like cave drawings. Nothing for me.

I came to the last car, but it was entirely free of fresh silver paint. I searched it even more carefully. There was nothing.

I hit the final car's back fin with the flat of my hand, as hard as I could. My palm stung. I pressed my hand against the hot metal, panting hard. It was here. It had to be. I must have missed it.

Or I was too late. Three days had passed since I'd seen her at the airport. She'd insisted that I come out here at once; she knew her message would be covered over sooner or later.

I walked down the row and started again at the first car, hunting more carefully this time, looking for my color under the newer words. On the third car, a glittery white paint caught my eye, fooling me, but it wasn't silver.

The next car had the picture of the rose. It was drawn straight up and down, ignoring the tilt of the slanted car. The green stem ended where the car met the ground, and it grew straight up, so that some of the petals touched the undercarriage.

All three of the flower drawings looked weathered, as if the paint had been there awhile. The gypsy would have seen this rose, then, and she must have guessed it would catch my eye. The words *Sex, Drugs, Rock-n-roll, Anna!* looked fresh, written thick and dark, as if Anna had gone over each letter twice. I leaned in closer. Under those words, I could see that something had been written in metallic silver paint. The gypsy may have used the rose as a marker for me, but some girl named Anna had taken a can of blue paint, her name, and her unhealthy priorities and wiped the message out.

I went backwards, moving right to left away from the rose until I found the place where the silver paint began, under the *e* in *Sex*. The writing was small, and two lines of text were buried under Anna's message. I could make out a capital letter *I*, then a *d*, and what I thought might be the top and the dot of a lowercase *i* that was framed by the capital *D* in *Drugs*. I could see the top half of the letter after that. It was a vertical line, so it could be a lot of things. Another *d*, maybe, or *b*, *k*, *h*, or *l*. Maybe even a *t* with a low crossbar; spray paint didn't lend itself to good handwriting. Anna had written her important philosophy in thick, broad strokes, covering the gypsy's smaller words at random, but I found an *o*, a *v*, another possible *o*, and an obvious *u* with a low, curved line after, like a comma.

The second line had more visible pieces. It started with an *ay*, and I could make out three letter bursts of longer words, *Sai* and *Cec*. It ended with a lowercase *a* and a smeared exclamation point.

I stepped back from the car, into the full force of the wind, trying to gauge the spacing of the letters. I put my free hand up to hold my hat on.

I di ov u, butting up to the picture of the rose.

Under that, *-ay t Sai Cec a!*

"I'd like to buy a vowel," I said, squinting at it, hating Anna and drugs and rock-n-roll and sex so hard in that blank second. She couldn't have painted over the tic-tac-toe game? I couldn't make the letters say *Berkeley*. Perhaps my mother was in a suburb or a smaller town nearby. Saint something? Santa Cruz didn't fit, and I didn't know California well enough to make a better guess. I shifted from one foot to the other, trying to remember the names of cities in California. I stared and stared, and then, almost involuntarily, I understood the first line of the gypsy's message:

I did love you. And then a comma and my name in picture form. I was already shaking my head in flat negation when the rest of the missing letters filled themselves in for me, and now I could see the whole thing.

I did love you, Rose. Pray to Saint Cecilia!

I shook my head. That couldn't be it. Pray to Saint Cecilia? If she was going to tell me to pray, why not to Monica, a beaten wife herself, or a hard-ass like Saint Paul? Saint Paul and the gypsy both knew all about abandoning a life in midstride. Cecilia was the patron saint of music, and there was no way praying to that pious warbler could ever make me safe.

I leaned in close to check the space below Anna's message for more silver paint. There wasn't any, so I searched the car's whole side, expecting to see more peeking out from under something fresh. There was none to be found. I kept going, on to the next car and the next. I dropped to my knees to check each car's belly, crawled to read the inside of the ones with no doors.

There was nothing else for me.

I walked back to the car with the rose on it and stared through Anna's message at the silver words. I tried to make the few letters I had picked out say something else, but I couldn't. Once the message filled in—*I did love you, Rose. Pray to Saint Cecilia!*—I couldn't unsee it.

My body turned itself sideways, and my hands came up into the good batter's stance I'd learned in Little League T-ball. I'd played from the time I was five until I was eight. After that, no one was around to take me to practice, but my body still remembered how to choke up. I gripped the narrow neck of my Coke bottle as if it were a miniature slugger. I swung it as hard as I could at the car. The bottle hit the spray-painted rose where the petals met the edge of the car's underside. The blow shivered the thick glass so hard that it cracked into five or six pieces. I felt those shivers move all the way up through me to become a buzz in my teeth as I watched the shards fall to the ground. I was left holding the neck with a single, jagged slice of glass jutting out from it.

It looked like a weapon. Something a person would have in prison, wicked and curved and slim. I dropped it, fast, and it jangled when it hit the other shards. I stared down at the green glass, glinting in the soil.

"Oh, I'm sorry," I said, and my voice dripped acid. "I did love you, Coke bottle."

She'd made me come out here. She told me I had to kill Thom Grandee if I wanted to live. I'd put bullets in my dog because of her. Saint Roch tried to speak, and I said, "Shut the hell up," to him. He didn't know how Gretel was. None of them did, this chain of saints bobbing in my wake, and these saints all came from her, too, didn't they? She was the one who had always called them. They'd answered her in ways they'd never answered me before today.

The wind that was their breath had smelled so sweet to me, like summer coming. A long time ago, on a day like this, she had knelt with her arm around Rose Mae's shoulders. Rose wore poppy-colored running shorts and pigtails. It was kindergarten field day. They watched the other girls line up, all taller than Rose, with longer strides.

She was praying into Rose Mae's ear, calling Saint Sebastian, patron to all athletes. The exact words were lost, but I remembered the low burring of her voice, calling him and calling him, until Rose could see him. He stood on her other side, looking down, shot through with a thousand arrows that bristled out of his body like bloody quills. His eyes were white hot and fervent. One arrow had pierced his cheek and gone out the other side, and when he grinned, Rose Mae saw the post going across his mouth like a horse's bit, and his teeth were rimmed in blood.

All the girls were in a line. Rose squirmed away and trotted fast from Sebastian to join them.

Instead of a starter pistol, there was Mrs. Peirson, the gym teacher, counting down. Three, two, one, go! Rose took off. There was no way she could win. She was the shortest girl in the whole class. But Sebastian came fast up behind her. From the corner of her eye, she could see his shafts bounce as he ran. He bristled and dripped.

Adrenaline washed into Rose Mae's blood, a push like a big red wave. She put her head down and tore forward. She could see him keeping leering pace as she ran her guts out and kept running, past the hundred-yard mark, past the booth where they sold Cokes and Popsicles, though she could hear she was being called. "Stop, Rose Mae. Stop! Stop, you silly." The crowd around the broad jumpers rose up in her path to block her.

Rose felt hands on her, lifting her, swinging her body high, and she almost screamed. It was only her mother, who had run on quick little feet to catch up. Sebastian was gone, but he had indeed wrought a miracle. Rose Mae placed second.

My mother had called saints when she lost her keys, when we were late, when we were hungry or sad or tired or jubilant. These saints that I had called today were hers. Cadillac Ranch was hers. Shooting at my husband, the bullets in my dog, these were all hers. I was doing what she wanted, obedient and dumb as that five-year-old who got a red ribbon because her mother called a saint stuck through with a thousand arrows and scarier than Satan.

Behind me, the trail of saints popped one by one, like soap bubbles, misting the air and then becoming nothing. I pulled off the baseball cap. I was too hot to stand it any longer, and Cadillac damn Ranch was the one place in Texas I felt certain I would not run into my husband. The wind caught my sweaty hair and slung it around, snarling it. I let go of the cap, and the wind took it and tumbled it away across the field. My hair whipped into my face, and I could smell the sulfur of gunshots in it. I lifted my hands to my nose and breathed in more sulfur and fruit sugar clinging to my palms.

For the first time since I'd gotten up and cooked Thom's butter-logged breakfast, I felt like I was living wholly in my body. I gathered my hair up and held it in a wad at the base of my neck with one hand, glaring at the gypsy's message. I was surprised the layers of paint didn't blister and bubble and flake off and disappear under my angry gaze. Those words should be burned away. They were insulting on so many levels. Not the lowest of which was, she had written, *I did love you,* in the past tense.

"Smug," I said, and turned my back on the Caddies. I was done looking at them. I walked toward Mrs. Fancy's car, my feet smashing down hard into the soil, every step an angry stab at the earth itself.

She'd said Thom Grandee would kill me if I didn't get him first. I had failed, and yet the earth still turned and Thom and I were both still breathing, because the reading wasn't about me. It was all her.

I had reached the road. I stamped at the asphalt to get the soil off my shoes and because the stamping felt good.

The first card was loss. That was hers. She had lost me. Her marriage had been the thing that was made of swords, and no one knew that better than the girl who had spent her first eight years growing up inside of it. My mother was the hanged man, the one who'd had to choose, and she had chosen herself.

There was a phrase for what her child had been to her. I knew it from the black-and-white war movies Thom and I rented to watch on the weekends. An acceptable casualty; that was what they called those poor fellows that the generals decided they could spare ahead of time. I was the thing she left in her place when she saved herself, and I was still sitting in it, in a place so like hers, it was easy for both of us to mistake who owned those cards.

I got in Mrs. Fancy's Honda and slammed the door so hard behind me that the car's frame shuddered. The most terrible part was, now that I had seen through all her layered gypsy scarves and figured her out, she wasn't here for me to tell her. I couldn't shove her nose down into the truth. All the Stephen King book had given me was a city and a state, and unless I wanted to hire a plane to skywrite a message over Berkeley, I couldn't tell her a damn thing.

What was left? What could I do?

I could get home. I felt my mouth drop open in a perfect O and my eyes widened. "They shot at you?" I said. Better. "They *shot* at

you?" I could act surprised. I could go see if my dog was going to
live. If only Gretel was alive, then I could sleep bug cozy next to my
husband tonight in our soft bed.

In the black-and-white movie Thom and I had watched not two
weeks ago, they'd sent some French guy to have his head lopped
off. He'd lifted his pointy nose and walked to the guillotine, calm
and noble, saying, "The blood of kings flows in my veins."

Well, screw that. The blood of assholes flowed through Rose
Mae Lolley's. My mother had just proven that. She was not going
to rescue me. She could take her empty *You are welcome* offer of a
haven and stuff it directly up her ass. I'd sooner go to hell than go
to California now. I didn't need her, anyway. I'd forgotten, in the
wake of seeing her, that I could damn well handle Thom Grandee.
A woman who couldn't would have been dead nine times over by
now. I set off for home.

My foot, heavy in its anger, had shoved the gas pedal down. I
was going a good twenty miles over the speed limit. I made myself
slow. The last thing I needed was to be pulled over now, with an
unregistered gun in the car and no ID. And I was only speeding
because I was angry with that gypsy. Surely Thom was off the road
by now. He must be at the vet, please God, saving Gretel. Or he
might be at the police station.

Even now, this speeding, it was about the gypsy, too. I should
have been home by now, unloading the dishwasher and practicing
my surprised face. But instead I'd wasted an hour creeping around
a wheat field looking for an empty love note she'd left with no way
for me to write her back.

"I'm going back there," I told the blessedly empty car. "I'll live
through this and soothe Thom down, and then I'm going to take
a rotisserie chicken and fruit salad and some paint and Gretel and
Mrs. Fancy, and go out to Cadillac Ranch." I would cover *Sex,
Drugs, Rock-n-Roll, Anna!* and the silver remains of the gypsy's
message with graffiti of my own.

I would be sure to bring red, so I could freshen up the hippie chick's flowers. Beside the rose, I would write the word *Jim*, with a tiny heart for the *i*'s dot. Then a larger heart after his name, point up and humps down, so it looked like a pretty girl's bottom. Jim upside down hearts Rose. Those words and pictures had been on the cover of every one of Rose Mae's high school notebooks. It would feel good to write them again.

Then when the gypsy returned, she'd see I'd left no answer. She wasn't my loss. There would be nothing for her, and my doodle would stick in her throat, pointy as a fish bone.

My loss was Jim Beverly. I'd thrown that fact at her at the airport like it was monkey poop, something to offend her as she'd gawked at my life like a tourist. Now it seemed like it was true. Rose Mae'd been soldered to Jim Beverly's right hip bone from third grade on, through most of high school, for more years than Rose had had a mother.

In grade school, after the boys were divvied up for kickball, Jim had picked her first from all the girls, every time. Rose Mae got free lunch in middle school, and Jim's mother packed him one from home. He'd always shared his fresh fruit and eaten half her chalky brownie. In high school, she'd written his reports for civics, and he'd done her dissections. They'd traded virginities in tenth grade. He was the boy she first saw naked, too, though that was years earlier, when they were only nine. Rose had made him show first.

They'd met in the woods behind the elementary school. He had turned his back, pulling down his shorts and underwear very quickly. His T-shirt hung down so only the lower half of his bottom showed. She saw two beige squares with a crease between them, flat and small, like the crimped edge of the Post toaster pastry she'd eaten for breakfast.

"Now you," he said.

Rose turned her back. She was so spindly that she barely had a butt at all, more like a little slice. She reached up under her dress, careful not to raise the hem, and pushed her cotton underpants down. Then she quickly flipped the skirt up and back down, yanking up her panties a scant second after. She turned around to face him. It was summer, and the Alabama woods were so lush that even the air seemed green as the sunlight filtered through all those trees.

"Want to do fronts?" Jim asked.

Rose shrugged and they stood there for half a minute, maybe longer. She said, "You first."

"I did butts first."

She waved that away. "Everyone has butts. You first."

He shrugged and pulled his shorts down again, this time using his other hand to raise his T-shirt, just a little. His thighs were pressed tight together, from nerves, she thought, and it pushed his testicles forward into a wad, so that the whole thing looked like an upside-down pansy. His pale, smooth penis was the rounded bud tuft at the center.

"It's nice," Rose said, surprised.

"Now you," he said, yanking up his shorts.

Rose scuffed one foot at the dirt, not looking at him.

"Now you," he said again, more insistent because she had one over on him; it wasn't equal anymore.

"Rose Mae!" he said, but it seemed to Rose there was no way to make it equal. She was only a little pad of fat there where he would see. All her interesting pieces were tucked under.

"I want to be fair," she said, eyebrows coming together. He nodded, uncertain.

She left her panties on and began lifting her dress. She crumpled the hem of it in her fists as she went, pulling it high so that he could see her belly and her skinny rib cage. Her trunk was a mess of dark, welted flesh that began at the panty line and went up, swelling her flat chest where her breasts would one day be. The bruises were all fresh. Her mother had been gone almost a year now, and her daddy had only just started.

Jim's eyes widened. She thought they got darker, too, but it was only his pupils expanding. The black ate up the blue to a little rim.

"Can I touch?"

Rose shrugged. He stepped forward and reached out one dirty brown boy's hand to cover her belly, tracing the mottled black and purple in a soft pet that ended at her nipple. Then he pulled back his hand as if her skin was hot.

"We're even," Rose said, and let her dress go, the hem falling back down around her knees. He didn't bother to nod or say yes. It was obvious that they were.

Instead he said, "I won't tell," and Rose nodded, solemn.

We neither of us told, not ever.

"He was the loss," I told the gypsy. I hated her for not being present to hear.

I was exiting 40 now, in Amarillo proper, three minutes from home. I should have kept that baseball cap. I was too recognizable with my hair down. My cheeks felt flushed and I had a familiar coiled feeling winding itself up inside my belly. I hadn't noticed it happening under the anger, but I could trace it back. It had started when I thought of Jim Beverly and his brown, square bottom, how it looked like toaster pastry tabs.

That ass never changed as he got older. It hardly got bigger, and as he grew up, it stayed his narrowest point. By high school, his short, muscular thighs had been wider. Above that tight ass, his spine had dipped into a smooth slope of ribs and ropy muscle that led up to his broad shoulders. The thing in my belly coiled tighter.

"What the hell is wrong with you?" I said aloud. I'd spent the morning shooting at my husband, and now my body was readying for sex. After a moment, I nodded. My body was wise. It knew how to handle Thom Grandee.

I was turning onto my own street now, heading for our squatty ranch house in the middle of the block. I was almost to Mrs. Fancy's when I saw Thom's familiar blue Bronco with its wide white stripe was parked in the middle of our driveway. Worse, there was a Chevy truck pulled in behind, huge and black and gleaming like a custom job for the devil himself, if the devil bought domestic. It belonged to Thom's parents.

The Grandee clan was gathering, and Thom had beaten me home.

CHAPTER

⁓

4

TIME KEPT ROLLING FORWARD, and Mrs. Fancy's car kept right on rolling with it. I sat helpless on my butt inside of both, toted forward in a horrified, slow-motion promenade down my own street. I was almost to Mrs. Fancy's drive now, with my own driveway up next. Tom's Bronco and the black truck stood out in my vision, crisp and sharp-edged. Our house looked brighter, too, more real than the rest of the neighborhood. It was a fifties ranch house, built flat, but even so, it was doing its damnedest to loom at me.

The previous owner had ruined our brick by coating it in sickly pastel paint. It was like Crest toothpaste, a matte, grained aqua that looked pure icy with mint. Now that color stung at my eyes, and I felt them watering up. I forced my head to turn away and found myself looking up Mrs. Fancy's drive. My hands followed the way I was looking, and the car turned and started up the slope.

My left hand reached up to the sun visor, and I pushed the button on the automatic garage door opener. I rolled smoothly into the garage, snaking under the rising door. I didn't wait. I double-punched the button and had the door heading back the way it had come the second the Honda's back end was through the opening. It took that garage door a solid year to grind its way closed, but finally it touched down, blocking out the sunlight.

I sat listening to the Honda's engine tick its way toward cool, watching the digital clock on the dash: 10:37. Thom and his parents were probably powwowing in the living room, smack in the middle of the house. That room had a huge picture window that faced the street, and if one of them had happened to be peering out from between the curtains, I wouldn't have to wait long. Even if they hadn't been watching, the garage door's noises might catch Thom's attention; he knew Mrs. Fancy was out of town. To my ears, the damn door had roared and growled like a bear on fire, hollering to get word about his predicament to his relations in Alaska.

The clock's last number changed: 10:38.

I didn't hear Thom's big feet lowering the sea level of Mrs. Fancy's yard as he stamped across to kill me. I didn't hear him bellowing my name. It was quiet and dim in the tidy garage. I waited to be sure. If any of them had seen me driving Mrs. Fancy's car, the best place for me was behind the wheel, ready to drive like hell. There was no way to explain Pawpy's gun or where I'd been while someone was shooting at the Grandees' eldest boy.

The clock numbers rolled over again. Still no Thom. No rumble of Joe Grandee or Charlotte, his shrill, piping wife. *Clear,* I thought, and felt my body break out in a wash of fresh sweat, as if my skin had been holding it in like breath.

I was already moving, snatching Mrs. Fancy's keys out of the ignition and grabbing up my book and the bag of gun chunks. I fumbled and almost dropped the whole armload as I scrambled out the car door. I clutched my things to my chest and struggled upright. Every minute counted now, as each was one more minute's absence I had to explain.

What the hell was Thom doing home? And with his parents? I had thought he'd be at the vet, unless Gretel was— I couldn't bear to finish the thought.

The garage had a door that opened into the peachy-colored kitchen. I went inside and spilled my things across Mrs. Fancy's countertop. Thom had been shot at, for the love of holy God, didn't he have some things he needed to do? But no, he'd come home and holed up with Joe and Charlotte, and he must be wondering where the hell his Ro was, especially since the ancient Park Avenue I drove—monkey-shit brown and wide as a tugboat—was still parked in our garage. That car was a hand-me-down from Thom's mother. Joe called it a courtesy car, because we'd gotten it for free. Considering the gas it ate and the sheer number of abrasive Fifth Amendment bumper stickers Joe had plastered across the back of it, I thought it might have been more of a courtesy to simply tell me that walking everywhere would keep my ass toned.

Mrs. Fancy's yellow cat, Phil, came barreling up and started hollering at me. I blinked stupidly. I'd forgotten to feed him this morning when I was over here stealing Mrs. Fancy's car. He spat out a row of short, urgent mews, like his stomach was a bomb that needed to be defused and we had to get to the Purina bag. Now.

Thom should be at the police station. He would have called the police, no doubt. He had to have. I had seen it on his face, that moment when he realized this wasn't someone shooting, it was someone shooting *at*.

Also, I'd hit Gretel at least once. Wasn't the vet obliged to call the cops? Or was that only people doctors? I'd logged enough time at the ER to learn that they had to call the cops for any gunshot wound. Hell, they wanted to call the cops for me every time, and that was only bruises and cracked bones, not bullets. By now they knew me so well, I figured I could show up with a sinus infection and the charge nurse would ask if I wanted the police out of sheer habit.

There was this one poky-nosed nurse in particular who always pushed me to "notify the authorities." She was a skinny, pale thing with permanent yogurt breath, as if she herself might be fermenting. Last time, she'd laid one of her hands, pink and soft as a mouse paw, on the wrist that wasn't broken and said, "You don't have to live like this," while my very flesh tried to creep off me to get out from under her touch.

"I fell downstairs," I said in my best bored voice, staring through her.

"Last time you said you had a ranch house, Mrs. Grandee," she said, and I was so surprised she'd remembered that I almost met her eyes. But I didn't. I'd come to this ER two or three times a year since my marriage. Our third year had been hard; I'd been in five times. I was a pro by now, and I kept my stare aimed at the wall over her left shoulder.

I said, "I fell down someone else's stairs," in that same bored voice, shuddering my good arm out from under her palm. I almost would have preferred the cops. Cops didn't get all moist and mothery.

Phil blurted out another desperate meow, winding through my ankles like a furry serpent. "I'm working on it," I told him, but I was staring at the outline of the gun chunks in the plastic bag.

I needed a hiding place for Pawpy's gun, and a damn good one. I couldn't sneak it home, not with Thom and a herd of God only knew how many Grandees over there. I tried to think of a place Mrs. Fancy never used, but it also had to be someplace I could get to easily and retrieve it without notice. "Guest room closet," I said, and I didn't realize I'd spoken out loud until Phil answered me with a squeak of aggrieved sound that was too bitchy to be called a mew.

"Wait your turn, Phil," I said. I grabbed the bag and the book and went on through the archway to the living room. Phil ran on ahead of me, all the way to the hallway with the bedrooms on it. His sides joggled, giving chubby testimony that late breakfasts were a new injustice in his life.

Mrs. Fancy's house was laid out like ours inside, only exactly backwards. There were two bedrooms besides the master, one she kept made up in case of company and one she'd turned into a sewing room. I went into the guest room. My first thought was to jam the bag under the bed, but Mrs. Fancy kept her house spotless. I could imagine the clunk she would hear the next time she ran the vacuum under it.

I slid open the closet door. Bingo. The bottom was lined with shoeboxes. I dropped to my knees and lifted the lid of a box on the top row. It held a pair of black suede peep-toe pumps that were a good two decades out of style. The box beside it had a pair of strappy red sandals with a high, jeweled heel. These must have belonged to her younger self, the one who looked like the dead sexy woman at the airport. It wasn't likely Mrs. Fancy would come digging in here anytime soon. I closed the lids and got on all fours to choose a box from the bottom row. Phil came up behind me and butted my hip with his head, insistent. I couldn't push him away; if I got cat dander on my hands, I'd spend the rest of my day sneezing.

"Phil, you asshole, give me a sec," I said. The shoeboxes were in nine stacks, each four or five boxes high, all the way across the bottom of the closet.

I chose the lowest one in the farthest back corner and pulled it out. I didn't register that it felt too unbalanced to hold a pair of shoes until I was already knocking the lid off.

The box was full of baby things: a silver cup, handmade pink booties, a baby book. There was a spritz of dark hair, fine as silk, in a Ziploc bag. A folded piece of old paper rested on top.

I'd gone looking for a hiding spot for me, but I'd discovered Mrs. Fancy's. I rocked up to a kneel and picked the paper out and opened it. It was the birth certificate. In the first-name slot, I read the name Ivy. I glanced down it, looking for a date. The certificate had been issued in 1972, four years after I was born. Ivy's father was listed as Harold James Wheeler, and her mother's name was Janine Fancy Wheeler. Janine was the daughter Mrs. Fancy was visiting right now. The one who had supposedly had her first baby last week.

I'd stumbled upon the secret flotsam of a sad time, and now I was digging in the private pieces of a grief that belonged solely to my friend. I put the birth certificate back. I put the box back, too, exactly as I found it, and then I moved to the opposite side of the closet.

I pulled out two shoeboxes from the last row on that side and found some sleek red pumps. The other held cloth espadrilles. I wedged one of the pumps into the other box, and then I wrapped the Target bag tight around the pieces of my gun. I put that bundle in with the single shoe. Phil weaseled up beside me and poked his sniffy head into the box that held the gun. I herded him away with the lid so I could close both boxes up tight and slide them back into their places.

I slid the Stephen King book behind all the boxes, resting on its spine with the cover pressed flat to the back wall. I got up and closed the closet door. Phil ran ahead of me down the hallway back to the kitchen, anxious and yelling. I took a minute to fill his bowl up—it was that or get Pawpy's gun back out and shoot him—and at that thought my hands shook, scattering pellets that Phil hoovered up immediately. I wondered where Gretel was. If Gretel was.

I couldn't walk across the yard and home and find out, though. Not while I stank of shooting and flop sweat and green woods. The truth was all over my skin.

I went to Mrs. Fancy's green-tiled guest bathroom and borrowed a washcloth. I didn't have time for a shower, and damp hair would be suspicious in its own way, so I took a whore's bath in the sink. I washed the gun smell off my hands with Mrs. Fancy's apple-scented soap and then swabbed out under my arms and between my legs. The mirror told me I still looked like sweaty hell, but that was a good thing. That could work for me. I threw the wet washcloth into the hamper and headed back to the kitchen.

Mrs. Fancy kept all her poisonous Comet and Pine-Sol in easy reach under the kitchen sink, like me. Neither one of us had babies to worry about. I opened the cabinet and grabbed the first thing that came to hand: Lemon Pledge. I sprayed a fine mist of it into the air like it was perfume and walked through. I grabbed the 409 and sprayed a jet directly on my hands and wiped them through my hair, hiding the smell of shooting as if it were a lover's musk.

I started to put the 409 back, but then I changed my mind and started pulling out all Mrs. Fancy's cleaning supplies. I stood them up in a scattered line on the counter and then got her vacuum out of the hall closet and left it in the middle of the living room for good measure. Set dressing, in case Thom came over to check my story.

Time to go home. My heart started banging against my ribs like it was fighting to get out. I paused to take deep breaths, ten of them, until I felt quieter inside. I set my face to its familiar sweet expression and walked out the front door, my steps steady and unhurried.

Our aqua house glowed, fiercely cheerful, bouncing the morning sun at me hard. The low roof was mostly flat, but there was a sloping point that rose up over the front door. It struck me that it looked like our house was wearing a jaunty hat several sizes too small for it. It was silly looking, and the mint-fresh color made it sillier. It didn't look like a house that would have a wolf inside. Today, it held at least two.

Still, this was probably the first time in my marriage that I'd ever been pleased to have Thom's parents over, especially his daddy. Joe had no trouble wrestling his boots off and thumping his bare feet up on our coffee table like he owned the place. In a way he did; the Grandees gave us nine thousand dollars for the down payment. It was a gift, not a loan, Joe said. Out loud, he said it. Frequently. In public. By now he had to have been repaid twice over out of Thom's considerable store of banked pride. I didn't think of it as a gift so much as another way to keep Thom feeling indebted. If Joe paid his eldest son what he was worth for running all three Grand Guns stores, we'd have been able to afford our own damn down payment, and on a house two steps up from Chez Crest.

But today, I was glad to think of Joe Grandee filling up the house like packing peanuts, pouring into every bit of open space. There would be no room to breathe, but on the upside, Thom and I would be suspended and separated. He could not crash into me.

I opened my front door. Just inside was a tiny square room with parquet flooring, a closet-size space that hoped to be a foyer when it grew up. Through the archway that led to the living room, I could hear Joe Grandee holding court. I'd come in midtrumpet, and I don't think anyone heard the door swing open over him.

"—married almost five years. What are you waiting for? I thought the one upside of you marrying a damn papist was we'd get a passel of grandkids. Your mother, she kept saying in the car, what if those shooters hadn't missed? What would you have left behind you on this earth?"

I waited in our wannabe foyer, caught by a silly hope that Thom would choose this moment to tell his father to pull his head out of our business and stick it up his own back end where it belonged. But there was only the familiar silence that meant Thom was supping, spoonful by spoonful, on his daddy's crap. It would surely go even sourer in his belly.

"Your brother here, he's bull's-eyed twice on Margie, and they got married half a year after you. What's wrong with you, boy?"

A small, square piece of the parquet floor extended into the living room, surrounded by our oatmeal-colored carpet. I stepped onto that wooden island, directly into my living room. "I'm on the pill," I said in the mildest tone I could muster, and immediately I had four sets of eyes on me.

"That's a little more information than I needed, missy," Joe said. "And where the hell have you been?"

He was hulked upright and angry in Thom's own easy chair, centered in the room. He was past fifty, and age had blunted the sharp edges of his athlete's body, but he was still broad-shouldered and solid. He had his booted feet set wide apart and flat against the earth. He leveled the question as if he had a right to the answer, staring me down like he was King Shit of Poo-Paw Mountain, as my daddy would have said. I felt my eyes getting narrow above the fake smile I'd drummed up for him.

Everything in the room seemed to turn inward to frame him, starting with his own wife. Charlotte was perched on the end of the sofa closest to him with her spine straight and her spiky knees pointed his way. Charlotte wasn't at ease even at home in their own dry-aired mansion, and in my house she sat stiffer than a cardboard cutout of herself.

Larry, the middle Grandee boy, stood on Joe's left, angled toward his daddy as well. He had a broad forehead and a Roman nose like Thom, but under that, his face waffled away in a chinless slide. He was an accountant, and he kept the books for the stores. Joe must have folded him up like the luggage he was and brought him in the cramped backseat of the big black truck.

"What brings alla y'all over here in the middle of the day," I said politely to Joe, but my gaze shifted quickly, almost against my will, going right to Thom. He was at the opposite end of the sofa, sitting way too still. His eyes looked like two pans of something left too long on simmer on the stovetop, seconds away from smoking and going black.

"I believe I asked where you've been, first," Joe Grandee said, stern, like he was the wronged, shot-at husband in the room. I was surprised he wasn't shirtless and barefoot, guzzling milk straight out of the carton while he questioned his son's wife.

It was all the more insulting because I understood what he was really asking. The only question that truly mattered, the one that only my husband had a right to ask. I could read its echo in the crackling air around Thom's head, three words repeating in an endless loop:

Who is he. Who is he. Who is he.

"I was next door," I said, jerking my thumb in the direction of Mrs. Fancy's place. "Now what are y'all doing here?" I pulled my eyebrows together, trying to look puzzled. "Is Gretel out back?"

Thom's stony face did not change at the mention of my dog. Neither did the words he was thinking at me.

Who is he was a refrain familiar enough for me to recognize it banging around his head. He started with *Who is he* and finished by putting me in the hospital. We'd had this conversation plenty, though there hadn't ever been a he. I'd never stepped out on Thom Grandee. I'd never so much as pointed a toe in the direction of that doorway.

"Next door?" Joe said, sounding so skeptical that I might as well have said I'd spent the morning skipping on down to hell to bring the devil some cool, sweet tea.

I nodded and sent Mrs. Fancy a mental apology for the lie I was about to tell on her. "I'm cat sitting for our elderly neighbor. She comes home tomorrow, so I was giving her place a good cleaning. It was all over filth."

Charlotte's spiky fingers flexed on her knees. She somehow managed to look down her short peck of a nose at me, even though she was seated. "You could have left a note," she said in her needle-thin voice. Charlotte was made entirely of angles. Even her small boobies were pointy, so sharp that it was a mystery to me how none of her boys had lost an eye while trying to breast-feed.

"I got Margie and me a set of them mobile phones, Thom. I can track her in a second," Larry said. Mystery solved. Larry had clearly never been breast-fed.

I had to squint to keep my eyes from rolling in their sockets. Track Margie, my butt. Larry lived chained to Margie's leg in the few hours he wasn't chained to his daddy's. He seemed happy enough grazing on whatever scant grass he found around their ankles.

The phone suggestion didn't even register with Thom. He didn't so much as spare his brother a grunt.

Who is he.

"I wasn't expecting company," I said. I plucked at my dirty T-shirt, then ran my palms down the sides of my ancient jeans. Exhibit A. "I must look a mess." I picked my scraggled hair up off my neck and raised my eyebrows at Thom. Exhibit B, and I hoped he could read my answer in the air around me as clear as I could read his question: *Do you think this is what a girl wears, how she does her hair, when she goes out to meet a lover?*

I couldn't stop myself from thinking that if I ever did step out, this would be the way. I would go to and from his arms in a ponytail, wearing clam diggers, no makeup on. I'd look like I'd spent the day gardening instead of on my back. I blinked at the thought, and on the inside of my closed lids I saw Jim Beverly's sweet and boyish monkey face again, his long upper lip and his flat nose, his eyebrows waggling as he made some joke and pulled me down to lie beside him.

"Look at me," I said again, quieter, to Thom, only to Thom. "I'm all over dirt and cobwebs."

Thom passed his big palm down over his face, slow, as if he'd been born with a caul and was only now rolling it away. He looked me up and down with fresh eyes. I prattled on. "You should have seen under her beds. I'm surprised I didn't find Jimmy Hoffa buried there in all that filth. I should run grab a quick shower."

I started to turn away, but Thom surged to his feet. My breath caught. He was so fast. His long strides carried him around our coffee table, eating up all the room between us. I took two panicked steps backwards, until the wall stopped me. My hands came up.

Thom steamrollered straight toward me with his bright eyes blind. He was seeing only the shape of me, as a thing to break, as if his parents and his liverless brother weren't clotting up our home. He pushed through my hands like they weren't there, but then his arms folded around me instead of rising up against me. I found myself pressed hard against him, my nose smashed flat against the broad slab of his chest. He buried his face in my hair and inhaled, drawing in sweat and ammonia like he was sniffing daisies.

I smelled him, too, the dark clove scent of my husband, and my eyes closed all on their own. My arms snaked their familiar way around him, and all at once it felt like we were alone in our house.

"They fucking shot at me, Ro," he said into my hair.

"They what?" I said, glad he couldn't see my face. "Who? What?"

"On my running trail," he said. "They took a couple of shots at me."

"Oh, my Lord," I said. I fake struggled, as if trying to get back to see him, but he held me tight. I turned my head sideways and pressed my ear against him, my face hidden against his arm. The thump and rumble of his heart struck me as beautiful, and I felt my eyes tear up, as if I hadn't caused this mess.

"They shot *at* me, Ro. Like they meant business."

"Who were they?" I asked, embracing his use of the plural.

"I don't know," he said, pulling me closer, too, hard enough to squeeze out half my breath. "I have to tell you something, Ro. She's fine. Okay? She will be mostly fine. But one shot hit Gretel."

"Gretel?" I said. We were finally to the place in the conversation that I cared about, and I couldn't seem to process the word *mostly*. This time I struggled for real, trying to lean back away from him and see his face, but he clamped me even harder. When he spoke, his voice was flinty, close enough to losing control that it scared me into stillness: "Ro. Please don't give me any crap about running your fat-ass dog right now."

"No, baby," I said. "Only what does that mean? Mostly fine?"

Tom sighed and shifted, easing his controlling grasp. "She got hit high in the shoulder. The vet had to take the leg. But she came through fine. She's sleeping."

My knees were glad for Thom's solid body. I trembled and leaned. "Take the leg?" I said. Those words made no more sense to me than "mostly" had.

"Shoot, she won't even know." Joe bulled his way back to the middle of the conversation from the easy chair. I started and felt Thom's reflexive jerk, too, as we remembered together that the room was full of all the wrong Grandees. I wished Margie were here or Thom's youngest brother, Peter. Margie taught middle school science, and that's a job that trains a woman to brook no crap. Nothing Joe said ever fazed Teflon Peter, either. He was a beautiful pothead who dropped in and out of jobs and colleges and the beds of pretty young women with good-natured, unshakable ease. But when Joe spoke, Thom turned away from me, one arm still across my shoulder, so the single thing we'd been split and opened to face Joe.

"I had a hunting dog lost a leg when I was growing up," Joe went on. "Trip, I called him. Get it? Trip? After he got used to it, he didn't remember he'd ever had four. He didn't remember his name used to be Blue, either. They aren't the brightest things, dogs."

Larry and Charlotte nodded in unison, like this was wise enough to be engraved on tablets and handed down the mountain. Commandment Eleven, Thy dog shalt have three legs and like it.

I looked up at Thom, trying to call him back, and asked, "What did the cops say?"

He made a scoffing noise, and he stayed facing his daddy. "Kids, maybe? Poachers? They didn't take it too serious."

Joe shook his head, disgusted. "Damn cops, checking boxes. They aren't going to do a damn thing."

I tried to look anything but relieved. Thom let go of me to pace up to the top of the room. He took long loping strides like a riled zoo tiger.

"I want to go see Gretel," I said to his back.

He wheeled on me and said, "She's going to be fucking fine, Ro."

It got very quiet.

"No call for that," Joe said. No one used the f-word in front of Charlotte. Not when Joe was in the room, anyway. Joe pulled it off as good ol' boy gentlemanly behavior, but I understood him better than that. It was one of the thousand ways he let the world—and his sons—know that his wife was not his equal. Joe shifted in the chair, prepping to rise, and I think we all could feel how electric the air had become, even thick old Larry.

I was trying to think of what to say, of what Thom's Ro would do. It wasn't coming natural. I didn't feel like Thom's Ro. I felt cornered, and I felt Rose Mae rising; excepting fire and locusts, she was the last thing needed in this overcharged room.

I made myself walk across the room toward my husband, trying to block his view of Joe with my small body. He was so on the edge, I knew if Rose Mae pushed him, even a little, the room would be all over blood in seconds. Mine, no doubt, though if God was merciful and just, it would be Joe's.

I took another step to Thom. I was small and he was so very angry. I didn't understand why Rose felt so excited, almost hopeful. Why she was putting her hand on his broad chest and why his flesh shuddered at her touch.

"Baby," I said, "I'm so glad you're all right. That's the only thing that matters. That you're all right."

It was the right thing. He wheeled back into his lopy pacing. After a moment, Charlotte wrinkled up her nose-peck at me and said, "It's nice you're helping your friend, next door, but you might want to have that shower before you go check on the dog. Or before you go, well, anywhere."

Thom's eyebrows beetled back down as he walked the room. My bullets and his daddy had put him as on edge as I had ever seen him. His ears pricked and his brow furrowed at every little rumble.

"A shower sounds like a good idea," I said, treading careful, trying to see what Charlotte had said to rile him. Then I had it. Me helping my *friend*. Thom and I didn't have friends, neither of us. He came to me for food, for sex, for talk, for play, for violence, and he had no other needs. We were closed together like two halves of a clam's shell. If I had a friend, she would notice long sleeves and scarves in summer, and unlike Mrs. Fancy, women in my generation had not been trained to look the other way.

It wasn't as if Thom and I were hermits. We were friendly enough with couples at church, and I was in the Ladies' League and helped with food and clothing drives. Sometimes I went to lunch with Margie, but her job and her young boys kept her too busy for it to happen often. Thom hunted with his brothers and his father, and he played on the Grand Guns softball team. Every other Sunday, we choked down his mother's dry-meat roast at an all-family dinner. But Thom didn't like me to have phone calls or girls' night at the movies. That sort of thing brought us back to *Who is he* every time.

I said to Charlotte, ultracasual, "I'm going to have to talk to Mrs. Fancy's son or whoever that is who mows her lawn. She might need to go to assisted living. She seems like a nice enough old lady, but that house . . . well, look at me, and you'll get a clue how bad it was."

I could feel Thom's hackles lowering as I spoke, but his fingers still fisted and uncoiled in angry rhythms as he paced. It wasn't good, having me in the room, untouchable in every way that mattered.

I said, "I think I will grab that shower."

I took silence as permission and got out, fast-walking all the way down the hallway to our master bedroom. Gretel was alive. I wouldn't think about her leg now. I couldn't. She was alive, and I was not alone. Those were the main things. The vet had said she would be mostly fine. Mostly.

I didn't realize Thom had followed me until I was inside our bathroom. When I turned and saw him, I almost screamed.

"I told them I'd be right back," he said.

He came at me and I backed away, but he was so fast. He bullied me backwards to the wall, and I was half-terrified and half-excited, not knowing which thing he wanted. My hands were flat against his chest, and I looked up, trying to read his face. He kissed me then, hard, first on my mouth and then on my throat with his mouth open like he was trying to eat me up. Big Bad Wolf kisses. His hands on my body gripped me hard enough to hurt.

"You smell like lemons," he said.

"I'm filthy," I said.

"I don't care."

"Your parents are just down the—"

He interrupted me. "I don't damn care."

"Your daddy—"

He came back to my mouth again, eating my words, and all at once I was as ready as he was. Kissing him felt slick and secret and dirty. This was like high school sex, male hands seeking desperate paths through my clothing with a room full of parents right down the hall.

"Hurry," I said, and he shoved my jeans down around my ankles. I kicked one foot loose. He jerked his pants down, too, not bothering with the buttons. He lifted me and flattened my back against the cold tile. His mouth was on me, and he was grinding into me, hard and good with only the thin cotton shield of my panties between us, and this was like high school, too. I closed my eyes against the sunshine, and there was Rose Mae Lolley, rampant in my head with her Jim Beverly.

I kept my eyes closed, and the world tilted and was darker, and Rose Mae was in Jim's car after a game, parked up by Lipsmack Hill, her shirt pushed up and her bra unhooked. I peeked through my lashes, gasping, and there was Thom in the sunshine with his face twisting and his eyes open. I closed my eyes, and Jim had one hand between Rose Mae's legs, rubbing her through her jeans, and Thom said, "I thought I was going to die, Ro."

I said, "They missed. They missed."

All the while in my head I heard Jim Beverly whispering to Rose Mae, and Rose's hands remembered what it was like to touch Jim, too, her clever fingers counting the buttons on the fly of his Levi's, endless crazy-making touching through layers of denim and white cotton. She would cup and grip the outline of him, learning by feel this thing she hadn't seen since they were nine. It was a rigid line of heat that felt nothing like the little-boy pansy blossom she'd seen.

Thom snaked one hand between us and ripped my panties away. Then he was in me, breathing hard, his face buried in my 409-filled hair. He said, "God, it's like screwing Mr. Clean," but he was grinning. I could feel his teeth against my scalp.

I closed my eyes and heard the ten-year-old echo of Jim Beverly's voice in my head, saying, "I'm going to kill him. I'm going to kill your worthless daddy, if he lays one hand on you again." Jim's hand gripped the undercurve of Rose Mae's ass, pulling her against him to grind as he said, "I'll slip in at night and hold a pillow over his face while he's passed out." Jim's fingers followed the inseam of her jeans. "Who would know? Some drunk smothers while passed out? That must happen all the time."

Thom was in me, each thrust pushing me up the wall, his face in my hair, just as I liked, and inside I was tipping over. Ten years away, Jim Beverly's words blew through Rose like a wind, lifted her and sent her into someplace new and dazzling. We met there, met and melded for one moment, so real that I heard that old remembered whisper in my own ear. "I'll kill him for you," Jim Beverly said. I opened my eyes and saw my husband's face.

Far away, in a car parked up by Lipsmack Hill, Jim's hand still worked between Rose Mae Lolley's legs. He hadn't known that Rose Mae had finished. He was still living blindly in the space where her hand cupped him. But I was wholly in the present. Here in my bathroom, I laughed and arched into Thom in the wake he'd caused. I felt so good. We both felt so damn good.

That laughy sound from me, so happy, and the way I flexed my back up pushed Thom over, too. We breathed in four or five times together, big cleansing whoops of air, and then his arms lost strength and he let me slide down the wall to thump onto my bare bottom. He relaxed into a lean against the countertop. I pulled off my shirt. My bra was torn, the cups hung down over my ribs, and my jeans were in a bunch around one ankle.

I grinned up at him and he whispered, "This is nuts."

He shook his head and began packing himself away and pulling his shirt down. Half his vinegar was gone, and yet he still smelled dangerous. I was spent, but Rose Mae was a wild thing in me, rioting and pleased.

As soon as he got his shirt tucked back in, Thom said, "I have to go out there. Take your shower," and he was gone.

I took my time, letting hot water pound down on my shoulders while my conditioner set for ten minutes. Even after I got out, I stayed in the bathroom, slowly moisturizing every inch of my skin and then blowing out my long, thick hair.

I think I already knew what Rose Mae wanted to do next. It wasn't what I wanted. I didn't let myself even think it. I didn't let myself think at all. I didn't want to wreck the good peace I felt in my whole body in the aftermath of sex. I didn't want to start again.

I aimed the dryer at my roots to get some volume, staring into the mirror. Rose Mae Lolly stared back at me, not thinking either. She didn't have to think. Her day would come, a day when Thom would hurt me bad enough to loose her. I closed my eyes against her patience. I dried my hair by feel, but she was still there, chockfull of something close to smug. All she had to do was wait.

CHAPTER

❧

5

GRETEL CAME HOME. Her empty shoulder was a white cone of bandages. The missing leg seemed to puzzle her more than it distressed her. She'd try to lay her head down on her front legs, then pop back up and make thinking eyebrows at the place where it used to be. Five seconds of brain work was enough to make her too tired to keep on; she'd cock her head at an angle that looked to me like the dog version of a shrug and lie back down to sleep.

She fast mastered a three-beat lazy canter, and she got around the house and yard just fine when she chose to heave herself up off her favorite snooze rug. I tried to drown my guilt in gratitude to God for the small mercies that had been afforded me. She had lived in spite of me, and though one leg down, she was exactly her same dim and lovely self.

For the rest of that week, in celebration, I made what I called manfood, the meaty dinners that Thom liked best. Pork roast with potatoes and baked apples. Turkey pot pie. Stuffed flank steak. The meals were too heavy for me, but if ever a man needed some comfort food, it was Thom. He stomped around with two creases between his eyebrows that pointed straight up like horns.

While I'd holed up in our bathroom drying my long hair and trying not to think, Thom's daddy must have kept on force-feeding him all kinds of crap. One piece in particular had gotten way down wedged in Thom's belly. He was grinding and churning at it, but it wasn't breaking down. I could see how it chafed him from the inside out, this thing his daddy had stuffed down him. I'd seen this all before.

I'm not sure if Thom understood his daddy's last visit was the reason he was so set on picking a fight with me, but I sure as hell did. I owed Joe Grandee thank-you notes for more than one prior bone crack; Thom may have delivered them, but they were presents Joe had bought and paid for. So I cooked soothing foods that made Thom logy and sleepy, and I tried to live quiet in the corners of our rooms until he'd worked it out.

On Wednesday, Thom looked down at the meat loaf on his plate with one lip curling, as if I'd served up possum sushi. It was a beautiful meat loaf, too, made with half ground pork and lots of sage like his mother's, only I didn't overcook mine until it tasted like a chunk of mummy. He didn't so much as lift his fork.

"I was hoping for that sour cream chicken you do."

He had his wrists resting on the edge of the table, and I watched his hands flex and unflex. He looked to me like a bad storm coming. Like a bad storm almost here.

"I've bought everything to make it at the grocery," I said. "I'll make that chicken tomorrow."

"I wanted it tonight," he said, mulish.

I thought, *And that's the battle cry of every spoiled toddler.*

I didn't say it. I knew this game. Hell, I had helped invent it. But I wouldn't play. I couldn't afford to anymore. Rose Mae was biding her time; she knew that I had glimpsed the path she'd set. It would not take much to get me walking down it.

So I showed him some teeth and kept my brow smooth and my tone mild. "Why don't you go watch the news? I can throw that chicken together in maybe thirty minutes. I'll use the meat loaf for sandwiches. That'll be so much nicer for you this week than deli ham and cheese."

His brows moved inward, puzzling up together, and he looked

at me like he wasn't sure whose table he'd sat down at. I wasn't sure, either.

"That's ridiculous," he said.

"I know," I said. "But if you really need that chicken for your day to go right, then I want you to have it."

Now he looked almost forlorn, as if I'd abandoned him.

"Thom," I said to him, "I'm trying." It sounded to me like a plea. I didn't want the gypsy's cards to be for us. They fit her life just as well as they fit mine, and I was doing my damnedest to prove it had been her draw. I couldn't do that alone. "I'm trying so hard."

His gaze dropped to his plate, and he took a big sniff of air into his lungs. I watched his chest expand. I'd always loved the workings of his thick, sleek body. I loved to put my ear to his chest and feel the boom-thump of his heart, then slide lower to hear the gurgle and sigh of his belly hard at work on something I had made.

When he finally spoke, his voice came out so quiet that it was like he had a secret he was whispering to the mashed potatoes. "I see that," he said. He started eating, so I did, too. A few minutes later, chewing, he said, "This is delicious." He sounded surprised.

I said, "Good," in a truly pleased way. I didn't say, *"No shit, Sherlock. My meat loaf tastes great and water is wet and your name is Thom."* I blocked those words in with a bite of salad and swallowed them with a gulp of sweet tea. He watched me struggle to get it all down. I managed it, barely. We found ourselves grinning at each other across the table like children, while under it, Gretel thumped her tail against the floor; usually when I said the word *good*, with such sincerity, I meant her.

He said, "I'll try, too." I watched him, wary-eyed, and he added, "I mean it, Ro."

I nodded, and then we picked up our glasses and drank, watching each other over the rims, like we were solemnly sealing a deal with sweet tea and cool water.

The next day, when he came home from work, he paused and stood silent in our cubicle of a foyer. I was sitting on the sofa, waiting for a timer in the kitchen, and I heard him stamping and breathing in that tiny space, but he didn't say anything. When at last he stepped through the archway, it was as if he'd left his father and his job and the bills and his temper in the cube behind him.

On this side of the archway, we holed up, honeymoon style, eating a quiet dinner and then watching a rented movie with a lot of kissing in it. I sat wedged between Thom and Gretel on the sofa, snug and pleased. By morning, everything seemed fresh-made between us.

It occurred to me I should have hidden in the bushes and taken a couple of potshots at his fool head years ago. It was turning out to be downright good for both of us. I think he was pleased to be alive, and me, I was scared of the secret thing Rose was planning next if he couldn't join me in playing nice.

I kept the house so clean, even Thom's mother couldn't have found a dusty corner with white gloves and a microscope. Thom and I ran together most mornings, going way too fast to bring Gretel, and at night we sat on the sofa, breathing in the orange oil smell of our clean house. We watched a lot of college ball, and I rooted for his teams, even when Bama was playing. If no one we liked had a game, we rented old movies or played gin rummy after dinner.

Four days a week, I cashiered at the gun store, and I didn't let myself bitch to Thom about still making minimum wage, although Joe Grandee was making that harder and harder.

A week into our truce, a salesman didn't show, and Joe asked me to help customers as best I could until he could get in a replacement. I'd been raised up with guns, and I sure as hell knew more about our stock than the missing fella. My best times with my daddy had been when he took me out shooting. I'd ask a thousand questions about zeroing or muzzle velocity, then lure him into musing about who made a better .45, Colt or Smith & Wesson, stretching our good hours into half a day. If Joe Grandee had ever looked past my boobs up to where I kept my brains, he'd have had me on the sales floor years ago.

I'd been working the floor maybe half an hour when an obvious fat fish came in—midlife crisis fellow with a salt-and-pepper comb-over and three-hundred-dollar pointy-toed cowboy boots. He was looking, he said, for a little home protection.

"Nothing flashy," he said, meaning nothing expensive.

"Of course not," I said. "Guy like you, you want something sleek and plain, with enough power for the job at hand. Not some silly cowboy gun that's all show."

Ten minutes later, I had his fingers curling around a gorgeous black snub-nosed revolver that cost over a thousand bucks.

"I like how that looks in your hand," I said, and I let myself sound breathless. I leaned over the counter to get a better view, biting my bottom lip.

I sent him out the door with the revolver and ammo and a gun safe and a cleaning kit and a couple of packs of the overpriced cinnamon gum we kept by the register. He swaggered out hips first like he was toting ten pounds of extra penis, swearing to come back and take a look at our rifles before hunting season.

I didn't realize Joe had come out from the office. He was standing in the doorway to the back, watching me run the endgame. The next day, when I came in to relieve Janine, she stayed perched up on the stool, shaking her head at me. I thought I'd misread my schedule, but Joe said, "Derek had an emergency, darlin'. Cover the floor for him until I can get a replacement?"

When I clocked out six hours later, Janine was still running the drawer and Derek's "replacement" had yet to show. After that, it seemed like some member of Joe's sales team needed sick leave or vacation every other shift I worked. It didn't take a genius to figure Joe was cutting their time because I was better. Meanwhile, I got the same four bucks and change an hour I would have gotten if I'd spent the time under the Golden Arches saying, "You want some special sauce on that?"

Still, I didn't fight the Joe Grandee party line: Grand Guns was a family business, so I was building up our own future. It was only to myself that I added, *And helping Joe buy himself another big-ass Harley-Davidson.* After all, that big-ass Harley would be part mine on the merciful day the Lord got tired of Joe pooing up the earth and called him home to heaven. Or wherever.

At home, I sat on Thom's lap and nibbled his edges and tempted him to bed early. I gave him cheerleader sex, bouncy, full of gymnastics and genuine enthusiasm. In my head the words went like this: *Thom, Thom, he's our man, if he can't do it, no one can.* Rose would echo, *If not, I have another plan.* I cut her off right there, making damn sure I never thought a different man's name while Thom Grandee's hands were on my body. I pushed away all memories of other hands from days long past, and I didn't think about old promises made on Alabama nights hot enough to be the sweetest kind of sticky.

Not when I was awake, anyway. Some nights, my sleeping self would see Rose Mae, no more than fourteen, haunting the woods behind Fruiton's old elementary school, waiting for Jim Beverly to shimmy down the oak tree outside his bedroom window and come join her. She'd wake me up, too sleep-logged to stop myself from remembering how it went the night Rose Mae decided to see for herself what manner of pleasure her daddy found in drinking.

The moon was near full that night, lighting the way even as it set. It was so late, the tree frogs had shut up and gone to sleep. This was hours after every kid with a decent human mother had been called home and fed and tucked beneath a blanket. Rose Mae waited in the clearing that she and Jim had made their own when they were nine, watching Jim Beverly come loping through the trees to meet her.

He said, "Hey, Rose-Pop," in a whisper, though they were far from any other ears. He kissed her mouth, then set about building them a campfire. He was an ex–Boy Scout, so he knew to clear a hollow down to the bare dirt and bank it in stones. Rose gathered twigs and sticks to feed it. When it was crackling and cheerful, they sat pressed together, side by side.

"Did you get something?" Rose asked.

Jim pulled a flat bottle out of his back pocket. Amber liquid glinted in the firelight. "Whiskey. I stole it off Lance," he said. Lance was his oldest brother. "I hope it makes you happy because when he notices, I'm a dead man."

He was grinning that lopsided smile that got her every time, his thin upper lip showing too much gum. She couldn't help but grin back.

Rose Mae said, "Lance can't fuss. If he starts to kill you even a little, you tell him you'll rat him out for that fake ID."

Jim cracked the seal and screwed off the cap, then sat, holding it. The fumes coming out of the lip smelled to her like someone had bottled her daddy. Jim started to bring it to his lips, then stopped. Started to lift it again. Stopped.

It was Rose Mae who began. She wrapped her hand around Jim's on the bottle and guided it to her mouth. She test-drove her father's method, drinking as if the liquor was shoes and toys left out on the floor and it was her tiresome job to put the mess away. She swallowed, then coughed in hard barks that sounded like a circus seal she'd seen once on TV. Air in her mouth brushed against the sour mash taste, reactivating it. She clamped her lips and breathed deep through her nose to keep the cheap whiskey from coming right back up.

Jim watched her until she'd blinked away the water in her eyes and was breathing regular again. He took a big sip and rolled it around his mouth before swallowing. He made a "bad medicine" face, but then he took another big sip and rolled that one around his mouth, too. He made that same face after each of his turns, as if the harsh taste continued to surprise him. They passed the bottle back and forth until it was empty, not talking much.

They set the empty bottle by the fire.

"This don't do shit," Rose said, but her voice sounded funny to her, and she started giggling.

He started laughing, too, and said, "What's funny?"

Rose stood up and the ground tilted and swayed under her,

as if their private clearing had floated out to sea without them noticing.

"It does things," Rose said. "Stand up."

The night became snapshots and flashes. Rose would remember it only in bursts: Jim and Rose running the narrow trails. Jim hollering and Rose shushing. They spun off each other into trees, then came back and grabbed each other and wrestled, practicing a kind of making out that was more like fighting than kissing.

Then he had her on the ground, on her back, her jeans-clad legs around him, feeling the rigid line of his cock straining toward her through the denim. She tried to turn her face from the whiskey smell on his breath, but he put his mouth on hers and sucked her air out, and his hips ground into her. She bucked, close to panic, and he rolled over to let her on top for a breath.

He flipped her again, and her back landed on a short slope. They rolled together into blackberries that clutched and hurt and broke them apart. He thrashed free, pricked and bloodied. When he grabbed her hand to pull her to her feet, she saw the face of some other Jim, a secret face the whiskey had loosed. He grinned, big teeth gleaming, and Rose understood that both of his faces belonged to her. He helped her out of the blackberries carefully, the two of them peeling away the thorny vines. He drew her close again, sweet now, and she could smell the liquor on him, and the whites of his eyes looked as hard and shiny as the skin of a boiled egg.

That was the first time he put his mouth against her ear and whispered, "We could go to your house and make your daddy stop."

"Stop what?" she said, because the hitting wasn't something anyone talked about, though surely people knew. Fruiton had a mall, three high schools, and too many churches to count, but it was at its heart a small town. Of course they knew, even though Rose Mae was a pro at covering for her daddy, and Daddy did his part, too. He never hit her in the face. But things like this were always known, tittle-tattled by women over back fences, whispered in the hollows between teachers and preachers: *All is not right at the*

Lolley house. But it wasn't a thing that got said loud and plain in front of folks that would work to stop it. It wasn't said plain even between Rose Mae and Jim. Sometimes, making out, he'd push her clothing around until he found hurt skin, and then he'd put his fingers, reverent, on her bruises. It felt so good to have him know her in this way, but they didn't talk about it.

"Stop what?" she said again, to make him say it out loud at last.

But he answered, "Stop everything. Stop breathing."

She laughed, an uncertain sound.

He was still whispering, face-to-face now, so close their noses almost touched. The whiskey on his breath made her eyes water. "Drunks like him, they must smother in their sleep alla time. I could finish him for you. Do you want me to, Rose-Pop? Do you want me to make him quit?"

He looked cold and capable, laying out murder for her like wares on a blanket. All she had to do was nod. It dizzied her, made her small. She could feel how the whole great world heaved and spun and dangled itself in space. She shoved him away and managed four steps before she found herself on her knees, throwing up.

She threw up for a long time, it seemed, and then she crept sideways away from her vomit. She came to some clear ground, under a loblolly pine, far enough away so all she could smell was the tang of its dropped needles. She lay down on her belly, pressing her cheek into the cool, firm ground, and her eyes closed and that was all she knew.

A few hours later, walking home with Jim through the woods with the morning sun an overbright punishment, she didn't know if she would get home and find her daddy dead or not. She hadn't said yes, but she knew she hadn't said no, either. The idea of her daddy being dead was like something from television. She could see herself in a slim black dress at his funeral. It was distant, and she didn't truly believe in it.

On the path ahead she saw matted fur, an animal, stretched

out like a sleeping thing, but too still. It was a calico cat, someone's little pet, lying on its side with its legs stretched out long and
crossed at the ankles like a sleeping lamb's feet. Its head had been
turned around backwards.

She stopped. She had this crazed moment of absolute conviction: Jim had done this. His arms were allover scratches. He had
picked up the cat and turned its head around and her father was
dead and she had let Jim do it and she did mind, after all.

It came back to her, how strongly Jim had meant his offer, how
she had seen him wearing the face of a thing that was capable of it.
All at once she didn't want to go home. Jim was a weapon with a
hair trigger, and the simple act of not saying no, of saying nothing,
had been enough of a breeze to pull it. The little cat was actually
and really dead, and Jim had made it so, and it was permanent and
serious and awful. She did not want to go home and see what else
Jim had left for her.

Then Jim said, "Poor thing. You think a fox got him?" in such
sorrowing tones that the idea stopped feeling true. The Beverlys
had a fat white cat named Moses that would sit in Jim's lap and
purr as he rumpled it. How could she have thought this boy could
ever kill a cat?

Jim said, "Rose-Pop, don't look." She closed her eyes and felt
him walk her past. She wanted to look back over her shoulder at it,
but he put an arm around her, stopping her, and said, "Poor little
thing. I'll get you home, and I'll come back and bury her."

She looked down at her own hands, and they were as scratched as
his arms. The blackberries, she remembered. She was better protected,
was all, in long sleeves that hid the bruises her daddy had put on her.
It was from the blackberries, and she knew her father would be passed
out safe and whole when she got home, ready to wake up even more
hung over than she was, ready to start another got-damn ugly day.

Something in the woods had gotten the little cat, had picked it
up and turned its head backwards and put it back. It was sad, and
that was all. Nothing to do with them.

But Rose Mae and I both knew that the story would have been different if she had only said yes. If she had had one less drink or one more, whichever would have made her head nod, even slightly. If she'd said yes, she knew where Jim's feet would have taken him once she was passed out safe in the needles.

When they came to the fork where they split to go their own ways home, she said to him, "We're not doing that again."

"No," he agreed.

"I don't like you like that," she said. "I won't be with you like that."

He said, "I don't like me like that, either," with such a ring of trueness in it that she reached for him, but he was already turning and walking away.

Not even a year later, after they'd taken a blanket to the top of Lipsmack Hill to become lovers for real, this offer to kill her daddy would come back. It was something he would whisper to her, his mouth warm and wet against her hurt places. He lapped them like a cat. It would not sound true. Sometimes it sounded like comfort, and other times it was young and angry, blustery even. But she never forgot seeing the Jim who had meant it, that capable thing the whiskey had let loose, and these nights, I was dreaming of that capable thing, too. I woke up smelling the green woods where I had waited for him.

Whenever the dream woke me, I would stand up and get a drink of water. I would pace the hall and plan the next night's dinner, maybe make a shopping list, until the last lingering smells of those long-ago woods were gone from me. I had to fill my head up with right-now things.

A clean home, good gun sales, better meat loaf, best sex. These things let me stay inside each minute as it happened. I trained my thoughts away from the future, and I didn't dwell on gypsies or cards, especially not the hanged man with his snarling wolf hat, his bound hands. "*Those were for the gypsy,*" I whispered when my imagination tried to make me be the girl inside that burning tower.

If I had a marriage made of swords, then we were both trying our damnedest to stand shoulder to shoulder only, weapons pointed outward, watching each other's back.

Spring waned, the blooms full-blown and readying for summer, until one day I barked my shin on an end table. It hurt like a son of a bitch. I sat down to rub it, watching my skin swell, the flesh already darkening. Pale skin bruises easy, and I knew it would be purple by tomorrow. I nursed my rising lump, and out of habit, I found myself checking all over for other parts that might need ice or attention. I couldn't find so much as a twinge. I realized I was milk-colored and smooth all over.

We'd never gone so long before.

CHAPTER

6

THE DRY AIR GOT crisp with heat around the edges, and we were coming to what I'd always called icebox weather. Late spring was my favorite time of year. I wasn't much of a baker, though thanks to the stream of goody plates Mrs. Fancy brought to morning coffee and left behind, Thom thought I was. Still, I could make a decent lemon chess pie, and the weather was right for it. I got a pan of lasagna in the oven and then put my Cuisinart together and made the pastry. I was rolling out the crust when Thom came into the kitchen and boosted himself up onto the counter across the room from me.

Before I could speak, he said, "Why don't we have a baby?" with the emphasis on the word *don't*, so it didn't sound like a suggestion. It sounded puzzled, like he was looking to understand why one of the spare rooms wasn't already covered in teddy bear wallpaper and piled high with Huggies.

"Hey, what's in your jeans?" I shot back. It was the familiar start line to an old conversation I liked to have with him.

He grinned and said, "Why, Mrs. Grandee, that's where I keep my fine ass."

I said, "That's right. Why are you fine ass–ing up my counter-top, the very place I'm going to fix our salad?"

He hopped down onto his feet and leaned instead. "Excuse my buttocks, ma'am, and tell me, why don't we?"

I said, "There's a lot of reasons why."

He nodded, slow and thoughtful, and then he said, "The Catholic thing."

"That's part of it," I said, surprised that this was what he'd bring up first. Back in Kingsville, where we got engaged, my Catholicism hadn't seemed like such a big thing to him. At college, he'd had the whole of Texas stretched between him and his stick-up-the-butt Protestant family.

Charlotte, who'd been born and raised in a border town, believed it was the excessive Catholic breeding of Mexicans that was wrecking Texas. Joe was a more practical racist, who understood that without illegal immigrants he might have to pay a decent wage to get his yard done. But he agreed that it wasn't a religion for upright, gun-store-owning white folk. Things had looked a lot different to Thom once we were in Amarillo with his daddy asking me across the dinner table, "Are you a *practicing* Catholic?" in the same tone he might use to ask if I was a practicing cannibal.

"You don't go to mass," Thom said. "You don't go to confession."

I'd gone a few times, when Thom's daddy took him to a big gun show in Houston or Atlanta. It had caused a lot of friction early on, so confession, like coffee with Mrs. Fancy, was something I did on the sly.

I said, "Give us a child until he is seven . . ."

"And he'll be a Catholic forever," Thom finished for me.

"The church had me till I was eight. It's easier on everyone if I go to y'all's church on Sundays, what with your folks acting like incense and praying to the saints and votives is straight up witchcraft. But you don't stop being Catholic because you stop going to mass. I may be in your church, Thom, but don't ever think I'm of it." I stopped pinching the edges of my crust into a ruffle and turned to face him, leaning back on my own piece of counter across the kitchen. I kept my body relaxed and my tone light, but I looked him in the eye, and he knew I meant every word I said. "I am not going to wreck my figure and squeeze seven pounds of baby out my personals and spend the rest of my life raising something up unbaptized, just so it can get old and die and go to hell."

Thom was nodding, but it was thoughtful-like, not agreement. When he talked he sounded easy, but he was as serious as I had been. "You're on the pill, Miss Catholic, so where are you going?"

"Purgatory, for my sins," I said. "I hope I squeak into purgatory. And I'll have earned every damn millennium I spend there."

I turned to the fridge and got out my bowl of filling, beating it with a fork to refluff the beaten eggs. He didn't go anywhere, but he didn't say anything, either, not until I was pouring the mix into the crust.

"Do I have to be Catholic?" Thom asked. "Or just him?"

I heard it as an echo of Thom's old, favorite question. *Who is he.* There had never been a him, but just the asking led toward fists and fury. I could feel little hairs pricking up on the back of my neck, and my hands slowed down. "Who is him?"

"Or her. It could be a her," Thom said, and I realized he meant the baby. "But Grandee men, we tend to throw boys."

I found my spine relaxing, and I said, "I gave you up as hell-bound years ago, sugar. But I can't raise a Presbyterian baby."

"I can live with that," Thom said. "I mean, I'm good with that."

I shot him a skeptical look over my shoulder and scraped out the last of the filling with my spatula.

He said, "I'm not converting, but if you need me to go sit through mass with you on Sundays to be a family, I can do that. It's not that important to me."

"It's important to your daddy," I said, peeking over my shoulder at him again.

All at once those two spiky creases were running up the center of Thom's forehead, and I gave all my attention back to my pie. But his voice came out even as he said, "This won't be his kid, Ro. I don't see as how he has a say in where our baby gets his preaching."

I had to bite back words then, about how Joe stuck his Roman nose into everything and Thom let him. Instead, I swallowed and said to my pie, "Church is not the only reason, Thom."

"I know," Tom said. "Money."

I'd been thinking of Thom's temper. But more than half of Thom's rages and all our money came from Joe. I figured money was a back road in to what we both knew was the real subject. When he spoke, his voice had settled into serious tones.

"I'm going to talk to my father on Monday. We can't raise kids living in this school district, so there's a move to consider. You'll want to be home, and that means we'll be losing your little checks, too. He has to see that.

"I'm going to tell him straight up how much I ought to be making. I've asked around, and I've even been down at the library, doing some research. I have a pretty good idea what I'm worth, and it's a helluva lot more than my current salary. I have it all on paper. I made a graph to show him what other men doing my kind of job here in Texas get paid.

"I made an appointment. I put it in his book for next week, like any employee would. When I began, he said he didn't want to start me out high because I was his kid. He wanted me to earn my way up, and I respect that. I think that was even good for me, because now I don't take anything for granted and I know what work is, which I sure didn't learn in college. But I've put five good years in, and these days, he's doing less and less as I do more and more. I've grown into doing a pretty big job."

"I'm not the one you have to convince," I said, turning back around to face him.

He was smiling, and his posture was loose and easy. He said, "Sorry. I've been practicing this in my head for days, getting myself ready to say it to him."

"What if he says no?" I asked carefully. "If he starts in on that 'Boy, you're building your own future, this is sweat equity' stuff, and all it really means is no, what then?"

Thom said, "Then it's time for me to find another job. I've been practicing how to say that to him, too."

He sounded so sure of himself, so calm and confident. I was close to believing him, and I realized my floury fingers had come up to worry at my bottom lip. I made my hand drop and I said, "You are going to give your father an ultimatum?"

"I wouldn't put it like that," Thom said, but he shrugged with the easy jock confidence that had always before deserted him when confronted with his father. My jaw dropped and my eyes went wide.

"You are!"

"About time," he said, shrugging, so cool. I realized I was staring at him like a middle schooler with a way bad crush. "So what do you think?"

I blinked. The most important things were still sitting unsaid in between us. I was on the pill because it seemed to me the lesser sin. I'd never let him put a baby in me, on purpose, when I knew with such certainty he would punch it right back out. I couldn't see a single way that it would be any different from penciling in an abortion and then trying to get pregnant in time to make the appointment.

But I thought of the sole purple bruise on my shin, lonely in this new marriage we'd been making ever since I had hidden in the woods and taken those shots at him. It reminded me of a line from a story I must have read a thousand times as a girl. "She would of been a good woman," a character says, "if it had been somebody there to shoot her every minute of her life."

The story was by Flannery O'Connor, and she'd been a southern Catholic, too. Like my mother, who had left O'Connor's stories and a hundred other books behind when she left us. And like me, who'd read each of those books over and over. We were rare things, southern Catholics, swamped in Baptists and hemmed in by Methodism. Maybe O'Connor had been telling me something, one pope's girl to another.

Six weeks was such a small time, for Thom and for me, especially when I held it up against the years that had come before.

Still, it wasn't only the time I had to measure. Thom was offering me my religion back, like it was a gift. Presbyterians skipped a step, going straight from group confession to communion, as if absolution was a simple thing that slept at my feet like Gretel, waiting to be called. They didn't understand penance.

When Rose Mae brought me back to that crazy place where I called violence to me like it was my lover, if I had my religion back, I could learn to go to the priest instead of Thom. A few hours on bent knee with a rosary might still even Rose Mae Lolley. Hell, worst case, I could go dredge me up a nun. I still remembered the precision of Sister Agnes's ruler stinging my palm from catechism classes long gone; no one understood crime and punishment better than a savage little nun.

Meanwhile, here was my husband, telling me he was ready to face his father directly and say a thing Joe wouldn't like. I didn't know this man, but I loved him. God help me, how I loved Thom Grandee in this moment.

I said, "Why *don't* we have a baby," with that same odd emphasis, as if I, too, could not imagine why it hadn't happened already.

"Why don't we," he asked, and this time it did sound like a suggestion.

I said, "I can't stop in the middle. It will mess me up. But when this cycle ends, I won't start the next month's pills."

He ran right at me, fast, and I was not afraid. He picked me up and spun me. My floury hands left white prints against the dark blue of his shirt, and I clasped them around his neck. He carried me back across the kitchen, and I felt my ballet flats slip off and plop onto the floor.

He boosted me up onto the very countertop I'd fussed at him for sitting on earlier. Then we stilled, caught up inside a quiet kind of happy. He stood between my knees with my bare feet dangling down the counter on either side of him. We stayed there kissing with our mouths mostly closed for long minutes, innocent, the kind of making out I'd only seen practiced by teenagers on eighties sitcoms. We breathed each other's air, peaceful together, solemn and pleased inside of our decisions.

Thom was still Thom, so pretty soon the kissing got serious, and his hands took a wander up under my skirt.

"When we have kids," he said, "we won't be able to do it in the kitchen."

The casual way he said it, "when we have kids," got me flushed. I laughed and said, "We're not doing it in the kitchen now, buster. The countertop is the wrong height, and if you're thinking about that cold linoleum floor, I suggest you rethink."

He grinned and kept on kissing me. I hopped down and we stood pressed together, me on tiptoe, mouth to mouth by the cabinets. We began to move like slow dancers, swaying our way to the living room, shedding clothes as we went. He had me right there on the oatmeal-colored rug, and I had him.

While we were busy, my lasagna burned up around the edges. When we were finished, we were so starved that we ate the middle right out of the pan, standing naked in the kitchen, side by side with two forks. I put the pie in to bake while we were showering, and then we ate the middle out of that, too, for no reason other than we wanted to.

The next morning, once Thom had gone to work, I checked my wheel. I had seven pills left before my cycle ended.

I took one little white disk and laid it on my tongue, then washed it down with a sip of my morning cran-grape. I looked at the new empty space on the wheel, and it felt like the start of a whole new countdown. A week and change until the start of something lovely.

I tried not to think about how not so long ago, Rose Mae Lolley had been counting down the days and hours and minutes in an opposite direction, moving toward his death. She was quiet for now. Too quiet. Unriled and still biding. She had no faith in this new Thom that did not seem to carry her match inside of him. She had no faith at all.

Five more pills taken, and the day came when Thom had scheduled his meeting with his father. We didn't make love that morning, though he woke up ready and Lord knows I was willing.

"Game day," he said, like he was back in college and this was a morning after one of the first nineteen times we'd made love, all the times before he'd first hit me. Back then we were still busy being pretty for each other. I think even then I knew a day would come, a lost game, a failed test, when I would needle out the Thom I had seen at the diner. The one who had banded with Rose Mae to play a cruel trick on his own date.

One day he dropped an easy interception at a practice. Later, when he couldn't get my bra unhooked, I stepped away and turned to face him. I reached for it myself, saying in a sly voice, as thin and sharp as needles, "It must be national fumble day," and he backhanded me across his small dorm room.

He stared at me, shocked at himself. Rose Mae, banged loose, opened her bloody lips into something that was half grin and half snarl. "Not the face, baby. What will the neighbors say?"

This morning, though, that Thom was far away, and I was done calling him. Thom suited up, khakis and a power tie, a navy sport coat pulled on over his starched white shirt. He left with his head set to a cocky angle.

I was full of ants. I phoned Mrs. Fancy and canceled morning coffee, not fit for even her easy kind of company. At two, right when his meeting started, I pulled my secret stash of votives out from the bottom of my tampon box and lit one on the tub rim. I prayed for a long time, about fathers and justice, calling on Saint Joseph. I felt my prayer was heard, but the air stayed still, unmoved by saint breath. I was glad. Beckoned saints belonged with my mother in California, a place that I would never go, in a future I would not step toward. I put out the votive and prayed the rosary for good measure.

Only once through. I thought Thom might come home early, right after his meeting. I wanted to greet him at the door, off my knees and smiling. By three-thirty, I'd sprayed Lysol to cover the sulfur smell the match had left and put away my rosary, hoping this might be the last time I had to hide it.

He didn't come. I thought sure he'd at least call, but four P.M. came and went with no phone ringing.

I started to feel a green and mossy sickness slow growing in the pit of me. I ran the vacuum over my already clean carpet and told myself no news was good news. I told myself he wanted to see my face when he came in, smelling like win, carrying sparkling wine and field daisies. At five, I went and got my green bottle of Coke out of habit, though Lord knows I didn't need the caffeine. I drank it while I prepped scalloped potatoes and put pork chops in marinade and chopped up mushrooms and bell peppers and tomatoes for a salad.

Dinnertime came, and he still wasn't home. I quit hoping it had gone well.

I decided maybe it was good he'd stayed away. He was walking it off. He was making plans. He was getting a leg up on job hunting. In my opinion, leaving Grand Guns altogether would be fifty times better than a raise. I ate a piece of bread and opened another Coke to settle my stomach. I walked from room to room like a restless spirit haunting my own house. Gretel followed me, pressing against my legs every time I paused, her eyebrows so worried that eventually I put her out in the back.

It was after eight when at last I heard his Bronco pull into our drive. I ran for the door, then stopped and went instead to the sofa. I perched myself on its edge, spine straight like a schoolgirl's. I held my warm Coke in one hand, its base resting on my knee, and waited for Thom to come in and tell me if it was half-full or half-empty. The drapes were closed over the picture window. I sat myself as still as I could and listened for the sound of his keys jangling against the door.

He walked in like his whole body was made of springs. His eyes were too bright, as if he had fever. I found I was making myself be small, sinking and curling back into the cushions. I thought, *No. We have promised to be different now.* It *had* been a promise, those shy declarations that we would try, exchanged over meat loaf. For the last six weeks, we'd treated those words as solemnly as the vows we'd re-cited in front of his father's Presbyterian minister. I tried not to think that those un-Catholic vows had been worthless, too, in God's eyes.

He stood still in the center of the parquet island.

"It's done," he said.

"Good," I said, neutral. "Good for you. Are you hungry? I can have dinner on the table in half an hour, maybe less."

"We compromised," Thom said, never his favorite word; in his mouth right now it sounded downright filthy.

"That's wonderful," I said, hating the fake of it, the forced chirp I heard. Here I was again treading careful with my husband, and I made myself stop bright-siding before I found myself dancing, as eager to please as an organ-grinder's monkey. It was fine. He was tense, but a talk with his daddy was always a challenge.

"You did a hard thing, and I'm proud," I said, and that was true.

"Here's what *he* decided," Thom said, and I didn't like how he pushed down hard on the word *he*, like Thom himself hadn't got-ten a say. "*He* says, when you get pregnant, then my salary moves up halfway toward what I want. After the baby, we get the other half," Thomas said. "That seems fair, right?" he said, not like he was asking really, but as if he was ordering me to shore him up.

"That seems perfectly fair," I said, although it didn't sound so much fair as it sounded like Joe Grandee demanding to stand in our bedroom with a metronome, setting the beat while we made him a grandchild. Thom seemed to know anyway, like he could hear the thoughts under my words. He looked at me with his eyebrows beetling down and his mouth set so firm, it was a lipless slash. I saw his pulse in his temple and the curl of his hands, and for the first time since summer I felt a trickle of scared dribbling down my spine. It passed a bright drop of Rose Mae's excitement, going the other way on the same path.

"I've got me one bad-ass headache. Can you keep it down in here if I go back to sleep?" Thom said.

I could see how on the fence he was. We'd been here before, and I could push him either way. I felt Rose unfolding, creamy and pleased and ready for her boy, the one I loved, the one she'd love to shoot. I knew what to say. *Sure, sugar, have your nap, but then can you run retrieve your balls from out of your daddy's pocket? You'll need at least one if you're gonna give me that big money baby.*

That would tip him over, surely. I could see how bad he wanted me to say it. It would be permission. More than that. It would be an invitation. Rose Mae wanted it as well, to step out of dreams about Jim in the green woods and be present, wanted me to push him so he'd push back. She wanted me to admit I knew the silent, secret thing she'd planned.

He waited and I waited.

I didn't say it. I didn't want it. I thought, *This is my last chance, if I want to be Ro Grandee.* I thought of how sweet Thom could be with his brother's roly-poly boys, and I wanted the last six weeks to keep going on forever. I kept my mouth shut and nodded.

Still he didn't move. He stayed on the parquet square. His hands were at his sides, but his fingers stayed slightly curled, yearning to be fists.

"I'll keep it so quiet for you," I said, and my voice came out sweet, barely above a whisper. My heart had to work, beating hard to make my scant and shallow breath be enough to go around. He didn't move, and my body released a clammy, instant sweat. Thom stared at me, and I waited, slick and trembling. Finally he nodded.

"Okay, then," he said. It came out sounding defeated, but I heard it as permission to exhale. "I just need quiet."

I nodded, dead silent, and he turned to go. The moment I saw the back of his blond head, my spine became a noodle. I felt like I'd been through a siege and the last forty seconds had taken a solid hour. My fingers were made of jam and string; I thought I might drop my half-full Coke. I picked it up off my knee and set it on the end table beside me. My hands were shaking, and I misjudged the distance. I heard the overloud clack of glass bottle on the wood. We both did. It went off like a gunshot in the silent room.

Thom turned back to me instantly, a fast wolfy wheel-around.

He thought I'd meant to bang the table, and I saw the ugly relief spreading across his face. He came at me with total purpose. He came so fast.

Adrenaline dumped into my blood. I leapt off the sofa and took off, the Coke bottle still clutched in my hand. I hadn't made it three feet before he reached out and tangled his fingers deep into my long hair. He dug his hand in close to the scalp, then fisted it. He yanked me through the air back toward him, and I felt and heard the rip of a thousand different hairs tearing loose at the roots. I think I screamed.

My feet lost all purchase with the earth, and my body swung back toward the fist coming to smash into my back beside my spine. My back bowed like my body was trying to fold wrong-ways around the blow. The air pushed out of my lungs, out of my very blood. The world went dark red and I was spinning, dangling by my hair like a punching bag. His other hand came toward me again and again in fast, hard jabs, thumping into my hip, my side, my gut. He hit me so hard that the swing of my body away unbalanced him, and he had to step in closer. I felt my feet touch ground, but he still had half my weight and my scalp felt torn and I could hear my hair still tearing.

It was close to stopping then. I felt him shift to stopping. But my hand was still curled around cool glass, and I was at Cadillac Ranch, looking for my mother, remembering how it felt to swing. The glass had shivered into something like a weapon. I smashed the green Coke bottle into the middle of his face with all the force I had. His eyes widened and I saw surprise, then disbelief. Blood came out of his nostrils in two shocked jets. Then his eyes were animal eyes, and I couldn't see my husband at all.

He shook me by my hair, and I felt more skin and hair ripping from each other. I screamed, and he shook me and shook me, and inside I could hear all my bones jangling together. I lost my grip on the bottle as he hit me and kept hitting me until I lost time and myself and there was only him hitting me.

I think he threw me then. I hung in space for one cool, unrippled moment, and then a wall rose up and stopped me hard and I slid down it.

I couldn't find up, but from sideways I saw how he ran at me and kicked out. I folded around the jackhammer of his foot. Something stabbed me in my side, as if his shoe had been tipped with a white hot blade. My chest was burning. I couldn't breathe. I heard my screams stop, and all I heard was whooping bird noises as I gulped at air and got nothing and whooped and got nothing. He kicked my shoulder, and my head snapped back into the wall again, and I was falling into some black and airless place where there was only someone small and lost, done playing, hurt, wanting her mother to come and get her.

Choose him, the gypsy had said. She had flipped the cards for me, and I had done it wrong. She was saying something else, something urgent, telling me to pray to Saint Cecilia, but all I could hear was Thom's voice saying, "Dammit, Ro . . . Ro? Dammit."

I couldn't answer either of them. I could only make that awful bird noise again, that whooping. I recognized the sound. It was the sound of me not breathing. Not breathing was a hazy place, and pain was a box of kittens who had curled up all around me. I could feel warm, furry pockets of them pressed into my ribs and back and hips and belly where his fists had touched. Still more nested in my hair and wrapped around one shoulder like a stole.

"Ro?" I heard him calling to me from far away. His hard voice had unraveled. He was ready to let his fingers drift gentle down over me, searching under my skin to see if my bones had cracks. He wanted to kiss the hurt places, and his eyes would be full of sorry.

I couldn't answer. I had no breath, even to say I hadn't pushed, that this day was on him, only him. I felt an airless coiling in the space where there had been spent peace before. It was Rose Mae Lolley, saying they were my cards after all. She remembered crouching in the ditch at Wildcat Bluff. For a moment she had owned my hands, and if she'd had another second and a half to aim, we wouldn't be here now, not breathing. She raged at me for failing. I tried to hold myself still, to stay there in the woods and be Rose Mae, to do it over, to claim the cards as mine, to choose him and not me. I tried to stay. It went black anyway, and I was gone.

I woke up smelling antiseptic and the fermenting tang of yogurt.

"There you are," a woman said. I knew the voice. Even more, I knew that strawberry-vanilla breath.

"I fell downstairs," I said to the ER nurse I hated very most. The words came out creaky, automated.

I heard the cluck of her tongue, and I managed to slit one eye to see her lavender scrubs and her moistly sympathetic eyeballs, too close to my face as she bent over me. I heard the tick and beep of some machine.

"You could have died, you know," she said. "He's getting worse. He's come pretty close to killing you before, but not this close. You should let me call the cops."

I tried to nod, but it hurt too badly, so I said, "Okay. Have them arrest the stairs."

Her nostrils flared. "This isn't what love feels like, Mrs. Grandee. One of your ribs snapped and stabbed you in the lung. It collapsed. Your shoulder's dislocated, and your scalp's a bloody mess. You married a set of stairs that's too damn big and too damn angry. Next time, he'll send you here in a zipper bag. The cops will come then, believe it, but it will be too late for you."

"I know," I said.

"And that's all right with you?" she said. Now she sounded angry. "You're going to let him kill you?"

I didn't answer. I let my eyes drift shut. The thing I'd tried not to see was in the front of my head now, and I was Rose Mae and Rose Mae was me, and neither of us wanted to unthink it.

An hour-long blink later, and Thom was there, holding a huge bright spray of wildflowers. His nose was swollen, and I felt instantly, savagely pleased. He looked at me with sorry, bad-dog eyes, ready to pet his Ro, as if she was still spread thick as putty over Rose Mae. He should have known better. We'd been married five years. I wondered how he could look at me, limp in my hospital bed, and not see he'd beaten his girl clean off me. I was Rose Mae Lolley, almost alone in a hospital bed, waiting to be released.

"Hey, baby," he said.

"Hey back," I said, and my voice came out rusty and weak. It didn't sound like the me I heard in my head. Thom heard my weakness as permission. He set the flowers down and came to sit in the chair by my hospital bed.

I'll never unlove you, Jim Beverly had said to me, once, twice, a thousand times. I saw my whole plan now, out loud in my head, and I accepted it, as easily as I accepted Thom picking up my limp hand and holding it.

Thom looked at me and I looked at the white pebbled ceiling until he asked, "Want me to put the game on?"

"Okay," I said. He let go of my hand to get the remote, and I slid it under the covers to hold its mate. He kept the sound down low. I lay in the bed, feeling how slowly time unfolded around us, feeling how little time mattered.

It hadn't even been ten years since Jim had last said those words to me. *I'll never unlove you.* I found I still believed him. Thom turned and smiled at me, hesitant. I smiled, too, a glowing thing that made Thom's empty hands flex.

"They got you on the morphine, huh?" he asked.

I didn't answer. I was smiling at Jim Beverly. I would track him down. I would remind him.

Thom said, "So we go ahead. With the plan." He still looked hesitant, almost timid.

"Oh, yes," I said, absent and smiling, not sure what plan he was talking about. I had my own. Jim Beverly had promised me long ago that he'd kill before he'd let anyone hurt me again.

"We'll talk about it when you're off the morphine," Thom said, turning back to the TV.

Nothing to talk about. Him or me, and I had chosen. I would find Jim Beverly, and I would see if his offer still stood.

PART II:

❧

THE GIRL LEFT IN THE TOWER

Amarillo, Texas, 1997

CHAPTER

℘

7

I WAS FLAT ON MY back in a hospital bed for three days, pressing the button to flood my veins with morphine every time the machine counted down to zero and let me. The drug was pumped into my bloodstream through a tube, but after I pressed, it was as if I could see it coming down from the ceiling in icy chips of soothing white. They built up and blanketed me. I lay still and cool underneath, like a creature with no heartbeat, healing and waiting to reanimate.

Long before the timer worked its way down to zero and allowed me a fresh dose, the pain would sharpen, and I would sharpen with it. It took all my concentration in those clear and aching moments to hold my wounded body still. I wanted to rise up, to smite the glass that covered the fire ax in the hall and take it up by the wooden handle. I would use it to lay waste to Thom's hale body and then hack my way through the wall of my hospital room and leap away into the blue like some teeny, slighted pagan goddess. I longed for the lovely echoes of the thunk that ax would make when it met flesh, for the feel of something rendable between my teeth.

I had to make my body rest, because right then, breathing in and out was painful. Leaping and smashing, hell, even standing up straight was beyond me. I hunched and crept my way to the bathroom and back. I would fail, not out of sentiment and weakness, as I had when I was laying for him in the ditch at Wildcat Bluff, but simply because I didn't have the juice. Even wholly healed, my five-foot frame could not move so openly against him. So I waited and pressed the button for more morphine to hold myself at bay.

While the drugs force-rested me, my mind wandered in an endless loop around and around one subject: How would I find Jim Beverly?

I didn't think about the why. I knew the why with a lovely, black clarity that was chafing hard at poor old Ro Grandee. She was in shreds and strings around me, a web of desperate tenderness for her Thom, trying to rebind me and hamper all the ways I was going to move. It was Ro who had given him a final out on my second day in the hospital.

I was quieted by drugs, blankly watching Thom's broad back as he walked away after his lunchtime visit. He was heading back to work. Ro's remains were sorrowing after him with every speck of energy she still possessed.

I heard myself say, "We should call it quits, Thom." The words fell out in Ro's soft tones, deliberately pitched to let him decide to hear or not, as he chose.

In less than a second he was back, bent over me with one huge hand on either side of my head, flattening the crackly hospital pillow, pushing into the mattress so my head tilted back to stare directly into his face. Half his mouth was pulled down, like he was stroking out, and the surface of his eyes looked so flat that I couldn't see myself reflected in them.

"You will not start this shit again," he said. One hand moved to encircle my throat and he leaned in even closer, so I could smell coffee and sweet milk on his breath. "We're married. I will fucking end you."

He shoved himself up and away, using the pillow and my throat as launch pads. I watched him cross the room in long, loping steps. My mother's cards had told me plain that it would come to this.

Him or me. One day soon, his rage would break its chain and come to kill me. If I slipped back inside the skin that was Ro Grandee, I would stay and waffle and find excuses for both of us until I was dead.

I listened to the stomping footprints as they moved down the hall and died away, and then I said, "I'm gonna choose you, baby." It came out loud and clear, a declaration to myself and what was left of her.

Then I watched the numbers on the machine count down, time leaking away. When they said zero, I pressed the button. For a few hours, morphine boxed up the whole mess of my marriage and put it away like a never-to-be-finished jigsaw puzzle. It pressed me lower and lower, into my loop of endless longing. How to find Jim Beverly? I didn't think beyond that, not even to what Jim would be like now and what methods would best win him to my cause and what harm he might actually inflict on Thom, who had four inches and forty pounds on the boy Jim had been the last time I had seen him.

I didn't even think about where I might go after, and whether Jim would be there with me. I did not imagine us holding hands and skipping into the muddy sunrise of a rainy morning. This was choosing, not romance. Jim was a tool, much like my Pawpy's gun, and I'd find a way to aim him when the time came. Guns and men had always been the things I worked best. Guns had already failed me.

I concentrated solely on looking for a way to track a boy who had disappeared himself so thoroughly that his own overdevoted mother and the state cops had failed to find him. He'd left me near the end of our senior year, during a week when we'd been technically broken up. Ever since the night Jim and I had shared stolen whiskey, trying to understand what fueled my father's love affair with drinking, I'd refused to be with him if he had even a sip of something alcoholic. It wasn't only that I wouldn't be his girlfriend. I wouldn't be in a room with him.

He used the days when we separated to catch up on the benders that were his right and privilege as a star quarterback in Alabama. I suspected he got caught up on his rightful share of tail, too, but I never asked. Jim drinking was not the Jim I wanted, and those days did not belong to me.

His last night in Fruiton, he got crazy wasted at a party. I was at home, trying to be small and good and quiet, a mouse in the house, so as not to rile my daddy. In two days or three, I fully expected Jim to show up at my house with his head set to a cocky angle. He'd say, "Hey, Rose-Pop," like nothing had happened. I'd say, "Hey yourself," and look mad until he scuffed one foot in the dirt, sheepish, and said, "Aw, hell, Rose, I got out of hand. Come on down off the porch, and let me buy you a cherry Coke? A root beer float? Hot cocoa? Nothing says I'm sorry like a beverage with a lot of sugar in it." I'd shake my head with fond exasperation, come down, and take his hand. We would be us again, and that would be that.

Instead, sometime after midnight, Jim crashed his Jeep into a pole. He walked away from the accident, leaving a trail of beer foam and angry footprints stamped deep into the dirt as he made his way back to the highway. A couple of passing drivers saw him hitchhiking, his thumb pointing away from town. He disappeared himself, a brilliant magic trick, emphasis on trick, and it had been played on me.

I couldn't make sense of it. I wandered Fruiton High blind and naked as an unearthed mole, uncomprehending. Then it had come out that Jim was failing his senior year and would lose his scholarship to UNA. He'd lost almost everything, and he'd walked away from me, the one thing he should have been certain of, the one thing that was still his. Not forgivable. The day after I turned eighteen, I had done the Greyhound bus version of Jim's hitchhike out. I'd disappeared, too, never to be found.

In the lovely, morphine-covered landscape where I lay, looking for a path to him, it dawned on me that I hadn't disappeared, after all. I'd tried, but I had been found. My mother had found me.

Her presence at the airport was not merely a hideous coincidence.

She had come to Amarillo specifically because I lived here; she'd come to put her eyes on me. She'd sat low in the coffee shop across the parking lot to watch me pimp Joe Grandee's guns, or crouched down in a rented car on my street, watching me bend and dig in my garden. She could have been making Amarillo pilgrimages for years now. No way to tell. The only certainty was that she knew I was there long before I caught her at that airport. The proof was at Cadillac Ranch. She had left a message on the cars a day before our eyes had met.

I did love you, Rose. Pray to Saint Cecilia!

She'd left it to soothe her conscience and invoke her favorite saint in a place where she could be 99 percent certain I would never find it. But in coming to my city, she'd left a speck of working room for whatever minor saint was in charge of chance meetings and graffiti. He was on my side, no doubt tittering on my shoulder as he brought me to the airport in perfect time to catch her leaving me again.

The only question that mattered now was, how had she found me? Because if I could be found, then so could Jim Beverly.

The hole my own slivered rib had stabbed into my lung resealed itself. The hospital pulled my pretty morphine tube, and I started a new, less intense romance with Percocet. I was still bad off, but I could breathe, so they released me.

Thom drove me back to the house, bracing me in the seat with pillows and taking it easy on the curves. Once we got home, he put one arm close to his own side and bent it at the elbow, so his forearm was a ballet bar I could cling to as we made our way from the car back to our bedroom. I creaked my way down the hall like a granny, trying to walk in a way that favored my hurt places. There weren't enough working pieces of myself to take up the slack, so I had to favor Thom.

He helped me lower myself into the bed, plumping up a ridge of pillows behind me so I could see the TV if I wanted. He gave me the remote, the book I'd been reading, and another pill to wash down with a cool cup of water from the bathroom. He reached to smooth my long hair away from my face, but something in my gaze paused him. He took his hand back. Wise move.

"I'll tell my dad you're still under the weather this week. He can get Kelsey to cover your shifts," he said, sweet as sugar cereal. He was treating me like something breakable, which is different from how you treat something you yourself have broken.

I let my body lie in our bed like it was a hole-covered log, waiting for squirrels and spiders to find it and nest. Only Gretel came, flopping down with her spine a solid line of warming comfort against my calf, my faithful napping partner. Thom brought me hot cereal and scrambled eggs in the morning, Cup-a-Soups with crackers and sliced cantaloupe at night. Invalid food, with Percocet for afters. I ate it without tasting, mending through the tick of each long second, and my mind spun in a circle like a lazy Susan with a single idea on it: How did my mother find me, a thing that deliberately went and got itself lost?

When Thom came to bed, we lay on our own sides, both flat on our backs. My cold will was a ridge of Puritan pillows running in between us. But the fourth night, my body had healed enough to turn and shift without pain waking me. I fell asleep, and Ro Grandee crept over, seeking her husband's heat. He came to her as he always had. We woke up face-to-face, our pieces tangled and tucked around each other. I unwound my limbs and took them back without looking at him. He let me go.

Thom posed little threat in these days. He was ashamed and yet so sated that it was like a bloat, making him sweet as he tended to my body, his favorite toy. He worked to heal it, same as I was, readying it for rough play. I was safe with Thom; right now, Ro Grandee was the danger.

I was back in her house, with the pretty ocean blue coverlet and sheers she'd picked, her willow-patterned china in the kitchen, the remnants of her light perfume tainting the air of the bathroom. I'd lived inside her familiar, comfortable skin for years, until it was me, until I had no choice in it. But to let myself be Ro again now was suicide, the only irrevocable sin. The drugs that held me back in the hospital were holding me too still in her territory. I felt her as a creep, growing on back over me like fungus. It could not be allowed.

When Thom brought my breakfast on a tray, I handed him back the Percocet and said, "Could you bring me a couple, three Motrin, please? And a great big cup of coffee?"

I downed the coffee and ate every bite of my cheese eggs. Thom left for work, and I could feel myself waking up, truly waking, as last night's pill spent itself in my bloodstream and was replaced by the caffeine. The first thing I realized was that I was filthy, covered in a waxy coat of my own mank. My hair was limp and greasy. I creaked to my feet and took a long shower, scrubbing myself so hard that it was like being peeled. I made the water scalding hot. When I got out, I was pink under my fading bruises.

I opened the closet and got an eyeful of Ro's swirly skirts in springtime colors. Sweet flats with bows and buckles and embroidered daisies. Clingy lightweight sweaters, all long-sleeved. I slammed the closet door, as repulsed by these things as if they had been hand-sewn from human skin. I went to my dresser instead and dug out a long-sleeved T-shirt and a pair of the old Levi's that I wore on heavy cleaning days.

The jeans were pale blue and baby soft from a thousand washings, and they sat easy against my bruises. My rib cage pinged as I shifted, and I could tell by how the jeans fit that I'd gone barn-cat scrawny. Still, I felt whole and ready for movement, but only from the neck down. My wet hair was a heavy reminder, pulling at my sore scalp. I dried it on cool, then I bundled it away into a low ponytail and braided it. It still felt like the braid had a barbell tied to the end. I pulled it over my shoulder, where it hung past my breast, heavy and hers.

I didn't want it touching me. I wanted none of Ro's things touching me, and the long hair my husband loved felt like a most offensive bit of Ro-ness. I strode to the kitchen and yanked my meat shears out of the butcher-block knife rack on the counter. I thought I could lop that braid off in one fell swoop, but it was too thick. I had to squeeze the handles open and shut and saw at it with the blades to get it off of me. Finally the last connecting hairs yielded, and the braid slithered down my back to the floor. My head felt so suddenly light that it was like being dizzy.

The braided cable of hair looked like a long, glossy pet that had coiled up at my feet. It was sleek and dark, more than a foot long, so thick that I doubted I could get my finger and thumb wrapped all the way around it. I looked down at it and felt no remorse. I felt no connection to it at all. It was nothing more than a brown black rope that Thom could damn well never hang me from again.

I picked up the braid and walked back to the bathroom. I think I meant to put it in the trash, but I caught sight of myself in the mirror and stopped. I was ten pounds too thin and two shades paler than paper. My shorn hair hung around my face in a ragged tangle, longer on the right side than the left. I had kaleidoscope eyes, spinning with a hundred different colors of pure, naked crazy. For the first time in years, I was face-to-face with Rose Mae Lolley. Even my clothes were hers, faded and ill used enough to have been found in a church box. I was cold all over, predatory, and it showed in my face. Every line of my body said, *Down to black business, up to absolutely nothing good.*

I'd been Rose Mae in accidental flashes over the years, most recently in the ditch at Wildcat Bluff. This was the face Jim Beverly had seen, I felt certain, that night we got drunk and ran through the woods, and the rustle of ferns and branches was the crack and snap of tiny bones. Thom knew this face, too. It had been reflected in the mirror of his gaze the first night I met him, back when I was slinging eggs and corned-beef hash at Duff's Diner. Stirring spit into his date's drink had been a stopgap measure to keep me from boiling half her face off with a pot of scalding coffee. He'd known what he was getting, same as I had. But those were forays, a creature taking peeks and darts out of its pretty, placid home.

In the mirror I was as ugly and iridescent as a de-shelled hermit crab, fleshy and exposed. I hadn't been this nakedly myself since the morning I left Fruiton, Alabama.

When Jim left me, it was as if he'd ripped my skin off and toted it down the highway with him. The very air stung me. I wandered the halls of my school drugged with loss and rage. I stopped turning in my work. Tests were passed out, and I sat through them, not even lifting my pencil. It was all I could do to hold myself still with the air and sunshine touching the raw and blinking object that I was. Graduation came, and I sat home through it, knowing I had flunked and not caring. I sat through summer like it was a prison sentence.

I thought I might hear from Jim on my birthday. I held myself afloat with the idea: He would call. He would tell me—and only me—where he was. He would say he'd only been waiting for me to turn eighteen, so that no one could come looking for us.

The day came, and the phone stayed silent. Then my father clocked me a good one for the high crime of walking to the kitchen, my back to him, when he was thinking he might speak to me. Kidney shot. I lay on the floor where he had put me, and I understood that Jim would not rescue me. If I stayed in Fruiton, this was my life. This was all I could be. No dear and worthy girl could be rebuilt under my father's fists.

I packed a canvas duffel bag and slept a fitful few hours until the Greyhound station opened. Daddy was passed out on the sofa, dreaming like a dog with his bare feet hanging off the edge and twitching as he chased down rabbits or naughty daughters. I had a little money of my own, but I decided that final punch would cost him the nine dollars in his wallet as well as the sacred "whiskey twenty" he kept in his bedside table for emergencies.

There was leftover Tuna Helper in the fridge and half a pan of mac 'n' cheese, too. It could be days before he ran out of things to microwave and realized I was gone. I wanted him to realize sooner.

There was a big print of ships in a harbor hanging above the sofa, over Daddy. It had been my mother's. As a girl, I used to pretend she'd stepped into it and gotten on a ship and gone someplace that I could follow, the way Lucy and Edmund had floated across a painted ocean back to Narnia. I was grown up now, and I understood she left on purpose, through the front door. I was about to follow her lead.

I looked at the print, all that deep blue water hanging over Daddy's head. I thought about the gas can in the carport, how it would slosh, unwieldy, if I lifted it and carried it back here. It was more than half-full because Daddy never fed the mower. It was cool inside our small brick house in the hour before dawn. A fire sounded nice.

Instead I turned myself, went to his room, and I stole his pistols. I took Pawpy's both for protection and as a punishment; it was just about the only thing of Pawpy's Daddy had. I took both his newer ones to hock, as if they were my rightful dowry. I'd have taken his deer gun, too, but it didn't fit down in my duffel.

My last act was to dig a shedding Crayola paintbrush out of my childhood toy box. I took a coffee mug to the neighbor's yard and scooped up a generous cupful of the dog crap that had leaked out from their dyspeptic standard poodle. I took these tools back to the sofa and used them to write, "Later, Gater," onto the hanging print of ships at harbor. The ships and the docks were brown, and the sea was a storm dark blue. The words were hard to see, and I wondered how long he would stagger around the house, hung over and gagging, checking his shoes and sniffing and cussing, before he found my billet-doodoo.

Considering he was passed out helpless, considering that I had a swollen kidney and two loaded guns, considering how raw I was, he was damn lucky that was all I did. If he had stirred, if he had so much as cracked an eye, he would have seen the face that I was seeing in the mirror now. If he'd said the wrong word to me in that moment, then as sure as God made all the pretty fishes, I'd have put a hole in him.

I reached out and touched the mirror, disbelieving. The girl inside the glass reached at the exact same time, raising her hand on her side to meet mine, fingertip to fingertip. The glass was showing me an accurate reflection, showing me that she—I—was way too easy to read. I had to camouflage myself.

I rummaged through Ro's flowered handbag to find the keys to my hand-me-down Buick. I drove downtown, still clutching the coil of my hair, to a place called Artisan Salon and Day Spa. I knew Charlotte Grandee paid this place a small fortune to keep her hooves sanded down and her gray covered. I had never so much as stepped inside. Thrifty Ro got her split ends trimmed at a place called Mister Clips for eight meager dollars. I did my pedicures at home. Artisan wasn't a place we could afford, but that one glimpse in the mirror had told me a faked smile and some Maybelline blusher wouldn't cover half my sins. Damn the cost; Thom owed me this, and more. Hell, all the Grandees owed me. I circled Amarillo's small blocks until I found a parking space that would hold my ancient tank of a car.

I walked into the ultramod reception room, and the lone blonde waiting to have her frosty tips refreshed gasped at the sight of me and looked away fast. One manicured hand raised itself involuntarily to touch her own thick curls, like she was scared whatever had happened to me might be catching.

I looked past her to the young man behind the apple green check-in station and said, "Do you take walk-ins?"

He looked up, his mouth already shaping the word *no*, but when he saw me, his lips froze into a kissing shape around the unsaid word. I had the long rope of my former hair coiled around one wrist, and I lifted it and let it unfurl and dangle.

The air came out of him so fast that it made a woofing noise, and he said, "What did you do?" He sounded slightly awed.

"I had a bad idea," I said.

"I'll say," he agreed, fervent.

I was used to men looking at me, but not like this. I felt my eyebrows come together, and I blinked hard. "I'm not getting out of the house much, these days. I haven't . . ." I swallowed so loud that it sounded like gulping, and then I felt my mouth opening up again. "My husband died. Quite recently." Instantly I had to fight to keep an inappropriate grin from spreading across my face.

I had not spent my week on bed rest making up drug-induced, cheerful Disney-rip-off songs about a world with no Thom Grandee in it. My only thought had been how to find Jim. Test-driving widowhood with the salon's tanned godlet-style receptionist as my witness was my way of saying exactly and out loud why I was looking for my lost love. The boldness of it, the truth of it, moved through my body like a wave of black pleasure. It was the confirmation of a thing that had already been decided, a long time ago, in an airport. Maybe even by someone else.

The receptionist said, "This is clearly an emergency." He had big hazel eyes, shaped very round, with a down tilt to them that made them seem sadder for me than he probably was. "Let me see what I can do."

The blonde said, "Rexy, I am in a hurry today . . . ," giving me a sidelong glance. It was the look a well-fed person who was enjoying an excellent cold lamb sandwich might give a homeless fellow or a hungry dog.

"Faye will be ready for you in five," Rexy told her. "Maybe four." He turned back to me and said, mostly for her benefit, "You, my dear, you are past what Faye can do. Miles past. I suspect you've crossed the border and left Faye-country altogether. You require Peter."

The blonde's eyebrows lifted and she looked me up and down, clearly wondering what made Rexy think I rated. I looked back, bottom lip atremble, and I made my eyes go big and soulful, like those single-teared orphans that get painted onto black velvet. Her gaze broke first. She picked up a glossy magazine and put it up in front of her face, a wall I couldn't climb over. It was *Architectural Digest*, and Charlotte Grandee got that chichi rag every month. I realized this blond thing probably knew Charlotte. They certainly looked of a set, and this was Charlotte's spa.

I wasn't worried, though. I currently looked nothing like the pretty Ro Grandee in the wedding photo at Charlotte's house, and the godlet hadn't asked my name. If I so much as whispered the word *Grandee*, though, I had no doubt this blond creature would be on the phone with Charlotte before the door had closed entirely behind me. She'd be delighted to reveal that Charlotte's low-rent Alabama daughter-in-law had been seen poor me–ing her way into Artisan via the fictional death of her eldest boy. I might enjoy that, actually. But it would be tempting fate to let Thom's mother hear this fiction right before I made it fact.

Rexy came back and said to me, "Follow me now, hon." The blonde made a huffy throat noise, and Rexy gave her a shit-eating grin, his teeth as white and square as peppermint Chiclets. "Faye will come for you in bare seconds, Sheila. She has sworn."

I followed him through the archway down a long moss green hallway lit by wall sconces. There were doorways on both sides, some closed with signs on them that said things like "Shhh . . . Massage in process!" and "Aromatherapy Room."

I whispered, "I'm sorry about . . ."

"Pish, Sheila? Bottle blondes on the wrong side of forty need us more than we need them, believe it. She's about sixty percent spackle as it stands."

I chuckled, but now I was thinking about how much folks like to bond over a bit of gossip, how nasty good it could feel to talk ugly about outsiders with your own kind. That must be how my mother had found me. She'd asked her own kind.

Fruiton was a small town, and if a single person had seen me toting my gun-stuffed duffel bag to the Greyhound station at dawn, stomping away from the remains of my life, then the whole town as good as knew. The right people, if asked, would have been happy to relay this information to her.

I followed Rexy all the way to the back, to a more brightly lit, deeper green room with a gleaming sink and a sleek black stylist's chair. He presented me to a short, slim man beside it who looked way too young to be cutting hair.

"This is Peter. I leave you in his capable hands," Rexy said.

Peter's hair was an artful tousle of multishaded gold. Up close, I could see fine lines mapped around his eyes and two deep creases framing his full lips, so he had to be at least into his thirties.

He looked at me and tsked, then said to Rexy's back, "You weren't exaggerating." He walked forward and circled me, then reached down and grabbed the braid I was still holding in the middle. He lifted it without taking it out of my hand, feeling the weight. Then he let the hair go and touched the ragged ends where I'd cut it off, his soft fingers brushing my cheek. I found myself leaning into the touch like a petting-hungry stray cat.

He said, "Poor sugar. What do you want?"

That stopped me, because I hadn't a clue. I only knew what I did not want.

"I can't look like this," I said.

"No. It isn't good for America," he agreed, so overly grave that it made me laugh. He led me over to the sink and settled me in the chair. I leaned back and rested my head in the sink while Peter washed what was left on my head. His fingers moved in a vigorous, painful rumple across my sore scalp.

"So, you want to look 'not like this.' That's not terribly specific, is it?" Peter said, rinsing the shampoo and reaching for a bottle of conditioner. "Why don't you tell me how you think you look, and I'll go the other way."

"Skinless," I said.

He laughed out loud. "I meant your hair, sugar."

"Ruined. It looks like angry hair."

"It does look a little . . . fraught," he said, smiling down at me, then he shrugged and said with perfect confidence, "Whatever you did, I can fix it."

I believed him. With his low-down, slinky voice, he could say anything and most people would believe him. I let my eyes drift closed as he worked a thick cream that smelled like gardenias through my hair.

My mother was in California. I thought of it as her place now, like she'd walked all the way around the state, peeing endlessly to seal the borders so that nothing from the life she'd left could follow. She couldn't have gone all the way back to Fruiton to track me. Coming halfway, just to Amarillo, must have nearly killed her. No. She would have called folks in Fruiton who were her kind. This would be both the admittedly sparse ranks of southern Catholics and shitty mothers, of which there was no shortage.

One of them must have tattled, told her I'd gone to the bus station. I'd had a crap waitress job near the bus station in every town I'd paused in. She'd simply tracked me from Greyhound to Greyhound across the country, all the way to Amarillo, without ever leaving her new territory.

This was how I could find Jim. I could call the kids I had gone to high school with, and they would talk to me, because I'd been one of them. They would tell me, their peer, more than they would have told the cops or their parents back then. Telling cops or parents would have been ratting him out; it was obvious Jim had not wanted to be found.

"Let's promenade," Peter said, and I started, my eyes popping open. I stood up and let him drape me in towels and a slick black poncho. As he led me across the room, I hung my braid over one arm and rummaged in my purse for a pen and a piece of scrap paper. I needed a list of people back in Fruiton who were my kind, who would talk and tattle to me.

Peter took me straight to the chair and sat me down. The leather was butter soft and the seat gave under my weight, cupping my ass like a lover and supporting my sore back better than my own bed at home. Charlotte Grandee was used to sinking her pointy back end into chairs like this. Artisan was giving me a taste of the life she took for granted. I settled myself down in the seat, acting like it was rightfully mine, as if my mother had given birth to me while sitting comfy in this very chair and I'd never yet moved off it.

Peter picked up a pair of slim silver scissors and then paused, considering me. He walked around me, looking at me from every angle.

I braced my paper on my purse and wrote, "THE LAST PARTY," at the top. I wrote Missy Carver's name first, because the party had been at her house. Missy had a divorced mother who went on lots of dates, so the party had almost always been at her house.

"I'm ready. Are you ready?" Peter asked. He made it sound the right kind of dirty. Like I was beautiful enough to tempt him, but he was much too gay to be a real threat.

"Hell, yeah," I said. This was part of what rich wives like Charlotte and the blonde outside paid for, this safe, flirty assurance that they still had it.

"No input? I'm taking blades to your head, sugar-pie. Are you comfortable saying, 'Go mad, Peter, and make me a goddess'?"

"That sounds great," I agreed. "Let's go with that goddess thing."

Peter went to work with the scissors, the blades rubbing up against each other like cricket legs. I didn't watch him cut. I didn't look at him at all, and he seemed to feel me being finished with the conversation, because he dropped the flirt and went quiet.

Under Missy's name, I wrote down all the varsity football players that had been in our grade. They would have been at that party, certain. Those names came easy: Rob Shay. Chuck Presley. Benny Garrison. Car Kaylor. Lawly Price. Back then, we always called the football boys by their first and last names, as if they were rock stars instead of boys we'd known since grade school.

I looked up, thinking, and accidentally met Peter's eyes in the mirror.

"Prospectives?" he asked instantly, like I'd hit his on switch. He glanced down over my shoulder at my list.

"Guest list," I said. "For a party."

"Lots of boy names. Looks like my kind of shindig." He waggled his eyebrows at me.

I looked deliberately away. The girls' names were harder to recall. I hadn't been the kind to have close girlfriends. Hell, I still wasn't. I never got in the habit. This was partly because most of my wardrobe came from Fruiton Baptist's annual clothes drive. The popular girls, with their pom-poms and sleek ponytails, recognized my outfits, and some were crass enough to greet the pieces in public like old friends. If I hadn't been the quarterback's girl, they wouldn't have talked to me at all. I wouldn't get much from the girls, anyway. Pretty had bought me an in with the fellas, but I had never been *their* kind.

Peter watched as I added the name of every girl Jim Beverly had taken out during the couple, three times a year that we'd been broken up. I wrote quickly. My hand could barely stand to shape the letters. I remembered all seven effortlessly, because for the short time each had been with him, I'd chanted their names under my breath all day long. *I hope you get run over, Dawna Sutton. I hope bears eat you, Louisa Graham. I hope you get run over and* then *bears eat you, Clarice Lukey.*

"It's still a mister-heavy list," Peter said. "And why not? A good mister-ing will do more for your pores than any product I have here." He cocked his eyebrow to a rakish angle, so charming, but I wasn't as easily seduced as his regular Sheilas and Charlottes.

I said as kindly as I could, "Stop."

"I'm sorry. I'm a horror," he said, sounding more pleased than apologetic. He gathered the front of my hair and clipped to the top of my head. "Your lips say stop, but your eyes say you're half in love with me already. You're the kind who likes bad boys, I can tell."

Bad boys, he'd said, and our eyes met in the mirror again. I found myself staring at him as if I were looking down a deer gun barrel, like I saw his handsome face framed in sights. I wasn't Charlotte's kind, and in that moment, he knew it.

"Sugar," I said, grinding the word into him, "you have no idea."

I saw whatever lived under his hypercharming ease flash recognition, and then he drew back like he'd been bitten. His gaze dropped. He coughed and shook his shoulders, then his hands got busy in my hair again. I finished my list in silence, but not an angry one. I was more comfortable than I had been since I'd walked in and Sheila had given me that bitchy once-over.

When he finally spoke again, his voice had lost its indulgent purr. He sounded less Hollywood gay, less flirty, but somehow warmer. "What are you going to do with that long braid of your ex-hair?"

"I'm not sure." I packed my list and pen back in my bag. "Maybe I'll make a lanyard."

"Is it virgin?"

"Virgin?" I asked. I found myself smiling at him as I said, "I was married five years, so it's certainly seen a few things."

He chuckled and said, "All at once, I'm glad my own hair can't talk. I meant, do you use any kind of chemical on it, to straighten or curl it? Or do you dye it?"

"No," I said. "That's the color I was born with."

He set down his scissors and said, "May I?" I handed over the cable of hair. He lifted the braid and smelled it and said, "No one in your house smokes, and I would know. You can't get that smell out of hair. This has got to be five inches around. And so healthy. You must take vitamins. Do you drink? Do drugs?"

"You mean other than my pet heroin addiction?" I said, a little put off, and he laughed.

"I'm not asking these questions to be nosy. Hair this thick and long, gorgeous color, virgin, this can be worth a lot of money."

I sat up straighter and asked, "How much is a lot?"

"Hundreds." He handed the cable of hair back to me and let my front hair down out of its clip. "So you lost your husband quite recently?"

I nodded, thinking, *Very recently. In fact, any day now.*

"Is it safe to assume your finances have changed?" he said. I looked away. "I ask because, among my many hair-related talents, wig making shines. I do custom jobs. Local but very high end. I could sell one made out of this hair for a couple thousand. I'd give you six hundred for the raw material. Now. Today."

I turned my head to look up at him, directly. "Six hundred? Is that a fair price?"

He nodded. "I went to Catholic school. The first thing they taught me was that people who cheat teeny, big-eyed widows go straight to hell. It's quite fair, for what's essentially my clay. What makes the finished wig worth more is the work I'll put in. It will be head art by the time I'm done, and some poor balding—and wealthy—Amarillo brunette would be thrilled to have what I could make out of that perched on her head."

"Six hundred," I repeated. That would buy a lot of long-distance phone calls to my kind in Fruiton. Once I had a bead on Jim, it would cover a bus or plane ticket to get me to him.

"I'd throw in this haircut, which is no small change," Peter added.

Still, something in me balked. I felt my hands fisting around the long cable, imagining some woman, a wealthy stranger, wearing my hair to play bridge, probably with my mother-in-law and the woman who'd snooted me in the waiting room. The brunette would give me a dismissive hair flip for even door-darkening a place like this; if I took the money, she could be flipping at me with my own ex–crowning glory.

"You think it over, sug—" Peter stopped himself and grinned, rueful. "Just think it over, lady friend."

He swapped his scissors for the hair dryer. He used a round brush, and it hurt my sore scalp something fierce. I closed my eyes, clutched hard at the cable of hair, and endured it. My mother, a beauty, had slept with pink foam curlers pressing into her head most nights, willing to trade some pain to get pretty. But that was before she'd run to California to grow her locks out long and plain and dress like a gypsy. Now I'd cut my hair off, but it didn't make me like her. I was still here, fighting to keep my life, still willing to trade pain to get pretty.

The dryer shut off. Peter turned the chair, and the mirror showed me a woman I didn't know. She had a razor-sharp bob, the sides slanting down into points. The haircut was too angular and edgy for Ro Grandee, too polished and sleek for Rose Mae. I reached up and touched the back, feeling how he'd shingled it. My eyes looked larger, and the cut had honed my cheekbones.

"Thank you," I said, staring. I looked more sophisticated, but also younger, as if he'd cut the last five years of my life away. And good riddance, the woman in the mirror was thinking. I could read her mind in the set of her jaw. "Thank you," I repeated. Even the second time, it didn't seem like enough.

"I'm quite fabulous," he said, offhand. "Hair is important. Frame the face, lift the spirits. Imagine how happy the next lady who loses the cancer lotto here in Amarillo would be to have yours."

Those words changed my picture of the wig-wearing lady. Now she looked like I had looked this morning, pale and wasted, crazy-mad and crazy-scared. She wasn't playing bridge. She was in a hospital waiting room with her hair gone brittle, falling out in patches, and she didn't give two goat shits if they let trash like me into her country club or not.

She wasn't the true reason my hands had closed around my braid. The true reason was, if I took this secret pot of money, the ability to travel, to leave, became suddenly much realer. I was waffling, and it wasn't Ro Grandee making me go spineless, either. Artisan was not her territory. This was something else.

I could see myself walking in a grove of lemon trees, smelling the ocean, the points of my new hair swinging. My mother had said to me at the airport, *You are welcome.*

But that picture was wrong. I would be traveling to find Jim Beverly, to fight to keep my life, not leave it. I opened my eyes and looked at this new, sleek woman in the mirror, all lavender eyes, pale skin, cupid's-bow mouth. "Do you remember?" I would say to Jim. "Do you remember what you promised?" I smiled, and the me in the mirror smiled back, a lush and knowing smile that would make any man remember.

The scenery in my head changed. I was walking toward Jim down a city street, then down a red clay road, then through deep green woods like the ones we'd made our own in Alabama. He could be anywhere in the country. There was no reason to think he would have landed in California. I felt my fists loosen. I held up the braid toward Peter.

"I don't have anything else to do with it," I admitted.

He took it from me and put it on the shelf in front of the mirror. The points of my short hair swung, brushing my cheek, as I stood up. I liked how it felt, and I liked how the wings fell to hide my eyes when I kept my head down. I peeped out between them as Peter took out his wallet and peeled six fresh one-hundred-dollar bills out of it. I took the money.

On my way down the hallway that led back to the waiting room, I ducked into an empty massage room and closed the door. I pulled out my makeup case and made myself up, fast, like I used to in the girls' room at Fruiton High, back when my daddy said I was way too young and got fisty if he saw me in mascara. Smoky eyes with a pale and glossy mouth. Jim Beverly's girl.

When I got back to the waiting room, Sheila was still sitting there, waiting. I came through the door, hips swaying, not caring now if she recognized me. She was jiggling an angry foot and staring daggers at Rexy, who was saying, "Faye has sworn before all the gods that in two minutes she'll be ready for you. Not even two. One. Mere seconds. Not even—" He stopped talking as I entered. They both turned to me and did double takes, his elaborate and theatrical, hers almost affronted.

I said, "It lives!"

Rexy gave me a frank-eyed assessment, then said, "And it's gorgeous."

"Thank you," I said, smiling wide. He meant it. I could hear it in his tone and feel it in the amped-up wattage of Sheila's glare. She looked ready to leap over the stack of fashion magazines on the coffee table and ruin my day and her French manicure by tearing my throat open. I turned and showed her all the teeth I'd bared for Rexy, then put my nose up and swanned out past her, thinking, *No wonder I don't have any girlfriends.*

It wasn't completely my fault I was so friendless, I thought as I got in my hand-me-down Buick to head back to the house Joe Grandee helped us pay for. I was hemmed in, surrounded by Grandees. They were wrapped all around my life, like the prickly pink foam that lined our attic and kept the cool air from getting out. All I had was Fat Gretel, who was too dear and dim to remember my secrets, even if she'd had a mouth shaped right for telling them. I couldn't count Mrs. Fancy. She had never been *my* friend.

She'd befriended Ro Grandee, and for her own reasons, which I could not begin to fathom. She never asked about the days I disappeared, convalescing from viruses that were not going around. She knew, of course. She wasn't stupid. She'd been conditioned to overlook these things, to be complicit in Ro's life, and I was done with that. I was looking for my ex-lover to break the Sixth Commandment. I planned to snap the Fifth as a bonus. Genteel Mrs. Fancy could not possibly approve.

I hadn't banked friendships in the same way I hadn't banked money. No exit strategy. I should have had a secret stash already, saved out dollar by quarter by dime. My mother had. As a little girl, I'd watched her refill an empty bottle of a brand-name shampoo with generic, and then she'd pay the difference to her flowered-shoe bank in the top of her closet.

"Our secret, Rose Mae," she told me. At seven years old, even before, I understood that if Daddy knew about it, that money would go away. So it stayed our secret, even though it was not *our* stash. It was hers alone, money she banked so she could leave me. Sometimes she'd peel off a five and drive me to Fruiton's teeny mall to get a cone at Baskin-Robbins. Double chocolate chip tasted sweeter when it felt stolen, and though I did not know it at the time, every treat she bought me was of double value. Each dollar spent on me meant she had to stay another day, setting her back from the magic number she needed to escape. I wondered, how much was enough to let her go but not enough to pay my way as well? Hard to calculate the exchange rate on thirty bits of silver.

It was more than I had now, that was certain. I owned two pairs of flowered shoes, but the toes were empty. I'd never padded the grocery bill and kept the difference. I'd willfully not thought to, as another way I could not be like my mother. But it had also saved Ro the bother of having any real choices to make about breaking with her husband.

I caught sight of myself in the rearview and took a moment to admire my free, expensive haircut. Screw the forty cents for shampoo; I bet a cut like this cost plenty, plus the tip. History told me Thom was guilt soaked enough about putting me in the hospital to shell out for it. I pulled into the next bank I saw with a drive-through ATM and withdrew $120. I added the sheaf of twenties to Peter's crisp hundreds.

At home, I stripped naked and then stood in front of my closet for a long time before I could force myself into one of Ro's swirly cotton skirts and a matching sweater. Her clothes were alive, brushing my bare skin with a squirmy kind of touching that I felt all over me, every time I moved. It was close to unendurable, and it made her real in a way she hadn't been since he'd put me in the hospital. I shuddered my way to the bathroom to touch my pulse points with Thom's favorite perfume, my muscles twitchy under Ro's brushed cotton.

I went in costume to the kitchen to make dinner, pulling the biggest knife out of the wooden block and cutting up too many tomatoes. When I'd hacked up the entire basket, I went after the cucumbers. I was making enough salad for an army, but I couldn't put the knife down. The hand I'd wrapped around the solid wood of the handle and my shorn head were the only pieces of me that felt right.

I was mincing a second onion when I heard the Bronco screech up outside. The car door slammed, and ten seconds after that our front door crashed open. I stayed where I was in the kitchen, making the onion into even squares. When Thom came banging into the room, I turned toward him. I held my knife at a casual angle in my right hand, pointing at the floor, but my grip was so tight that blood could barely move through my fingers.

"Where the hell have—" His voice cut out abruptly, and he stared at my head. "You cut your hair."

"You like it?" I said. Ro's trembly voice. Ro Grandee's binding clothes.

"You cut your hair?" he repeated, a question this time. He was breathing fast and deep, nostrils flaring on the inhale.

I worked to make my voice steady and my own. "I needed a change." I did a slow spin, modeling for him with the knife still pointed down, my fingers needling at the lack of circulation.

"I called you five times," he said while I was turning. "I had vendor meetings all damn day, and I'd get out of one and call you and go into another still wondering where you were."

"So what do you think?" I touched the point of hair on the left side of my face. He stared at me, not seeing me at all.

"I think you shouldn't fucking disappear like that," he said.

"Thom Grandee," I said, and I had the tone mostly right now, mock stern and almost pouty, but under my control. I lived in my knife hand and kept breathing. If I knew Thom, I'd be peeled out of these clothes soon enough. "You would be a total loss as a detective. Where do you think I was today?"

He compressed his lips and blew air out his nose like a frustrated bull. "Getting a haircut, obviously. That's not the—"

"Not any old haircut," I interrupted. "This haircut came from a spa downtown. It cost one hundred dollars."

That drew him up short, and his eyes refocused. I could

practically hear the gears change in his brain. "A hundred dollars?"

I nodded. "Plus tip. Also, I have never had it short before, so you need to stop your yapping about I don't know what-all right this second and tell me if you like it." Perfect.

"Holy shit," he said, but he didn't sound mad now. "A hundred dollars, huh?"

"Foldy green American," I said. "I got it done at that place your mother goes." Whatever red wave he'd been riding when he came through the door was receding. I set the knife aside, casually, though it hurt me to uncoil my hand from it. "I needed a pick-me-up, baby. I've been feeling lowly."

"I've noticed," he said.

I swayed toward him, slow across the kitchen, and as I moved I grabbed the bottom of Ro's clingy sweater and pulled it off over my head. All at once I could breathe easy, and Thom couldn't.

"When I couldn't get you on the phone all day, I thought . . ." He trailed off. I hadn't bothered with a bra.

I knew what he'd thought. Some variation on *Who is he*, spiced by the idea that I had left him. He'd come home ready to hunt me down, and instead he'd found a pink-cheeked wife, out of bed and smelling like freesia, making him a supper. His only punishment was a hugely overpriced trip to a salon, so slight a rebuke that it was practically a gift to him. I paused in the middle of the kitchen to unzip Ro's skirt and let it drop. I stepped out of it and gave it a small but savage kick. It slithered away from me across the well-waxed floor. I hadn't bothered with panties, either.

His gaze roamed up and down me as I came to him, and he said, "I never cared for short hair, but you look beautiful. Hell, you'd be beautiful shaved bald, but this is gorgeous."

"It dern well better be, for a hundred bucks," I said.

"Plus tip," he said.

"Plus tip," I agreed, and stepped into his arms.

He pulled me close, careful, trying to be gentle with my healing body, but I sucked his bottom lip into my mouth and bit down, hard enough to sting. It felt good. I ran my claws down his back, scraping his skin, then put my hands flat against his chest and shoved off, hard and fast enough to surprise him. I pulled free from his arms. He reached for me, but I turned and ran naked away from him down the hall. He followed me, as he had always followed me.

I turned at the bedroom door, let him catch me. I kissed him again, not sweet, plenty of teeth. He lifted me up, walking me back into the bedroom with my feet dangling. He threw me backwards, so I was briefly flying, the cool air a pleasure on my naked hide. I landed, bouncing against the mattress. Then he was on top of me, and I wrapped my legs around him, dug my heels into his ass, and pulled him into me. I bit down hard into the meat of his shoulder. He reared back and I dug my heels again, drawing him in.

We rolled in the middle. I got on top and rode him like a pony. When I came it was like the sound of thick glass shattering in me, a crashing, and then I was full of bright shards that chimed against each other as they slivered up my insides with a sound like jagged bells. Then it was his turn, and I rode him down till he was nothing, till he was lying in a heap, deflated, his eyes half-closed and no one home behind them.

He took the sex as if it were simple and delicious and carried no message, and then he slept. He didn't even know it was good-bye. I lay beside him, smiling but not pretty. I felt it as a broad stretch of my mouth that showed my whole, panting tongue to the air, and the air tasted warm and full of musk.

From then on, every time I took him to my bed it was good-bye like that. Just as every time he hit me was a reminder of how permanently I was going to say it.

CHAPTER

8

THE NEXT DAY, as soon as Thom left for work, I gathered up Ro Grandee's floaty skirts, her sheer, fitted cardigans, and her lace-trimmed blouses and bundled them into the washer. I added a packet of red Rit fabric dye and started the machine. Heavy-duty. Hot water. Extra spin cycle. I left Ro Grandee's wardrobe to ruin itself and walked over to Mrs. Fancy's in my Levi's and the shirt I'd worn to Artisan.

I was lifting my hand to knock when the door sprang open. Mrs. Fancy let out a peeping yip noise and hopped back. Ro would have jumped back, too, like a moving echo, but I didn't so much as twitch. I lowered my arm and waited. Mrs. Fancy put one hand to her chest, breathing in, then covered her mouth. Her eyes got bright and her shoulders shook, and I could tell she was laughing behind her hand.

"Lordy, Ro, you like to give me a heart attack," she said when she could speak. "Look at your hair. I didn't even recognize you. Why, you're lovely all bobbed."

I'd been missing morning coffee for more than a week now, but she didn't ask. She never asked. It had made her Ro Grandee's perfect friend, but it made me angry now. Angry enough to feel just fine about all the ways I planned to use her. Even angry enough to steal from her.

"You're going out?" I asked.

"I was heading to my reading club up at church. Did you—" She stopped talking and peered at my face. "Did you need something?"

"I need to borrow your phone," I said.

"Oh, has your phone gone out?" Mrs. Fancy asked. She peered around the door frame to look at my house like a concerned owl, blinking against the morning sunlight.

"No," I said. "I need to make some calls, long-distance. I'll pay you for them, of course, it's just not something I want Thom to see."

"A surprise?" said Mrs. Fancy.

"Oh, yes," I said, utterly truthful. "I'm planning a surprise."

She leaned back, and her sparse eyebrows came together. "Come on in," she said. Her papery hand closed around my wrist, and she towed me across her threshold. Her living room had a square of parquet by the minifoyer, too, but the carpet surrounding hers was blue. We stood on the fake wood island, and now she was looking at my clothes. "Spring cleaning day?"

I shook my head, trying to sound sorry instead of triumphant. "A pair of Christmas socks got in my laundry."

"Oh, honey!" she said. "What are you going to do?"

I waved it away. "Trinity Methodist runs a good secondhand store downtown. I'll get some things."

She tutted and said, "That store is run by a bunch of dirty hippies. I bet those clothes are full of lice."

"I'll wash them," I said, impatient. "May I use your phone while you're at book club?" I came down hard on the last two words, reminding her she had someplace to be.

"You'll want to use bleach, or a color-safe bleach alternative," Mrs. Fancy prattled on, completely unreminded. "Lice eggs are so hardy."

"Mrs. Fancy," I said, "I know how—"

She grabbed my arm and interrupted, her gaze bright. "You know, we're of a size. I bet I have some things you could wear!"

That derailed me, the idea of heading into my gun store shift later in one of her old-lady pantsuits, stretched out in the bum and with matching sweaters that had three-dimensional, sequined scenes of forests in the fall and snowmen at Christmas.

It must have showed on my face, because she started laughing. "Not what I wear now, you silly. I've kept my favorite things for years now. You'd look darling in my old peasant blouses or my mod minidresses. I see girls your age in outfits like the ones I've saved all the time. The stores call it vintage, but that's only so they can charge more."

She seemed perfectly content to natter on about fashion until I grew old and withered up too much to wear a minidress.

"I'd love to try your things on," I said, and I grabbed the edges of my shirt and pulled it off over my head. She stopped talking. Her gaze flicked to my soft cotton bra, then lower, taking in the slow-fading patterns, olive and mustard and palest sunrise blue, that were still mapped across my breasts and belly.

Her gaze skittered off me sideways, and she put one hand to her throat. I half expected her to close her eyes and loudly chant a recipe for fruited Jell-O mold or tell me how to get wine stains out of the carpet, some small, domestic spell to ward away the ugly story my skin told.

Instead she said, "Come away from the windows, or you'll be giving the postman a treat."

She walked away from me, through the den and down the hallway that led to the bedrooms. I followed in my jeans and bra, my old T-shirt crumpled in an angry ball in my left hand, saying, "You're missing your book discussion."

"Never you mind," she said, and went on into the guest bedroom. Phil came in with me, and he jumped up on the flowered comforter. He yowled at me, sensing the tension that Mrs. Fancy was delicately ignoring.

She opened the closet and started pushing things aside. "I haven't saved much of anything from the last ten, fifteen years. My knees put me in ugly shoes about then, and I stopped caring. Anyway, eighties fashion is like jumbo shrimp or pretty ugly—what do you call those things, where it can't be both? But the seventies, that was a fun time for clothes. Look at the colors! I have quite a few dresses from the fifties and sixties, too." She flipped through the hangers until she came to a row of brightly colored blouses. She pulled out a poet's shirt in bright blue floaty cotton and turned to me. I reached for it, but something on my face made her hug the blouse to her chest.

"You're different, Ro." It was more than Ro Grandee's own husband had noticed, even when I was naked and riding him. Points for that, at least.

I steeled myself, and then, more for expediency than for Mrs. Fancy's own sake, I pulled Ro Grandee's face on over mine, blanking my eyes and upping the wattage of my smile. My body curved into her good-girl's Catholic posture. Immediately I felt the mistake. I could not empower her this way. Ro was suicide, and slipping her skin on was as delicious and fatal as the first drag off a cigarette after days of being quits. If I did it enough, I would no longer be able to help it.

In a single moment of looking through the tissue-thin filter of Ro's eyes, I recalled what it felt like to love Mrs. Fancy. I could see how each thing she had felt regularly had put lines in her face, all her favorite feelings permanently remembered by her skin. Now her eyes crinkled up, and the vertical creases around her mouth deepened. These particular lines were so fixed that she must have made this face at least a million times before I met her. It was concern, tempered with such love and ready mercy that it had to have originated for her children. She was making it for me now.

I shook Ro off me, fast, and said, "Let me try that shirt on."

She took the blouse off the hanger and held it out to me, but she did not let go. We stood joined by it, each holding a shoulder.

She searched my face, and then she said, "You're leaving your husband." She spoke quietly, but her tone was plain: She was crowing.

"Do you see me packing?" I said. Good Lord, what an awful choice of words. "My things, I mean. I am not packing my things."

But Mrs. Fancy's mind was not on guns and double meanings. Her fingers clutched her half of the blue blouse and she said, "Who are you calling that you don't want him to see, long-distance? Someone you can go to? When you leave him?"

"I'm not leaving him," I said, but her eyes were as bright and round and hopeful as a spring robin's. "I'm thinking things over, is all." Her reaction made me ashamed to be taking advantage of her. But not enough to stop me. A lie came to me then. It wasn't a lie I'd planned. I'd heard something like it on *Oprah* once, and it tumbled down out of my memory straight into my mouth. I opened wide and let it out. "I want to talk to some people back in Alabama, the ones who knew me before I met Thom. I want to remember who I was before."

She narrowed her eyes at me. "That sounds like shrink talk." She didn't sound like she held with that. She probably didn't hold with *Oprah*, either.

I said, "I don't have the money for a shrink. I've been . . . talking to my pastor." The pastor at the Grandees' church was a wobbly-necked fellow who dyed his hair shoe-polish black. His office smelled like tuna fish and ranch dressing, and Joe and Charlotte Grandee's tithe paid a goodly piece of his salary. He was a social club Presbyterian whose sermons were written to butter open the wallets of his wealthier congregants; a drunken barn cat could fart out better advice than I would expect to hear coming out of the other end of that man.

Still, I could tell Mrs. Fancy liked this idea, even though she said, "Are you sure your pastor hasn't been talking to a shrink?" She still held tight to the blouse with one hand. The hanger dropped from her other hand to the floor, and she didn't even notice. "At least there's some God behind it. I don't trust that muddled-up Freud stuff. Such a pervert! Ladies wishing they had penises. Why, I never heard of such. The only penis I ever wanted was properly attached to Mr. Fancy, where I could get some good use out of it."

A muffled squawk of laughter got out of me. She'd surprised me for the second time in as many minutes, and she didn't look a bit sorry. She had a sly smile pulling up one corner of her mouth. She leaned in and smoothed back a piece of my hair, tucking the end behind my ear so she could look me directly in the eye. My surprise held me still for it.

"I had a good marriage, Ro. In all ways good, and it made everything else good, too. I'm not ashamed of that. It's what I want most for you." She petted back the other side of my hair, her fingers lingering as she tucked it behind my other ear. "Leave him. Today. My church works with some people that would hide you. They run a facility for women in . . . your situation."

"Women in my situation, huh?" I said, wry, shaking my head at both the idea and her delicate phrasing in a room where my bruises were so loudly displayed. I breathed in deep, through my nose, and smelled her baby powder and mothballs and the drifted-down scent of yesterday's baking. This was Mrs. Fancy's territory, and until this moment, I'd assumed only Ro Grandee had a place here.

In the house where I grew up, the kitchen had belonged to my mother. The air said so with vanilla and cinnamon, the same way the orange blossom soap in the bathroom made that place hers, too. The den was Daddy's. He filled it with the smells of salt and beer and the angry sweat that comes from watching your team lose hard at baseball. The bedroom smelled mostly his as well, and the hall where he'd worn down the carpet pacing and drinking on the bad nights. My room was mine, so it smelled like me, which registered in my own nose as nothing.

The day before she left, my mother had gone into her kitchen and packed a PBJ and red grapes into my brown paper lunch bag. She should have put a hunk of mutton in, or sliced kiwi, feta cheese, some strange food I'd never seen, to prepare me for her long-planned disappearing act.

She gave me only my usual lunch, my usual quick kiss goodbye, and I ate that lunch. I brought home the bag to reuse the next day. My faith that there would be a next day's lunch was so basic, I didn't even think of it as faith.

Maybe she *had* gone to a shelter. She'd been a woman, as Mrs. Fancy said, "in my situation." I had no way to know. She'd gotten out of a bad marriage, but she hadn't taken me with her so I could learn the route. She hadn't even dropped a trail of bread crumbs for me to follow. She'd only set my mouth, giving me her taste for called saints, good books, and angry men.

My throat felt closed. I couldn't open it to answer Mrs. Fancy. I'd come here to steal from her, but now a connection formed in my head, sudden and complete: I would steal from Mrs. Fancy and go to California. It felt true. Predestined, even, as if my mother had left me a secret something else: her ability to see the future, so mighty a gift that I didn't need cards.

I tried to keep my face still, to not let my expression show Mrs. Fancy a map that she could read. Not California, I reminded myself. I had no reason to believe Jim Beverly had landed there.

Mrs. Fancy was waiting patiently for me to answer. I said, "A shelter won't take Fat Gretel."

"My son could take Gretel. He has a fenced yard and a lonely German shepherd," Mrs. Fancy answered promptly, like she'd thought this out years ago and was five steps ahead with arguments and logic front-loaded to shoot down my objections.

I looked down at my feet and said, harsh and raw, "I only want to borrow your phone."

She looked like she wanted to say something else, but she read the mulish shape of my mouth correctly and settled for, "Try the blouse on."

I pulled it on and turned to the mirror hanging over the old-fashioned dresser. The shirt was soft cotton, long, but it gathered at the waist with elastic and showed my figure. It had a drawstring neck and bands of pale yellow ribbon and embroidered flowers near the ends of the sleeves, the conservative side of seventies hippie wear. My mother'd left a closet full of clothes like this in Fruiton.

Wearing it, I could see that the new haircut hadn't given me high cheekbones, it only showed them off. They were hers, like the down tilt to my mouth and the sharp-etched line of my collarbone. I blinked, long enough for it to be more like closing my eyes against the sight of my mother's child. Still, it was better than seeing Ro. At least my mother had gotten out of her marriage alive, something that was utterly beyond Ro Grandee.

"This will work. Thank you," I said.

Mrs. Fancy was already flipping through hangers, pulling out peasant blouses with angel-wing sleeves and button-down disco shirts with nipped-in waists. She laid them out on the bed in a pile, six or maybe seven of them, then added a couple of pairs of embroidered belled jeans and three minidresses in bright, mod patterns.

"What about shoes?" Mrs. Fancy asked.

"I'm good on shoes," I said instantly. The last thing I needed was for Mrs. Fancy to go digging in her old shoeboxes. One of them would feel way too heavy and rattle with loose bullets when she lifted it. I felt my gaze flick to the box that held my Pawpy's gun. I willed myself to look away, but not before I realized a couple of the shoeboxes on that side stuck out an inch or so beyond the rest because I'd stuffed my mother's library book behind them.

Mrs. Fancy did not notice, though. She was caught up staring at her own box of secrets on the other side. Her head was down, and her body had canted itself slightly toward it. I didn't much want her thinking hard on that box, either, since I was planning to loot it.

I said, "Help me carry this stuff back to my place. I'll make coffee?" trying to pull her away, but she didn't move.

When at last she spoke again, her voice had changed to something small and strangled. It didn't even sound like hers. "Did you know that my daughter, Janine, had another child? Before she had little Robert, I mean. Years ago. She had a baby with that bad man I told you she had married."

I'd guessed this. I'd also guessed that it had come to no good end. Mrs. Fancy's box held mementos from a babyhood and nothing more: booties and a clip of hair, but no first attempt at ABCs, no child's ballet shoes, no dried flowers from a pressed corsage. If my mother, out in California, had boxed up souvenirs from my childhood, then hers would end with a bag of baby teeth shaped like shoepeg corn and a five-sentence book report on *Beezus and Ramona*.

"I didn't know," I said.

She turned and walked away to the other end of the room. She twisted open the blinds and looked out the window that faced the backyard, her back to me and the closet. Our houses were called starter homes, but there were more retired folks in our neighborhood than young couples. Ender homes, more like. The backyard had a flat space near the back windows where a swing set could go. Mrs. Fancy had a birdbath there with a pansy patch around it. She said, "That's why she married so young, hardly more than a baby herself. Ivy came too early. Poor little thing. Poor little both things."

Her voice was steady now, loud enough for me to hear her even with her back to me. Each word came out formal and precise, like she'd been invited to speak to the Rotary Club six months ago and she'd been practicing this talk in her bathroom mirror.

"The baby's lungs didn't hardly work, but that sweet thing tried very hard. She'd twine her fingers around my pinky and clutch on. That's why Janine named her Ivy. She was born with that fierce grip."

Now Mrs. Fancy's shoulders shook, and she paused and breathed deep in and out. Ro would have gone and hugged her and soothed her into silence with pats and there, theres, but I stayed where I was, smelling useful information and almost hating myself for it. At last she said, "Ivy lived four months. Janine thought she was in the clear. We all did. One night, Ivy stopped breathing. She stopped everything. To this day, no one knows why. Babies sometimes do that.

"Janine didn't leave him. I couldn't make sense of it. They'd married because of Ivy, and then there wasn't any Ivy anymore. He was hell, and I was sure his fists had something to do with the baby coming early. Still, she stayed. I couldn't fathom it. Now I see you, no babies to hold you, staying and staying. You've stayed years now, so there must be parts of it that are sweet. There must be other parts that are so regular to you, you've come to think this is what life is like. You can't see there's other ways to live." She turned away from the window and looked at me, and I could see the whites of her eyes had gone red, but she wasn't quite crying. "Ro, I'm telling you. There's other ways to live."

I held myself still. I had no answer I could say to her.

She said, "My Janine, she cut her hair all feathery down the sides when she was pregnant. Before, it had been all one length, with bangs. She got heavy with the baby, too, soft in her belly and legs.

"After, she stayed with him, but she started growing the layers out of her hair. She took the baby weight off, too. Slowly, walking every day, eating more salad. One day, I think she looked in the mirror and saw how she was back to being herself. Her same long hair. Her same flat tummy. She looked like the girl she'd been before she got stupid in the back of his car after a dance." She sighed, a private sound, telling the story with her face to the pansy plants. "That's when she left him."

"Mrs. Fancy," I said, to get her attention. When she turned and met my eyes, I said, "What you said doesn't sound like shrink talk. It sounds like good sense. That's all I'm doing. Trying to remember the girl I was before him, and be that girl again."

That seemed to make sense to her in a way my stolen *Oprah* explanation hadn't. She blinked twice and then said, "Fine. If using my phone helps, come over and use it. If I'm not here, you have my spare key. Just know that I will drive you to my church's safe house the very moment you are ready."

She turned, suddenly brisk, and walked to the door. I could see her wanting out of the room where Ivy's things were secreted in a shoebox, where she'd said Ivy's name.

I said, "If you want to try to get to your book club, don't let me hold you."

She checked her watch, then nodded. "We read *A Prayer for Owen Meany*. That book has a lot of God in it, but it was quite dirty." She gave me a slight smile. "I'd like to catch the last half. You can stay here and finish going through the closet, if you like. Take anything that suits you."

She left me there, alone in the room with a box that held a perfectly good birth certificate. I was pretty sure I had seen a Social Security card, too, among the relics. It had been unlaminated, soft around the edges. The certificate and the card, to me these were the only mementos that mattered.

With these things, I could get a new driver's license. Ivy Wheeler. The name went with my new haircut, maybe with these clothes. I could travel under this other name and leave no trace of my comings and goings. If Thom became suspicious, there would be no trail for him to follow. When I found Jim Beverly, and then when something untoward befell my husband, the police would find no tattling bus route or plane ticket.

First I got my roll of bills out of the zipper pocket of my handbag and put them in what I thought of as my shoebox, nestling the cash up next to Pawpy's gun. The bills would come to smell of gun oil, like the money at Joe's stores always did.

Then I slid Mrs. Fancy's box out from its place in the stacks, and I toted it back to the guest bed. I set it down on the flower-covered comforter by the stack of blouses. Phil, in the automatic inconveniencing way of cats, had moved. Now he was nested on top of the blouses, shedding.

I felt a faint reluctance when I reached to open the box. I'd looked at Mrs. Fancy through the filter of Ro's kinder eyes. She'd pushed my hair out of my face with such sweetness, and though she hadn't been able to look at my bruises directly, she had spoken of her daughter's husband in a clear response to their presence in the room. I wondered if this shoebox really was Mrs. Fancy's. Perhaps this was Janine's box, too painful to have close, but too close not to have. I wished I believed it. I'd have no problem stealing from Janine.

I turned from the closed box to the phone on the bedside table. It was easier to pick up the receiver and dial Information. When the connection was made, I said, "Fruiton, Alabama,"

"What listing?" the operator asked in a bored voice. I said the first name that came into my head. I heard the clack of keys, and then she told me that there was no Lawly Price in Fruiton. I gave her another. She had plenty of Presleys, but no Charles. Not even an initial C. The football boys had moved on.

"What about Shay?" I asked the operator, who was already tired of me. "You have a Rob or Robert Shay?" I spelled the last name for her.

The operator said, "No, ma'am. Is that all?" in an exasperated tone.

I said, "No, ma'am, yourself, that's not all. Look for a Carson Kaylor."

"I do have a C. Kaylor in Fruiton."

"I'll take it," I said.

Car picked up on the second ring. He sounded sleepy, like I'd woken him up. He coughed, then made a throwaway "Heh," sound, so short that it was almost swallowed, and the "lo" stretched itself out long, tilting up into a question at the end. It was pure Alabama, and hearing that accent washed off whatever coat of sticky sugar Mrs. Fancy had put on me. I was Rose Mae Lolley, the prettiest damn girl from Fruiton High. Boys like Car Kaylor had always been as malleable as Play-Doh in my hands.

"Car! I swan, I'd know your voice anyplace," I said, and flipped the lid off Mrs. Fancy's shoebox with two fingers.

There was a pause, and then Car said, "Holy smoked hell. This can't be Rose-Pop Lolley?"

"Right first time," I said. It gave me a little shiver. No one but

Jim had ever called me Rose-Pop. "I was lying around thinking about old home folks, and I thought I'd see if I could find you."

Talking to Car felt like a good kind of creaky; marriage to a man as jealous as Thom had held my flirty girl muscles still for too long. Now I was stretching them, remembering the moves.

The folded birth certificate was right on top, and I lifted it out and set it aside. I looked down into the box. A rattle. A square of pink cotton, maybe cut off a swaddling blanket? A soft rabbit with a bell inside him.

I gave the contents a stir while Car yapped about his job laying floor for Home Depot, but it didn't unearth the Social Security card. Car was telling me about his job's great benefits package, but I nudged him off the now, asking about his old high school girlfriend. I was casting about for a crafty way to bring up Jim, but I didn't have to. Our star quarterback's vanishment was the single largest event that happened in my class's four-year run. Car brought it up himself.

I poked around in the box, hunting that card, and made the kind of interested, admiring noises that encourage men to talk more. Car had only the dimmest recollection of running into Jim on his last night in Fruiton, though he confirmed Jim had been at Missy Carver's party. "Truth told, I was wasted, Rose Mae," he told me. "I think Jim was hanging with Rob Shay and Jenny."

"I don't remember Jenny," I said. I found I'd taken my hand out of the box so I could poodle one finger around in my hair, just as if he could see me. I dropped my hand and moved the belled rabbit out of the way. Underneath him I found a teeny book with a picture of a pink rattle on the front. I knew if I opened it, I would see someone's best penmanship listing Ivy's date of birth, weight, and inches. Maybe a page to record her first smile and another for the first time she rolled over. After that, the pages would be blank.

"Sure you do, pig-faced blonde. Pig-faced in the cute way," Car said. "Jim was wasted, too, at that party. And he didn't stop drinking there. I remember they found beer cans busted open all over his wrecked Jeep. You never did hear from him?"

"No," I said. Jim had last been seen on the side of the highway, pointing his thumb away from me.

"If you was my girl, I would have called you at least before I took off," Car said. "Oh, wait. Weren't y'all broke up?"

That irked me instantly, for no rational reason. I moved the baby memory book and flung it, harder than I needed to, out of the way. I still didn't see the soft, unlaminated card I'd clocked before, and this was irking me as well. "Just for a day or two. We'd have gotten back together," I said, trying not to let my sudden wash of red temper color my voice.

"Still, that's probably why he didn't call you, Rose Mae. Y'all was broke up," Car said. He sounded now like he was explaining a very simple thing to someone who was maybe not too bright. All at once, I wanted to reach through the phone and slap him sideways. Back in high school, he'd had these meaty, round cheeks that were already yearning downwards, hoping to become jowls. I could imagine exactly what my palm would sound like, smacking hard against one.

"We always broke up when he was drinking," I said, quiet, trying not to get sharp.

He laughed. "Shoot, you musta ditched his ass three, four times a year. Rob Shay had a nickname for you, did you know that? He called you 'Delicious Hitler,' because you were hot, but you gave Jim righteous hell if he so much as licked the dew off a beer can."

"That ass," I said with forced cheer. I'd always liked Rob Shay, but the red wave of angry I was trying to squelch had put a shake in my voice even so. I couldn't help but add, "We always came back to each other, Car. Us breaking up didn't mean a thing."

"Well, it meant he didn't feel like he had to call you afore he went off," Car said. He still sounded doggedly overreasonable, pushing me past my desire to slap and deep into throttling territory. His tone changed to coddlesome, and he added, "What about you? You still single? You still fine? You was so fine, Rose Mae."

"Naw. I turned gay and got super fat," I said. "You take care, Car." I hung up. I was breathing hard, like I'd taken a sprint across loose sand.

I picked up the folded birth certificate and felt the slickness of the paper between my thumb and index finger. Official paper. Legal. A paper that meant something in the world outside my closed front door, if I could find the card that went with it.

All at once I realized how shortsighted I had been: If I took these things, I wouldn't need to find Jim Beverly at all. I was dumbstruck by the simplicity. With a new name, with a new identity that clipped four years off my age, with real ID, I could truly become a different person, a person Thom Grandee would never find.

"Ivy Wheeler," I said. I didn't know who that was, but I'd bet she had a razor-sharp bob and never wore ballet flats. The real Ivy and I already had at least a few things in common. She'd been a southern girl with a shithead for a father, just like me. I picked up the plushy rabbit with my free hand, wobbling him back and forth to make his tummy bell jingle. I could see Ivy, living somewhere green and unfamiliar with a few hills and a cool breeze. Fig trees and lemon groves.

Dammit, it was California. Again. I gave the rabbit an angrier shake, but all he had in him was sweet, light bells, muffled in his stuffing. Ivy'd also had a mother who couldn't stand to leave. Even after Ivy died, her mother couldn't bear to leave the man Ivy had come from, couldn't leave the rooms where Ivy had breathed and cooed and slept.

"Wonder what *that's* like," I asked the rabbit. He had an earnest, cream-colored face; this was not a rabbit who got sarcasm. I tossed him back on the bed and kept digging, looking for that Social Security card. Screw California. If I was Ivy, I could go anywhere. Thom could search for his Ro, angry and ready to end her, but I would have ended her already. He could live out his life in Texas, free of me, with his big red heart still thundering away inside him.

Ro Grandee wanted this last part so badly: the simple fact of Thom alive and in the world. As soon as I recognized this longing, this deep yearn of hers to leave Thom breathing, I understood the reason.

Ro Grandee wanted something to go back to.

I pulled my hands out of the box as if it had suddenly gone heated. How long could I stand to be out on my own? After Jim, heading west from Alabama all the way to Texas, I'd always found myself a man. Patently bad ones, happy to give me a ride off the edge of the world since they were heading that way anyway. I'd traded them out the same way I traded out cities, never learning how to trade up. Thom was the best of the lot, the only man since Jim that I had loved.

I had a few hundred bucks and an ancient revolver to my name. I'd be broke and dead lonely in a strange place, trying to scratch a shallow, safe hole in the chalky dirt. I was getting close to thirty years old, and that would still be true, no matter what Ivy's ID would say.

How long until a dark night came when I longed for the devil I knew so badly that I let Ro Grandee creep up over me and call him? She would tell him where I was. She would say, "Thom. Come and get me," and let him decide what that meant. The gypsy had told me there was no simple way out of this marriage, that it would come down to him or me.

I couldn't find the damn card anyway. I tossed everything back in the box. Stealing from Mrs. Fancy, especially after how she'd treated me today, felt flat wrong. Tracking Jim, that was the main thing. I put the lid on and picked up the box to put it away, but Phil had slithered off the bed without me noticing. As I stepped toward the closet, he threaded himself between my legs, pitching me forward. The lid flew right back off and everything inside the box went airborne, arcing across the room.

The booties separated and dropped, and the birth certificate sailed sideways like a paper airplane that had been badly folded and thrown all wrong. The silver cup pinged off a baby spoon and rolled until the wall stopped it. The rattle and the belled bunny plopped down side by side in a chiming patter. Everything hit the floor in a second, two at most. Except one thing. Ivy's Social Security card must have gotten stuck inside the baby book, hiding, but now it fluttered out as the book dropped. It caught the air exactly right and fell slowly, slicing back and forth, riding the air like a moth wing.

As it fell, I had time to think the words *coin toss*.

Then it landed. I dropped to my knees, already gathering objects, but I was looking toward that card. It landed writing-side up. My hands stopped their busy tidying. The day I'd seen my mother in the airport, she'd been tensed to bolt from the moment our gazes met. She was grabbing her things to run when she fumbled her tarot deck. The cards slid and scattered, and almost all of them fell facedown. Every card except one fell facedown.

That one card had told her that she had to stay. She'd refused to tell me which card had shown itself and paused her, but its message had changed her course and then mine. Now Ivy's Social Security card had fallen faceup, as if it too had something to say.

I knee-walked to the card and looked at it, really looked at it, for the first time. When I had opened the birth certificate before, I'd skimmed the name *Ivy*, taken in the birth date, but then my gaze had gone right to the words *Janine Fancy Wheeler* and stayed there. I hadn't read it carefully. But here the message was, plain and obvious, no mysterious swords or burning towers. The card's top and bottom were edged in red-and-blue scrolling. Sandwiched between the curlicues were nine numbers, dark against the white card, and three words in plain black type: Ivy Rose Wheeler.

Janine had named her baby Ivy Rose.

I left the card where it was and reached instead for the Ziploc bag. I opened it and carefully lifted out the tuft of baby hair. It was clipped into a pink bow barrette with tiny teeth, made to hold fine strands. It was dark hair, but a lot of babies are born with a head full of dead black hair. It lightens as it meets the sun, or it falls out altogether and brown or blond or red stuff grows in under.

This tuft didn't look like that. It was a true dark brown, as rich and glossy as mink. I tilted my head forward so the wings of my bob closed around my face, and I held Ivy's little tuft up against my own hair. Ivy's all but disappeared, so close were they in color.

Half an hour ago, Mrs. Fancy had reached to tuck my hair behind my ear, her fingers lingering in the strands as she told me all the good things she wanted for me.

"Oh, shit," I said to the room.

I packed up the rest of Ivy's baby things with the reverence they deserved, putting the hair back and getting all the air out of the Ziploc bag, checking the silver cup for dings. I saved out the Social Security card and the birth certificate, and then I put the box away.

I put Ivy's papers in my purse. I would go to the DMV tomorrow and get Ivy a driver's license. I'd need to find a family of local Wheelers and lift some of their junk mail for proof of address. That would absolutely be a felony, but it would be my first, because taking these from Mrs. Fancy wasn't stealing. She'd said, "Take anything that suits you," and Ivy Rose could suit me to a tee.

But only if I first made damn sure Ro Grandee had nothing to come back to.

I would use the ID to travel invisibly, to find Jim, and I'd be Rose Mae long enough to get him to burn my bridges for me. With Thom gone and Jim beside me, I'd be ready to rebuild myself into someone nicer. With nothing to go back to, Jim and I would be entirely free.

CHAPTER

9

I FOUND HIM.

It took ten long days. Every night, I played my own version of Scheherazade for Thom, 1,001 pieces of tail, taking the tension out of his broad shoulders when he came home from Grand Guns. It eased me, too, this endless, brutal sex that left us both as spent and wasted as a beating, but only an eighth as sore. He did hit me once, but only a glancing backhand. Another day, after a run-in with his daddy, he shoved me into the wall. These were squalls, though, over before they truly started.

He didn't get angry enough to flip my mother's final card and end me, and I didn't get angry enough to pour Drano into his corn chowder and go stomping off, vindicated, to prison. When the sun went down, we took the day's frustrations to our mattress and hurt each other just enough. The nights bought me the days, and every day, I stole time on Mrs. Fancy's phone, hunting for Jim Beverly.

By sundown on the tenth day, I knew exactly where he was.

"You're different," Thom told me that night, in the dark. We lay side by side on our bed with four inches of cool air in between us. I could feel sweat, mine and his, drying on my skin. Gretel, with her usual impeccable timing, had hopped on the bed and flopped down between my calves two minutes after I'd come like a screaming eagle and thrown myself backwards off him. Her snores and the warmth of her had soothed me close to sleep, but when I heard how flat his voice had gone, my eyes popped open wide and my nerve endings tingled.

"It's a haircut, Thom," I said. "It's a couple of new tops."

"I mean you're different here," Thom said. His big hand thumped the slice of bed between us for emphasis.

"I don't know what you mean," I said. It sounded like a lie even to me.

"Every night, Ro. That's a lot, even for us."

"Are you complaining?" I said, boosting myself up on my elbows, incredulous.

He made a short, hard, barking noise. It was a scoff or a laugh, hard to tell in the dark room. "No. But that thing, with your back to me . . ."

I lay back down and asked, "Reverse Cowgirl?"

"Yeah, that," he said at the same time I said, "Giddy-up," trying for levity.

He went on as if I hadn't spoken. "You never used to like that. And you do that thing with your teeth now, and that scissoring thing. That's all new."

I could see where he was going. When a wife brings home new bedroom tricks, a certain kind of husband starts to wonder where she learned them. I turned on my side and looked at him. My eyes had adjusted, soaking in the moonlight coming through the sheers. I could see his profile etched against the windows, but it was too dark for me to get a good read of his expression. I didn't need to see to recognize the thought behind the words. *Who is he.*

It had always been his most dangerous question. For him to ask it, even obliquely, was a harbinger. It was a more dangerous question now, because the answer was no longer Ro's endless, true assurance of fidelity. Now the answer was, *He is Jim Beverly, and in four days, when you head to Houston with your daddy for that gun show, I am going to Chicago to righteously screw him until he remembers his promises. I am going to reclaim him.*

Reclaim was the right word, because Jim was living in sin with a girl from Fruiton High. Arlene Fleet was her name, and she hadn't even made my call list, though I remembered that scrawny, dark-eyed weasel quite clearly. Jim had never dated her officially, but rumor had it she'd put out for every member of the football team and half the county besides. She'd stuck in my brain because she was the only person at Fruiton High to ever suspect me of stealing.

She saw me nab a chocolate cookie from her pretty cousin Clarice. Clarice was a leggy blonde with honey-colored skin, and Jim Beverly *had* dated her. I'd thought Clarice's smile was both too dim and friendly and too wide and white, so that she looked to me like the love child of a cannibal and a Labrador retriever. Still, a lot of boys went for her, including mine.

Stealing her cookie was a victimless crime, as I'd never once seen Clarice Lukey eat dessert. I planned to slip the treat into the sad brown paper sack of this kid whose crunchy mama packed his lunch every day: spelt bread with nut butter and homemade yogurt that smelled like baby urp.

I drifted by with my best underwater walk and palmed the cookie. When I looked up, Arlene Fleet's big eyes were aimed my way across the table, glossy black and blank as an animal's. After that, she seemed to be creeping around the edges of every room I was in, staring at me with that same fever-bright, accusing stare. Her name did not appear even once in my notepad, as I could see no possible connection between a scrub like Arlene Fleet and my quarterback boyfriend, but she had him now. Not for long. If I could soothe and feed and sex Thom through the next four days, he'd be off to Houston. I'd go to Chicago and take Jim back from her.

"Honey," I said to Thom. "Sugar. Of course it's different now. You know I'm off the pill."

He turned on his side toward me, and now the moonlight was entirely behind him, making his hair into a faint gold halo. I could see nothing of his face, and my own was pointed directly into that scant light. My eyes must have glittered at him in the dark, hard and shiny as a feral cat's, too reflective for him to read them.

"I thought about that. It seems like that would make a girl . . . mushier," he said.

I laughed out loud, a harsher sound than I intended, and said, "Like they make babies on TV? Slow? With the covers up? You want to get all missionary, Thom? If you like, I can stare up at you all weepy and think about Pampers while you pump away. That sound fun?"

"No, thank you," he said. "Don't be like that. I thought you'd want baby making to be more romantic."

"I don't feel romantic," I said. "I feel more like, I don't know. Primal."

"That's pretty clear, Cowgirl," he said, and I could tell by his voice that a little smile had snuck up on his face under cover of this darkness.

"That's Reverse Cowgirl to you, bub," I said, making my voice sound smiley back. "Mrs. Reverse Cowgirl."

"So we're having *National Geographic* sex," he said. "Primal."

"You bet," I said, and that was true, because nothing was more primal than survival. Reproduction was absolutely not going to happen. Ivy Wheeler, proud new licensed driver in the great state of Texas, had driven her sweet ass directly to Planned Parenthood. I'd committed some identity fraud to get a supply of pills that would not show up on Thom Grandee's insurance. Three wheels' worth were hidden under the bathroom sink in my tampon box, uneasy roommates with a votive candle and the rosary beads I prayed through as a penance every time I took one. To Thom I said, "We are leopards making more leopards. We are sharks making more sharks."

"If you want to do it like leopard sharks, I'm your boy," Thom said, his tone light, but another thirty seconds passed before he lay back down.

Who is he had been pushed back, but it had not gone away.

Thom was searching for his Ro, wanting her sugar-talk that could change on a dime to a sass-mouth, wanting her penchant for yielding to him and enraging him by turns. I would not be her for him, not for five minutes. I couldn't afford to be her for thirty seconds, but Thom's favorite question had surfaced, and that meant I was running low on time.

It had taken too long to find Jim. I'd had to rely on the information of the kids who'd been my kind, football boys, mostly. I'd learned early there was no point calling the girls, especially the ones that Jim had dated, when I tracked down Dawna Sutton.

She was now a social worker up in Boston, and she ended the conversation forty seconds in, saying, "Yes, I remember your piece-of-shit disappearing boyfriend. I hope he's dead and frying deep, deep, deep in deepest hell. As for you, I don't think you spoke more than nine words to me in school. Meanwhile, a live baby with a crack problem got pulled out of a Dumpster this morning, and I have to find a place for him. Your 'good old days' chat can go suck it." She hung up.

None of the girls Jim had dated had cause to feel any more friendly than that toward me, so I stuck to folks that did.

After days of dead-end conversations with boys who had last seen Jim at Missy's party, I got aholt of Bud Freeman, former linebacker, currently married to Clarice Lukey. Judging by the noise at their house, she'd pumped out about a thousand angry babies for him. No one else had even had an inkling of where Jim spent the blank hours between leaving Missy's and wrecking his Jeep, but over the thunder of rioting toddlers, in the middle of a walk down memory lane, Bud told me. He said it off the cuff, almost in passing.

According to Bud, Jim Beverly was out at Lipsmack Hill with Arlene Fleet the night he disappeared. My breath stopped. Lipsmack Hill. With Arlene Fleet. I knew perfectly well there was only one reason to go up on top of Lipsmack. I'd traded my virginity for Jim's on a scratchy picnic blanket atop that very spot.

I asked Bud for Arlene's number, but Bud snorted. "She won't talk to you. She lit out of Alabama close to ten years ago, and we ain't seen hide nor hair of the girl since."

"No kidding," I said, and another memory was surfacing. One time, when Jim and I were broken up, a pack of cheerleaders tried to get a rise out of me by saying they'd seen Arlene wearing his letterman jacket. They told me Jim had been walking Arlene down the hall with an arm around her shoulders. I'd said, "Charity work, clearly," in a breezy voice, though I'd felt it like a fast, pointy elbow to the kidney. A few days later, Jim and I were back together, and I'd forgotten it. I asked Bud, "Do you know where she's living?"

"Chicago, and she don't truck with nothing or nobody from back home. She's ass-rat crazy, Rose Mae."

"Like, in an institution?" It was a fair question. Arlene's mother had spent more than one "vacation" at the special hospital over in Deer Park.

He chuckled. "Well, I reckon not. But she's crazy. She ain't even been home to see her mama. Ain't talked to Clarice for more than a minute on the phone for years now, and as kids Arlene was welded to her hip. I couldn't hardly get my Clar alone for half a minute."

I didn't answer. I myself had zoomed out of Alabama like the state itself had lit my tail on fire. I had not spoken to my own father in more than a decade. For me, Arlene's behavior lived next door to normal.

"She married?" I asked. I was remembering something else, too. I'd seen Arlene with Jim together once myself, at the movies.

Bud said she wasn't married. She was teaching college English at a big state school in downtown Chicago. But she had a fellow, he said. One who was comfy enough to answer the phone at her place. They'd never heard a word about him from her. No name. Not even an admission he existed.

It was a lot to process. Arlene Fleet had been with Jim out at Lipsmack the night he disappeared. Arlene had followed me all over school for months, watching me like . . . like the other woman might. She'd had his jacket. I'd seen them out together. Arlene had fled Fruiton the same way Jim had, same way I had, the first red second she could. Now she was half a country away, living with a mysterious man. She wouldn't visit home. She never told her family about her fella.

As I got off the phone with Bud, it struck me that she and I were of a type. The other girls Jim had dated had been as unlike me as he could find. Tall girls, redheads and blondes. Arlene had been a teeny, dark-haired, waxen thing. She was like my photocopy, but pale and fuzzy round the edges, made on a broken-down machine.

I tapped Mrs. Fancy's phone button to get a dial tone, then punched in 411. "Chicago, Illinois," I told the operator. "I need an address and a phone number for Arlene Fleet. Two e's."

It was that simple. She should have changed her name or ditched her family altogether, as I had done. And was about to do again. I tapped the disconnect button again and dialed Arlene's number. Three rings, and she picked up.

"Hello?" she said. Almost a decade in Chicago, and her accent was still pure backwoods Alabama. "Hello?" she said again, sounding like me before some Texas got up inside my mouth.

Behind her I heard another voice, asking her something from across the room. It was deep, a man's voice, not a boy's. I strained to catch the tones. It could be Jim. Older, with a wider, deeper chest; I could imagine him sounding like that. But it wasn't the voice that made me sure. What made me sure was the way Arlene Fleet shushed him, nervous and immediate. Her voice was worried, much louder, when she said, "Who is this?" into the phone. "Who is this?"

She had him. He was there, and she was hiding him still, all these years later. I made my voice husky and tried to talk like a Yankee. "Wrong number. Sorry." It came out sounding like a Muppet with a cold, but it worked.

"That's okay." She sounded a little too relieved, and she hung up a little too quickly.

I stood breathless with triumph, my hand still curled around the phone. He was there, and he was with her because she looked like me. Arlene had been a fetal kind of pretty back in high school. If she put on a little weight, grew some boobs, learned to smile, we'd be even better matched. I felt my whole body flush. Jim Beverly remembered. He was hearing me every time she spoke in that thick accent, touching me every time his hands reached for her slight, pale body. I could go to Chicago, knock on Arlene's door, and Jim Beverly would open it. He was living with the shadow, but I was his real thing. I could knock on her door and take him back. Easy as that.

The four days after I knew where Jim was were the hardest of all. Thom could smell it in me, a deep-set, bubbling purpose. He had no idea what it was, but he was dead sure he didn't like it. I picked up every extra shift at the gun shop I could get and even instigated a dinner with Larry Grandee and Margie. I volunteered Thom and me both to clean out his mother's garage. I kept us too busy to give him time to ponder, too public for him to tear me open and read the new name written on my heart and lungs and guts.

The morning of Thom's Houston trip felt like the tail end of a countdown. While he was in the shower, I slipped outside with a razor-sharp fillet knife and cut our phone line. When he came out, rubbing his hair with a towel, I had the receiver in my hand and I was glaring down at the phone.

"Our phone's gone out," I said, my back to him, tapping and tapping at the button in a manufactured pout.

Thom had to come over and tap the button himself and hold up the receiver and shake it and hear no dial tone. He said a few choice words, and I laid a soothing hand on his damp shoulder.

"Never mind, you'll miss your flight. I'll call from a pay phone and get a repair guy."

"When we land, I'll call you at the store," Thom said.

"I'm not working today," I said, and he gave me a long, level stare, too many wheels set turning in his brain for my comfort.

Driving him to the airport, I had to work hard to keep my hands still on the wheel, to not jiggle or twitch. I put my gaze on the road, and the car ate the last miles between me and a brief window of freedom.

"Baby, your eyes look overbright. Are you sick?" Thom asked.

"I'm fine," I said.

"You're so quiet," Thom said.

"I'm fine," I repeated, and then I veered sideways into a gas station parking lot, opened my door and leaned out and threw up all my breakfast.

"Yeah, you look fine," Thom said.

I flapped one hand back over my shoulder at him and puked some more.

When I finally sat up, he was looking at me with one eyebrow up, his expression a hybrid of concern and I-told-you-so. "Do you need me to stay home?"

It was mostly a courtesy, as it would take a disaster on a par with one of Egypt's ten plagues for Joe to let his eldest off the hook for this trip. A delicate wifely puke out a car door wasn't going to rate. Even so, I practically hollered, "Lord, no!" at him.

I said it way too fast, way too fervent. There was a pause between us, and in that space, Thom swallowed a whole bag of thunderclouds. They didn't seem to be agreeing with him. "You seem pretty set on getting your husband out of town," he said. His whole body flexed like a fist, closing and tightening beside me.

I gulped, pitiful, and added, "No woman wants her best fella watching her throw up. I can't think of a thing more likely to kill the air of mystery." I gulped again and tried to look wan. Wan should have been an easy sell, tense as I was, thick as the air in the car had become.

"But if you're sick . . . ," Thom said. Heavy emphasis on if. *Who is he* had climbed into the car with us, and that question had the power to keep Thom home, Joe or no Joe.

The hanged man card was coming, and there was no stopping it. I could only hope to put it off and get him on that plane. Then I'd go get Jim and set him like a wall between us.

"Maybe I'm not sick at all," I said, desperate. "Maybe this is something else? We've been trying awful hard."

He didn't know what I meant for a second, and then his eyebrows came together. "This fast?"

"Why not?" I said. "Maybe we hit it right out of the gate."

"You think?" Thom asked, and I saw a faint easing in the line of his arms and shoulders. I dropped wan and tried to look bloomy.

"Sure. According to Larry, the Grandee sperms are so ever-lovin' mighty, he knocked up Margie by standing upwind and thinking about Cindy Crawford. Maybe it runs in the family."

His eyes brightened and he leaned in to kiss me without thinking. I put a hand up over my mouth. "Yick, no, baby. I need some gum," I said, and he actually laughed.

Two hours after Thom and Joe's flight left, I was on a plane of my own to Chicago, throwing up again, this time into a wax-lined airplane sick bag. I'd lucked into having someone's unflappable granny for a seatmate. She patted my back and said, "There now, get it all out. You'll feel better." Then she made me drink a fizzy water.

I got off the train from the airport at a stop that was smack in the middle of downtown Chicago. I stepped out of the station into a steel grid that seemed to grow straight up out of the concrete, towering all around me. The streets were dead straight, cutting the buildings into orderly blocks. I had a map of the city, and I'd planned a route to Arlene Fleet's apartment. I walked quickly, swinging my outsize macramé purse. Along with all my regular purse things, it held a change of clothes, a can of pepper spray from Grand Guns' stock of lesser weaponry, and a ticket that said Ivy Rose Wheeler would be flying back to Texas tomorrow.

Out of sheer habit, I smiled at the folks coming down the side-walk toward me, but their gazes slid off sideways like my skin was slicked in grease. They didn't look back. Everyone who passed was doing busy things: a man barking into his mobile phone, a gaunt woman who almost hit me with her swinging briefcase, a herd of pretty girls in jeans and clacky shoes. Everyone was going to their own places, as orderly and single-minded as ants.

They were like the moving pieces of a beautiful machine, each a cog that churned and clicked its chilly teeth against the teeth of other cogs, uncaring. It was nothing like small-town Alabama, where the local paper did a human interest story if someone's mama released a particularly loud fart in church.

Even in Amarillo, I was someone known and noticed. Hell, I was Joe Grandee's daughter-in-law, and he was on three billboards, five times larger than life and grinning like a possum, cradling a gorgeous shotgun. Over his head, black letters read, "You know Joe!" And across his chest it said, "Grand Guns. For Amarillo's Big Shots." Joe's outsize eyes seemed to track me anytime I drove past one of those boogers.

Around town, especially with Thom, I felt watched by all the folks who did, indeed, know Joe. But this place had swallowed Arlene Fleet up for more than a decade. I felt a twinge of some-thing ugly in the deeps of me, and it shocked me to realize it was envy. Back in high school, if anyone had told me I'd be marching past a fifty-story Chicago building one day, shivering in a peasant blouse and envying Arlene Fleet, I'd have laughed until something busted.

She was such a skinny, creeping critter, twitchy as a rodent. As a child, I'd been capable of envy for orphans starving to death in far-off darkest China, but never once had I felt a green yearn toward Arlene Fleet's life. Her mama bounced in and out of the nuthouse, and a bat-crap crazy mother seemed a flat step down, even from a willfully missing mother like my own.

Now she'd come to this foreign place and let it eat her up until she was unseeable inside it. I realized I was, too, for the moment. No one on planet Earth had any idea where Mrs. Thom Grandee was. If a car smashed into me and killed me, Ivy's ID would lead nowhere. For this one day, a thousand miles from home, I'd been swallowed, too.

My route led me out of Chicago's skyscrapered center. The foot traffic was lighter here, and the sleek steel buildings gave way to Greek restaurants and coffee shops. The walk to Arlene's had looked much shorter on paper. I wished I had taken the time to figure out a bus route. The held-over cold of the sidewalk came up through Ro Grandee's trouser socks and thin-soled flats, until each step felt like the sidewalk was stinging me.

I stopped in front of a video rental place to check my map. The store was about the size of a walk-in closet, and it had an age-faded feature poster of *Flashdance* still in the front window. That movie had come out when I was a teenager. I found myself staring at the display, puzzled, disoriented, as if moving toward Arlene had moved me back in time to high school and leg warmers and spiral perms.

A scroungy guy with about fifteen visible tattoos was sitting on the sidewalk. "It's a front," he said, as if I'd asked about the poster out loud. "They have a huge back room full of porn."

He had a blanket spread on the ground beside him, canted back a ways into an alley. He raised his eyebrows at me and gestured at a jumble of objects on top. "See anything you like, doll?" It seemed the blanket was a store. Everything sitting out on it was inventory.

In the middle, I saw a pair of scuffed-up yellow boots. They stood up tall among fake Coach purses and scraps of silk fronting like Hermès scarves, and they were the only things that looked comfortable with themselves. Even their dings had a mellow buttercream glow, and they were my size. I could see the number in faded print inside the lip.

I found myself pausing, drawn, my cold feet aching. The only pair of boots I owned had kitten heels. They rested in my closet with strappy sandals and flats with bows, all the dainty accompaniments to Ro Grandee's ruined wardrobe.

Ivy Wheeler is a woman who wears cowboy boots, I decided. And I would know. After all, I'd just had a taste of what it might be like to be Ivy Wheeler, unmoored and unknown, eaten by a city.

I squatted by the blanket. A dollar sign and the number 40 had been scrawled across an index card leaned up against the pointy right toe. Too much. I touched the card with one finger and said, "If they fit, I'll give you half that," to the tattoo boy.

He sized me up, taking in my macramé bag, my ancient jeans, trying to read my money. I lowered my head, looking down at Ivy's boots.

He didn't say anything, so I started to rise. Then he spoke up. "Gimme the twenty. Whether they fit ain't my problem."

Most of my remaining wad was in a Ziploc bag in my underpants, but I had three twenties and some smaller bills tucked in different spots, each miniroll trying to look like all the cash I had. I chose the twenty in my bra, just to mess with him. Pulled it out slow.

He cool-boyed it right to the end, and then his eyes shifted, taking an involuntary glance south. His gaze flicked back almost instantly, but I had one eyebrow up, waiting for him. He grinned at me, caught, the smile crinkling the blue star he'd inked on his cheek, and we liked each other for a second.

I kicked off my flats and left them on the sidewalk like bits of shed skin. The boots slid on so easy, it was as if some other girl with feet shaped like mine had walked in them for a year, breaking them in for me, readying them for this moment. As I walked away, tattoo boy was already putting my flats on the blanket to sell to someone else who needed a change.

My pace quickened. The porn place had clued me in: Arlene wasn't living in the world's best neighborhood. It was getting dark, but I didn't have far to go. Jim Beverly was less than a mile away from me right now, maybe sitting down to dinner with her. I could picture him touching her dark hair, remembering the silkier feel of mine.

The sun was gone by the time I found her apartment building. I saw her listed on the row of call buttons: Fleet—4B. I hit a button on the intercom, two numbers under hers. Nothing happened, so I went down one more and tried again.

This time a male voice came through the speaker. "Yeah?"

Arlene had failed to rinse the long taste of Alabama vowels out of her mouth, and I could sound like her, easy. "It's Arlene Fleet, from 4B. I locked myself out."

A second later the door buzzed, and I pushed my way in. Her building had no elevator, and the door by the stairs said 1B. I was breathing hard by the time I got to Arlene's floor, and my heart was banging itself against my rib cage, both from the stairs and from being this close to seeing Jim again. I paused, listening.

Arlene was home. I could hear her rattling around inside 4B, her voice raised. She wasn't alone. Her shrill yaps were punctuated by the sound of the deeper, male voice I'd heard behind her on the phone. I couldn't make out any of the words through the old building's well-made walls, but they both sounded angry. I pressed my ear against the door and a second later felt the wood shudder as something on the other side hit it hard and bounced off it. Arlene? In my mind's eye I saw her slight body ponging off of mine, only an inch or two of wood between us.

Was Jim hitting her? My Jim had laid heavy hands on me only once, when we were blind drunk together on that long, wrestling night in our green woods. If he was hitting her, then he was drinking.

The male voice dropped in volume, going almost inaudible, and Arlene's raised up, so strident and high that she sounded like an angry budgie. I pressed closer, as if yearning alone could melt oak and push me through it, trying to hear him. His words sounded clipped, sharp and fast like drumbeats, but he was very angry, and Chicago could have whittled down his accent.

Was he drinking? I wasn't sure that I should knock if he was. Jim drinking was not the Jim I wanted. I was surprised my banging heart didn't do the knocking for me, an endless thudding gallop against the wood. Perhaps they did hear me, because the door flew open, spilling me all the way onto my ass. I landed face to crotch with a pair of knife-creased khakis.

I went scuttling backwards crab style. When I saw the coffee dark skin of his hands, I knew he wasn't Jim. I looked up at him. He was a tall black man with a trim waist and broad shoulders. He was better looking than Jim had ever thought of being, too, with a long, straight nose and sharp cheekbones and a full mouth. He was too good-looking for Arlene fucking Fleet, that was sure. I scrambled to stand up. He must have been a foot taller than me, but I wanted to take him on, punch his face in, for the crime of not being the right man.

"What the—," he said, and he stepped toward me. He was so big. I scrabbled in my purse for my pepper spray. I whipped it out and aimed it at him, pushing down hard on the trigger, but nothing happened. He stopped in his tracks, boggling at me. I pressed and pressed, and nothing came out, while he dared to keep on standing there, existing, and not being Jim. Not being a single thing like Jim, even. I'd come halfway across the country, spent most of my cash, only to be wrong. I pushed harder, wanting to watch him claw at his eyes while Arlene and I kicked the shit out of him. My new boots had steel toes.

"I heard you yelling," I said to Arlene. I sounded breathless.

"Whoa," the guy said. He put up his hands. "Calm down."

I said to Arlene, "You go for the soft parts. And then we run while he's down." I pressed again, and still no spray came out. I gave the can a fast, angry shake.

Arlene Fleet wasn't even looking at me. Her focus was all on her fella. She was talking to him now, continuing their fuss like I wasn't standing pumping my finger up and down on the unresponsive pepper spray trigger, trying to blast him into blindness.

He kept his hands up but turned to talk to her as if I wasn't hardly there.

As I watched their body language, my adrenaline began to leak away. This was Arlene's mystery man, and she was serious about him. She didn't have Jim in there, too. This was her guy, and he was hidden away from her family for the high crime of not being a white boy. That was all. He also threw her into doors, but, hey, with her family, I'd bet that was less of an objection than his skin color.

Jim wasn't here. He never had been.

At last he turned to me and said, "I was just leaving."

"Bet your ass you are," I told him. I had stopped trying to press the trigger down, but I still had the pepper spray's round, plastic eye trained on his face. Now I could see the problem. I hadn't flicked the safety off.

"He was only trying to help you up," Arlene said.

He skirted me, careful, hands still up, then turned and went on down the stairs. Arlene started to go after him, but I blocked her path. Even if Jim wasn't here, had never been here, Bud had told me that Arlene had been the last set of eyes alive in Fruiton to see him on the night he disappeared. I wasn't finished with her. Not by a long shot. I stayed in her way and said, "They're almost all sonsabitches."

When I couldn't hear her fella's big, angry feet stamping down the stairs, I lowered the spray. She wheeled on me, black eyes snapping, and I got my first clear look at Arlene Fleet. Maybe he wasn't too good-looking for her, after all. Her skinniness had shifted into something sleek and trim. She looked as flexible as a bendy straw. Her face had lost that feral look, and anger brought a flush to her pale, high cheeks. Her skin was perfect, except she had a crease, what my mother had always called a temper line, running vertically between her eyebrows.

That line deepened, and she said, "Rose?"

She hadn't even recognized me. If she'd run off to Chicago to be with Jim, even if she'd swapped him for the black guy later, she would have recognized me right off. Women don't forget their rivals. Still, something had happened between them back in Alabama. There was only one reason Fruiton High kids went up on top of Lipsmack. I tried to ask her, but she'd turned her temper from her fella to me, and she overrode me.

"I haven't seen you in ten years. I didn't even know if you were alive or dead, and quite frankly, I didn't much care. And now you are standing out in my stairwell, apparently eavesdropping on me and my boyfriend?" She seemed to have it in her head that I was there on some crazy-ass mission from her family, to get her back to Alabama. "How the hell did you even find me? What are you doing here? What do you want from me?"

I plastered the nicest smile I could muster up onto my face. I needed an in, something that would make her talk to me, the way mentioning my pastor had eased Mrs. Fancy. All I really knew about Arlene Fleet was that she'd been kind of a whore and her mother was a nut job. I wasn't sure how whores bonded, but I doubted I could get her on my team by sprinkling some Jesus. Maybe *Oprah* and therapy, a wash with Mrs. Fancy, would work on the child of a crazy woman.

"Okay, Arlene. I guess you never were one for social graces. That's fine," I said. "It's kind of a long story, but if you want the short, standing-in-a-stairwell version, I can do that. I got in a fight with my therapist, and now I'm on a spiritual journey. Congratulations, you're my next stop."

She didn't rise to my shrink bait. She held up one hand to stop me talking and said, "If this is some sort of Twelve Step thing, making amends or whatever, fine. I forgive you. Now I need to go catch Burr."

"Forgive me for what?" I said, dumbfounded. I wasn't the one who'd stalked her all over school. I hadn't gone up on Lipsmack to have a mysterious and likely horizontal powwow with her boyfriend. We did a three-step dance in the hallway as she tried to get around me again.

I altered my tack slightly. I'd heard her fella pitch her into a door, so maybe she was a romantic now, Ro Grandee style. "Wait, Arlene, one minute. I'm sorry I sounded snippy. I really do need your help. I'm only doing what you're trying to do, too. Going after the one that got away."

She paused then, and her eyes got cagey. "Whatever this is, it can't have anything to do with me."

This was the first time she'd stood still and truly listened to me since the door flew open. I kept going, winging it. "But it does, indirectly. See, my therapist said I get crappy men because I go looking for them, not because men are mostly crappy. She thinks I choose assholes because that's what I think I deserve, blah blah, masochism, blah blah, low self-esteem. You know how shrinks talk."

"No," Arlene said pointedly. "I don't."

"With your mother? Come on." That hit her low, and she took a step back. I followed. "Anyway, she's wrong. I've been thinking through my romantic history, looking for a guy I picked who wasn't an asshole. If I can find just one, then my shrink is wrong and it isn't me, it's the men. And there is one, I know it. I remember. But I need you to help me find him."

"Find him?" she said. Now she was truly edging backwards, and I followed her, because that caginess in her eyes had deepened, and she knew where this conversation was going. I hadn't been all wrong. She knew something. I followed her step for step in a backwards dance that I was leading, even though her feet shuffled first. I got in close, kissing close, predator close, nailing her down and holding her with sheer animal will.

"I have to find Jim Beverly," I said.

His name rolled out into the stairwell, and its presence changed her. She became in the space between those two words the ugly weasel I'd known, the one who had followed me all over Fruiton High, scrutinizing my every sneeze and shuffle as she tried to catch me stealing. Her shoulders folded in and her face went white as poached chicken. Her throat clicked, like she was trying to dry-swallow a mouthful of mini-ball shot. Her eyes went wide. She was afraid, as if she was so allergic to his name, its very syllables could swell her throat closed and stop her breathing.

Two seconds at most passed, then she went leaping wildly backwards into her apartment and slammed the door. I heard the bolt slam home and the rattle of a chain.

I stood panting in her stairwell. "Arlene?" I called. I tapped at the door.

Nothing. I knocked again, harder.

"Arlene? This is ridiculous. I need maybe five minutes of your time," I called. My new steel toe shot out and kicked the door as hard as I could. It made a satisfying clap of angry sound.

The only response I got was a barrage of obnoxious music coming through the wood.

Arlene Fleet knew. She knew where Jim had gone and why, but that information was locked up inside with her.

I was powerless to get it out.

CHAPTER

❧

10

THE NEXT MORNING, I lay for Arlene outside of the classroom where she was teaching. Ambush time. Her job offered no easy door that she could lock between us. She wouldn't want a scene, and I was willing to stage an entire opera on the campus green, complete with hair rending and the wailings of the damned, if that was what it took.

I leaned up against the wall with my new boots crossed, trying to look relaxed and in control. By the time she came out of the room, head down, deep in thought, my shoulders were aching and my knees were trembling with the effort it took to hold the pose.

"Hey, Arlene," I said.

She did a double take that ended in a recoil. "How did you find me?" Her voice came out in a mousy scratch.

"They gave me your course schedule up in the English Department."

"No," she said. "I mean how did you know I worked here, or my address? How did you even know to look in Chicago?" She was clutching a soft leather satchel like a briefcase, and now she shifted it in front of her so it was between us.

"Oh, that," I said. "I talked to Bud."

"Bud Freeman?" Arlene sounded incredulous now. "My cousin Clarice's husband?"

I nodded, and she turned away from me without another word and walked off at a good clip, heading out the front doors and across the quad.

I boosted myself off the wall and came after her. She wasn't running, exactly, but it was close. I trotted to keep up, relentless. With the whole green lawn of the quad in front of us, where could she go?

"Hold up, Arlene. I just need to ask you a couple of questions and then I swear I won't bother you anymore."

Then she did start running, actually running away from me, like I was some sort of vampirous animal that had crawled out from under her bed to make a God's honest try for a daytime chew on her vitals. I broke into a lope, too, raising my voice.

"I called your cousin Clarice, but she wasn't home and I ended up talking to Bud. He told me you talked to Jim Beverly, the night Jim wrecked his Jeep."

Arlene stopped so fast that I barreled into her. His name had retained its magical effect on her. It was like she'd been hypnotized at a party once, and now the words *Jim Beverly* made her body jerk and panic. We stood facing each other, exactly eye to eye. She was breathing hard, as if we'd run a marathon together instead of dog-trotting halfway across a quad.

"I didn't talk to him," Arlene said, but she came down hard on the word *talk*, and I stepped in a little closer, pressing my advantage.

"But you saw him?" I asked. I grabbed her arm, trying to make her look at me. "Where was he? What was he doing?"

She pulled away so hard, I almost overbalanced. "I don't know," she said. "There's nothing I can tell you about this."

Then I did make her meet my eyes. I willed it fierce, and I thought his name like a talisman, thought it so hard that it was like she heard it and her mouth trembled and her unwilling eyes met mine. When I had her, I said, "I don't believe you. I know you saw him."

She wet her lips with her tongue, as if she was about to speak.

Her gaze darted away and then back to me, away and then back. She made a throat-clearing noise, and then all at once she wheeled and bounded away again, tearing her arm out of my grasp. She went so quick that she ran right out of her shoes. She left them lying in the grass by a stand of four oak trees, and then she dropped her briefcase, too, like she was shedding.

I watched with my mouth hanging open as Arlene Fleet bounced and grabbed a low branch. She went shimmying up one of the trees, barefoot monkey style.

"Arlene?" I called. "What are you doing?"

She didn't answer, picking her way from branch to branch, climbing so high that if she lost her balance and fell, her bones would snap and crackle against the earth like kiddie breakfast cereal.

"Arlene, this is ridiculous," I yelled up at her. "Get down here."

A crowd of students was gathering, smelling drama, but Arlene ignored us all. She crammed her tiny butt into a fork, sitting way up in the tree as stoic as Tiger Lily, her long dark hair blowing back from her face as she pointed her nose into the wind and stared out across campus.

I hollered, "You can't stay up there in that tree forever. You have to come and talk to me." No response. I cast about wildly for an idea, and my gaze landed on her loafers. "If you don't get down here, I am going to take your shoes!"

One of the kids who was watching gave me a poisonous look and said, "You are not taking her shoes." The kid snatched up the loafers before I could, and then her friend grabbed Arlene's briefcase for good measure. They marched indignantly to the side with their prizes, standing over them like a pair of pimply avenging angels.

Arlene stayed where she was, as still and absent as a catatonic. She had somehow made the world go away and me with it.

"Oh, that's so fucking Zen, Arlene," I hollered. "You get your ass down here and you tell me where he is!"

Behind me, I heard one girl say to another in wise tones, "Oh! Boyfriend trouble."

The other said, "Are they twins? Was he screwing twins?"

I wheeled around and snapped at them, "I don't look like her." I almost screamed it, really.

The two girls exchanged a nervous glance, then they turned away and started walking. The first one said to her friend, "Jeez, what did he *do* to them?"

"He didn't do a single fucking thing to me," I yelled after them. They sped up, the first one peeking back over her shoulder at me with wide eyes. I realized that if someone asked her to find the crazy lady in this picture, she'd have to flip a coin to choose between me and Arlene Fleet.

They were out of range, but I said it anyway. "He didn't do a single thing to her, either."

Even as I said it, I found that I did not believe it.

I turned back and stared up at Arlene on her perch. I'd thought to ambush her at work and threaten to make a crazy scene, but she'd out-crazy-scened me. Her reaction to his very name was immediate, and the only word for it was terrified. She knew about Jim Beverly all right, more than I did.

Something had happened between Jim and Arlene, and now his very name put Arlene three baby steps from prancing naked off a building singing the "Gloria." Only now, with her body trembling up in the treetops and her mind gone to a happy place, with me baying up at her like a foaming mad hound dog, was it occurring to me that those two things had to be related.

"What *did* he do to you?" I asked, too quiet for Arlene to hear me, even if she had chosen that moment to come back inside her body. All at once, I felt so light-headed that I had to put out a hand and steady myself on the oak's broad trunk. I'd puked up everything I'd eaten in the last two days. I was exhausted, too. I hadn't gotten much sleep last night. This close to finals, the school's library was open twenty-four hours. I'd camped out there, sharing a crackly vinyl sofa with a blond girl who was trying to absorb her engineering text by pillowing her head upon its cover.

I pushed off the tree and started walking, leaving Arlene Fleet to sit up there until the Second Coming if she wanted. I could stay in Chicago and pop out at her from under bushes and out of dark alleys, but she wasn't going to tell me where Jim was or what ugly thing had happened between them.

I left the campus, retracing my path down the same indifferent Chicago streets I'd walked yesterday. Then it had felt as free as swimming naked. Now, being so unknown and unmoored was frightening enough to put me close to tears. These were not my streets. The only person I knew in this city was building herself a marriage much like mine, and she hated me.

Whatever Jim had done to her, it was very, very bad. I knew he was capable of very, very badness. He was capable of anything. There had been something in Jim that had spoken to me, monster to monster. The reverent way he'd touched my bruised belly. The calico cat with her head on backwards. I'd only seen glimpses, had guesses, but it was real and there, or else I would not have come to Chicago to retrieve him. I'd been looking for a weapon, and I'd thought of guns first and then Jim Beverly. That should have told me something.

My body was too achy with tired to keep on walking. I crossed the street and caught a bus that was heading east, back toward Arlene's crappy neighborhood. I sat up front, in the handicapped seats that faced sideways, resting my face against the cool silver pole.

Jim had always been so sweet with me. But I'd known then and I knew now that I'd been held separate from the darker pieces of his life. Hell, I'd been held separate from most of his life. On Friday nights, after the football game, we'd go off alone. The "Hot Donuts Now" sign would be flashing at the Krispy Kreme. I'd have coffee and a doughnut, and he'd have coffee and six doughnuts, just the two of us. His hair would still be damp from the showers, and I'd put one hand on his neck and run it up and down the back of his head. The velveteen and springy wheatgrass feel of his buzz cut was a pleasure.

No other football boys would be there. None of their steady girls came, ever. It was a rathole in Fruiton's small and seedy downtown, with bright blue-green Formica counters and pumpkin-colored vinyl on all the stools and booths. It looked like a demented and slightly color-blind Auburn fan had been cut loose in there to decorate. Our fellow customers were bums, drifters from the Greyhound station, and Fruiton High's small population of stoner kids. The stoners liked to stare through the huge plateglass window behind the counter, watching the big doughnut machine crank out the good stuff. We sat, a closed unit of two, and watched them watching. We were the only two sober kids in the building, on the block, maybe in the whole damn town. Everyone we knew was grunt pumping cheap beer over at Missy Carver's house.

Friday night, off-season, meant Jim's parents would be sitting across from each other at the brand spankin' new Olive Garden, silently eating chicken Parm with endless breadsticks. I remember one Friday when we sat at that counter for over an hour, waiting his parents out. At nine, we drove by Jim's house to check for his dad's car. His folks were still gone, and that meant they'd decided to catch the second show at the movies. The caffeine, the sugar, they had been warm-ups. The house was ours for the next ninety minutes, and we went inside to get our real fix.

"Date night for the grown folk," I said to Jim, pulling off my hand-me-down dress and dropping it to the floor. I'd worn someone's pretty lace cami instead of a bra. It had a stain on the back, but Jim was focused on my front. "After dinner, I bet your dad says, 'Hey, Laura, you want to see a movie? Or go home and do it?'"

"Shut up," Jim said, laughing, reaching for me, sweet like always.

I imitated his mom's prim, high voice. "Movie, please! I like to gander at that Clint Eastwood for a couple hours, before."

"This is so not the time to talk like my mom," Jim said, hands on my cami. "Don't you ever pick the movie, Rose-Pop."

He pushed the cami up and stepped in closer, fingers moving

careful and reverent down the chain of boot-print bruises that ran from my rib cage to my hip and down my thigh. The darkened flesh felt hot to him, he'd told me once, like it had fever. I pretended he was rubbing them away, but I knew better. He liked it.

We were seniors. That was the year sex changed for me. It stopped being something I did for him because I loved him, loved the kissing parts and closeness and the smell of him. Something opened up for me that year, my body finally catching up to my choices, coming to understand all the things he was learning to do to me on his squeaky brown bunk bed, top and bottom. He knew exactly how to touch me, how to move between my legs to please me, but always, always, his lips and fingers came back to haunt the spots where I was blackened and punctured and ruined.

He never hurt me himself. In fact, he'd once gotten in a fistfight with my daddy on the lawn, telling him to keep his hands off me. I needed sweetness, and Jim gave me that. The other thing I needed, I got plenty of at home. I took hard roundhouse rights on the sly from Daddy, separate from Jim. What had Jim Beverly been getting on the sly?

He'd gotten it from Arlene Fleet. And Dawna Sutton, too, I realized. On the phone she'd said she hoped Jim was burning deep, deep, deep in deepest hell, an extreme consequence for a three-date relationship in high school, unless something truly ugly had happened between them.

I dug around in my bag for my notepad and a pen. I started writing Arlene a letter. I tried to remember everything I'd said to her, to keep it in character. It was part apology, but mostly, its purpose was to let her know I could find out what I needed elsewhere. I assured her I would not be troubling her again, because I owed her that much. I folded it up and wrote her name on the outside of it. I would leave it on her door, and then I would be out of time, in more ways than one.

I hadn't let Mrs. Fancy take me to her church's shelter. I couldn't.

Ro Grandee was harder to peel off myself than leprosy. I knew if I got scared and cold and lonely enough, Ro would bring me back to Thom. I'd wanted to remove that option, remove Thom from the earth. In the hospital, then at home ruining my ex-wardrobe, even yesterday as I puked my way across the country, I'd been so careful not to think of how things would be after, when Thom was gone and I was left alone with Jim.

I hadn't wanted to think of it, because I knew already. It would be the same thing. Before I got rid of my last bad man, I was making damn sure I had another man just like him already lined up. Jim was every boy who had ever belonged to me, from my daddy on down, and I hadn't understood what that meant until Arlene Fleet had scrambled up a tree and made me understand: Thom was suicide, and Jim was Thom in a different body. A permanent end to Thom did not end my need for him.

I took inventory. I was almost out of money. I didn't know this city, and I didn't have a single friend here. The most valuable objects in my purse were a fake ID, a can of pepper spray, and a plane ticket back to Amarillo. If I was running, the start line could not be Chicago.

I had too much I couldn't leave in Amarillo. My dog. My Pawpy's gun. Rose Mae Lolley's ID and bank card, which would let me clean out our checking account. But at four this afternoon, my shift at Grand Guns started, and if I wasn't there, some over-helpful Grandee or another would alert my husband that his Ro had gone AWOL.

After I left the note for Arlene, I went back to the airport, and I caught my flight home.

What the hell else could I do?

CHAPTER

❦

11

I WAS FIFTEEN MINUTES LATE, but I made my shift at Grand Guns. Two sales guys, Derek and James, were holding down the fort.

Derek said, "There's the princess now," when I came in, and looked meaningfully at the clock. Derek was kind of an asshole.

The Grandees' main store had tables of accessories and sales items in the center, but most of the serious inventory was locked inside cases that ran all the way around the three back walls. The rifles were on vertical display in glass-front cabinets. In front of them, glass-top display tables holding the pistols were connected in a U-shape. There was an aisle running all the way around between the rifles and the pistols where the sales guys worked. On the right side, near the doorway to Joe Grandee's office and the storage area, there was a table for the register. It had a butcher-block top instead of glass, and James was sitting behind it on what was usually my stool, minding the till. He didn't give me any crap, though, just did a drawer check and signed out to go work the floor.

I slid into my place and tried to look like I was working, but my gaze kept stealing to the phone. Any moment, Thom would call to check up on me. I'd practiced lines in my head on the flight home. I wanted to sound bored and a little lonely for him, completely regular. After my shift, I could swing by the bank and clean out our money, then I was smoke. I'd have a twenty-hour lead time before Thom's flight landed tomorrow.

An hour later, I still hadn't heard from him, and that wasn't right. He knew my schedule. Another half hour passed, and I was considering calling his hotel when I heard the door that led from the alley behind the store into the storage area crash open. Joe Grandee called, "Grab that other box." Then I heard the unmistakable sound of Thom's voice calling back, "I got it."

The air left my lungs in a *whoosh*, and I couldn't get more in. They weren't supposed to be back until tomorrow. I took three desperate panting breaths and tried to make my spine unstiffen. Thom came out of the door that led to the offices. I felt him behind me, felt the push his big body gave the air. He came up right behind me and said, "Hey, baby."

I turned on the stool toward him, trying to look pleased and surprised, but as soon as I saw him, my face froze. Thom was different. I could see it in every line of his tall body. I could smell it on him. I gave him a smile close to one of Ro's, and he curved his lips up at me, but his eyes stayed dry and flat as matte wall paint.

"I thought you were coming back tomorrow," I said. He didn't make a move toward me, didn't touch me or lean in to kiss me, and that was wrong, too.

"I couldn't wait to see you," he said, but he didn't sound eager. He was in the doorway behind the low glass-top display cases, nothing between us but three feet of cool air, quickly growing cooler. I got up off the stool and went to him and lifted my face. He leaned down and put a kiss on my mouth. His lips were hard and tasted foreign, not like Thom, as if he'd been eating tamarind and cumin on the sly. As I turned to go back to my stool, he gave my ass a slap, hard enough to sting.

"There's my girl," he said.

Joe appeared in the doorway behind Thom and said, "Help me get this crap out of the truck."

Thom nodded once. He was rubbing at his lips with the hand that had slapped my ass, as if he was balming them up with what that had felt like. He turned and went into the back room.

"Help me" in Joe Grandee language apparently meant, *You go get the crap out of the truck while I throw my jumbo-manly key ring in the drawer by the register, grazing your wife's titty in passing, and then plop down on my stool.*

"Go give Thom a hand unloading," Joe called to the two salesmen. "Ro and I got things under control out here."

James and Derek went on in the back, and Joe and I sat on our stools, his by the door, mine behind the register.

"What are y'all doing back?" I asked, trying to look anything but panicked.

"Hell if I know," Joe said. "Thom worked the show like a whirly-dervish all morning. Then he said he was done and flying home. I could come or not." Joe was different, too. Not to such an extreme, but something had changed. I'd long wished he would keep his greasy eyeballs off my ass, but now his gaze kept drifting to my belly. He made significant eyebrows at my abdomen and added, "Why don't you tell me why we came back early?"

"I don't know," I said.

He waggled his eyebrows at my belly again and said, "I figured we came home to get us some good news?"

"That's nice. What happened?" I said.

That surprised him enough to make him drag his gaze up off my body to my face. I was surprised they knew the route. "Thom said on the way to Houston *you'd* have some good news to tell me, once we were home."

He shifted his eyes right back to my stomach, a gloaty smile spreading across his face, and all at once I remembered puking on the way to the airport. I'd implied to Thom I might be pregnant, to get him on the plane.

"I do not have good news to tell you," I said, and I bit down hard on the last word.

Thom ducked his head in through the doorway and said, "Where do you want that box of brochures? In the files?" He looked only at his father, not even glancing my way, and I felt it again, this overwhelming sense of other coming off him.

"Nah, set 'em by my desk," Joe said. "Your wife here says she doesn't have any news to share."

Thom's flat gaze finally shifted to me again, and I felt a chill run up my spine at the ice in it. "I'm sure she will soon," he said. "All the way home on the plane, when you were saying I was so quiet? I was wondering to myself what the baby might look like."

"He'll have the Grandee nose," Joe said. "Both of Larry's do."

"Maybe not," Thom said, with too much meaning behind it, right to me. He went back into the offices.

Joe was showing me all his teeth.

"I'm not pregnant," I snapped.

"But Thom said—"

"I was wrong, Joe. Now can we drop it, please?"

There was silence between us for maybe thirty seconds, and then Joe said, "I think you should go to a lady parts doc, Ro. Make sure all your bits work."

I spun sideways on the stool to face him. "Good Lord! We only just started trying." I was angry that I felt I owed him even that much of an excuse. "Keep your mind out of my pants, please, Joe." I wanted to say more, but something was off with Thom, way off, and I couldn't afford to get into it with his daddy right now.

"You think it's Thom, huh?" Joe waved one hand around at all the weapons lining the walls and cackled. "That'd be rich. A Grandee man shooting blanks!"

"I'm not at all worried about Thom," I said in the coldest voice that I could muster. Inside, I was so worried about Thom, I felt like my spine was shivering itself into bits.

"Me neither," Joe said agreeably. "You're the one that worries me. Your family was Catholic, after all. You should go see a doc."

I felt my eyes going narrow, drawn into the conversation in

spite of myself. "I don't think a gynecologist can cure Catholicism," I said. "I don't even think that's something you can see with a speculum."

Joe grinned, genial and intrusive. "A Catholic only child? That says to me your mama had something bunged up in her works. You could, too."

I stood up, furious, just as Thom stepped back into the room, right between us, and a good thing, too. He glanced from his daddy, sitting splay-legged and relaxed on his stool, to me standing with my shoulders braced and my hands curling up into fists.

"What did I miss?" he asked.

I said, "Your daddy is a little too interested in the state of my Catholic vagina." I was breathing hard, eyes on Joe.

"Oh?" Thom said, the single syllable tolling low, like a warning bell. His wrongness, the not-Thom-ness of him, froze me in place and killed my temper with his daddy. Thom said to his dad, "Pop, you want to go take a look, see if we put things where you want 'em?" and that didn't sound like my Thom either.

Joe looked back and forth between us, puzzled, as if he sensed it, too. Finally he nodded and said to Thom, "Come on, then, I'll show you how I want to shift things around."

"Derek and James can help," Thom said. "I need a minute. I've yet to say a proper hello to my wife."

Joe pushed his lips into a down pout, but he went. Thom didn't come toward me, though. He leaned in the doorway and crossed one foot over the other. "So. What *has* your Catholic vagina been up to while I was gone, Ro?" The words were right. It was a Thom-style line, and it should have made me grin, but the tone was all wrong.

I stared at him, wary. "Just hanging out in my underpants, like always."

"Is our home phone fixed?" he asked, and with such purpose behind the question that I felt myself go very, very still inside.

"The guy is coming tomorrow morning," I said.

"Mmm-hmm. Here's a funny thing, Ro. I already know what's wrong with it."

"You do?" I said. I swallowed, way too loud. I was suddenly pleased to have Joe and two sales guys in the store. I did not want to be alone with whoever the hell this was.

He nodded. "I was worried about you, sugar. Alone in the night with no working telephone. I called Larry from Houston and had him go by the house, check on things. He said the phone line had been cut. Deliberate. Now, who would do that."

It didn't tilt up at the end like a question, but I answered it like one anyhow. My voice came out high and breathless. "Kids, maybe? Teenagers?"

"I don't think so," Thom said.

My fingers moved up to press my forehead, and I don't think I'd ever hated Larry Grandee more than I did at this moment. That chinless bastard must have been delighted to check up on his brother's wife.

"Larry said you weren't home," Thom went on.

"Oh," I said, faint. "I had some errands."

"Yeah," Thom said. "So I had him go back again, late."

"Oh," I said again. I couldn't look away.

"You never came home last night, Ro."

Who is he?

I felt my face flush, deep and hot, obvious, a confession. He was still and so controlled, but any second I felt that he could calmly put his clenched hand through my face, all the way into my brain. His eyes had never been so cold on me before, or so at peace.

This wasn't temper. This was a fundamental shift. He believed I'd stepped out. He'd added up my strangeness over the last ten days, my new wayward bedroom tactics, my overnight absence, and drawn an inevitable conclusion. He would end the game for good now, no winners.

Ro Grandee's husband had been peeled away, and I was seeing the thing that lived underneath. I stood in the middle of Grand

Guns eye to eye with the hanged man, and his face was smooth and rested. A muscle jumped in his cheek, twice, and the rest of his face stayed as still as a corpse's. I could see my own death reflected there.

"I think you should drive me home now," he said. "This is something we should talk about alone. You and me."

"I have another two hours on my shift, baby," I said. I let my body shift into Ro's good-girl posture. No danger in being her now. Looking at him, I knew that there was no Thom left for Ro to go back to.

The new Thom had one thing in common with my husband: He did not know who he was looking at. He had sensed a difference in the hospital and while I looked for Jim, but he'd never understood his Ro was gone. It was the only advantage I had, and I smiled Ro's guileless smile at him, because I was damn well keeping it.

"James and Derek can handle it," Thom said.

"I better wait until Janine gets here. I was a couple minutes late and Derek was already being a dick about it." I could not get in the car and leave with him. If I went off with this man alone, it was the last thing I would ever do.

He shrugged, but his expression did not change. He didn't even have one to change. He was blank and still with cold, black purpose. "Derek will get over it. Get your purse." He stepped forward and closed one hand around my wrist like a manacle.

"Thom!" Joe called from the back. I jumped, but Thom stayed still.

Thom didn't answer. We looked at each other. He was thinking snake and bird, but it was snake and snake, and I was not done yet.

"You better see what your daddy wants," I said. "Sugar."

Joe appeared in the doorway. "Thom, boy, get your ass back here. I can't find that Mauser."

Slowly Thom's neck turned, his focus leaving me. Joe's influence held, even with this creature.

He said to his father, "Okay. I'll find it, but then I think I'm going to grab Ro and cut out early. I'm tired and I want to take my best girl out to dinner."

"Sure." Joe shrugged. "It's been slow, Derek said."

Thom looked at me, his lips curving into a smile. This was chess, and he'd just hemmed my king. His goal was to get me off alone, and I couldn't let that happen. I couldn't win in a straight-up fight. He was so much bigger. A gun could level the playing field, and guns were all around me, but Thom was as good with one as I was, maybe better. Him or me. If he took me off alone in the car, armed or not, it would be me.

"That sounds great," I said, working Ro's best perky. "We should go to Rollo's and have crab legs." They were Joe's favorite. "You want to come eat with us, Joe?"

Joe paused, tempted, but the ploy failed. "Too much to do. Plus you kids need to get working on that other project we've been discussing." He waggled his eyebrows at my belly in that same too interested, pervy way. "Come on, Thom."

"Just a sec," Thom said to his daddy. I smiled, trying to look sweet and clueless, but Thom had been hunting with his daddy since he was six. He lifted his head and breathed in a huff of air, smelling fear. If he walked out of this room now, he suspected I'd run like a deer. He was dead damn right.

"Give me your keys," Thom said to me. "I'll grab my bags out of the truck and move 'em to your car after I find this gun." Check.

"Sure, baby," I said, no hesitation. I dug my keys out of my purse and handed them over. That threw him off balance. He wasn't expecting me to give up my escape route. I smiled as I handed them over, Ro's smile, pleased to be getting off work early and taken out for seafood.

His hand closed around my keys. He hesitated, not sure what he was missing.

"Thom," Joe said, impatient.

"All right, then," Thom said. He turned away.

Ro's expression dropped off my face and shattered on the floor.

This was my one advantage: I knew what I was dealing with, and he did not. I was Rose Mae fucking Lolley, and I wouldn't go trotting off like a lambkin to my death.

He was barely out of sight before I was moving, grabbing Joe Grandee's jumbo-manly key ring out of the drawer by the register. The Buick had been Charlotte's before it was mine, so of course Joe still had a key. He had a key to our goddamn house, too. For once the fact that Joe's big sniffer was jammed hard into every crack of my life was working for me. I fisted my hand hard around the keys to keep them from jingling and ran, light and soundless, toward the front door.

I pushed it open and the bell chimed.

"Welcome to Grand Guns!" I cried out, loud and cheery to the empty store. "What can I help you find today?"

I slipped out the door and crossed the parking lot at a sprint, trying to find the Buick key on the overloaded ring as I fled. I barreled into the side of the car. My hands were so sweaty, shaking, I could hardly get the key in the lock.

I fumbled and twisted and got the car door open. I jumped in and started the engine. I risked a glance at the store. The front door was still closed. I threw the car into drive and floored it.

As I turned out of the parking lot, I saw Thom come out. He moved slow and deliberate, staring after me, implacable. He knew I had no place to go. I took the first turn I came to to get away from his gaze. Then I drove for home as fast as I dared.

I wasn't sure how big my lead would be. I had Joe's truck key on the ring, and that would buy me time. Joe would hold him back some, asking petulant questions about why his wife had taken off like a gazelle with his key ring. James lived close and usually didn't drive to work, and Derek was an asshole. If Thom couldn't borrow one of their cars, he'd have to wait for Larry to come get him or for Charlotte to bring Joe's spare keys over.

I drove like the very devil back to our house. It would cut my lead to stop at home, but I didn't have a choice. Gretel was there, and the first thing he would do would be to snap her neck for the crime of being something I loved.

The weather had been fine, so I'd left her in the backyard with triple rations by her doghouse for the thirty hours I'd been in Chicago. That made it go faster. I left the Buick running on the curb with the door open and ran across the yard to the back gate. I called her and she came slow-trotting over, wagging, pleased to see me. When she reached the fence, she stopped, puzzled, sensing my agitation.

I flung open the gate.

"Take a walk? Take a walk?" I said, trying to sound cheery. I failed, and her eyebrows stayed worried, but the words were familiar. She came through the gate and stood panting up at me as I peeled the Buick key off Joe's ring and dropped the rest of them onto the lawn.

I didn't dare take time to pack. I didn't even go inside my mint green house. Instead I ran fast to Mrs. Fancy's, Gretel trotting close on my heels, and pounded on her door. No answer.

She was not home, and Thom had my keys, including the one that unlocked her front door. I paced the porch, twice. I should leave. Who knew when she'd come back? I couldn't afford to wait. I started down the stairs, then paused. Gretel whined, nervous.

"Let's take a ride? Take a ride? Let's go!" I said. Gretel knew these words, too. She turned and ran to the Buick and hopped into the open door, taking up her rightful spot on the passenger seat.

Meanwhile, I peeled a paving stone out of Mrs. Fancy's front flower bed and toted it back to the porch. I lifted it, shoulder high, and smashed it through the narrow window by her front door. It shattered the glass and fell through, landing on the square of parquet flooring with a clap. I saw a yellow streak as Phil ran to hide. I reached through the hole and unlocked the door.

It cost me two precious minutes to run to the guest room closet and snatch Pawpy's gun and my real wallet out of the shoebox, but I felt better once I had the gun. I grabbed my mother's library book, too.

Mrs. Fancy had a place for Gretel at her son's, she'd said. She knew a shelter that could hide me. But I couldn't wait for her, and anyway, everything in me said it was too damn close. There was no place in this city, in this state, where Thom Grandee couldn't find me. He was coming toward me now. He'd keep coming. He always had, since the day I'd seen him through the window at Duff's Diner, walking jaunty and confident back to claim me. The only thing that had changed was his purpose.

I got in the car and started driving, away from my Crest-colored house and from all the roads Thom might be driving down if he was coming toward me from the gun store. Gretel whined, wanting me to open the passenger-side window, but my car was easy enough to spot without her big head hanging out, licking wind.

"Shush now, Gretel-fat," I said.

I drove as quickly as I dared for Highway 40. A red light paused me at the turn. Highway 40 stretched all the way across the country. If I turned west, it would take me to California, where my mother waited for her book.

At the airport, she had told me I was welcome. Ever since, I'd been flat haunted by images of Ivy Wheeler in a lemon grove, of living in a cool and hilly place. Ivy would be safe and new, just born, a creature with no husband and no history.

I found myself staring down the highway to the west. My mother had been offering me a place, but it was not a place she'd made for me. She'd saved money in her flowered shoe, planning all the while to leave me behind. She'd made plans that did not include me. She'd packed my regular brown bag lunch and sent me off to school with her regular quick kiss on my cheek. Then she'd left, and I'd come home to find the world had changed.

She'd remade herself, rebirthed herself as a gypsy, but she hadn't brought me with her and showed me how. Ivy Wheeler was only a haircut, some borrowed clothes, and a pair of steel-toed boots.

I faced west and said, "Fuck you," to my mother. "*You* aren't welcome."

The light went green and my hands were on the wheel, turning it. My foot jammed the gas pedal down. The car lurched forward with a screech, turning away from her, leaving two lines of burnt rubber, curving toward the east. I knew the South. I could go to ground there. Scared, yes. But too damn mad to lie down like Thom's good girl and die.

I ran home.

CHAPTER

12

I POINTED THE BUICK EAST, and I took all fifteen hours of driving straight up, neat, like a shot of Jack. The wind was behind me, and I felt it as wolf breath, hot and stinking of old meat, raising the hairs on the back of my neck.

I pulled off the highway only when my tugboat of a car needed another tank of gas. The Buick was a guzzler. I fueled up on these stops, too, on black gas station coffee as fumy and potent as the brew the car was drinking. I bought Gretel some kibble and got a jar of peanut butter and some crackers for myself, but I was scared too sick in the pit of me to eat much. I started off driving as fast as the Buick would let me, but I made myself drop to eight above the speed limit. I wasn't sure which ID to use if a cop stopped me; I didn't want to swap to Ivy so close to home, nor did I want a ticket in Rose Mae's name, pointing out my trail.

Gret sat up in the passenger seat beside me, snuffing my hair and jamming her wet nose against my ear, worried and vigilant and driving me bat crap. Once we got out of Texas, I opened the passenger-side window for her. She poked her face out through the narrow crack to huff the air of Arkansas, a mix of larch trees and armadillo poop that kept her attention all the way to Tennessee. There she finally calmed enough to sleep with her big head in my lap, making a drool splotch on my jeans.

By the time I hit the Alabama State line, I hadn't slept in close to thirty hours, and that had been some fitful dozing on a library sofa in Chicago. My joints were aching, and I had a dry, rattling cough that hurt all the old cracks in my ribs whenever it got away from me. All the caffeine I'd dumped into my empty stomach made me feel like my eyeballs were jittering in their sockets; the road looked like a drunken state worker had painted the yellow lines in slightly wavy. My peripheral vision was shrouded in fog.

In Arkansas, I'd decided that if I was running, Birmingham was my best bet. It was a big enough little city to get lost in. I could sell the traceable Grandee Buick for some cash as Rose, then leave the city as Ivy to sully my trail. I could go anywhere then, maybe down to the Florida Keys. I'd get a waitress job serving drinks made with key lime and coconut, invest in flip-flops and a red bikini. If I was running.

By the time I crossed into Alabama, I didn't think I was.

On our second date, I'd told Thom my father was dead. Daddy was so dead to me by then that it didn't even feel like a lie. Thom knew my mother had left me as a child, so Fruiton was the second or third place he would look for me. He'd certainly comb Amarillo first, and it was a good-odds bet that Kingsville, the town where we met, might pull his attention next.

Going to Fruiton gave me solid lead time and the home field advantage. It was my best shot if I was going to lay a trap instead of running.

The air grew warmer as I went east, and the Buick's AC was for shit. I drove into my old hometown with all four windows mostly down. Fruiton already smelled like a small-town Alabama summer: hot asphalt and secondhand fry grease, overlaid with deep green pine. Pollen hung in the breathless air, giving every outdoor surface a thin yellow glaze. When I'd lived here, Fruiton's singular air had been so familiar that it was invisible. I'd forgotten the feel of it dusting up my nose.

I pointed the car toward my old house, Gretel awake and back to sticking her boxy head out the window, her tongue collecting dust. My car hadn't had a working tape player in years, so I had the radio on a gospel station. In Fruiton, the only music choices were gospel or country music, or I could swap to AM talk and get a bellyful of angry men hollering about politics or Jesus or both.

I was so tired, I needed both hands on the wheel now just to keep the car going straight. My route took me right past the old Krispy Kreme that Jim and I had frequented. It was working hand in hand with the Church's Chicken next door to oil the air. Looking at it gave me déjà vu, which was stupid.

Of course I felt like I'd been here before. I had. A thousand times. But this was ten years later, and Bickel's Drugstore had turned into an Eckerd. The empty lot was now a Tom Thumb with three newfangled gas pumps. It was enough change to make me feel like I was being reminded of a place instead of actually being in the place.

The last time I'd been down this road, I'd been walking to the bus station. I'd worn someone else's shoes, like now, with a hand-me-down blouse and Levi's much like the ones I had on. I had probably been cleaner, though.

Another five minutes and I passed the entrance for Jim's old sub-division, Lavalet. It had seemed right fancy to me back then, with a pool and a clubhouse and the name spelled out in curly metal letters on a low brick wall beside the entry. I opted not to turn in, heading instead for my own old neighborhood. I had no desire to ring the doorbell and say to his mother, "So, Carol, you ever hear from your youngest again? . . . No? Not even at Christmas?"

I doubted they still lived there, anyway. No sane person would choose to stay in a house that reminded them every minute of someone who'd left and not ever once looked back. Normal people moved away from sorrow as soon as they could. Folks less whole, sanitywise, took my daddy's route. Daddy had raised me in the house my mother had abandoned, drinking until his vision blurred too much to focus on all the bare spaces where my mother wasn't standing. He drank so much, some days he had to furrow up his brow and squint to aim his fists proper at me.

There was a chance, small but real, that if he hadn't drunk himself to death, he would have stayed on in that house after I left, too. Now that I was heading toward him, I was surprised at how vague my visual memories of him were. It seemed the people that I remembered most clearly, every tick of expression and cadence of speech—Jim Beverly, my mother—were the ones who had left me.

My father was mostly a shape in my memory, short and broad with wide hands. I remembered his craggy Irish face and angry eyebrows from pictures, not from real life. The clearest things were the sour mash smell of him, the hard, fast feel of his fists, and his low and burring voice.

Still, Thom had no idea my daddy was alive, much less that he was meaner than a snake, tougher than boot leather, and better with a gun than any man I'd ever seen, Thom included. My daddy was as bad as Thom, and he owed me. And there was no danger I would stay on with him, the way I would with Jim Beverly. My nicer memories—shooting with him, piggyback rides, pushes on the tire swing—were buried under the ten years after my mother left us. He'd beaten any chance at auld lang syne right out of me. If he was still around, I was the bait, and he was nothing more to me than the steel jaws of a trap. Thom would surely look for Lolleys in the Fruiton phone book as a way to find me, but he would not expect to find his way to me blocked by a no-longer-dead daddy, much less my daddy's arsenal.

A mile past Lavalet, I crossed Bandeer Street and left the mall-and-Olive-Garden side of town. Fruiton had no railroad, but even so, this side of Bandeer was the wrong side of the tracks. I turned left at a run-down strip mall that still held a Salvation Army thrift store and a Dollar General. Another left put me onto my old street.

All the houses on Pine Abbey had been built in the sixties: low ceilings, one central bath, a harvest gold or avocado stove and fridge set in every galley kitchen. The houses squatted low, as if they thought they were down on Mobile Bay, in hurricane country. I went a mile down the road, to what in a nicer neighborhood would have been a cul-de-sac.

Not here. Pine Abbey simply ended, blunt as the eraser end of a pencil, with a dirt track cutting through the middle of the wild back lot. The track began just over the curb and disappeared into the woods. Daddy used to drive me down through on Saturday afternoons to do some shooting.

The branches would scrape the car's paint when we shoved our way down that track. It didn't matter. Daddy bought beater cars and applied duct tape, spit, and cussing till they ran for him. He would drive one until the engine fell out, then sell it for scrap and get another. The track ended in a sloping meadow. We would stand at the lowest point to shoot, setting up our targets so they had the hill behind them. We shot at two-liter soda bottles rifled from the trash of our Pepsi-drinking neighbors. We drank only Coke, and Daddy wouldn't shoot a Coke bottle. He said that for a southerner, blasting away at a Coke bottle was close to sacrilegious.

Daddy filled the bottles with water to weight them. Our bullets tore through them and then spent themselves safely in the dirt of the hill behind. We'd take turns shooting until they fell into plastic rags.

The first time he let me shoot a real gun, I was maybe five years old. It was a sunny afternoon, and the warm brown whiskey smell on his breath was light. His mood was good. He watched me taking careful aim with my pellet pistol, and he said, "Rosie-Red, I believe you're ready to try something a touch mightier."

He loaded a .22 for me and talked me through the kickback. He tucked in spongy orange earplugs for me, and I sighted on the Pepsi bottle. I squeezed steady, pressuring the trigger toward me until the gun bucked in my hands like a live thing. The shots rang louder when I could feel them. The .22 seemed powerful and sleek, yet it did what my hands said. I could feel the reverb of it in my whole body, and I squeezed again and again and again. I felt bullets moving out from the pit of me, down my arms, and then out the barrel. I held steady and shot till the gun was empty.

Daddy wove his way over to the Pepsi bottle and held it up. We watched water streaming out of several holes.

"Shit, baby. I think you nailed it. Three, maybe four times," he said, admiring. "If you wan't so pretty, I'd say it was a shame you wan't born a boy."

"Who would wanna be a boy," I said, and spit.

Daddy laughed and said, "Dead-Eye Dickless."

I laughed, too, though I didn't get the joke. I only got that this was a good, good day. My mother was at home, making us lasagna, and my daddy was pleased with me.

Here at the dead end of Pine Abbey, my red brick cube of an ex-house sat on the right, the last in the row. The house across the street was its mirror image, except the trim was cream instead of brown and they had an old VW Beetle rusting away in the carport.

The carport of my old house was empty. Maybe he'd wised up and left the haunted place where his two-person family had abandoned him one by one. Or maybe he really was dead.

Now that I was here, it seemed ridiculous to think that my actual father was sitting inside on the sofa. It was like expecting the copy of *Watership Down* I'd set on my bedside table a decade ago to still be there, facedown and splayed open to the chapter where the rabbits first meet Woundwart. But at the same time, I couldn't imagine him making a checklist and packing boxes and renting a U-Haul. If he was alive, this was the only place I could imagine him existing. The empty carport might only mean he was off working or between cars.

I wondered if he would recognize me, and I felt my ab muscles go tight on the strength of memory and instinct, as if prepping for his welcome-home blow. A blast of hot red temper came steaming up my throat from my belly. If he was here, he fucking owed me.

"Sit tight," I told Gretel. I turned off the car and rolled up all the windows to half-mast to keep her in but leave a cross-breeze going.

I got out of the car and marched across the patchy lawn, chin up, shoulders set. My eyes burned, full of sleep-sand and dry from staying open way too long. Even so, I walked tough, like a kid going to touch the front door of the neighborhood's spooky house on a dare. I jumped up onto the concrete slab that served as a porch, out of breath from just this short burst of angry movement. I had to breathe in short pants to keep from activating the dry cough that was waiting in the bottom of my lungs. I bypassed the door, going instead to kneel by the living room's open window. I put my face against the screen and cupped my hand around my eyes to block the sunlight, so I could see into the living room.

A little girl, maybe eight or nine, sat on the floor with her dark hair hanging in strings around her face. She felt my gaze and looked up, staring back at me with her big, glossy eyes. She didn't seem surprised to see me, or particularly scared. She put a finger up to her lips and said, "Shhh. Daddy's sleeping."

For one crazy second, I thought I must be looking back into the past, seeing my young self, warning grown-up me away. I knew from science-fiction movies that if I touched her, we'd both melt or burn up or explode the world.

I blinked hard, twice, and put one hand up to my aching forehead. Looking around, I realized that the room was a right-now place, not something from my past. There was nothing in it that I recognized. A long, puffy green sofa sat against the wrong wall of the den. Ours had been brown with dark gold flowers, and it had been against the front wall, between the window I was looking through and an identical one farther down the porch. The coffee table was different, too, flanked by a vinyl wingback chair and a stack of cardboard moving boxes. There was a big TV in a hutch, showing a Bugs Bunny cartoon with the sound off. We'd had a smaller TV on a sanded plank table.

The little girl had a slew of Barbie outfits scattered across the floor. She was working a naked Barbie's long legs into a spangled tube dress.

"Hello," I said, quiet through the screen.

The girl's hands were still working to clothe her doll, but the dress stuck at Barbie's flared hips. She said, "I'm not s'posed to talk to people I don't know."

"I'm not a stranger," I said. "I used to live here when I was your age. This is the house where I grew up."

She got curious then, tilting her head sideways. She set Barbie down topless and stood up and came over to peer at me through the screen. "Then what's your name?"

"Rose," I said. "Rose Mae."

She nodded like I'd passed some test and said, "You made the marks."

"Marks?" I repeated.

"On the wall," she said. "Daddy's mad about it. I know you made them because it says your name."

"You have marks on your wall that say my name?" I asked, and when she nodded I said, "Can I see them?"

She tilted her head the other way, considering. "You'd have to come in."

"Yes," I said. "Can I come in and see them?"

After a thinking pause, she shrugged and said, "I don't mind it. It's got your name, anyways."

I stood up and met her at the front door. She swung it open for me, and there was a squeak of hinges at the end that was so familiar, it made my teeth ache.

I stepped inside. The carpet had been changed. When I was growing up, it was a dark gold, so thin in places that I could see the woven plastic matting glued to the floor. Now they had a mottled khaki Berber. The little girl pointed at the front wall, where our sofa once sat. A crudely wrought chest stacked with three more moving boxes filled the space.

"Daddy painted when we first moved in, but they're all floating back up through," she said, pointing at two words and a host of dark marks on the wall. "Like ghosts, Daddy said."

The writing was all contained in an invisible square, exactly under the place where my mother's big framed print of ships in a harbor had once hung. The lines were thick, drawn on with a laundry marker. If the print had still been hanging, all the writing would have been hidden perfectly behind it.

At the top, someone had written my name, "ROSE MAE," in all caps. Underneath my name were long horizontal lines that ran from one edge of where the frame had been to the other. The higher horizontals were covered end to end in tick marks, thousands of them, all made of four vertical lines close together, then a diagonal slash drawn through to make five-packs.

Some were deep black, and some I could see only faintly as they worked their way up through the paint.

I said to the little girl, "This was done with a Sharpie, and that stuff will come up through paint every time. I've seen it come through wallpaper, even. Your daddy needs to prime the wall with this stuff you can get at Home Depot. It's called Killz."

"Killz," the little girl repeated. "I'll tell him."

I reached out one hand and set it flat on the cool wall, cautious, as if the marks had been scorched on and were still smoking. They were as mysterious and unreadable as flattened Braille. I slid my hand down, counting horizontal lines.

There were nineteen. The top line was about one-third covered in tick marks. I started counting across by fives, moving my hand over them.

The kid said, "It's a hundred and thirty-eight on that row. I counted before."

I kept going. She was right: 138. There were even more ticks on the lines under. They filled every line, until they stopped midway through the eighth line. The last ten lines had no ticks at all.

"I think my mother made these," I said.

The little girl said, "Mine works in a doctor's office," as if we were trading facts about mothers. "And she's in school to be a nurse."

"That's a neat job," I said absently.

My mother had kept my name and a strange count not five feet away from where my father's recliner once sat, angled toward the TV. The air was thickening around me, and it was harder and harder to breathe.

"I'm not going to be a nurse," the little girl said, confident. "I'm going into space."

"That's a neat job, too," I managed to say.

The little girl said, "My Skipper doll has on a nurse outfit. Want to see?"

"Sure," I said, but the pit of my stomach had gone sour. My eyes burned, and the vision in the corner of my eyes had grayed out farther. I was peering at the marks now through a tunnel of fog. The lines on the wall seemed to flicker, as if the lamp was putting out candlelight.

The girl trotted over and held up Skipper-as-nurse, too flat-chested to fill up Barbie's uniform.

"That's awesome," I said, already up and moving. "I have to go." It was true. I couldn't breathe the air inside this place for one more second.

"Bye," she said.

I hit the front door at a dead run, the squeaky hinge I remembered squealing at me like it was laughing. I bolted to the center of the small yard, dizzy again, gagging, but I had nothing in my belly to throw up. I coughed instead, hacking so hard that it bruised my throat. Gretel was standing in the passenger seat, her head thrust as far out the half-open window as it could go. She loosed a long, houndy noise, halfway between a bark and a howl, worried.

"Hush, Gret," I told her when I stopped coughing. I was still bent over, my hands on my knees. The grass was thin with spots of black Alabama dirt showing, just as I remembered. Leprosy lawn, my mother had called it. A decade had passed since my feet had walked off this browning patch of grass, yet it still hung on in the same state of wretched decay. The grass, at least, hadn't changed.

My stomach flopped inside me like an air-drowning trout. I hung my head down low to get in a good breath. The little girl might have come after me, but when I looked up, I saw her across-the-street neighbor had come outside. He'd already left his porch and was standing on his own tiny leprosy lawn, facing us.

He was a skinny old man with big, down-tilted eyeballs. His lower lids had sagged down so much that they'd bagged and gapped open. It seemed to me that if he bent down to get his paper, his eyes would roll right out of his head, dangling down on their stalks. He was bald on top, with strings of grayed-out hair in a straggled ring around his head.

He looked at me and his mouth dropped open.

"Holy shit!" he yelped.

I glanced behind me. No one. He pointed at me. His mouth stayed open. A thin string of drool came out of it, running down his chin and hanging free with a droplet of weighty water on the end. My stomach lurched again.

He came at me, moving across his lawn in a galumphing lope. He sped up as he came, arms spreading wide. His fingers splayed, and he staggered toward me like the mortal remains of some long-dead former love, reanimated. He hollered again, but his words were drowned out by Gretel's sudden chain of warning barks.

I was already dancing backwards, scrabbling in my purse, my fingers closing first around my lipstick, then my keys. He was still coming at me, drooling, a zombie crossing the asphalt to embrace me, maybe get a bite. Gretel was thrusting at the window, trying to shove her too-big shoulders through and get between him and me.

The man passed my car, coming onto the lawn in a herky bound, and at that moment, as if I knew desperation magic, my hand closed perfectly around the cool metal cylinder I'd been seeking. This time, I remembered to flick aside the safety with my thumb. Just before he touched me with those big, splayed hands, I lifted the pepper spray and blasted him right in the face.

I sidestepped and kept moving backwards, almost falling, avoiding blowback the way Thom had taught me when he gave me the spray. The neighbor stopped abruptly and blinked, and then he screamed. He screamed like a woman, high and shrill. He dropped as if all his bones had suddenly been teleported out of his body. His hands came up to scrub and scrub at his face. He flopped onto his back, and his heels drummed the lawn. Gretel barked and barked in a deep-chested flurry of angry sound.

I stood over him, no idea what to do next, as he screamed again and then again. I looked at the teeny can, impressed.

"Are you okay?" I asked him, loud, so he could hear me over my dog. The question seemed inadequate.

He ignored me, kicking his legs like a shot deer. His scream changed, going longer, until it was an endless keening. I took that for a no.

"Stay put," I told him, then put my hand on my pounding head. The guy was obviously not going to pop up and trot to Hardee's for a chicken sandwich. "I mean, hang on. I'll go on in your place and call for 911."

I went first to the car and put my hand on Gret's head to calm her. "I'm fine," I told her. "I'm fine." She panted and chuffed, staring at the man, her back fur standing straight up. I was pretty damn impressed. When Thom and I fought, she went under the bed till it was over, same as she did in thunderstorms, the coward. I'd never had occasion to see her react when I was threatened by a man outside her pack.

"What the fuck?" another man's voice said behind me. I looked over my shoulder and saw a bare-chested fellow in stripy pajama bottoms standing up on my old porch. Behind him, the little girl stood in the doorway. "What the fuck?" he repeated.

"Daddy said a Word," the little girl said to me, awed.

"He came at me," I said. Gretel was bristling at the new guy now, and I said, "Easy, girl," in the most soothing voice I could muster.

I looked down at the neighbor. He'd stopped kicking, and his keening had thinned to a whine. He was just about out of air. He took a long, choked inhale. He tried to sit up, peering at me through his fingers.

"Got-dammit, girl," he said.

I knew him then.

He took his hands down from his egglike eyes. The whites had gone hot pink, bright as Barbie's tube dress, and tears streamed out of the corners. His nose had two lines of clear snot running out of it, and his body was thin and frail, an old man's form. He didn't look much like his old self. But I knew him.

"Hi, Daddy," I said.

"I mean, got-damn," my father repeated. He put his palms against his eyes, pressing and snuffling. "I thought you was your mother. I thought you was Claire."

The guy in the pajama bottoms came down the step, barefoot, picking a careful path across the lawn.

"Mace or pepper spray?" he asked me, tilting his head toward the can.

"Pepper spray," I said. I looked at the can still clutched in my fingers as if I was surprised to find it there. I flicked the safety back on and dropped it into my purse.

"That's a mercy," the guy said, then added to my father, "You got any Maalox?"

"Naw, Bill, I don't," the skinny shadow of my daddy said, sitting flat on his butt in the grass. "I got Tums. You can go get you some if your got-dammed pizza lunch is bothering you while I sit here going blind."

Bill ignored that and said to me, "Help me get him up and to his house, will you?"

"I am not fucking touching him," I said, my tone very mild.

My daddy was a wreck. He'd gone and withered himself up, and the hands he used to claw at his face trembled and were thin and wasted. He was no match for Thom Grandee. Hell, at this point he'd been no match for me. I wanted to kick him for it while he was good and down. I said, "Why don't you go blind. We'll see how you like that," directly to him in that same mild tone. I was panting, and each breath felt like something sharp, poking me low in my lungs.

My father said, "That don't even make sense."

"Well, good, then," I said, and that didn't make sense, either.

"Okay!" Bill said, businesslike, and the little girl and my daddy and I all turned our faces toward him, as if he'd called everyone on the eternally dying lawn to order. He had a rounded chin and full cheeks that made him look younger than he probably was. He had good, broad shoulders and a sprinkle of dark hair on his chest. The beginnings of a beer belly lapped the top of his pajama bottoms. He walked past me and helped my father to his feet, calling to his daughter, "Hey, Bunny? Go get the Maalox out of the medicine cabinet, can you? Bring it across the street to Mr. Lolley's house?"

"Umkay," Bunny said, and disappeared from the doorway.

Bill drew one of the sticks that used to be my father's meaty arms over his shoulder and walked him back toward the other house.

"Don't you go nowhere," my daddy yelled at me as they walked away. His voice came out burbled and thick, as if more snot was filling up his throat, getting behind a host of other snots that were lining up to head on out his nostrils. Bill wrestled him across his lawn and onto the porch. As they went in the door, my father was still hollering over his shoulder, "Don't you disappear! Don't you go!"

I paused, shaky and panting, my hand on Gretel's head and my heart pounding away in my chest like it was trying to get out and follow him. I stood like tacky lawn art and the Alabama sun blazed down and it seemed to me like I was hotter than that sun. My eyes burned as if I'd pepper-sprayed myself. I pressed my hands to my forehead, and they felt like lovely blocks of ice.

Bunny trotted back out with an economy-size bottle of Maalox. I opened the car door for Gretel, who positioned herself at my ankle and walked in time with me like a sergeant, hackles at half-mast. The two of us followed Bunny across the street. The front door floated open, wavery, and my cheeks were so hot.

Gret and I stepped inside, and when I crossed the threshold I passed back in time, ten years or more. I got instant vertigo. I put one hand out to steady myself, and it landed on the key table beside my mother's old blue vase, still filled with her dusty, plastic tulips. I pulled my hand away like the table was made of human bones, gaping all around me. It wasn't our old house, but the floor plan here was the same, and my father had laid all our things out exactly as I remembered.

"Where are you?" my father bellowed from the kitchen. "Where'd you go?" He sounded desperate, almost plaintive.

I couldn't answer, goggling through fog at all the furniture and knickknacks of my childhood. Everything in the room was ten years older than the last time I had seen it, and looked it. The center of the brown and gold sofa sagged, as if it had been used for such an endless string of disreputable purposes that it had given up and bent beneath them.

"Bunny? Bring the Maalox to the kitchen," I heard Bill calling over my daddy's yowling. Bunny trotted obediently toward his voice.

My mother's ship print, so sun-faded that it looked like a photocopy of itself, was hanging in its designated space above the sofa. It had a ruined patch in the bottom corner. Daddy must have used the wrong kind of cleaner to take off my dog-shit good-bye note. Daddy's recliner was still angled toward the TV, looking as lumpy and ill used as the sofa. The plank table was there at the other end of the room, and on either side stood my mother's bookshelves. My father had made them for her back when they first got married, and she'd filled them top to bottom with her favorites. Less beloved books rotated in and out of a box in the coat closet. I turned, help-lessly drawn, and opened the closet. I smelled mothballs and old paper. Sure enough, there was the same wooden liquor store crate, old books stacked three deep under the hanging coats.

I walked across to the shelves, and the carpet felt like the floor of one of the ships in the picture, pitching and roiling under me. I grabbed the side of the shelf to stay upright. My mother had kept her books arranged by author, hardbacks and paperbacks jumbled in together. The top of each row humped up and down in uneven squares, like a row of poorly carved jack-o'-lantern teeth.

I trailed my hand along the fourth shelf down. Nine books in, my fingers came, as I knew they would, to Rudyard Kipling. I pulled out the book club edition of *Just So Stories* with the plain black cover I remembered, the title embossed in gold leaf on the front.

My father hollered from the kitchen. "Hello? . . . Hello? Don't you disappear!"

I put the book back and followed his howling call back to the kitchen, Gretel trotting close and anxious by my side.

Bill, still barefoot in his PJs, had my daddy bent over the sink. He was washing Daddy's eyes out with what looked like a thin gruel of Maalox and water. He nodded to me, calm and firm, holding my daddy's face down in the sink with one solid arm. Daddy was struggling a little, but he stilled when I came in.

"There you are," Daddy said. "Oh, there you are. Don't go away. I have a speech I want to say for you. I have it on a paper. I been waiting so long."

I ignored my father entirely and made my eyes click dryly in their sockets to look at Bill and only Bill. "How'd you know to do that? With the Maalox?"

"I was a med tech. Army," he said.

"Thank God you didn't leave," Daddy said to me, bent over, his blue T-shirt riding up his back. I could see two sharp knobs of spine in the space between his shirt and his jeans. He was so thin, his very skin looked worn down and sheer, like any minute the bones would press up through it. Thom could break him in one hand. He was useless. "I been waiting here to say my speech. Can you go get my paper? I wrote it all down in a paper in the drawer over yonder. The drawer in the phone desk." He aimed his words down into the sink, and his voice still sounded thick with snot. I could hardly make him out.

"I'm Bill Mantles. I'd introduce you to Mr. Lolley here, but I take it you two know each other?" Bill asked me, all ironical.

"We've met," I said.

"Can I pet your dog?" Bunny asked. She was at the other end of the galley kitchen, sitting in front of the built-in desk, in my mother's old chair. She'd turned the chair around to watch her dad, and she was swinging her feet back and forth. They were too short to reach the floor.

"She's a little het up," I said to her. "Give her a sec."

Bill kept rinsing, and my father kept talking into the sink, asking me to go get the paper out of the desk drawer so he could read me his speech. Even his voice had aged and gone thin, and his ropy-looking arms had deep blue veins bulging up all over them. He looked like a photocopy, too, as bleached out and ruined as the print of the ships hanging in the other room. I tried to let his voice run past me and go down the drain the same way the running water was going.

"The army gave you a class on pepper spray?" I said to Bill. I spoke loud enough to drown my daddy out.

Bill nodded. "I had chemical weapons training."

"My daddy was in Desert Storm," Bunny said, proud. The chair's ladder back blocked the drawer my father was asking me to open. Her feet swung back and forth, back and forth.

My father saw where I was looking and said, "Yes! That drawer! That drawer!"

I stayed put. Daddy could go to hell and read his speech to Satan. If I stayed here, Thom would come and give him the chance sooner than he might like. "You still work in the medical field?" I asked Bill, like I was making small talk at a church social, like I couldn't feel each heartbeat like a gunshot in my aching head.

Bill's cheeks flushed a faint pink, and he kept working on rinsing out my father's eyes, not looking at me. "I'm not working right now."

"Daddy's home with me," Bunny said, and the prideful tone had gone to defensive. *Little tiger*, I thought, staring at me from the chair with her eyes gone fierce. "He takes care of me."

"You're lucky. I wish I'd had that kind of daddy, growing up," I told her, and she looked away, mollified. "I wish I had one like that now." It came out heartfelt, the truest thing in the room.

Daddy said, "Rose Mae? Ain't you gonna get my speech?"

I didn't answer. Bill let go of the scruff of my father's neck, but Daddy stayed bent over the sink, dripping. Bill said, "Okay, Gene, take a swig of this Maalox. Rinse it around and then spit it out. Do that a couple times. You might want to swallow some, too. How do your eyes feel? Are they— Wait a sec. Your name is Rose Mae?"

I nodded. "Rose Mae Lolley."

Bill said, "From my wall?"

Daddy finally stood upright. He took the bottle and tilted it back, mercifully plugging up his word hole with it. He swished the Maalox around a couple times and spit it out, then said to me, "The bank called my loan on the house. Bill and them have had it, what, six months now, Bill? It was empty a long time. This place is a rental. I took it so I could watch out the wind-er for you and Claire."

I'd forgotten that, how he always said "wind-er" for window. It was strange because he said words like *meadow* and *follow* properly, but window had always ended in his mouth with an -er.

"Wait a minute," said Bill. "What?"

"Bill wants to know how your eyes feel," I said.

"Good," my daddy said. He turned to Bill. "Good." His nose was still running. Bill handed him a paper towel to wipe it, but his eyebrows had puzzled up and his brow had creased.

"You should thank Bill," I told Daddy.

"Thank you, Bill," Daddy said, obedient, then he turned back to me and added, "Look, Rose Mae, everything is the same."

"You used to own my house, is that what you meant?" Bill asked, putting it together.

Daddy was looking at me, though, speaking only to me. "I knew you'd come. I watch our old house alla time, when I'm home. I put the TV on for noise, and what I do is I watch for you and Claire right through that front wind-er."

"That's kinda creepy, Gene," Bill said. The kitchen seemed crowded now that Daddy was standing up. Too many hearts beating in the room, too much carbon dioxide. My vision was down to a pinhole now. My lungs rustled in my chest like dried-up leaves. I kept my eyes on Bill, and Daddy was a thin wraith in the fog beside him.

"I watch for you when I'm not working," Daddy said to me. "I have a good job now, Rose Mae. At the Home Depot."

"I hear they have good benefits," I said. Someone had told me that recently. I turned to the girl. "Your name's Bunny?"

She was still sitting in the chair, pulling my gaze with the tick-tock swing of her pendulum feet. She giggled like I was the silliest thing she'd ever seen.

"My name's Sharon."

I blinked, confused and swaying.

"Hand me my speech out that drawer, won't you, Sharon?" Daddy said, and then to me, "I'm not good at talking things, so I wrote it down exactly, what I need to say."

Someone said, "I do not want to fucking hear it," really loud, gunshot loud, in the quiet kitchen. The someone was me.

"I think we should head on home, Bunny," Bill said.

Sharon hopped out of the chair and threaded her way past Daddy, to her father.

"Nice to meet you," Bill was saying. "Sort of." He put one arm around Sharon and they went past me, out of the kitchen.

Now there was nothing in front of me to look at but my father. I said to him, "What do you mean, everything the same?"

"I'm in the program, Rose. I got my five-year pin in January, but I been stuck on step nine, waiting for you and Claire. Please won't you let me read it to you?"

"Every little thing? Exactly the same?" I said. The air was thin and hot in my dry lungs. I was panting louder than Gretel. I followed Bill and Sharon into the living room, listing hard starboard as if my feet were borrowed or brand new. My father came after me. My body felt as unwieldy as a bag of sand, but I went straight to the sofa and made my heavy body climb up onto the cushions. I grabbed my mother's faded ship print and jerked it off the nail. I slid it down behind the sofa, leaning it against the wall.

Bill and Sharon were at the front door. I heard Bill's sharp intake of breath, and then he said, "Holy crap. You did that to the wall? At my house, too?"

He meant my name and the black tick marks. My father had reproduced them here exactly, only fresher and darker. These had never been painted over.

I said, "My mother did the ones at your house."

At the same time, my father said, "Claire made them ones at your place."

"You ruined my damn wall," Bill said, more aggrieved than angry.

"It was Claire," my father said, and then added, surprised, to me, "You knew these were over there? You knew she wrote your name?"

I was trying to count the marks on the first line, to see if he got it right. There should be 138. But the lines kept waving and changing places with each other. I had to start over before I got to 50.

"You have flat ruined that wall," Bill said. "Bunny, we need to get out of here before Daddy loses his temper."

"Killz," the little girl said to him, seizing the moment to pass on my message about the paint primer.

Bill misunderstood her. "Not *that* mad, silly," he said.

I only got to 35 this time before the lines shifted sideways and tricked me and made me lose my place again. I started over, but now the lines were broadening in front of me, each black mark spreading into a puddle and blending into the next.

"Rose Mae," Daddy said, clambering up onto the sofa beside me, "you don't look so good. Bill, hold up."

The lines met, and the whole wall was black. A rich darkness, thick like velvet, spread and unfolded over everything around me. I fell down into all that darkness and was lost.

CHAPTER
13

I RAN ON A GREEN FIELD, and the sun was so hot that I felt flesh melting off of me like wax. Saint Sebastian ran beside me, bleeding from a hundred arrow holes, the shafts tearing his skin as he ran. "Faster, please," he said.

I looked over my shoulder. Thom was coming, bounding along at a quick and steady pace that ate up the ground I'd put between us. His face looked both cheerful and implacable, mouth smiling, but he had the eyes of a dead thing.

"Forget him," Sebastian said, the quills in his arm bobbing as he pointed behind Thom. "Run. We're going to win."

I looked back. Behind Thom, I saw my kindergarten class, chasing me in their field day T-shirts. My mother cheered me on from behind them. She looked young and fresh, cool as a cucumber, but I blazed so hot that steam came off my skin.

"Those are little girls," I said to Sebastian, angry he was worried about a field day race when Thom was coming. I ran on in a panicked scramble. Thom followed us, loping toward me on the balls of his toes, almost jaunty. He was the only thing cooler than my mother in the whole hellish landscape. He wasn't even winded, and his arms ended in axes.

I ran and ran, until I was so tired that my run was half stagger. Thom kept coming. He would always be coming.

"He's not after *you*," Sebastian said as we broke through the tape and won the race. Sebastian pulled me to the side. Thom ran right past. I looked down and saw my flat chest in a sweaty field day T-shirt. Thom did not know me. Then my mother was there, lifting me up, swinging me and whooping, and a rush of air was a cool balm on my blazing skin.

Sebastian put a kindly hand on my shoulder when she set me down. Now his arrows were more like quills, growing out of him. He looked like Mrs. Tiggywiggle from the book my mother read to me at night, only with a halo instead of a mobcap. This was how he'd looked in my head the first time my mother called him for me. I had forgotten.

We turned and walked together across my elementary school campus to the edge of the woods. Thom was there, behind a temporary classroom trailer. He stared down into a hole, oblivious to us. It was a pit trap, and when I looked down into it, I saw he'd caught me. Crouched in the bottom, Rose Mae Lolley reached up to draw a vertical slash in the dirt wall with one finger, marking time. Like any prisoner might.

"You understand?" Sebastian asked. I did.

The trap here was not for Thom. Fruiton was a trap for Rose. I had come here to trap her and leave her in it. I nodded, and Sebastian smiled kindly down at me. "Let's go find your mother. The sack races are starting."

"You aren't scary," I said to him. He'd changed after my mother left. That was when I began remembering Saint Sebastian as an open wound, grinning a bloody, broad grin and chasing me.

"What's that, Rosie?" Daddy asked me.

"He wasn't scary," I said, miffed at having to repeat myself when my throat was burned so dry.

"Her fever's broken," another man said. "We need to keep pushing fluids." I knew the voice. Bill. Bill Mantles from my old house across the street.

I cracked an eye, and I was in my childhood bed, lying on the saggy, sprung mattress, clammy with my sweat. Bill propped me up, half-sitting, and Daddy held a cup of tepid water to my mouth. I drank what I could, eyes closing. Bill's fingers poked a couple of pills into my mouth, dry and hard as perfect little pebbles, but Daddy flooded my mouth with more water and they went down.

"Sleep now," Bill said.

I tried to say I couldn't. Thom was coming. He was coming to kill Rose Mae Lolley. I had to get up and learn to kill her first. Saint Sebastian had showed me.

Bill pushed my shoulders, easing me back onto the mattress. I sank into it, and it parted under me like the waters of a river. The river swallowed me and pulled me under and moved me, past Thom, past Texas, all the way to lemon groves and cool air touched with brine. I slept, turning on my side to face the west. I heard my mother say, *You are welcome*, and I was.

When I woke up, the mellow sunlight coming in the window said late afternoon. Bill was gone, and Gretel was sprawled out against my side, snoring, all three of her paws twitching after dream rabbits. Daddy dozed in my old wicker chair. He had a piece of blue-lined notebook paper resting in his slack hand, crumpled up, with one corner ripped off. His feet rested on the edge of the bed. He was wearing grayed-out athletic socks with a big hole that showed me his heel, callused and cracked as rhino hide.

I was in my old room, exactly as I remembered it, with my white quilted blanket pulled over me. The closet door was open, and I saw the clothes I'd left behind still hanging in a neat row. A matted lion doll lay on the closet floor. Growlfy, his name was. My old green-glass water cup stood on the bedside table, an amber bottle of pills beside it.

Daddy's eyes opened as I propped myself up on my elbows.

"How long?" I asked.

"Couple days," he said, and I nodded.

"That's not so bad," I said.

"You was real sick." Daddy put his feet on the floor. I heard his old man's knees crackle as he bent them. I was wearing a faded pink nightgown with a bow at the top. My mother's. It had that musty, papery smell that gets into old cotton. I remembered her standing at the stove, making me eggs in this nightgown and her pretty housecoat. I sat all the way up and swung my legs out of bed. He said, "Girl child, are you crazy? Lie back down."

"I have to get up, Daddy. I don't have a lot of time." He rustled his piece of paper at me. Cleared his throat. "Not now," I said.

I stood up, and my legs were shaky and frail under me. I went down the hall toward the den, and Gretel got up and followed, tags jingling. I could hear Daddy coming behind her, an even sorrier dog, still toting his crumpled paper.

Daddy hadn't bothered to hang the ship picture back up. The ticks and lines stood out starkly against the white wall. I climbed up onto the sofa and stared at the marks, then up at my name. My father came up to the arm of the sofa, staring at me with his saggy, basset hound eyes, clutching his paper close.

"It's a calendar," I said.

I counted the ticks on the second line. There were 365. I'd known there would be before I started. Each line was a year. Each tick was a finished day.

My mother had been counting off the days literally behind my father's back. Marking time. Like any prisoner might. She hadn't begun at the start of their marriage, though. She'd begun at the start of me. The first line counted the days after my birth until the New Year. Then there were eighteen lines, each standing for a year she'd have to serve to get me to adulthood.

I remembered how she'd sometimes stand and face this wall, staring at the ships. As a child, I'd wondered why she didn't turn around and watch the TV on the opposite wall. Later, as a teenager, I remembered her ship staring as if it was clichéd foreshadowing, irritatingly symbolic. But now I wondered if she'd been looking at the print at all. Maybe she'd been staring through it, at all the days she'd marked off behind it, all the blank lines waiting to be filled.

She'd planned to stay another ten years, looked like, but she'd let herself out early. Time off for good behavior?

I didn't think so.

"What happened?" I said. "The day she left, Daddy, what did you do?"

He shook his head. "I came home and she was gone, same as you."

I wheeled on him, staring down at him from the extra height standing on the sofa gave me. "Bullshit."

"I swear, Rosie. I came home and you was sitting in the kitchen at the table waiting on your snack and had been for two hours, maybe more."

That was how I remembered it, too. Daddy had come home expecting to see my mother making dinner, same as always.

"She didn't plan to leave that day. Something happened." I was sure of it.

I turned around and climbed down off the sofa. Daddy still had his crumpled paper in his hand. His big droopy eyes were fixed on me, pitiful and pleady.

"I'm not listening to that speech, Daddy," I said in the kindest tone I'd used yet. "You want to say sorry? Say it by making me a sandwich. I'm starved."

"I got white bread and bologna," he said instantly, so eager that I felt a flash of something that was neither shame nor pity, but maybe kin to both. "I think there's a yellow cheese slice left."

"Whatever you have is fine," I said.

He turned to go to the kitchen. Gret and I went the other way, back to the master bedroom. There I found my mother's bedspread, covered in tea roses. It had a series of unfamiliar cigarette holes burned along the right side but was otherwise the same. Her garage sale lamp still sat on the bedside table. I bet if I opened the little drawer, I'd find her Day-Timer, circa 1977, cuddled up with a tube of ossified orange blossom lotion. The whole damn house was a shrine to the kind of family we had never been.

But here in this replica of a room, I found I could more easily remember the good days, too. Dove hunting in season with my daddy, watching him line up his shots, sharing out snack bags of Cheerios and raisins with his bird dog, Leroy. Sunday mass with my mother, who handed me the long wooden matches and let me light the votives when she prayed. Good moments, but we hadn't spent them as a family. I remembered me with Mother, me with him. I couldn't call up any happy memories of the three of us together.

At night, I'd lie in bed and their angry voices would come through the thin walls, followed by the thump and clatter of his hands meeting her body in hard ways. I'd hear an open-handed slap crack like a distant rifle shot, hear my mother's body banging into the walls. I'd roll out of bed and creep under it like Gretel in a thunderstorm, waiting it out.

Even so, they must have had some good times together, separate from me. After all, he'd kept the house the way she'd made it, as if still hoping any minute my mother would come strolling in and take off her flowered shoes and put them away in the closet. She'd fall down backwards on the bed with a tired sigh and say, "What a day. I'm glad to be home."

I opened her closet. On the top shelf, her shoes still stood in a row. Just the same, Daddy had said. When he'd lost the house he must have moved over here piece by piece, room by room, re-creating it exactly. There was only one gap in the line of seven pairs of shoes, a slot for the flowered canvas shoes where she'd kept her stash of money. Her running shoes were still there, as were her short black all-weather boots. It seemed odd that she'd left these sturdy, neutral things in favor of a thin-soled pair of multicolored Keds.

The day my mother left, she'd sent me off to school, and Daddy was working that week. She'd had all day alone in the house to choose what shoes to take, so why these? She'd probably put her stash in flowered Keds to begin with because she seldom wore them.

I'd been eight years old when she left. It hadn't occurred to me to inventory her closet. I flipped through her things now, and it seemed to me there wasn't much missing. Very few empty hangers were mixed in with the clothes.

I stared at that single gap in the row of shoes, as bothersome as a missing tooth. I reached up and began squeezing the toes of the other shoes, one by one. When I came to the black boots, the right one had no give. I pulled it down and jammed my hand down in there. I pulled out her money, still held in a roll with a pink ponytail band, just as I remembered.

When I popped the band off and fanned the bills open, I found it was mostly ones and fives. I did a quick count: eighty-two dollars. Not a lot. Not a stash, saved out for years while planning to leave her child like a reptile leaves a dropped egg. This was pin money, and she'd blown town in such a rush, she had not even come back by the house to pick it up.

I'd had her wrong, all these years. She'd meant to stick, for me. The tick marks, the abandoned money, these things proved it. Something had happened, and it had sent her careening across the country in the shoes she stood up in. It hadn't happened in our house, either, or she would have taken this pittance, at least.

Forget Florida and the Keys. Lime drinks and red bikinis had no charm for me now. I wanted to understand, and the answers were in California. I thought of her saying, *You are welcome.* She'd better have meant it, because she was sure as hell getting me now.

Or she was getting Ivy Wheeler, whoever that was.

In my dream Thom had come after Rose, bounding cool and determined over the blazing landscape, like a nightmare version of Pepé Le Pew. I'd read him rightly the last time I saw him, at Grand Guns. That had to be the last time I saw him, ever. I would not live through our next encounter, and he wanted that so badly, he'd never tire or waver. He would never stop hunting his Rose, so I had to leave her in Fruiton.

I locked my father out of his own bedroom and pulled my mother's nightgown off and threw it on the floor. I got in Daddy's shower and bathed, then got dressed in one of my mother's cotton skirts with a long-sleeved fitted tee. My mother's wardrobe, though twenty years out of date, favored lightweight fabrics and long sleeves, just as mine had back in Texas.

I spied a blue canvas satchel bag in the bottom of her closet, behind her wicker laundry basket. I pulled it out and set it on the bed. I filled it from her closet, choosing more hippie-chick skirts and blouses and bell-bottom jeans, two pairs with bright embroidered flowers, another pair covered with fabric patches. I rummaged in my mother's drawers and added socks and a couple of nightgowns. I drew the line at underpants. That was creepy, somehow. I'd pick up an eight-pack of cotton bikinis at Wal-Mart.

When I was packed, I grabbed the satchel and then walked fast to the bedroom door. Daddy was lurking right outside, holding a bologna sandwich on a paper towel. I took it and started wolfing at it. Daddy had his piece of notebook paper and the bottle of pills from the bedside table in his other hand. He rattled them both at me.

"Bill got these pills from his friend. He says you need to take them all the way down to the bottom," Daddy said.

I nodded with my mouth overfull. I felt a little better with every bite. Gretel, called off the bed by the sound of chewing, came and sat at my feet, giving me and my luncheon meat equally rapt gazes. I tore her off a corner. I glanced at the label on the pill bottle. I didn't recognize the name, but the drug ended in "-cillin," so I pocketed it.

"Thank Bill for me," I said with my mouth full. I pushed past Daddy and started for the door, my father's voice following me, now with a slight whine.

"Rose? Rose Mae? Don't you think of me at all?"

"Not really," I said. I opened the front door and looked out at

Pine Abbey. The sun was going down. The lights were on in the kitchen across the street, Bill and his Bunny presumably sitting down to dinner with Mrs. Bill.

My mother had walked out of that house one day, wearing her flowered shoes. No plan beyond the grocery store or a weekday mass. Something had happened, and she'd never come home.

"I think about you, alla time," my daddy said.

I looked at him over my shoulder and nodded. "It's harder on the left person." He blinked at me, puzzled, and I added, "It's better to be the one that leaves." I walked out the door, heading for his carport where the VW Bug was parked. He followed me.

"I only want to apologize," he said. "It's step nine. Can't you let me?" He rattled his note at me, Marley with a paper chain.

I shook my head and handed the last bit of my meal to Gret. Leaving everything of Rose behind meant ditching the Buick, but I couldn't exactly go Greyhound with Gret along. I had a wild vision of myself in the bus station wearing black glasses, trying to pass her off as a three-legged service dog as she pulled me sideways off my feet and stood up to try to lick the ticket seller in the face through the glass of the booth.

Also, the tickets would get pricey. I'd have to go the long way across America. The quickest way to California was Highway 40, but it ran through Texas, right through Amarillo, and that was insanity. I would not place my fragile body back anywhere near Thom's orbit. I'd have to go around, head north and then cross over through Kansas or Nebraska.

I said, "Your little rusty Bug here, does it run good?" When he nodded, I said, "Can I have it?"

He reached in his pants pocket and pulled out a jingly set of keys, tucking the apology into his armpit and working the car key off his ring.

"Rosey, if you listen to me read this, just once through, then my car is yours." He held both things out to me, the key in one hand, his sad bit of paper back in the other.

I peeled his crumpled apology out of his hand. "I'll take it, okay? You wrote it for me, and I have it now. You did your step." I tucked it down into my handbag, then reached for the key. He hesitated, fingers closing on the key.

"What about Claire? I'd need it to read to Claire if she comes back."

"She's not coming back," I said. "I'll pass it on to her when I see her again."

"Again? You seen Claire?" he asked.

"Yeah, Daddy," I said.

"She ast about me?" he said.

There was no good answer to that, so I said, "She lives out west now, and she seems fine. She lays cards."

"Vegas?" my father said. He must have heard "plays" for "lays." "I sure can't picture Claire in Vegas. You'll give her my speech?" I nodded, and he handed me the key. "You'll tell me when she reads it? So I can know I'm done."

"I guess I could," I said. "But listen, if anyone comes asking, don't say anything about this car. Don't even say I was here," I said.

"Is someone going to come looking, Rose?" Daddy asked.

"I'm afraid so. You never saw me, okay?" He nodded, and I climbed in the Bug. "I have to run out and get a few things, but I'll be back for Gretel, okay?"

"The pink slip is in the glove box," he said. I opened the box and found it under a stack of old maps. I had a pen in my purse, and he signed the car over to me, using its own roof as a desk, then handed me back the slip.

"That Buick, Daddy, you need to get rid of it. You can drive it down the trail and leave it in the woods, or if you know someone who'll take it under the table, you do that. Sell it for scrap. But no paperwork, you understand? That car has to disappear."

"I know someone who'll take it for the parts, no questions," he said. I nodded, unsurprised.

I started the VW. It sounded like some fireworks were getting it on with a bag of asthma in the engine box, but it ran. I backed out and left him standing there, empty-handed in his driveway.

I ran by Wal-Mart for underpants and a new toothbrush. I also got a good-size bag of Purina Dog Chow and some raisins and hard pretzels.

I got back in the car, but I didn't head to Daddy's. I hadn't come out for underpants. I was glad to have that off my mental to-do list, but I had really driven out to find a way to say good-bye to Rose Mae Lolley. It was time to peel her off me, same way Ro Grandee had been stripped away. Whatever she had been or loved or needed, it was time to run from it, fast, never looking back. The way my mother had walked away, in the shoes she was wearing, taking nothing from her past. Not even me.

The Catholic in me needed something more than a simple resolution. The blessing in the water was meaningless unless I stepped into the river. Wine to blood meant nothing if I didn't drink. I needed a ritual, a solemn act to start and seal the change.

I drove first to my old elementary school, but I found the woods behind, my woods and Jim's, had been shaved away to make room for a subdivision full of cramped, square houses in pastel colors. I pulled over to the side of the road.

The remains of my childhood were buried here. See-through young Jims and Rose Mae Lolleys must disturb the people's sleep, running through the walls to hide and show each other private things. The mortal remains of someone's calico cat would appear at midnight to stalk ghost mice across the cheap carpeting, chasing as best she could with her head on backwards.

The homes smelled as haunted as that neighborhood in *Poltergeist*, a movie Jim and I had watched on tape at his house maybe fifty times. "You moved the woods," I whispered to the pink and aqua cracker boxes, "but you left the bodies, didn't you?"

The Rose I was had begun in these woods with Jim, but the woods were gone. Someone's TV room rested on top of our clearing, and the blackberry bushes had been poisoned and dug out and dragged away for burning. I put the car in drive and passed the entrance, spine ashudder. I needed a place less changed.

I drove on out to Lipsmack Hill, my hands steady on the wheel. I found the hard-to-see turnoff onto the dirt path through the woods, the way still clear enough for the Bug to pass without adding to its scratches. I stopped in the grassy clearing where, if this had been 1985, in a few hours couples would park to tangle up and get some steam on their windows. I wondered if this year's crop of kids still came out here to get rowdy.

I opened the glove compartment and rifled through the maps. I'd seen a flashlight in there, and when I clicked the button, it surprised me by working.

I hiked the familiar path up through the trees, toward the clearing at the top of Lipsmack. I remembered the path so perfectly, I doubt I would have needed the light, even though the moon was only now on the rise. I'd been so aware of every inch, the first time I came up here with Jim Beverly. He'd been carrying that scratchy picnic blanket, both of us too shy and hopeful and nervous to talk much. My feet remembered how to walk it as my light swept the trail, searching for rocks and fallen branches.

At the top of Lipsmack was a flat patch of lush grass, and it ended in a sharp cliff that jutted out above a valley full of kudzu. I sat on the lip and clicked off my light, swinging my boots back and forth like Bunny had in my mother's desk chair. I waited while my eyes adjusted to the rising moonlight. The kudzu waved and swayed below me in the darkness like a deep green-black sea.

My mother laid cards. Had they told her I was coming west? The three she'd turned at the airport said a lot about her life, but only because my life had been modeled in a thousand unseen ways on hers. They were my cards, too, and they'd said that either Thom or I must die.

I'd played cowboys and Indians in the bushes out near Wildcat Bluff, but I hadn't been able to shoot him. I'd gone to Chicago, fooling myself into looking for a lost love because it made it seem like I was doing something other than staying and staying and staying until the day he killed me. Then I'd come home to Daddy and found him wrecked. What a pair we were, Daddy and me. I'd followed my chain of bad men all the way back to my very first, but it was useless. Neither of us was up to battling sugar ants for control of his dirty kitchen, much less the man I'd married.

I was tired of stalling. If the cards were right, if it was Thom or me, then let it be me. I wanted to leave Thom's would-be killer and his victim both to rot in the kudzu. I wanted to be done with the violent, angry girl my mother had created with her leaving, and I'd long been done with Ro.

I had come up here to say good-bye, but not to Jim Beverly. Not even to Daddy. I was finished here. Rose—and her trail—had to truly dead-end. I could never come back to Fruiton, Alabama. But I wasn't sure how to leave her, how to start fresh, to be someone else. If I peeled Thom Grandee's would-be murderer away, what the hell lived underneath?

I'd been someone else, before my mother left. A regular girl, maybe like Bill's Bunny. Jim Beverly and I had not been friends then. There was nothing in that girl to draw him. I didn't remember her very well. My mother had left her, so I had left her, too, not wanting to be a thing whose own mother couldn't love her. I didn't know her, but my mother must remember her and could help me remember, too. If I could abandon Rose Mae Lolley here, the way I'd left Ro Grandee back in Texas, I could start fresh. And after all, I wouldn't be the first asshole to try to find themselves in Cali-fucking-fornia.

I took off my wedding band, and the interlocking engagement ring diamond that went with it. My small marquise-cut stone glimmered in the faint light. I stared down at the sea of kudzu below me. It seemed like it could hold a thousand secrets. I closed my hand around the rings and reared my arm back, prepping to throw. I'd seen this done before in movies, a diamond hurled off a bridge or a ship, tossed into the woods from an overpass, or flicked out a moving car's window. It meant a permanent break.

I couldn't do it. I froze with my arm back, rings still fisted in my tight-closed hand. The pragmatist in me was totting up groceries and gas and even the cheapest hotels. I'd need to stop and sleep in real beds, to let my body heal. I'd been so sick. I'd need to eat good things, fresh fruit and soup, to get my strength back. I needed cash, fast and untraceable, and I could get it at any pawnshop with my ring set. I lowered my arm, even though without a sacrament, my resolution to start fresh as someone wholly new was weak. It couldn't hold.

I paused, torn, and then, like a gift, I heard voices down at the bottom of the hill. I cocked my head sideways to listen. I recognized them. Arlene Fleet and her angry fella.

Was she here looking for me? I tried to remember what my note had said, back in Chicago. I might well have mentioned Fruiton. She had a story to tell, a story that was so ugly she'd run straight up a tree rather than remember it. Her history with Jim must be haunting her so hard. I knew what that felt like. Perhaps she'd tracked me all the way to Alabama to try to lay it to rest by telling me, by telling anyone, at last.

I stood up and jammed the rings in my pocket. I could do this for her. I could play the part of a wounded Rose still hunting for her Jim. I would listen to her story, though I already knew it. It was my story, too. The details didn't matter. I would listen and then carry as much of it away for her as I could and dump it, for both of us. I would never think of Jim Beverly or be his Rose Mae again. I'd go get my good dog and blast out of here. I had a handwritten apology from Daddy and a long overdue library book that needed to be delivered.

The voices down the hill were getting louder; Arlene and her boyfriend were getting into it. It occurred to me that if I wanted a

symbolic gesture to seal my transformation, here it was on a plat-
ter. Arlene had found her own replacement bad man, and she'd
brought him right to me.

There was no more fitting final act for Rose Mae Lolley than
this: I would go down the hill and kick Arlene Fleet's piece-of-
shit boyfriend as hard as I could, right in the nuts. Then she and
I would run. I would listen to her, then be on my way. I felt my
grin go wide and wolfy in the darkness. I started down the steep
path in the moonlight, ready to begin.

PART III:

⌒

HANGING IVY

Berkeley, California, 1997

CHAPTER

❦

14

MY MOTHER LIVES somewhere in this city, maybe even on the street I am driving down. It is lined with skinny stucco houses, set close, growing like bright, rectangular mushrooms out of the hills. She could be walking down one of these narrow sidewalks, making her way between the houses and the parked cars that line the street.

Gret and I took the drive here in four easy days, going first north to St. Louis, then west through cowboy country. I drove with the windows down all the way. Desert air whirled through the car in a constant cyclone, catching up our hair and rifling through it, blowing all the Alabama off our skins. I wasn't halfway through Nebraska before even my regrets had been blown clean away. I may have kept a small one for Arlene Fleet's poor boyfriend. He'd turned out to be a decent fella, but I hadn't known that until well after I'd kicked his family jewels so hard that I was surprised they didn't shoot straight out his nose. Arlene had defended him like a miniature tigress, but after she'd calmed down, she'd confirmed everything I'd come to believe about Jim Beverly. Everything and more. I'd seen no point in dwelling, though, as I drove away. I was heading toward my lost mother and the answer to a question I'd been carrying for more than twenty years. I'd had no room for other thoughts inside the little car. I still don't.

I coast another slow mile through Berkeley, and the houses give way to neighborhood stores; my mother could be one of the shoppers meandering from coffee house to stationery shop to the futon store. It should be easy to spot her, given her penchant for bright and mismatched layers, but her strangeness is eclipsed by a white boy with blond dreadlocks, a six-foot black guy in a red dress, a turbaned girl dancing on a corner to music only she can hear.

Most of the couples I see don't match up in the usual ways. My gaze is pulled to a tiny Asian girl, straining up on tiptoe to kiss a tall, stooping black man, then a pair of Swedish-looking blond ladies holding hands, then a slim, attractive fifty-year-old Hispanic woman who is walking arm in decidedly unmotherly arm with a bulky guy, his pale head shaved clean and gleaming. He must be twenty years her junior.

My mother is close, perhaps even present, but strange works here as camouflage. I begin to understand how much little ol' Claire Lolley from Alabama must have changed in order to belong. She has done it, though. It is as if I can feel her heart beating, and it is the same heartbeat that the city has, a thready, strange arrhythmia that shouldn't work as well as it does.

I will find her. I am obeying the most basic drive there is. New lambs, blind and soaked in afterbirth, go immediately to their mothers. They know, and I know. She can blend into the landscape all she likes. I will find her. Watching for her, I drive right past the turn for the Berkeley branch library and have to go back.

The VW is used to the gentler hills of Alabama. It struggles to crest a slope so steep that I have to pump the brakes to keep the bald tires from playing sled on the downside. The library is a squatty brick building wedged in between an organic food mart and a gas station. It has slitty 1960s windows like my library back home—a little slice of familiarity in a city so strange, I feel like I have left my home planet—but it has no parking lot. The street is lined with meters with a two-hour limit.

I backtrack until I find a tiny half slot open on a residential side street with no parking limit posted. This space would defeat the smallest Honda, but I squeak the Bug back and forth, like I am sawing it into place. I make it.

Gretel and I get out and start walking back to the branch. It's the best place to start. Claire Lolley may have changed, but I can't believe she's changed so much that they won't know her at her local library. Back in Fruiton, she and I went to the library two, sometimes three times a week.

We are passing an Indian restaurant, and the air has a tangy, sharp smell. My mother had a similar scent, like ginger and other unfamiliar spices. Gretel lifts her nose to snuff. I do the same thing, just as a homeless fella comes up even with me. He is gusty and overripe, and I get a noseful.

He grins, showing me less than ten teeth, and falls into step beside me. He has a ragged swath of braided hair poking up out of the rag he has wound around his head, and his eyes roll around in separate ways. Gretel mutters low in her throat, a warning noise, as he leans in and says into my face, "You a bull daggahhhh!" with cheery relish. I stop, startled, but his message has been delivered, and he keeps walking.

"Just a harmless weirdo," I tell Gret, who has her hackles up. My voice calms her but not me.

The homeless fella catches up to an older lady in a peacoat who is walking along in front of me. He delivers the same message to her. She smiles at him and digs in a brown paper sack she is holding, then pulls out a sandwich and hands it to him. He takes it and hurries on, eager to tell all the women ahead of us that they, too, have been identified as bull daggahhhhs.

"The weird go west," I tell my dog. Anyone too strange for Berkeley must walk straight into the sea like a lemming to drown. Or possibly grow gills. If they are too odd for this city, there can be no place for them above sea level.

I hook Gretel's leash to the bike rack by the library's front

steps and tell her I'll be right back. Inside, I am greeted by the
familiar smell of musty books. There's a counter with two librarians behind it, and to their right, I see the low shelves and the
outdated computers of a typical reference section. The furniture
is covered in crackly blue vinyl. They are obviously underfunded,
the furniture and technology years out of date, just like back
home. The whole building could be swapped out for the library
in Amarillo and no one would notice. Not until they looked at
the librarians, anyway.

The closest librarian is a young woman, and I automatically
skip over her to look at the man at the other end of the counter. He
has a sheaf of dark hair falling over his forehead and a pierced nose.
His eyes are as black and shiny as oil slicks.

He looks up at me as I pause a few feet back from the counter
with my mother's book clutched close in one arm. He sees me, and
his shoulders tuck in and his spine bows slightly, as if a little bit of
breath has been pressed out of him by an unseen hand.

A pretty woman is a Christmas tree, my mother told me in the
airport. This fella is hanging things on my branches as his gaze
sweeps from my face all the way down my body to my hips and
then back to my face. Ideas fly from his widened eyes and land on
me like teeny, decorative burdens. He is giving me shyness, maybe,
some book smarts, and a certain yielding sweetness in the bed. The
oil-slick eyes get me, and I find myself hanging a few ornaments
myself, giving him deft hands and a sense of humor.

Ro Grandee would go lean over the counter and touch her hair
a lot of times, maybe touch his. She'd pinch and wheedle information out by turns. Rose Mae Lolley would simply hop over to his
side, get herself a fist full of testicle, and twist until he spilled. I
pause, uncertain, and then do the one thing that comes least naturally: I step straight toward the female librarian.

She looks soft, as if she's been raised in a box and purely milk-
fed, like veal. A line of teeny blue butterfly tattoos flutter out from
behind her ear, cross her collarbone, and disappear into her blouse.

I give her the most friendly, open smile that I can muster, put my hand out, and say, "Hi, I'm Ivy. Ivy Rose Wheeler."

She takes my hand and says, "All Swan."

I blink. "All what?"

"All *swan*," she says, smiling, then explains, "that's my name." She spells it for me, Alswan, then cranes her long neck at me, trying to look like she's at least some swan. She's got a good yard of extremely rumpled golden brown hair, wild, like she's spent the afternoon having cheerful jungle sex with Tarzan in the stacks. Tarzan kept her bra, looks like.

She's for sure younger than me and maybe prettier than me, which makes her about the last creature alive any of my former selves would go to for help; score one for the new girl. I plant myself in front of her and I say, "I found this book of y'all's. In an airport."

I hand over the Stephen King book, and Alswan flips open the cover to read the stamp. "This is ours all right. Thank you."

"The woman who left it, she also left something in it. Inside it. Something important. Or valuable, I mean." I'm practically stuttering. I'm not sure what kind of person Ivy Rose will turn out to be, but sadly, she's a terrible liar. At least to women. Perhaps, I think, this is because I weathered adolescence without a mother to practice on. Something else to put on Claire Lolley's long, long tab. "I need to get in touch with the woman who checked it out."

Alswan's eyebrows come together. "I can't give out information about our patrons. That's not . . . We don't do that."

"I understand," I say, nodding. "But I was hoping you could contact the person and tell her I'm here with the book." Alswan regards me with a healthy skepticism. I soldier on. "The thing I found, it's not something she can easily replace. She must want it."

Alswan's mouth purses up into a prim wad, as if, under the sex hair and the tats, the spirit of my hometown librarian is rising up inside her. Mrs. Blount once gave me this exact face back in

Fruiton, when she caught me reading D. H. Lawrence at thirteen. Alswan clearly has not bought what I am selling, but she humors me and says, "I'll take a look."

She turns her monitor, canting it so the back is squarely facing me. She looks back and forth from the book to her screen, typing in the numbers on the spine. She waits, squinting at her screen, while the old computer grinds its way to an answer.

I can't see the information that comes up, but Alswan says, "Oh," in such a tone that I know at once she recognizes the name. This girl knows my mother; she softens toward me immediately. As she turns back to me, she looks me up and down, fast. It's as if she is trying to see through my clothes, but not like her male colleague did. There's no sex in it. Curiosity, maybe some pity, but no sex. Her voice is considerably warmer when she says, "You're one of Mirabelle's girls! You should have said so."

"Mirabelle," I say, flat, so it could be a question or a confirmation. My mother's name is Claire, and as far as I know, I am her only girl. Still, the name goes with the gypsy clothes and long strings of hair, and the first thing people in hiding change is their name. My heartbeat picks up.

Alswan says, "Yes. Our book club meets at her house. Just wait over there, okay? I'll call her and tell her you are here."

"Okay," I say. I blink at her, suddenly short of breath, and she blinks back, all earnesty. I say, "Tell her it's Ivy *Rose*. From the airport. Tell her I'm the one who has her book."

"Don't worry," Alswan says. Her smile is now so warm and encouraging that I find it slightly creepy. "She'll remember you. She does this all the time."

"Thank you," I say, wondering what it is my mother does all the time. I have some doubt curling up from my stomach like a growing vine, trying to close my throat. What if this mysterious Mirabelle is not even my mother? Perhaps my mother stole the book from *her*.

I step away from the counter as Alswan picks up the phone. I do not go far. There's an "Our Book Club Recommends . . ." table just to the right, where some industrious soul has set up a display of novels. I pick one up and stare at the cover, straining my ears to pick up Alswan's soft voice.

"Mirabelle?" I hear her say. "It's Alswan, down at the branch." I try to look as uneavesdroppy as humanly possible, but Alswan turns her back to me and I can't hear what she says next.

After a minute, she turns back to look at me. I pretend to be lost in the book I am holding. I don't even know what it is. Hell, it could be upside down. I'm listening so hard, I've gone half-blind to compensate. I catch Alswan saying, ". . . five one sounds about right . . . Ivy . . . yes, dark hair."

Alswan turns away again. I wait until she hangs up, and then she's busy, writing something down on a piece of scrap paper. When she's finished, she gestures me over.

"Mirabelle's been expecting you." The breath rushes out of me in a *whoosh*, and I realize I have been holding it. My mother is Mirabelle is my mother. "See, I told you she'd remember! Her house is a short walk away, not even five minutes. I put her number down in case you get lost."

The paper says, "*Mirabelle Claire*," and then a phone number. Under that, Alswan has written detailed directions. I skim them. I am less than six blocks away from my mother's house.

Alswan is still talking. "She says she is about to start a reading, so you'll need to wait outside. She's sending Parker out to meet you . . ." Alswan falters. "That is, I didn't think. Do you mind a man?"

"Do I mind a man who what?" I ask.

"Oh, you know," Alswan says, and now she sounds a touch embarrassed. I look at her, puzzled. It's clear I don't know. "I thought you might be gun-shy."

A little Rose Mae Lolley gets out then, and I find myself smiling at her, showing quite a lot of teeth. "I'm not gun-shy."

"That's good!" Alswan says, almost as if she's proud of me. Like

I'm two and I just took a brave bite of my peas. She adds in a reassuring tone, "And anyway, it's only Parker." She dismisses Parker as a sexual threat with a wave of her hand, and I think this Parker must be eighty-five, or gay, or five feet tall with no arms. Or maybe she only means Parker is taken.

It suddenly occurs to me that Parker might be taken by my mother. She is sending Parker outside to wait for me, so they must be living together. They may even be married. They could have children for all I know, and everything in me recoils at this idea, my mother off in California raising a herd of babies that she liked enough to keep.

"Are you okay?" Alswan says.

"I'm sorry, yes," I say. I've fallen down a rabbit hole. I start to go, but Alswan puts her hand on my arm, stopping me. I freeze beneath it. I've never understood girly-girl friendships, all that hugging and squealing and air kissing. Girls can be so touchy-feely with each other. Me, I'm just touchy. But she seems sincere, and I'm so dizzy with hate for this Parker and my mother's imaginary children with him that I don't mind it. Much. She says, "You're going to be fine. I know Mirabelle. All you have to do is follow her rules, and she'll do anything for you. Anything."

I nod, solemn, though I haven't the faintest clue what she is talking about: One of Mirabelle's girls. Do I mind a man. Her rules. I'm wondering now if my mother has shed her gypsy clothes and become a madam. Or a matchmaker for lesbians.

Outside, Gret is sitting up waiting for me, her nose pointing straight at the doors she last saw me enter. "I didn't forget you, silly dog," I say. I unhook her and we fall into step. Alswan's directions are easy to follow, even with a detour to get my bag from the VW. I could drive the rest of the way, but as hard as it seems to park around here, I decide to leave it and tote the duffel.

We walk down the streets, my feet moving faster and faster.

Gret drags. A thousand dogs have peed out greetings onto the strip of green by the sidewalk, and Gretel wants to pause and sniff-read them all. I click my tongue at her, tug her along. I am close. I will see my mother—or at least her house and her maybe-husband—in four blocks. Then in three. Now I am almost running, questions stacking up with every step.

Alswan said she was about to start a reading; I assume this means she has some hapless new age seeker paying her to lay her weathered cards. Hurrying will only mean waiting longer outside with this Parker fellow, but I can't seem to slow. I am desperate to see the house where she lives, the man who shares it. Even now, accepted and on my way, I can't quite believe this Mirabelle is my airport gypsy, my long-lost mother.

It strikes me again how small the world can be and how hard it is to get truly and permanently lost. A couple of phone calls gave me Arlene Fleet. A library book is taking me directly to Claire Lolley, though she was all the way across the country hiding under a new name. My spine tingles, and I wonder how thick a trail of bread crumbs I have left for Thom Grandee to follow. I shove the thought away. He's seeking Rose Mae, and there is no Rose Mae anymore. There is only a girl named Ivy Rose Wheeler, running to her mother, now a scant two blocks away.

Questions from Alabama and Amarillo and new ones from the library are piling up into an avalanche that propels me forward toward her, fast, in spite of my heavy bag. Gret breaks into a cheerful three-legged canter to keep up with me, panting.

I come to Belgria, the street where my mother lives. It's an actual place, and I have found it, and now I am turning and now my feet are walking down it. I scan the sidewalk in front of the houses for Parker, her nonthreatening quasi man, the lover she's sent outside to wait for me.

All I see is a young woman, standing about four houses down, facing a sky blue house with a chain-link fence running around it. I'm at number 24, so that makes the blue house number 30. My mother's house. I slow and Gret tugs at the leash, but I want to study this woman before she notices me.

She's not looking down the sidewalk, watching for me. All her attention is on the house. She is in profile, her long hair hanging down her back, and she looks part Asian and part a lot of other things. She's leaning forward like a supplicant, and I read desperation in her tense shoulders. Her hands clutch and knead at the fence top.

As I get closer, I see she's talking to a man in the yard. Parker. Has to be. He's standing inside the fence, a few feet in front of the narrow, covered porch that runs the length of the house.

I give Parker the once-over, and I understand at once why Alswan wasn't worried that a gun-shy girl might get spooked. He's a long, narrow, pale fellow, his posture so slouchy that he's the droopy definition of nonthreatening. He's wearing a long-sleeved jersey over khakis and, God help him, mandals. He has a sharp, attractive face, but his heavy-lidded eyes and laid-back expression say he's about to carefully catch a porch spider in a Dixie cup and walk it out to the garden. Then he'll recycle the cup.

He has a couple of mutts lolling at his feet, Lab mixes, both floppy-eared and jet black. A third dog is standing on the porch stairs, a teeny Boston terrier with pugnacious shoulders. The terrier is the fiercest thing in the yard, man included, and he wouldn't even come to my knees.

I draw closer, trying to get a read on my potential stepfather. He's young, I realize. Closer to my age than my mother's. A lot closer. I find my lip curling up, wondering what the hell she's doing living with a fellow who is young enough to be her— I stop abruptly. Maybe Parker *is* her son. He looks Irish, with high, flat cheeks and a narrow jaw, his skull so angular that it looks like it has a few extra bones in it.

I come closer, close enough to hear Parker say, "It's Mirabelle's call, Lilah." His voice is set low, as mellow as his posture. He calls her Mirabelle, not Mom or Mother, but maybe children call their mothers Mirabelle in California. As for Claire Lolley, she didn't like motherhood enough the first time around to keep the job. Maybe the second time she kept the kid but not the title.

"Please," Lilah says. Her voice breaks in the middle of the word. "I can do it right this time." She sounds breathless and sorry and eight years old.

Just then Gretel clues in that we are approaching a yard full of dogs, and she jerks me forward, tail wagging.

"I can't help you," Parker says, spreading his hands as if he is showing the woman that they are empty. "Let me call Safe Harbor."

"No!" Lilah says, fierce. "I want Mirabelle."

Parker raises his hands to his head. His hair probably looks dark brown indoors, but the sun has found a lot of red in it. It's long, pulled back, and hanging in a tail almost past his shoulders. He's pressing the sides of his head like his brain is starting to hurt, and then Gretel jerks me forward again, chuffing.

The sound catches Parker's attention. He smiles when he sees me, raising one hand in an easy wave. The terrier hears Gretel, too, and he starts barking, alerting the Labby mutts. They rise, and the whole pack of them surge like a hairy wave to the corner of the fence closest to us, barking and wagging. Gret tows me to the fence corner, and all four of them thrust their noses through the links to snuff at each other.

When the dogs come running, the woman turns to see what they are racing toward. The side of her face that was turned away from me is mottled in spectacular purple and black, with violet and olive around the edges. Her right eye is swollen shut. The other eye is almond shaped, and its thick lashes are matted and wet. Pale women like me, we get red noses and splotch up, but this girl is a pretty crier, and the unmarked half of her face is lovely.

"Hi," I say, embarrassed, my gaze skittering sideways to meet her good eye. This is my mother's house, but this beaten woman makes me feel like I am an intruder here. Meanwhile, my dog sniffs and wags and makes a pack of easy friends, just like that.

Lilah stares at me, her good eye accusing, and she says, "She has my place?" She's looking at me but talking to Parker.

His eyebrows draw inward. "I don't think so," he says to her, then to me, "You're not Ivy?"

Lilah stares at me, hostile, daring me to be Ivy.

"Why aren't I?" I say.

"You're not . . . not how she described," Parker says.

I smile and say with almost no irony, "Maybe I've changed since she saw me last."

Lilah snorts. "Good luck." She is speaking directly to me, meaning just the opposite. "I hope you're perfect. You damn well have to be, here." She lets go of the fence and turns her back to me, starts walking away.

"Lilah! Do not go back home again," Parker calls after her. He comes toward the fence, all the way to the gate. "Let me call Safe Harbor!"

She flips him the bird over her shoulder and keeps walking. I come down the length of the fence, the dogs in step with each other on their separate sides. The Labs are dipping their front ends down, rumps up, asking in universal dog language if Gretel wants to play. She does. Only the terrier stands off to the side, suspicious, cocking one sprouty eyebrow up, then the other. I stop by the front gate. Parker is still watching Lilah walk away. She's pretty from the back, too, but I can tell from the careful way she's moving that the bruises on her face have plenty of company.

After she makes the corner, I turn to Parker and say, "I didn't mean to interrupt."

Parker's head tilts sideways at the accent. "Where are you from?"

Does he not know about me? The woman he lives with—our shared mother or his way-too-damn-old-for-him wife—is from Alabama.

"Where do you think I'm from?" I ask.

He says, "I don't know. Someplace south. Virginia?"

"Sure," I say. "Virginia. Why not." I say it like an asshole, my gaze pointy, staring sticks into his skin. He smiles, genial, oblivious, and I say, "So you're . . ." I'm not sure what to call her. My mother? The gypsy? I can't bring myself to say Mirabelle. Finally I settle on a pronoun, anonymous and plain. "So you're her, what?"

"Whose what?" Parker asks. "Lilah?"

I jerk my thumb at the house, to indicate my mother, and find I also can't say husband, stepfather, or, God help me, my brother. These words are all distasteful, and I don't want them in my mouth. I finally say, "You're her boyfriend?"

Parker looks startled, then laughs. "I'm Mirabelle's landlord."

"Oh," I say, nonplussed. "That's great. I mean, how great. For both of you, both." I've been so caught up studying the people, I did not look closely at the house. I see now that it has two front doors. The one in the center has a dog door set in the base. The second door is at the far right end of the porch, so I doubt this place is a true duplex. It's more like the house has a mother-in-law suite with a separate entrance. There's an unlit neon sign in the window beside the far door: an open hand, palm forward. My mother's business.

I feel stupid for being so angry, for jumping to so many wrong conclusions. "*Is* she married?" I ask.

"No," Parker says, looking me over. His expression is as bland as oatmeal. "She told me you had long hair."

"I cut it," I say.

"And she didn't mention the dog. It's like if someone has a unicorn tattooed on their forehead. You don't say they'll have on a red shirt. A three-legged dog is the kind of thing you mention first."

"She didn't know I had the dog," I say, then remember he's her landlord. "Is the dog a problem?"

"Oh, yeah. I hate the stinking things," he says, deadpan, while his mutts drip friendly slaver and try to goozle through the fence holes, jostling each other to be the one touching noses with Fat Gretel. I realize I'm grinning at him, so pleased to know he isn't any kind of dreadful kin to me. He smiles back and then points from one big mutt to the other and then to the terrier, saying, "Buck, Miss Moogle, Cesar."

I point and say, "Fat Gretel."

He squats down and addresses Gretel directly, threading his fingers through the fence so she can smell him. "Are you a good dog?" It's not rhetorical. She grins and pants joyfully into his face through the links, tail in a mad wag. "Yeah, you're a good dog. Okay, then." He straightens. "Come on in."

I block the entrance with my bag and then my body as he opens the gate for me, and Gretel and I slip in without letting his dogs out. He shuts it, and Gretel and the other dogs are winding all around, each trying to be the first to get a noseful of the other's butt.

Parker says, "Let her off the leash before she trips you."

I let Gret go, and they take off in a pack, even the standoffish terrier caught up in the pleasures of lapping the house with a visitor dog. Meanwhile, Parker takes my bag for me and crosses the small lawn, heading to the porch in a shambling, amiable walk that reminds me of Shaggy from *Scooby-Doo*.

He is talking at me loud, over his shoulder. "The stairs are in her reading room, so you can't get up to your room without tramping through the middle of her reading. Sorry. Can I get you some water? Or tea?"

"No," I say. "That woman, Lilah. She used to live here?"

There are three steps that lead up onto the porch, and Parker pauses on the bottom one. He turns toward me to shake his head, rueful. "Yeah."

"With Mirabelle," I say. "Before me."

"Not right before. She was three—no, four before you. She keeps coming back, though." He sets my bag down on the top step.

"Four before me," I say, hesitant. Parker seems to have no clue that I am Mirabelle's daughter. He thinks I am Lilah's successor, and I am starting to get a feel for what that means. My mother has been taking in stray ladies, the kind who have bad home lives and a lot of bruises. It appears to be habitual.

The three big dogs all come charging around in a pack, streaming across the yard. Gretel is keeping up fine on her three legs. They disappear back around the corner, the stubby terrier trailing behind and barking like mad.

"Safe Harbor is a shelter, for women?" I ask Parker. He nods, and I keep guessing, on a roll now. "Mirabelle works at this Safe Harbor place? This is like an annex?"

"Nah. Safe Harbor doesn't officially approve of Mirabelle's . . . what would you call it? Freelance social work?" There are a couple of wicker rocking chairs with padded seats between the two front doors on the porch, but Parker sits on the wide steps, to the right of my bag. He leans back in the sunshine, stretching out his long legs. His rumpled khaki pants are too short. "But one of their directors, Jane, calls Mirabelle on the sly when all their beds are full, and at least three of Mirabelle's, er, guests who didn't work out here have ended up doing really well over there. Not Lilah, though."

"Lilah can't come back here," I say. It is not a question. I've gotten a good feel for it now. "She broke one of Mirabelle's rules." Parker nods, and I add, "The girl I met at the library, she told me I'd be fine as long as I followed the rules."

I come closer and sit on the other side of the steps, my blue bag a chaste wall between us.

"Yeah. Lilah went back to her husband," Parker says. "I've never seen Mirabelle take a woman in a second time if they go back to the husband or the boyfriend."

I look at his feet as he talks. I don't approve of men wearing sandals, unless they are the kind for rafting. Open-toed leather shoes are girly. But I like his feet. They are very long and narrow and pale, like tusks of ivory.

"Are there a lot more rules?" I ask.

Parker looks surprised. "Your driver didn't tell you?"

"My driver?" I ask.

He shakes his head, confused. "You're pretty far west, Virginia. You had to come in with a Saint Cecilia?"

Everything in me goes still. "I don't know what that means," I say, careful to keep my tone even, to not let my expression change.

"The underground railroad?" Parker says, like he's reminding me.

"Underground railroad?" I repeat. "You mean, what? Like Harriet Tubman?"

"Yeah, like that. Only the Saint Cecilia railroad is for women in very bad situations. Mirabelle is one of 'em."

"Mirabelle is a Saint Cecilia," I parrot back, but he doesn't seem to notice I've turned into a shocked echo.

Parker nods. "I drive for her sometimes. Mirabelle will get a call, and she'll send me to pick a woman up in a public place and drop her fifty miles away at a mall or a library. I never see who brings the woman to the meeting place or who picks her up after me, so there isn't a trail. Mirabelle's houseguests are either local, or they come through Jane at Safe Harbor, or they're moved here by the Saint Cecilias. If you didn't come here with a Cecilia, then how did you end up way out here, Virginia?"

I'm floored enough to speak the simple truth. "I met Mirabelle in an airport. She told me I was welcome."

He nods and falls into a small, comfortable silence. I sit beside him, trying to keep my expression plain even though my heart is racing. Back at Cadillac Ranch, I'd dismissed my mother's message as meaningless, even heartless. But she had left me the directions I craved, after all. On the same car, under her past-tense love note and her insulting instructions to pray, I'd noticed silver letters telling me, *The Fun's at RODEO!* I'd assumed that was the gay men for peace, but now I'm wondering what would have happened if I'd put it together, if I'd thought to call that bar and ask to speak to Cecilia. Would I have been offered the chance to disappear?

My chill heart almost warms a speck toward my mother, but in its next beat I realize that if I hadn't run into her at the airport,

I never would have known that message was there. Even when I found it, it was so obscure that I hadn't understood it. It wasn't really for me. It was for her. A balm to her conscience, a way to tell herself she'd drawn a path for me and put it in fate's hands.

I'm breathing too hard, and the silence feels strained to me. It doesn't seem to be bothering Parker, though. He is stretched out on the steps with his face to the sun. I try to shake it off. So my mother has made an asshole move; by now, this should not surprise me.

Finally I turn to Parker and say, "So you have house rules—"

"No, no," Parker interrupts. "It's my house, but definitely Mirabelle's rules. I'm not really much of a rules guy." That's so obvious it makes me smile, even through my anger. He grins back, but when he speaks again he sounds serious. "I'm sure she'll tell you. I know you spend the first seven days inside. She kicked one girl out for being on the porch."

I snort, and I have to work to keep my tone mild. "Mirabelle's kind of a bitch, huh?"

Parker shrugs. "It's hard-core, but it makes sense. That girl's boyfriend was driving all over Berkeley with a harpoon gun, looking for her." I catch him stealing a glance at my left hand. I have no tan lines, but the skin at the base of my ring finger has a faint indentation where my rings used to sit. I fist my hand and sneak a glance at his. No sign of a ring there. "After a week, even the maddest man quits looking. Or at least they are less likely to come in swinging."

I nod. In seven days, a temper-driven man cools off. If only Thom Grandee were running on temper instead of something so much colder. What Thom is carrying around is practically immortal: a pure desire to put me in the earth. I have a sudden snapshot memory of his dead-eyed face at the gun shop, all his layers stripped away and only the reptile left, cold-blooded and foreign.

I remind myself he's looking for a girl who no longer exists. Even so, my hand jumps to the top of my bag, pressing in to feel the comforting hardness of Pawpy's gun.

"That makes sense. Any other big rules I should know?"

Parker shrugs. "The usual stuff. No drugs or weapons, like that."

My hand is pressing Pawpy's gun, and I startle when he says no weapons. He catches it, and his eyebrows rise.

"I have some chunks of an old gun," I confess.

Parker sits up straight. "You have a gun?" He says the words with the same vehement disbelief I would use to say, "You have a rotting snake carcass?"

"I have *pieces* of gun," I say. "Pieces can't shoot." Technically that's true. Pawpy's gun can't work until I load the barrel and slot it into place. But anyone who knows guns, my mother included, could have this revolver ready to fire in thirty seconds. Still, if this fella has ever touched a gun, I'll eat my boots. I open my bag and dig it out to show him.

His eyes are wide, watching me unfold the T-shirt I've bundled around the gun. I hold it over for him to see, resting my hands on the top of the bag.

He says, "I'm not sure Mirabelle likes people to have pieces of gun. I'm not sure I do."

"Not a shooter, huh?" I say. "I kinda guessed that from the shoes."

He looks at his own feet, then over to Ivy's scuffed cowboy boots, then back.

"What about my shoes?" he asks.

"They're pacifist shoes," I say. "You ever see a soldier wearing mandals?"

He laughs at that. "Okay, Boots, so your feet are saying you're an expert marks-lady-person?" He sounds more interested now.

I meet his eyes, direct and steady, and I say, "Oh yes. My boots say I'm fantastic."

His floppy awkwardness is dropping away. He's gone all comfortable inside his wiry body. Sandals or no sandals, now I am sitting with a man, the kind that Alswan might not so easily dismiss.

He leans in toward me. "Why would you want to be a fantastic gun shooter?" It's not rhetorical; he really wants an answer.

"It's fun," I say.

He shakes his head, doubtful, and says, "I've never had to fight off a 'fun' urge to go shoot Bambi in the face."

I say truthfully, "Oh! Me neither. Not that I have a problem with it—my daddy hunted to feed us. I went with him dove hunting, but I didn't shoot, and if he was after deer or rabbits, I stayed home. I can't eat an animal once I've met it all up close and fuzzy."

"So you've never shot at anything alive?" he says.

I picture Thom Grandee rising over the slope on the running trail at Wildcat Bluff, his Roman nose centered in my sights, but I meet Parker's gaze and do not blink or hesitate before I say, "Of course not." I have not lost my facility for lying to men, thank God. "Anyway, rifles don't do much for me. I'm a pistol girl, and I purely love to target shoot. As for these pieces, this gun used to be my grampa's. All I have left of him."

"A sentimental gun? That's bizarre." He reaches over and rolls the loose barrel doubtfully.

"Chunks of sentimental gun," I say. His fine-boned finger touches the barrel, which touches the shirt, which rests in my hand, and he puts out a spark strong enough to travel through all that and reach me. I feel it like a buzzing in my palm. "Maybe sometime when I'm out of quarantine, I'll take you to a range to try some shooting."

"Ha!" he says, like the very idea is absurd. He takes his hand away, but then he rubs his fingers together, as if he's setting the feel of the cool, slick metal into memory. After another ten seconds he says, "Maybe."

The door on the far end of the porch swings open. We both jump, as if we have been caught out doing something naughty. I rewrap the gun and stuff it down under a few of my mother's old clothes.

A well-dressed middle-aged woman in pricey shoes comes out. Parker stands up and slouches off sideways so she can use the stairs. Flirting over guns is my oldest and most comfortable territory.

While we were there, I forgot to be angry and sick with nerves, and he forgot to be nonthreatening. Now we are back where we began.

The woman nods to Parker and me as she passes us. The dogs have been tussling in the side yard, and they come running around the house in a pack to investigate as she steps around my bag and walks down the steps. They're covered in each other's suck and hair and look like they've been rolling each other through dirt and dead leaves. She takes one look and dashes out through the gate before they can leap on her and coat her in a filthy greeting.

"I should just go in?" My voice comes out shaky.

"Take it easy," Parker says. "She's expecting you. It's going to all be fine."

I have good radar for when a man's attracted to me, but now there's nothing but vague, innocuous friendliness. Shaggy-Doo is back. He stands up and puts a hand down for me. His fingers are cool, and he lets me do all the gripping and pulling as I stand up. He steps back from me at once, the second I am on my feet. This is a man who has spent a good bit of his time around women who are, as Alswan put it, gun-shy. He nods good-bye and shambles to the center door, going into his part of the house.

I pick up my bag and walk to the other door. I hesitate, raising my hand to knock, then putting it down. I square my shoulders. I live here now, after all. This is my mother's house. I will not stand by the fence like Lilah, wringing my hands. I will not knock to beg entry. I put my hand on the knob and it turns, unlocked.

Gretel is suddenly beside me, jamming herself in front of my feet to stop me from going through a door without her. I let us both in. My mother stands in the center of a large parlor. She is facing the door, waiting for me to walk through it. I do. I close it behind us.

My mother looks much the same as she did in the airport, in shawls and multicolored layers with her hair unbound. There's a knot in the hem of her floral overskirt, holding it up to show a blue skirt under. She's too old to wear her hair so long and all one length. It hangs straight down like Witchie-Poo hair, drawing my eye to all the places where her skin is beginning to sag. I set my bag down. We look at each other, holding silence between us. I am breathless.

"You brought your dog," she says. She would probably sound more pleased if I had brought in the Ebola virus. "Where did her leg go?"

Gret starts sniffing her way around the unfamiliar room, and I say, "I shot it off." My mother blinks, and I add, "It was an accident."

She does a faint double take. "I had a blouse like that." I touch the lace-trimmed edge of her old hippie shirt and she says, "And I had jeans like . . ." She stops, doing math in her head. "Those *are* my jeans."

"Yes." I pull at the waistband. I can't believe this is the conversation she is choosing. It fills me to the rim with instant bitchy. "I'm a little thinner than you were."

"Well, *you* never had a baby," she snaps, bristling up.

"*I* still have time," I volley back.

We stare at each other, surprised at ourselves, and she says, "This is absurd."

It is. She's right. But I can't think of a light conversation we could have that would not be absurd and that would not enrage me. If she mentions the weather, I will have no choice but to slap her. We can't talk dogs and jeans, not with all the history between us.

"So you went back to Fruiton. I assume not just to raid my closet. Was that wise?" she asks. Behind her, Gretel has found an open doorway at the far end of the room. She follows her nose through it.

"Probably not," I admit, and I can't resist adding, "Daddy says hey."

My mother's eyes narrow and then go all the way to slits as I reach into my back pocket and pull out his rumpled piece of paper, now folded neatly into a closed quarter sheet. It's been partially ironed by the pressure of my butt as I sat on it to drive. "He sent you a note."

She stares at the paper with a chain of fleeting expressions flashing across her face, as if I have first pulled a live rabbit out of my pocket, and now it is peeing on her floor.

I hold it out, and she says, "I'm not reading that." She sounds affronted by the very idea.

I shake the paper at her, rattling it. She makes no move toward it, so I look for a place to put it. It's a big room, done all in ocean colors, fifty shades of blue and a sandy beige. Behind my mother is a good-size wooden table with chairs on either side. Her tarot cards sit on top in a neat stack, flanked by lit candles. I am standing in what looks like a mini-store. By the front windows are delicate display shelves full of jewelry and gift books. Directly ahead of me, a staircase with a heavy banister leads up. Beyond the stairs, in the middle of the room between the mini-store and her reading table, a love seat is grouped with footstool and a small recliner. The wall opposite the stairs is lined with overflowing bookshelves. I cross the room to them and set the folded note down in front of what looks like a full set of Austen's novels.

"I told him I would give it to you," I say. "What you do with it now is not my problem."

I don't tell her about step nine or how badly he wants her to read it. If she's tempted to open it at all, that information would stop her cold. Knowing how badly he wants me to read it has certainly stopped me, for days and nights and thousands of miles. I have not so much as peeked at the salutation.

I suspect it will be different for her, though. If it was a note from Thom Grandee, even if it was given to me ten decades from this moment, I'd have torn into it already. Marriage is complicated, and Daddy's note is working on her in some underhanded way. Now I can see, under her layers and between the dark curtains of her hair, some vestige of the woman who tucked me in each night. The one who made my bologna sandwiches with extra mustard, just as I liked them. That woman's gaze flicks to the note and then away.

"He's fine," I say, as if she has asked and I am answering her question. "He got his five-year pin. AA."

Her eyebrows rise, and then she passes one hand across her forehead, as if manually wiping any interest away, pulling the expression right off her face. But I can see my mother coming more sharply into focus with every piece of history I invoke.

I say, "I saw where you wrote my name on the wall. I saw the marks you made, behind the ship painting." I've surprised her yet again, but she remains silent. I say, "I know, Momma."

That final word undoes her. It hits me, too, this awful name I have not uttered now for more than twenty years. She can't look at me. She's gulping air in little pants, trying to get it down into her lungs.

"What happened?" I ask, because it is time. This is the question that has pulled me all the way across the country. There's plenty more I want to know. I want to know how she found me and when she started spying on my life in Amarillo. I want to ask about the Saint Cecilias and the impossible-to-decode exit strategy she spray-painted onto the car out at Cadillac Ranch. I want to know which tarot card fell faceup at the airport, stopping her when every line of her body told me she was going to run. But this first question eclipses all the others.

It's all I've thought of in the car on the drive over, building scenarios in my head that could explain her sudden departure, each more soap opera silly than the last. I imagined that she hit her head and got amnesia, or witnessed a Mafia killing, or was abducted. I never came up with a single explanation I believed, and now that I am here, this is all I want from her: a reason I can understand. I say, "You hardly took anything when you left Fruiton. I even found your money, eighty-two dollars, left behind in your old black boot. What happened? Why did you go without me?"

She stares down at the floor. Time passes. Whole minutes, one after another after another.

Gret comes back in the room and her tail goes down. She gives my mother a wide berth and slinks low-bellied past her. She comes to heel and sits down looking worried. Fat Gretel, who would face-lick Attila and play Frisbee with Jack the Ripper, does not like my mother. My mother's downward gaze is drawn to my dog, and I can see it's mutual.

My mother stares at my dog, pressing one open palm to her chest, and I watch her slowing her heart with her strong will. She takes a deep breath, like she's about to start yoga, and then another. When she finally meets my eyes, hers are as empty and shiny as marbles. My mother looks right at me, and she lies to me in a voice as flat as window glass.

"I went to mass that day, and I was visited by a saint. It was . . . a vision. She told me I had to go."

It's like a slap. This is the question I've come to ask, three thousand miles. Instead of an answer, I'm getting a metaphor, and a shitty one at that. I've already figured out that she must have had help from the Saint Cecilias, but she sure as hell didn't learn about them through some mystical vision, and the metaphor can't explain how she could let them spirit her away sans child.

I say, "Why are you lying?"

My mother keeps talking in that flat, almost bored way. "She told me to leave immediately, and not look back. She said—"

"Stop fucking lying," I interrupt.

She doesn't acknowledge that I have spoken or that she has stopped. She is perfectly controlled.

She gives her shoulders a little shake, as if she is shucking off a cape, and walks toward the stairs. She picks up my bag and says, "I'll show you to your room."

"Why did you leave without me?" I demand again.

She starts up, slow, like her knees bother her, talking over her shoulder at me. "None of my friends know I have a daughter, Rose Mae," she says. "Please be discreet. I do not want to try and explain you. Nor will I explain myself."

I follow her, and Gret follows me, careful to keep me as a wall between her and my mother. I say nothing. There is nothing else to say right now. I don't even ask if her friends will find it odd to learn she has a strange woman living in her spare room. They won't. There is always a strange woman living in her house, hoping to escape a marriage made of swords.

My mother goes up step by step, toting my bag and talking like a bored tour guide. "The kitchen is through that open doorway in the parlor. Help yourself if you get hungry. I usually cook a hot dinner, and I'll make enough for two if you care to join me. There's a half bath in front of the kitchen, behind the stairs." She reaches the top, me right behind her, helpless to do anything but follow. "That is my room." She points at a closed door at the end of the hall. "That's the bathroom, between. And this is your room."

She opens the door directly at the top of the landing, and she is right. It *is* my room. Exactly.

A twin bed, a table, and a lamp sit at the far right corner, opposite the door. They are placed in the spot where the bed and table in my childhood room in Fruiton still rest. The dresser sits across from a comfy chair for reading and a floor lamp, also just the same as Fruiton. She's even put a writing desk and matching wooden chair against the window, as if she thinks her residents might have homework. The furniture is a hodgepodge of finishes that range from maple down to darkest cherry, and my bedroom set back in Fruiton was all white wicker, but the placement of each piece matches my girlhood room exactly.

"Holy shit," I say in spite of myself. "Did you do this on purpose?"

She looks at me with her eyebrows rising in a question. She doesn't even realize. I might not have caught it myself if I had not just been home. She and my daddy both are living in shrines they've erected to lives they themselves either wrecked or abandoned.

"Let me guess," I say. "The saint who came to you in your 'vision.' It was Cecilia." Her eyes barely widen, but I catch it. I go on.

"Yes, I went out to Cadillac Ranch. I saw your note. And if I'd gone to Rodeo!—if I'd hooked up with your railroad, I'd have ended up here, wouldn't I?"

The room says so. She's made this room for me, the same way Daddy remade our house for her. But my mother is shaking her head in a cold, vehement no.

"Never here," she says. "We would never take you someplace at all connected to your past life. I am the last person we would have brought you to."

"Against the rules, huh? Well. I came my own way. Cecilia's rules don't apply to me. Your rules don't, either."

She is watching me, wary. "I suppose not. Not really. But Parker and my other friends will find it strange if they see that. As a courtesy, I ask that you at least appear to keep them." Her formal speech is beginning to bother me. It's as if she's given up contractions for Lent.

"I've broken one already." I set my bag down on the bed and say, "I've got Pawpy's old revolver in here, and I'm keeping it."

All at once her eyes go avid. Her blank expression drops away. We have come to the piece of conversation she has been longing to have, while I was wanting to ask her what happened the day she left me. She straightens up and presses one hand to her lips.

"Pawpy's gun?" she says, muffled behind her hand. She takes a single step toward me. "Is that the . . . is that what you used?"

"What I used?" I ask. She's failed to give me the one answer I wanted most, and I hope she's asking something that will let me fail her back. She wants something from me right now, badly. I step in, eager to know, so I can refuse to give it to her.

"What you used instead of taking the railroad. What you used to end things. With your husband. You used Pawpy's old forty-five?"

Now I understand, and I feel a smile coming. I can't damp it down. It's almost an exultation, that I can look her in the eye and say with ringing, happy truthfulness, "Momma, are you insane? I didn't shoot my husband."

She tries to swallow and coughs instead. Her face crumples and her hands fist, and all at once she's furious. "Rose Mae, no! Tell me that man you married is not still walking on this earth."

"It's Ivy now," I say, so sweet now that she is wanting something and I don't have it to give. "I'm Ivy Rose Wheeler. You're the one told me it was him or me. I chose, Momma. I got rid of Rose Mae."

Her eyes snap, and now she is beyond angry. Her skin is wax, and her eyes have a fevered glow. Her nostrils flare, and when she speaks, her voice sounds deliberate and deep, each word dredged up from the diaphragm. "Rose Mae, you stupid child, why did you come here? Dear God, you should have gone with the railroad. Do you really think fate can be fooled? That it can be that easy? It doesn't matter if you keep my rules or not. Nothing you do will matter. Not as long as you are here, and he is breathing."

She steps back, out of the room, her hand on the knob. "Your business with Thom Grandee is not over." Her words are livid prophecy, intoned like she's Elijah calling bears, and then she closes the door. I am left shaking, alone in a pale blue room she's made to mirror mine.

CHAPTER
✧
15

I AM LIKE AN ANGRY five-year-old, holding my breath until I am blue enough to match her decor. I am giving her the silent treatment, except I am almost thirty, which means I do not crumble after ten minutes and weep into her skirts. Instead I meander around whatever room she's in, touching all her things.

She has appointments all day long, crystal junkies and new age woo-woos coming in for readings. Whenever one rings her windchime doorbell, she asks me politely, in formal language, to excuse myself. I've toted a Barbara Kingsolver book to my room, and each time I go up and close my door and read in silent, furious obedience. When I hear the client leave, I mark my place and come back down to steadfastly ignore her where she can see me do it.

She has lots of appointments, and many of her clients are her friends, too. I hear them air kissing at her, the rustle of hugs and cheery greetings as I go up the stairs. None of them are surprised to see my ass disappearing upwards. None of them ask to be introduced. They are waiting, I suppose, to see if I am going to stick. No sense befriending another Lilah. The way my room faces the staircase, sounds travel from the parlor directly up to me. I could leave the door open and eavesdrop, but I am more interested in *The Bean Trees* than bullshit fates invented by my mother.

After her eleven-thirty leaves, she turns on the red-palm window sign. Belgria is a busy street. In fifteen minutes, a drive-by supplicant is ringing her bell, wanting a peek at the future. I don't get to see the walk-in. She won't even open the door until I am in my room with the door closed.

Perhaps she is worried that this passing chimer will turn out to be my husband, come to kill me. Thom Grandee in the parlor with the wrench. That's ridiculous. Thom is looking for his Ro clear across the country. She is not there, and she is not welcome here. If he did know to look in Berkeley, I strongly doubt that he would stand politely on the porch and ring the bell, bearing murderous intentions like a hostess gift.

During our shared and silent lunch, my mother hooks another true believer with her sign. I am banished back upstairs halfway through my grilled cheese sandwich. I hear her answer the bell, and after a brief exchange, the door closes again, and there is no more conversation. This second potential walk-in must not have passed muster in some way.

I open my door and see her coming up the stairs with a basket of fresh laundry. She walks past me without speaking and goes down the hall to her room. She closes her bedroom door decisively, but I follow her and let myself in. She is standing on the far side of her queen-size bed, facing me. She has dumped out a jumble of bright cotton clothing on her wave-covered comforter, and she's folding it. Her lips thin as I enter, but she does not tell me to get out. Her room is done in the same endless blues as the downstairs. It's bigger than mine, but not as bright because her windows are covered with heavy drapes.

I come closer, stand across the bed from her. She has collected a blown-glass and crystal menagerie, and I sort through it, bored. I find sharks nested with seals, lambs cuddled up to lions, and no people: She's made paradise on the bedside table. I put rough hands on her unicorn, picking him up and flicking his silly garland of blue roses. "You're out of luck, buddy. No virgins here," I tell him.

"Be careful, Rose. That's breakable," she says, stern and maternal.

"I'm Ivy," I say to the unicorn, and set him down dead on his side.

Mirabelle's nostrils flare. She leaves the rest of her blouses in a scatter to wrinkle on her bed and goes back downstairs. I go back downstairs, too.

She sits down at her table, shuffling her cards. I see my father's note still sitting on the bookshelf, neatly folded, but now it is directly in front of *Persuasion*. I'm pretty sure I set it down closer to *Sense and Sensibility*. I don't think she's read it, but she must have picked it up and set it back down wrong, or at least pushed at it with one disgruntled finger. Its presence is eating at her edges. Good.

I go to the other end of the room to touch things in her small store. A bowl full of polished rose quartz shares a shelf with Saint Christopher's medallions. Crystal balls are lined up with no irony beside a display of hand-carved wooden rosaries. She sells tarot cards here, too, and books on how to read them. The decks are stacked beside prayer candles with the images of obscure saints frosted onto the tall glass tubes that hold the scented wax.

I pick up Saint Jude and check the label. Twenty dollars seems excessive, but then again, this is a *magic* candle. It says so, right on the sticker. A bastardized novena is printed on the glass opposite Jude, something between a spell and a prayer. I set Jude down and paw through the candles, finding a host of less familiar friends: Expedite, Lucy, the Infant of Atocha. They've left Mother Church and gone voodoo.

While my mother sits on her chair and shuffles and watches me, I take up the Saint Lucy candle. The spell on the back is a demand for Lucy to reveal a hidden truth or expose a liar. I hold it up to show my mother, modeling its useful marvels as if I am Vanna White. She stares deliberately away from me. I tuck the candle into the crook of my arm and keep shopping.

I have just picked myself out a beautiful green rosary with

hand-carved wooden beads when the doorbell chimes again. Her next supplicant has arrived. She starts to speak, but I know the drill by now. I am already heading upstairs. I put the candle and the rosary in my room, unpaid for. I rummage around my room for matches and find an old hotel pack in the writing desk, stuck way back behind some pale blue stationery and a veritable host of pens. Even the frickin' ink in them is blue.

I follow her rules all day: I don't go back to my husband. I don't use drugs or shoot anyone. I don't poke my nose outside the house. I use the back door in the kitchen to let Gret in and out to play with the other dogs or use the lawnly facilities, piously careful not to let a single toe over the threshold when I open it for her.

Gret spends the afternoon with Buck and Cesar and Miss Moogle, but at her regular dinnertime, I go into the kitchen and hear her single-footed scraping at the back door. When I let her in, I bend down to ruffle her ears; she smells strongly of curry. She must have availed herself of Parker's dog door while he was fixing his own dinner. I squat down and scratch her head in earnest, saying, "That's very naughty." She pants into my face, and she even has curry on her breath. Parker is encouraging her.

I eat my own dinner with my mother. She fried catfish in corn-meal, and she serves it with hush puppies and buttered peas. She may have lost her accent, but she still cooks like a southerner. We eat and bristle at each other on either side of the butcher-block table in her blue-and-cream kitchen. We are almost all the way through dinner when I finally realize that she isn't speaking to me, either. The silence I thought was my choice has, in fact, stretched both ways, and she has been as purposeful about it as I have been. I take a sip of sweet tea to clear my throat. I am now perversely ready for conversation.

"What really happened the day you left Fruiton?" I say casually, as if these aren't the first words I've said to someone besides Gretel and a glass unicorn in over twenty-four hours.

Her lips thin and her eyes narrow. She tilts her head sideways and speaks to her peas in an irritating singsong, like she's saying a catechism. "I went to mass and then confession. I prayed, and Saint Cecilia answered, telling me—"

I interrupt her with a loud snort, unladylike as I can manage, and say, "Cecilias. Plural. They're activists, Momma, not deities. You're telling me your underground railroad doesn't have kid tickets? You have to be this high to ride that ride?"

She glares at me and drops the singsong. "I was praying. It was an answered prayer. I had to shake the dust from my sandals and go, right then." It sounds rehearsed, a thing she has told herself over the years. She hasn't said it enough yet, though. Not even she believes it. But her voice gains conviction when she changes the subject, saying, "He's going to find you. He's going to come here and kill you in my house."

I shrug, unmoved. "It's good that you have hardwood floors, then. Easy cleanup."

She slams her fork down. "Stop it."

Now I understand why she's been mad at me all day. This is about Thom. She told me to do something, and I have blatantly not done it. The last time this happened, I was eight and she ordered me to clean my room. I chose to scrunch up in a blanket and reread *Charlotte's Web* instead, and when she came and saw I'd disobeyed her, I was grounded. I'm grounded now, too, in a way.

We finish our meal and go off to bed, reenshrouded in our separate, angry silences.

A second day passes, much the same, and then a third. Each night at dinner I play Beast to her Beauty, asking my single question, asking why she left me behind. She sticks with her story about being told in a vision to go at once, alone, and my dinners all stick in my craw.

By the morning of the fourth day, I've exhausted all my adrenaline. It's hard to stay angry when the sameness of every minute nibbles away at my resolve. My mother is waiting for a client at her table, and I am back in her store. I've practically memorized her limited inventory. I step to the blinds and stare out into the front yard.

Lilah is back. She's beside the gate, begging hands folded over the top of the fence, looking yearnfully toward my mother's place. I am so desperately bored that I think she might have the better spot.

"Come away from the window, Rose Mae," my mother says.

"Ivy," I toss over my shoulder. I do not move.

Lilah sees me, or at least my shape in the window. She straightens, craning forward. "Mirabelle!" she calls, plaintive and hopeless. "Mirabelle!"

I hear my mother get up from her table and come over. She's moving quickly, and when she comes up even with me, she grabs the cord and jerks her wooden blinds closed with a clack. We stand side by side, no view but the slats, and we both choose to stare at them rather than each other.

"You should go talk to her," I say.

"Why?" she asks, dry-voiced. "Do you no longer require the room?"

I make a slit through two of the blinds with my fingers. I see Parker has come out, trailing his pack of rowdy dogs. Gretel is among them, tripping along on his left heel. He's wearing a crumpled button-down shirt, extremely faded, with black cotton pants that flap around his ankles like pajama bottoms. The man should clearly not be allowed to dress himself. He's crossing the yard to talk to Lilah in that weird Shaggy-style walk, slumped down to be shorter, hands where she can see them.

"Come away from the window," my mother repeats.

I ask, "Doesn't he have a job?"

"Who?" my mother says. When I don't answer, she reaches to make a peeping slit between two blinds for herself. "Oh, yes. Parker teaches anthropology over at Berkeley City College. He keeps odd hours," she says. We watch Parker standing a good foot back from the fence, talking to Lilah, who is gesturing wildly and weeping.

My mother watches me watching, and then she says, "Why do you ask?" Her voice has sharpened.

"Just curious," I say. "He seems nice."

She laughs, but it is a hard sound, not at all amused. "No, Rose. Just no."

"Ivy," I say.

"When that man you married comes, he will eat Parker alive," she says. "From the feet on up."

"All I said was, he seems like a nice man," I say, and she says, almost running over my words:

"Exactly."

Parker leans earnestly toward Lilah. He must be repeating his offer to get her into a shelter because she shakes her head at him, vehement and angry.

"I've never really known one of those," I say in musing tones, mostly because my interest seems to bother her. "A nice man. I wonder what that's like."

"I'll thank you not to experiment on Parker. He lost his wife to breast cancer, and she was so young—still in her twenties. They were crazy about each other, too. It was a complete tragedy. He's had enough hard times without your mess."

Lilah is turning away, trailing disconsolately back up Belgria. Parker stays by the fence, calling after her.

"How long ago did she die?" I ask.

"A while," my mother says, cagey.

"A year?" No answer. "More than two years?" I ask. Nothing. "More than three?"

Parker turns away from the fence and walks back toward me, spine straight, sure-footed and easy. Shaggy-Doo is a costume, so familiar and well used that he can pull it on and shake it off between heartbeats. I'm intrigued now for real, not only because it bothers her.

"She died six years ago," my mother says, begrudging me the information. "But it could be six months or six decades and it wouldn't change *your* situation, Rose Mae."

"Ivy," I say automatically.

Parker is angling away from the porch stairs. It looks as if he's heading around to the backyard, with the dogs surging around his feet in a cheerful four-pack. He disappears from my line of sight.

"He wouldn't do you much good anyway. He's been celibate since Ginny died," my mother says, changing tacks. I make a piffling noise, frankly disbelieving, and she adds, "It's a euphemism, Rose Mae."

"Celibacy is a euphemism?" I ask, but then I get what she means. "You mean he's impotent?" I take her silence as confirmation. "How interesting, Mother mine, that you would know that."

"He is my good friend," she says, prim-voiced. "And he is not for you."

I turn away from the window and face her. "Who is he for, then, *Mirabelle?*" I ask. "Is he for you?"

My mother draws back, affronted. She turns away and stamps back toward her table, saying, "Don't be ridiculous," over her shoulder.

"I'm not. You two clearly get along, and he's not at all bad-looking," I say. "As for what's not working, they have pills for that these days. You could—"

"Rose Mae! Don't be vile," she says, hurling herself into her chair and glaring at me over the cards. "He's young enough to be my—" And then she stops. I feel the word she hasn't said like an X-Acto knife, slim and sharp, opening my gut.

A heated silence stretches in between us. I change the subject. "What happens if I leave? If I break your rule and step outside?"

"Don't test me," she says.

"I could go out in the yard, play fetch with Gretel."

"Do it," she says, the temper she's been low-boiling for days finally roiling and foaming over. "Hell, go out the front. Run after Lilah and tell her you're allowed outside though she was not. Hit her in the face with it, why don't you? Dance and holler. Call attention. Make it easy for that man who is coming here. Help him find you, so he can snap your neck like an eating chicken's."

She's so angry, she's shaking with it. I'm surprised at how much southern has come out in her speech. We stare at each other, and she's panting. My breath speeds up to match hers, and in this tense and ugly silence, her mellow doorbell chimes.

It's a hugely inappropriate noise. It startles her. We both look automatically to the other window and see the red glow of the sign seeping through the slats. She's left it on, and it has attracted a walk-in.

"Shall I get that for you?" I ask, as sugar-voiced as a flight attendant offering a blankie. I am at the front of the room by the store's display shelves, much closer than she is to the door. I step out and put my hand on the knob, mostly to prang her. But she draws herself upwards, setting her shoulders, saying, "No, Rose Mae," in the "thou shalt not" commanding tones of some risen minor prophet.

"For the love of Jesus Christ, Claire," I say, "can you not get that my name is Ivy?"

She takes a long stride toward me, not listening, intent on stopping me. I spin fast and swing open the door. Wide.

A pair of servicemen stand on the porch. They aren't in uniform, but they are young, with whitewalled hair. Navy or maybe marines. One is short and broad with a hard face shaped like a shovel, and when he sees me he whispers, "Hallelujah," through his teeth.

The other one is tall and skinny, and he hardly looks old enough to shave. He has milky skin and chocolate-colored puppy eyes that tilt down. He's swaying, as if his sea legs are telling him the porch is moving. They are sweating, both of them, and the potent smell of hops and tequila rises off their skins.

The shovel-faced one crowds the doorway, saying, "What's your name, honey?"

I lean back and say, "I think you have the wrong house."

The tall one smiles at me, too wide, his mouth shaping a leer that is almost comical. He crams in close behind his friend, filling the doorway. "We want to get our palms read."

I shake my head and say in quelling tones, "You boys do not want to get your palms read."

The one with the hard face thinks I'm being funny. He crowds in even closer and says, "You can tell *my* fortune, honey." He speaks directly to my breasts, as if he believes my nipples know the future.

The tall one smiles even wider, goofy drunk and harmless, but his friend muscles forward again, coming so close to me that I move back. He closes the space I make between us immediately, like it's a dance step, and now he is across the threshold. His friend follows, but it is not the friend who matters in this room. It is this short, broad fellow with his bull shoulders and thick neck, one hand reaching to cup his own crotch and give himself a squeeze, hot eyes on my waist and hips and breasts. I step back again, fast, almost stumbling as my heels hit the lowest stair. I step up on it to keep from landing on my back in front of him. The tall one pulls the front door shut.

My mother glides quickly across the room, inserting her small body into the space between me and the sailors. "Rose Mae. Go upstairs."

I back up another step, instantly obedient. I don't even correct her. I want to go. I'm afraid. It would be stupid not to be, but at the same time my fingers are tingling and adrenaline has been dumped into my veins and I am not bored now, oh no. Rose Mae Lolley only needs a little lead time. I keep backing up the stairs, and my eyes feel hot and gritty and alight, as if I have come on with a sudden fever. I keep my gaze and my feral smile on the short fella, promising him things, but maybe not the things he is expecting.

My mother is still between us, blocking the base of the stairs. She is small, like me. He looms over her and around her, but her words hold him more than her small presence. "Not so fast, sailor man. You have to pay to play. Come sit down." She glances over her shoulder to see I am not quite to the landing. "Rose. Go. Up."

I turn and run lightly the rest of the way into my room. Pawpy's gun is in the drawer of my bedside table. I snatch it up, the weight of it familiar and sweet in my hand. I slot bullets into the barrel, fast and slick, and then fit the barrel into its cradle with a satisfying snap.

I set the gun down long enough to pull off my boots. My sock feet whisper against the hardwood floor as I slip fast and quiet back to the landing.

I can hear my mother saying, ". . . two hundred dollars for the full read." It's a lot more than the price she quoted in the airport, but no one at the table is thinking about tarot readings. She is pretending to sell my sweet ass, while truly she is buying time. I know it's only a ploy, but I'm still offended that she doesn't charge more.

As I cross the landing, I hear the shovel-faced one say, "Me first, mama."

I hear the rustle of bills, and then my mother says, "Rose Mae will call when she's ready. Shall I turn the cards for you while we wait?"

The tall, milky one laughs, high and nervous, as I come creeping down the stairs. Shovel Face says, "Why not."

Halfway down, I can peer between the ceiling and the banister and see the two men sitting at the far end of the room at her reading table. Their backs are to me. My mother is across from them, eyes on the cards, shuffling. She has not lit her white sage candles. She is pale, and I can tell from the set of her mouth that she is more afraid than I am.

My mother says, "What's your name?"

"John Smith," says the hard case.

At the same time, the one who doesn't matter says, "Jamie."

I am four steps from the bottom now. I train my sights on the back of the hard one's head. My mother looks up from the cards and sees me over his shoulder. Her face flashes relief. She flips a card and says, "Well, John Smith, I've turned the nine of syphilis."

She flips another. "Now I've crossed it with the four of herpes. The cards suggest that you stop screwing whores."

"You bitch," Shovel Face says, and his chair scrapes back as he stands.

"I'm ready for you, John Smith," I say, sweet-voiced, and he wheels around to face me. He sees the gun, and when he looks into its round, black eyehole, it becomes all he can see. I am colors and vague shapes behind it. I could take my shirt off, and he would not address my prescient nipples now. The gun is the whole of me, and it has his complete attention.

I hear my mother say in a steady, even voice, "Jamie, who is Gloria?"

Jamie is staring at the gun, too, mouth open, eyes completely round, sitting with his hands resting on the table where I can see them. When my mother speaks, he blinks like he is waking up and says, "What?"

"Gloria," my mother says, steady and so calm. "Who is she?"

"My little sister?" Jamie says, confused.

"Does your baby sister want you out with 'John Smith'? Would she like to know you are paying to use broken young women in such an ugly way, catching their sad diseases?" My mother's voice is the voice of every mother, and Jamie can't look at her or even me. Not even the gun can keep his gaze off the floor.

Jamie mumbles, "How do you know her name?"

"I'm psychic, you moron," my mother says, cool, and then, "Now her phone number is forming . . . I see a seven. I see . . . a six? No. A nine."

Jamie gasps, but I speak only to the hard one: "I think it's time for you boys to go."

John Smith is still staring at the gun, but his mouth sets and he says, "Fine. Give us our money back, you bitches."

My mother starts to reach for it, but I smile and say, "She read the cards exactly right, honey. You got what you paid for."

My mother stills.

John Smith's initial fear is fading. Now he is calculating odds. He's measuring his brawn and his training against the space between his body and mine, his body's speed against my steady hands, wrapped around the old revolver. He hasn't a prayer, but he may well be doing the math wrong. He does not know Rose Mae Lolley.

"Or stay," I say in Rose Mae's voice, and cock the pistol. The shift and click of the metal draws out her pleased and creamy smile. "Please stay. I'd love for you to stay."

I am fervent, sincere, and John Smith is suddenly all done here.

They head to the door, Mr. Smith first and Jamie shuffling shamefaced after. I keep the high ground on the stairs, Pawpy's gun trained steady on John Smith's whitewalled head until they pass me and file outside. The door closes behind them, and my mother runs across the room to draw the dead bolt. Then the gun gets heavy and points itself down, aiming at the floor between my socks. My mother leans her face against the door, sides heaving. I uncock the revolver, and at the sound she whirls to face me.

"Are you stupid?" she says.

At the same time I say, "What was that?"

"That," she says, "is not uncommon. More than half the signs for readers are a front for whores. When *I* answer the door, johns know this is not a cathouse. But you, three buttons on your blouse open, your hair all mussed, you look like an ice cream. When I tell you to get upstairs before a reading, then Rose Mae, you get upstairs."

"Ivy," I say, but with no conviction.

My mother looks from my feet to the gun I've aimed between them to my eyes to the fever I can feel on my cheeks. My heartbeat booms away inside me like the drums of war.

"Ivy," my mother scoffs. "Look at you. You are only what you are, Rose Mae."

I scoff right back, "Then there must be only Lolley women in the room here, *Claire*."

"Don't miss my point," she says, her voice blade sharp. She stalks slowly toward me, coming up three stairs. She puts her hands over mine on the gun. I cling to it, and we freeze there. "Look at you," she says. "Look at you. Why is your husband still breathing, if you have all this fight in you?"

I shake my head. I have no answer. I tried to shoot him and I failed. Ro tried to live in peace with him and failed. Even now, if it was his head in the crosshairs instead of Mr. Smith's, my hands would not have been so steady. Even now, if he pulled his Thom-suit back on over the monster, showed up with flowers, said, "Ro, baby, come home . . ."

I would not go. But I would feel the tug.

My grip weakens as her hands get more insistent. I let her slide Pawpy's gun out of my fingers. She turns away, and I sink down to sit on the stairs.

"What the hell is wrong with you?" she asks the gun. There's no safety, so she breaks it expertly into its separate pieces.

"The pin broke," I say.

"I mean what's wrong with you, all you young women." She is pacing up and down her parlor, one chunk of gun in each of her waving, angry hands. "My friend's daughter, she cuts open her own skin to let the bad out. She's a child, barely in high school. What bad can she have in her? Half her little friends are starving themselves, or puking up all their food. It's the same thing, but the starvers say, 'Oh, I could never cut myself like that,' and the cutters say, 'I'd never marry a man who hit me,' but it's all the same thing. You are all killing your stupid, stupid selves."

I stay slumped on the stairs with no answer for her. I am so tired now. She is still ranting, her voice shaking with anger, as righteous as Ezekiel.

"My ten o'clock today? Bette? You saw her. She can't be more than twenty-five, and she's wider than most walls. She brought cookies with her, for me, she says, and sets the plate between us. She never took a whole cookie, but she sat there pinching bits off one cookie till it was gone, then another, pinch by pinch, until half the plate had been moused away.

"Then she points through the window, to Lilah mooning on the fence outside, and says, 'I don't understand how she can go back to him when he beats her. She might as well put a gun to her own head.' Meanwhile, Bette is so trapped and hemmed by all the fat on her that she can't breathe. She's killing herself, same as my friend's daughter with her razors. Same as Lilah." She pauses to point at me with one accusing finger, the rest of her hand wrapped around the barrel. "Same as you."

I stand up, grabbing the banister and hauling myself to my feet. "You are no different."

She snorts in rude denial. "I earned my new name, Rose."

"Please," I say. "Then how come you can't keep your eyes—or your hands—off that crumpled bit of scrap paper I brought over from Alabama?" I am gratified to see how immediately her eyes go to my daddy's note. "The one true princess of Zen, afraid to read a note."

"I am not afraid," she says, but now her righteous indignation has a crack in it.

The doorbell chimes again.

We freeze, then she makes a noise that's halfway between a laugh and a gasp and says, "That's just Lisa, my next appointment. I'll turn the sign off. You need to—"

"I know the drill," I say, and head upstairs to my room on shaking legs. I go inside, and the walls seem to have crept in closer to each other while I was downstairs. The furniture in its familiar configuration grates at me. I need to be someplace where there is more air. I turn around and around in my room, panting like Gretel.

I can't stay in here, because this room is full to the roof with the knowledge that my mother is right: I can say that I am Ivy, but I am only what I am. But I also cannot go outside. I feel it in the bones of me. Not because of her rules, or even because the two angry sailors may still be near; my mother's constant warnings must be getting to me. I can't go out, but I can't stand to be trapped in this room with myself just now.

There is a window over the writing desk. It looks out on a small piece of roof that hangs over the backyard. I go to it and flip the latch, and it rolls open easy at my touch. I snatch up Saint Lucy's candle and the rosary and the matches and step onto the chair. I get on my knees on top of the desk. There is no screen, and I crawl right out the open window onto the slope piece of roof that juts out under it.

I don't have much of a view. I can see a slice of Parker's backyard grass and the backside of the house behind this one. Still, I can breathe out here on the shingled slope, bathed equally in cool salt air and warm sunshine. I tilt my head up and look at the bright blue sky. I need to pray, and here I've found as good a shrine as any.

I put Saint Lucy down and light the wick, placing her in the corner where the gable offers shelter from the wind. I close my eyes and take up the beads.

I work my way around the rosary, trying not to think too hard on what it means that my mother is so right. New name or no, I have brought Rose Mae Lolley and Ro Grandee with me. I do not want to believe that they are in me, always. That they are me, always. That's a path of thought that leads me close to Thom, so it has to be a problem for tomorrow. I need to still my heart and stop my mind from racing. I pray all the way around before the ritual calms me enough to let me open my eyes.

Parker has come into the piece of his yard that I can see. He is centered on the lawn facing my direction with his arms up, palms facing out, and he is standing very still. He is stiller than I have ever seen a human being stand. Even my daddy, laying in wait in a deer blind, would twitch more than Parker. He is still wearing those floppy black pants that look like pajama bottoms, but he has taken off the shirt. He has a sprinkling of dark red-brown hair on his chest. He's pale all over, and his skin fits tightly over wiry muscle.

Finally his arms move, slowly. Then his whole body moves into a series of weird, slow poses that look like what might happen if kung fu and ballet had themselves a baby. He is fighting nothing, in slow motion. It's completely unhurried, but so controlled that after only a few minutes he is sweating. He stills and holds, then moves again, deliberate and fierce.

The third time he pauses, he holds for several minutes. I'm exhausted with the adrenaline hangover, worn out from worry, and it is incredibly pleasant to blank my mind and watch a male body move with such deliberate grace. It doesn't hurt a bit that the body in question has taut coils of muscle in the shoulders and a six-pack.

The dogs come streaming through the backyard. The big mutts run past Parker, brushing their friendly sides against his legs, but it is as if they do not exist. His gaze is turned inward, and his body moves, releasing measured and unhurried violence on monsters only he can see. Buck and Miss Moogle disappear from my line of sight, lapping the house, but Gretel pauses to watch Parker with her head tilted to a puzzled angle.

Cesar stops, too, but he's not interested in Parker. His ears perk up, going on yellow alert. He peers all around until he sees me on the roof. Then that tattling little shit goes right to red, cutting loose with a yappy string of warning barks.

Parker's concentration breaks. His hands drop and he follows Cesar's line of sight up to my rooftop perch. I lift one hand in a wave, busted. Parker shakes his head at me, chuckling, and I can see what he is thinking. He is trying to decide if I am rule breaking, if this counts as outside the house. Parker does not want me to end up another Lilah-at-the-gates. I want to explain, but I can't call down to him. Mirabelle will hear, and I do not want any more Mirabelle just now, thank you.

I turn and get on my hands and knees. I crawl my top half back through the window. I lie stomach down on the writing desk, butt humped over the sill, legs outside, and open the desk's shallow top drawer. I dig out a piece of the blue stationery and a pen and scrawl, "I came out here to pray." As I back through the window to the roof again, clutching my note, I also grab up a stone cat paperweight from the desk's top. I wrap the note around the cat to weight it, then toss it gently down in the yard. It's a testament to my goodwill toward all things canine that I don't aim at Cesar.

Cesar and Gret run to my note first and snuff at it, and Parker follows, more slowly. He reaches between the questing dog noses and picks up the packet. He opens it, but he looks at the cat, as if the note is wrapping paper.

He looks back up at me, puzzled. I shake my head and glare, frustrated with the silence. I blow out my candle and hold it up. I point at the note with my other hand. In the yard below, my good, dim Gret wanders away after Buck and Miss Moogle, still clueless that I am present. Clever Cesar stares up at me, more affronted than alarmed that I am on his roof, a place he knows good and well that people do not belong.

Parker gets it. He reads the note, then looks back to me, impassive. He hefts the stone cat in his other hand, as if weighing it. He holds up one finger in a "wait a sec" gesture, then he walks toward the house until he disappears from my sight.

I sit another minute, and he comes back out. He holds up a blue sphere about the size of a tennis ball. I spread my hands and he throws it lightly up in an arc toward the roof. It comes right to my hands as if I'd called it.

It *is* a tennis ball, dog-chewed into a disreputable state, wrapped up inside my rumpled piece of pale blue stationery. Under my note he has scribbled two words.

"*Me too.*"

I find I am smiling at him, a wide and foolish smile. Parker raises his eyebrows at me, asking a question. I understand what he is asking, and I feel suddenly shy. This is not something I have ever done with a man. With anyone, really, except my mother when I was very small. Even so, I nod, a shallow head bob that he clocks.

Parker walks to his place, and I take up my beads again. His gaze turns inward, and his arms come up and he turns slowly, punching deliberately out at nothing. I watch him as I click through the beads, the familiar words shaping themselves silently in my mouth.

We are praying together, each in our own way. His movements are still focused, but he is aware of me now. I am included. He is inside my circle, too, as I pray through the beads with every nerve I have attuned to him. Something like longing happens in my belly, and I am not sure what I am praying for now. Some freshness, maybe, a new start, a chance to go back in time, before Thom, and make some better choices.

This is the strangest date that I have ever been on.

When I finish my second circuit of the beads, the sun is going down. The temperature is dropping, drying Parker's sweat. He stops, replete, his arms hanging by his sides. I lift my hand and he lifts his in a silent good night. We hold there for a minute, looking at each other.

Nothing is solved. I don't know how to get free enough to be someone different. Even so, I feel comforted.

I turn and creep back inside, my mind blank. My mother has been in my room. She has seen me praying on my perch and gone away again. A plate is resting on the bedside table, and Gret lies on the foot of my bed with her ears cocked, all her attention on the food. Meat loaf, whipped potatoes, carrots, and a very large glass of red wine. I change for bed and share out bites of cooling supper with my dog. I do not share the wine. I drink the glass down to the dregs. It's early still, but I'm exhausted and the wine makes me warm and sluggish.

I climb in between the covers and I fall asleep. I sleep dreamlessly, sated, for hours, before I hear the sound. When it begins, I am dreaming of a sweet-faced, small brown cow. She is being led up a hill to a shed, and I cannot see the face of the man leading her. The noise she makes is fearful but resigned, a mourning noise, and her eyes are huge and brown with long lashes, very human. She knows where she is being led. She knows why the man's arms end in axes. She goes up the hill with him, lowing out her sorrow at her dreadful coming loss. Her feet thump into the earth, giving tempo as she moans a sound so grievous that it wakes me.

They are true sounds, the thump and wail, and they are coming from the parlor. The noise climbs up the stairs and gets into my bed with me as if the sound itself is sentient, a messenger to me, but speaking in a tongue I do not know. I sit up and blink, scrubbing at my face, disoriented. Gret lies tense beside my feet with her head lifted and her nose pointing toward the door.

The noise is so inhuman and unending that it takes me a solid ten seconds before I understand. There is no little cow. There is only one other living creature in this house.

This noise is pouring from my mother.

CHAPTER

16

I TURN ON the landing light outside my room and head down the stairs, an anxious Gret on my heels. My mother's sage candles are the only light in the room, except what pours down the stairs from the landing behind me. It takes a moment for my eyes to adjust to let me see my mother. She kneels beside her bookshelves, rocking herself to some inside rhythm as the terrible noise comes out of her. As she rocks forward, she dips her head so far between her knees that her forehead bangs the hardwood floor.

My mother's sound is awful and ongoing, as if she plans to push out every bit of moaning air she's ever swallowed and then not inhale, not ever again. I haven't heard a sound like this, so pained and betrayed, since I shot poor Gret up at Wildcat Bluff.

Gretel's ears cock forward, anxious and alert. She makes a houndy grumble, a sorrowing harmony weaving in and out of my mother's keening. My mother's head comes back down to the floor and she bangs it, hard enough to make that drumbeat noise.

"Momma?" I say.

Her sound cuts out abruptly, and she sits up, pulling in a gobbling breath. Gret goes quiet, too. My mother turns her head and looks up at me, and in the stairwell's light her eyes shine blood red. She's wept so hard that she's burst the tiny veins that lace her eyes.

Then her face crumples into fury, lids screwing shut, her mouth pulling open and down in a wide, stiff frown.

"Your first word was Daddy, Rose Mae," she says in a strangled voice. It sounds like my very name is choking her. I stop at the foot of the stairs, all the way across the room from where she kneels. My mother looks ready to bite. "Dada, more like. You couldn't say the y. You said it a thousand times a day. Even before you could talk, when you were a colicky, awful piece of screaming luggage, even then, he'd hang you over his forearm and walk and talk, and his very voice would soothe you." She's somewhere far ahead of me down a path of thought. I pass my hand over my face, trying to catch up. She asks, accusing, "Do you know what your second word was?"

My eyes are adjusting to the dimness in the center of the room. I see she is kneeling in a shower of white speckles, as if she has sprinkled herself with bridal rice.

"No," I say.

She brings her head down to the floor again, fast, bang. Then she sits back up and says, "Dog. Dog, dog, dog, dog, dog, every minute your father's fuckhead hound was in the room. I'm a cat person, did you know? I like *cats*. *You* were allergic." It's an accusation, irrational and furious. "You learned that fucking dog's name. Leroy. And cookie. And bird." Her voice goes up an octave, into a high-pitched, screaming parody of baby talk: "Birt! Birt! Then you learned to say no. That was your favorite word forever. That's still your fucking favorite word, I bet."

Her voice is raspy from the weeping, hard to understand, but now I've finally caught up to the conversation. "When did I learn to say Mama?"

"After no. After *cookie*, Rose Mae," she says, and the words are so bitter in her mouth that she rushes through to spit them all out. "After the goddamn dog's name." She scrubs at her eyes like an exhausted toddler. "Daddy's girl, always. You wanted *him*, riding around the house on his shoulders. Him dead drunk. I thought,

He'll fall and crack her little skull open, see how much she likes him then. You'd just laugh and laugh. Him reeling around in circles. He gave you a BB gun. You were three. Who gives a gun to a baby? Your daddy, that's who, and he never, never, never hit you. Never. He never did."

I stare at her, impassive. I am not going to lie to her.

"Tell me he never hit you," she demands. I say nothing. "He didn't," she insists. "Jack Daniel's had a good hold on him even before I fetched up pregnant, but it wasn't till after you came that I always, always got the shitty end of his stick. The hitting was my share."

"When you lived with us—," I start to say, but she interrupts.

"You got horsey rides."

I change tack but speak as if I am finishing the same thought. In fact, I am. "But then again you didn't live with us for very long."

The specks around her are not bridal rice. They are bits of shredded notepaper. The shelf space in front of Austen's books is empty. My mother has been kneeling and weeping and lowing like a thousand dying cattle in the remains of Daddy's note.

"Before I left—," she says, and stops.

I cross the room and squat down in the speckles, a good three feet away from her, out of her reach but where I can see her face. I say, calm and cold-voiced, "I don't remember a lot of that time, Claire. You talk like it was a family picnic for me. Sunshine days. I'll tell you what I do remember. I remember creeping under my bed, all the way to the back so I could press my spine against the wall. I could hear him going after you. I could hear you crying."

My mother is nodding. "Yes. Yes. He was a terrible husband. Terrible. But you loved your daddy."

I shake my head at her, incredulous. "Of course I did. I was eight. I loved him when I was nine, too, and he dislocated my shoulder. What other daddy did I have? I didn't even know there were other kinds."

She wants me to remember a shining father she has polished up in her memory. But I can't see him that way. It's like Saint Sebastian. I may have envisioned a kindly Tiggywiggle of a saint when I was little. Later I could only remember him through the film of my mother's abandonment, when he became a bloody mass of wounded, grinning flesh. I can only see my father through the lens of the decade I lived with him alone, after she walked and left me to him.

My mother scrapes up a handful of the shredded bits of note. She has torn at it until it is hardly more than paper molecules. She holds them out to me. "This was to you, not me. It was always you." Still I say nothing, and she throws the bits of paper at me. They catch in the air and then drift down in a cheery shower of confetti. Her arm drops and her hand is open to me, like she's pleading for something. A few bits of white cling to the palm.

"So what," I say. "So the note was to me? Does that mean you don't get to be the prom queen?"

She blinks, confused. "No, because . . ." She shakes her head, trying to clear it, and then says, "I need to know that when he tells you he's sorry for all those times he laid hands on you, he means after I was gone."

"Okay," I say. "If that makes it better for you, sure. You can have that."

Her breath comes out in a sigh, and she is nodding. Her right hand closes and comes up. She holds her fist against her heart. It's like I have pressed a gift into that hand, a shell or a pebble, and she's clutching it close to her now.

She leans in toward me, as if she is going to give me a present back. "You were always Daddy's girl, Rose. Even so, I swear to you, I swear to you, I thought about coming back for you a thousand times. But each time I'd imagine what you would choose. He was your first word. I came somewhere after dog." She opens her hand and swipes at her palm, cleaning the last bits of paper off it. They join the others spangling the carpet. She's calmed now, quite a bit. Something sentient has appeared behind her eyes again. She says,

"I thought the two of you might even do better with me gone. Him and me, we never should have been together. We worked on each other like poison, but he loved you. Even now, you're the one that mattered to him. The note made that crystal clear."

I can hear the sick pit of pure green envy in her voice. She left him more than twenty years ago, yet this still eats at her.

She'll never explain herself, but I finally know the thing I came across the country to learn. I have my answer, and it is simple and plain and ugly. It's nothing I ever could imagine when I was building soap opera plots featuring abductions, amnesia, and, most of all, her absolution. The truth is, she tried to stay. The time she marked off on her wall told me that. She left with close to nothing, perhaps because it was all she felt she deserved. But at the bottom of the mystery, there is only, ever this: She left me behind because she didn't quite love me enough.

I'm shocked to find I almost understand. I am her daughter, after all. We are very much alike. Other women, to me, have always been the competition. I try to imagine it, bringing a girl your man likes better than you into your own home, bringing her in with your own body. That is the only why there is.

I stand up, needing more space in between us. I go to her table, where her weathered cards are in a neat deck between the lit candles.

"When did you find me again?" I ask.

She stares after me, blinking, and it takes her a good thirty seconds to change tracks and find the answer. She sounds wrung out. "I hired a PI eight years ago. He found you waitressing in Catahoula, living with that mechanic."

"Steve-O," I say, and she waves the name away as unimportant. She is right. I pick up the deck and flip it over, spread it open in a fan.

"He took pictures. I thought you were with a man like that because I didn't leave soon enough. I thought you'd soaked it up from too many years of watching my marriage." Her voice breaks. "Then I wished, if anything, I'd left you sooner."

"That's comforting, Momma," I say. I don't know what any of these cards mean—swords and wands, wise horses, maidens in chains—but the art is lovely. Even the words at the bottom of some of the cards, strange words like "Temperance" and "The Hiero-phant," are written like calligraphy, with flourishes and scrolls and trumpets.

"I *did* love you, Rose," she says, repeating the first words she spray-painted on the car out at Cadillac Ranch. She isn't speak-ing in the past tense, to mean she does not love me now, as I once thought. She means she loved me even as she walked away.

I find the hanged man with his wolf-head helmet in the deck. I pick him up, examine him by candlelight. As I look at his placid face, his praying hands, I find I do believe her.

She did love me; she left me anyway. That one choice has shaped her life into this ruin. She's been flying across the country to spy on me for years now, never brave enough to speak to me. I wonder how many of my old haunts hold her aborted messages. I suspect she's left obscure directions for contacting the Saint Cecilias all over Amarillo, perhaps carved in the wood under my table at my favorite coffee shop or hidden in the graffiti-covered bathroom of the place Thom and I liked to go for wings and beer.

She hid the messages too well because she knew that if I went with the saints that helped her escape, she would never see me again. She told me that herself, that her underground railroad would never deliver me to any place or person at all connected to my past.

I set the hanged man to the side, faceup, and search the fanned deck for the burning tower. There she is, the abandoned girl forever waiting, framed by a window that already pours smoke. I lay it out beside the hanged man. My mother lives alone in a rented apart-ment with a guest room that must feel like a gaping hole in the center of her house. That room upstairs is my room, and it always has been, even while a chain of other young women slept there. She's tried for years now to fill it up with her sad Lilahs, and they have not been enough. The Lilahs, even the ones who got free, got divorced, got saved, they have all failed her. Even the ones who kept her rules have failed her, because none of them were me.

"I know you loved me, Momma." I do not add, *but not enough.* I do not have to add it. She knows her weakness already. Not loving me enough is the essential truth of her life. It's the thing that has broken her.

I have my answer, and it should be the textbook definition of unsatisfying. Even so, the inside quiet that I felt upstairs after praying with Parker is coming over me again. My mad is leaking out of me, slow but steady, like I've been punctured. Underneath, I find something that feels a lot like peace, and with it, a pragmatic understanding: I cannot stay here.

There is only one card missing from the reading that she gave me. I search through the deck and pull out the two of swords. That's the card I hold up to show her.

"No," she says at once. "You have to stay."

But the reason I could not leave the house earlier is in the room with us. She has said it over and over. She has known it all along.

I set the two of swords down in its place beside my other cards. I can tell my mother and myself that I am Ivy, but I cannot change myself to Ivy in Thom's mind. He doesn't even know I'm trying to change inside my own. That's why my mother was so angry to learn that Thom was still alive. She's seen enough bad men in her life and work to recognize the ruthlessness in my bad man. As long as Thom Grandee is alive, then he is coming. To Thom, I am always and forever his Ro, emphasis on his. I have betrayed him, and he cannot bear to leave me breathing.

My mother is shaking her head at me, an emphatic denial. I say, "I can't be anyplace or with anyone that has even a tenuous connection to my old life. I've left a trail. I found you with a library book, for the love of God. If I sit here and wait long enough, he'll find me and come to me at his time, on his terms. He'll kill me."

In the deck I find a picture of a girl with long dark hair in wind-swept loops. Gypsy hair. I pick it up. A strip of lace winds around her head, covering her eyes. She holds a slim sword in front of her, and she has an old-fashioned set of scales in her other hand.

She is readying to weigh my tarnished dime against my mother's reading, to weigh all the girls Claire Lolley saved against the one she left behind. Her scales will never come out even. Everyone in the room knows it, except perhaps my dog, watching me anxiously from the foot of the stairs.

I lay the fourth card down above my cards, and then I turn away from the table. I come closer to my mother and sit down on the love seat. Gretel trots across the room and jumps up on the cushion beside me. She presses close to me, trying to fit the whole of her walrus body into my lap. I push her shoulder, make her settle for laying her head across my thighs.

I scratch her ears, almost a reflex, and she nudges her shoulder up against my hip. The feel of the air in the room has her worried. It is still charged, but this is coming from my mother, not me. I came here with a thousand other questions, but almost none of them matter in the light of the one answer that I finally have.

I am almost finished here. Only one thing is lacking. I feel it as pins and needles at the center of my back, like an itch in that one place I can never quite reach to scratch. Daddy. I promised I would tell him when his note had been delivered. Now it has.

But it is more than that.

Punch buggy green, I think. Thom is coming. My father's car is one hell of a bread crumb, and it is parked a few blocks away. I hope the old Grandee Buick is already vivisected into untraceable parts, scattered over Alabama, but I need to know. Thom thinks my father is dead, but the name *Eugene Lolley* is printed plain in Fruiton's slim phone book for anyone who thinks to look for it.

I think I have always known that Daddy is my canary in the mine shaft. I have gotten what I came for here in California. Before I go, I need to know how far along Thom is on my trail, how much of a lead I have.

I go to get the cordless phone from the kitchen, pausing as I pass to blow out the sage candles. The burned smoke smell of extinguishing them overpowers the herbs. My mother watches me, sitting in her ruined heap. I bring the cordless phone back to the love seat, but Gretel has flopped around and spread herself out to fill the space. I perch on the armchair and dial my old friend 411.

The connection makes, and a woman asks in mechanical tones, "City and state, please?"

I say, "Fruiton, Alabama. Home number for Eugene Lolley." My mother's spine straightens, her shoulders tensing as the same neutral-voiced operator—it may be a recording—recites my father's number.

It's not quite four A.M. on the East Coast. Daddy should be home and sleeping. I dial.

I let the phone ring ten times, but he doesn't answer. I stand up and pace down to the store at the front of the room, my mother's eyes set on me as unblinking and cold as snake eyes. She sways like a snake, too, her top half rising up from her coiled legs, her arms wrapped tight around herself.

I let the phone ring on, twenty times, pacing back to my mother's reading table. Daddy still doesn't answer, and no machine picks up. I hit thirty rings. Then thirty-five. Forty.

I press the disconnect button, my brow furrowing. I saw my father barely over a week ago, and where the hell can he be at this time of the morning?

I call 411 and ask for Fruiton again, but this time the name I give is Bill Mantles, Daddy's neighbor across the street.

"Who is Bill Mantles?" my mother says. I ignore her, but Gret whines and sits up at the tension in her voice.

A woman answers the phone, but it's a grown-up, not Bunny. She sounds sleepy and displeased.

I say, "Is Bill there?" and then there is a distinctly female silence that has no sleepiness left in it and even more displeasure.

"Who is this?" the woman says.

"I'm a friend of Bill's. I—" I stop, because when I hear it out loud, I realize my father is also a "friend of Bill's."

"What friend?" she demands.

I try again. "I'm sorry to wake you, but this is important. Is Bill there?" It's a testament to what I've learned earlier this evening that I try not to sound bitchy.

"Do I know you, friend of Bill's?" the woman asks, and she's making no such effort.

I say, "We haven't met. Your neighbor across the street, Eugene Lolley? I'm his—" With my mother's gaze on me, I find I can't quite say what I am to him. I have not been his daughter for years now. I pause and inhale, and then I say, "My name is Rose Mae Lolley."

"Oh," she says, and then again. By the second "Oh," her voice has gone up an octave, high with urgency and nerves. "I'll get Bill." She sounds sorry for being sharp with me. Very sorry. Too sorry. I hear her saying, "Bill, honey, wake up . . . Bill?" Then she covers the phone with her hand or sets it down because all I can hear is a wordless murmur of anxious conversation.

I wait for Bill to come on. But I know already. I know it in the pit of me, and I stop pacing. I turn to my mother. She sees my face and rises, coming across the room to me. I feel a hollow ball of nausea curdling in my stomach even before Bill's voice says, "Rose Mae? I'm so sorry. I didn't know how to get in touch with you."

"How," I say. "Just tell me how."

"He got mugged," Bill says.

"Bullshit," I say. "That's not what you mean."

"Yes, it is, Rose Mae," Bill says, and his voice is very gentle, with the sweet undertones I remember him using every time he spoke to Bunny.

"What's happened?" my mother hisses at me.

I want to tell her, but I don't want to say a mugging. That's a lie, and the very word sounds silly. It is harmless words—giggle and clogging and pug dog—that are full of cheery g's. I want to tell her truer than that.

"My daddy got beat to death," I say for her, correcting Bill at the same time. My mother's body does a sudden half bend, sharp and shallow at the waist, but her face doesn't change. It looks like an invisible fist has punched her and she has eaten the blow, as stoic as a spartan wife. "Someone beat him until he died." I feel a scalding wetness on my cheeks, and I have to reach up with my free hand to feel that I am crying. Bill's pause is an affirmation.

Finally he says, "So you heard already. I'm so sorry. I couldn't believe it either." I don't answer. I'm gulping, trying to get air in, trying so hard not to throw up. My mother turns away to face her table. She is staring down at the four cards I have left faceup. Her shoulders begin to shake, and Bill talks on, filling up the silence. "I saw him earlier that same night, drinking down at Chico's." I know the place, I can see it. Ten blocks from his house, a one-room neighborhood bar with neon beer signs in the windows. "I tried to talk him into a ride home, but he was pretty drunk already and mad. I let him be. He had a good bit of cash on him, and I guess I wasn't the only one that noticed. He tried to walk home a couple of hours after I left. Someone— maybe a couple of someones—followed him from the bar. They rolled him too hard, you know? He hit his head on the curb and cracked his skull. He was a tough old guy, but they rolled him too hard."

Behind every word he says, I see the big hands of my husband. Not someone, it was Thom. Thom found Daddy, and Daddy is over now. My fault. I knew Thom would search Fruiton. I knew he would find my daddy and question him, but I should have realized Thom was too angry to save murder just for me in the sickest kind of fidelity. Under the wash of guilt, an ugly self-preserving part of me wonders what-all Daddy spilled under the persuasion of Thom's fists. What did he say before Tom helped the curb rise up and meet his head too hard? *Punch buggy green.*

"When?" I ask. My mother turns to look over her shoulder at me. Her body is still shaking, but her red eyes are desert dry.

"Two days ago," Bill says. "I identified the body, but you'll probably want to come here. There's things need doing—"

"Two days," I interrupt for my mother's benefit. She nods. "Bill, I can't talk anymore right now. Sorry." I hang up, and then I drop the phone and run ten steps into my mother's store and drop to my knees to throw up into a big bowl full of worry beads. When my stomach is empty, I turn and sit flat on my butt facing my mother, wiping at my mouth.

Thom Grandee was in Fruiton two days ago. He is close behind, much closer, much faster than I ever would have thought.

"We should call the police," I say, and my mother stares back at me, impassive. She has picked up the cards I laid out and is holding them in a fan. But which police? The ones in Amarillo? I could tell them they can help close a mugging case several states away, and all they have to do is take on one of the most influential families in the city. Call the cops in Fruiton? I'm not sure how to explain to them who I am and how I know an angry man in Texas rolled their drunk. Thom is no doubt already home and alibied five ways from Sunday by Joe and Charlotte and his middle brother, as loyal and ball-free as a neutered dog. I may only succeed in giving Thom a better bead on my location. "Should we call the police?" I ask.

"They never did me much good," my mother says. "I need to think." I look at her hand, pinching those cards so tight that her fingers are as white as fine china.

Upstairs, I hear my mother's bedroom clock chime one. We have come to the end of the witching hour, and I am wasting time. I have to go, and quickly.

But my mother moves first, walking quickly past me to the front door. Gret starts to climb down off the love seat, but I tell her, "Stay." I don't want my dog out in this dark night when Thom is coming. It's foggy out, and the wind pushes its way across the floor to touch me, misty and cold. It lifts my mother's layered skirts, swirling them around her calves. She looks more gyspy now than she ever did at the airport. More gypsy and less my mother.

"I'm sure we can fix this," she says, firm voiced, stuffing the cards into her skirt pocket. But my daddy is dead, and there is no we. Thom is coming, and there is no fixing.

She turns away from me and takes a deep breath, poised on her toes at the edge of the doorway like it is a diving board. Then she steps off, and she pulls the door closed behind her.

I stand up. I have to pack. I need to be a hundred miles up the coast of California and ready to swap cars by morning. I am at the foot of the stairs before it occurs to me to wonder what other trails of mine Thom might be tracking.

All at once, my heart skips a beat and I run back to the phone I abandoned on the floor and dive down to grab it, dialing a number that I know by heart.

Mrs. Fancy's machine picks up, and her soft voice says, "I can't get to the phone right now—"

I hang up. Mrs. Fancy has even less reason than my father to be out at this hour; book clubs and church committees do not meet pre-dawn.

I find I'm rocking back and forth. This is my fault. My father has taken a beating meant for me, and it killed him. If Thom has given another, mine by rights, to frail Mrs. Fancy . . . The thought does not bear finishing.

I dial Information again, thinking that my mother is going to have twenty bucks in 411 charges by the time I'm done. Then I almost laugh at the absurdity of worrying about my mother's phone bill, when Mrs. Fancy is not answering her phone and Thom Grandee is snaking his fast way up my still-warm trail, my father's blood on his fists, hungry to kill me.

Information gives me the number of her one son who lives locally. I dial Daren Fancy, and he picks up on ring four.

"Hello?" he says. One word, pointed into a sleepy, angry question.

"I'm sorry," I say, "this is Mrs. Fancy's friend. I haven't been able to get ahold of her, and I am very worried—"

He interrupts me, "No, no it's fine. She's fine. She's here."

I can breathe again. "She's there, with you?"

"Yes. Her house was broken into," he says. "She didn't feel safe staying there alone."

"Oh, that's wonderful," I say, and there is an awkward silence. "Not about the break-in, but that you have her, I mean." When I broke Mrs. Fancy's window to get my Pawpy's gun back, I may well have saved her life. I am babbling now. "That neighborhood is going to hell."

"No kidding," he says. "Two break-ins in a week."

My mouth is already shaping a fast good-bye, but at that I pause. "Two break-ins?"

"The first time they only broke a window. I suspect they got interrupted," he says, telling me about my own small crime. "But when they came back, they tore her whole house up. I guess her sugar bowl money wasn't enough. What did they expect, I wonder, a little old lady living on her husband's pension? They took up her knives and gutted her mattress, stabbed open every chair and sofa cushion, smashed her dishes, shredded all her clothes. She couldn't have stayed there even if I woulda let her."

Thom again, this time beating a house to death. I have to assume he has my notebook, all my notes. He has a name for the phantom other man, now. Jim Beverly. I am trying frantically to remember if I wrote down anything that would point him west, toward California. Into my shocked silence, Daren says, "Could you call back later? My mother is sleeping. We all are."

"Of course," I say, "I am so sorry. I am so sorry." I am apologizing for more than waking him, but he takes it at face value and hangs up.

I leave the phone on the floor and get up. I have to go. I have to go now.

I run upstairs and begin pulling my underthings out of the

dresser drawers and stuffing them pell-mell into my mother's old cloth bag. I am working quickly, both so I can go and to keep my brain from thinking about how my independent friend has lost her home and how I've helped kill my own daddy. I've killed the pony ride man I do not much remember, the son of a bitch who raised me hard, and that sad old sorry man I met a little more than a week ago. I've led Thom to them all.

I go to the closet and start tearing my clothes down off the hangers, but it is hard to see to pack; I must have started crying again without noticing. Gret is following me back and forth across the room, worried by the noises I am making.

As soon as I have most of my things stuffed inside the bag, I grab it up by the straps and go running downstairs. Gretel follows. Her leash is by the door, and I snatch it. Gretel's tail wags uncertainly. She knows something is bad wrong, but still, in her mind a walk is always a good thing.

I'm about to click the leash to her collar when I notice that the bag slung over my shoulder feels light. Too light.

It is missing Pawpy's gun. I cannot leave without that. Not with Thom's hot breath coming up behind me.

I shake my head, unable to remember where I put it. It was in my bedside table . . . I remember my mother peeling it out of my hands after the sailors left. I have no idea what she has done with it. I drop the bag to the floor with a thump and let the leash jangle down beside it.

I could tear her house down to its very foundations and not find it. I do not know my mother well enough to know her hiding places.

"Stay," I tell Gretel again.

I open the front door and stare out into the blackness beyond Parker's porch light. I can't sit here and wait like my good dog for her return. I step out onto the porch and close the door behind me.

I slip through the front gate and close and latch it behind me.

My mother can't be that far, but I have no idea what direction she may have taken. Perhaps she is only wandering her neighborhood, walking to clear her head. I head up the street, going from street-light to streetlight at a fast walk. I have the sidewalk to myself at this hour.

"Mirabelle," I call, walking. Then louder, "Mirabelle?" My pace picks up. "Mirabelle!"

Somewhere a window bangs open and a man yells, "Shut up!" I do not care. I call her name again and again, louder and louder. I am running now. I run all the way up one street, then turn and tear back down another. Somehow without noticing, I have changed words. Now I am yelling for my momma.

I have made this pilgrimage before. The first night she was gone, my daddy came home to find me at the kitchen table, waiting for my snack. We waited there for dinner, which never came.

I said, "Should we call the police?"

"She ain't missing," he said, "She's just gone."

Then my daddy quit waiting and started drinking instead. I waited, though, hours more, sitting in that ladder-back chair, wait-ing for my mother to come and put me to bed. I believed that if I got up and put myself to bed, then she would not come to do it, but if I waited, she would have to. The chair was hard, and I got so tired, and my daddy passed out on the sofa. I left the house and went looking for her, wandering up and down our street, calling her quietly so as not to wake my daddy. I called until I was cry-ing so desperately that I could only call by vowel, and "Momma" became long, shuddering o's and a's that sounded more like mourn-ing than hope.

It was close to dawn when I finally made my way home, hoarse and all wept out. I closed the front door softly behind me, and the click that latch made as it caught was an awful noise, final and heartless and mechanical. My daddy snored on the sofa; he'd never stirred or noticed I was gone.

I am calling her now, much louder. But I have left the houses behind me, and no one tells me to shut up or phones the cops. I am passing closed stores and offices, and I realize I have made my way to the library.

My mother is here. I see her across the street with her back to me. She is standing in the glow of the security light that hangs over the library's front entrance. She is talking on one of the pay phones that hangs in a bank of three near the door.

"Momma," I yell, and I run toward her. "Momma."

She turns to me, still talking into the phone. She holds up one finger in a "just a second" gesture as I sprint toward her. She turns and sets down the receiver as I come up the library's front steps. She nods at me, as if in pleasant greeting, and says, "I was on the phone, Rose Mae. Hush now. It's the middle of the night, and you really shouldn't be outside."

In the harshness of the security light, her bloodshot eyes look crimson and blind, but astonishingly calm. Not even the sight of me tearing down the street, hollering for her with my nose running and my cheeks striped black with wept-away mascara, has disturbed her.

I clutch her by the arms and say, "I have to get ahead of Thom. I have to go somewhere he won't expect, and then I have to lure him there. I have to set a trap somewhere and lure him there and kill him."

"Because that's gone so well for you already," my mother says with sarcasm so heavy that her mouth literally twists up with it.

"I let him kill my daddy," I say.

My mother puts her hands over my hands on her arms, deliberate and calm, and says, "You're going to rip yourself in half, Rose Mae. Calm down." She takes my hands off her and turns me toward the road. She puts one arm over my shoulder and starts walking, towing me with her out of the pool of the library's security light. "Done's done. I'm sorry about your father if you are, but his liver would have killed him in another fifteen minutes anyway." She shrugs, cold and pragmatic, as she walks me across the street.

"Where's my gun?" I say as she tows me along. "I need my gun."

My mother shakes her head, a decisive no. She uses her free hand to pull the thin sheaf of tarot cards out of her pocket. The hanged man is at the top of the stack, faceup.

"I was wrong, Rose Mae." She shakes the image of the hanged man. "This is a tricky card, and I read it wrong."

I stop dead. "Where is my got-damn gun?" I yell at her, invoking Daddy's favorite cuss.

"Shhhhh," she says, calm as a corpse. She starts dragging me forward again. "Look at you, crying for your father. You think you don't have at least that much mercy for your husband? You can have your gun if you want it. Go lay your trap, but you'll pause too long, and he'll kill you. If by some miracle you manage it? You won't come back from it. Believe me." I realize she is navigating back toward her house, the last place on earth I ever want to see. But my dog and my bag are there, and my gun is there, too, tucked away in some hidey-hole of hers. She turns her head to look at me directly. "I know what it is to do a thing you can't ever undo." She lets that sink into me. I look at her bloody eyes and see again what a broken thing she is.

I do not want to be her. I do not even want to be me.

"I don't know what to do," I say in a small voice.

She nods, turning to face forward again and picking up the pace. "Well, you can't run—not on your own. You'll leave a trail. And you cannot kill him. It'll ruin you. I think it will make you a woman you do not want to be."

"So what's left? I don't want to die," I tell her. "Thom is coming. I don't know what to do."

"You don't have to do anything," she says. We are turning back on Belgria Street, and she offers me a small, encouraging smile. "I finally fixed it. I did what I meant to do years ago, what I should have done the first time I came to Amarillo and saw what you'd married."

I sniffle, and my head is starting to ache. "I need my gun."

"You don't have to kill him, honey," my mother says, like she is soothing an overwrought toddler. As we pass under a streetlight, I see her face has gone smooth, and in spite of her bloodied eyes she looks at peace, a good ten years younger. "I came to the pay phone to call the Saint Cecilias. I couldn't call from the house—they have very strict rules about leaving a trail."

We are back at the house. She closes the front gate behind me, and it clangs like a prison gate. Even so, I let her tug me up the stairs, back inside to where my anxious dog is waiting by her leash.

Instantly, all the fucking blue closes in on me. This whole house. Blue kitchen, blue bathroom, blue parlor, her blue-green bedroom. Even my room is infested with it. I want to be someplace that is restful and painted white.

Even so, the sound of her voice, her firm hand on my arm, these things pull me up the stairs.

"It's all set, Rose Mae. The Saint Cecilias will come tomorrow night, around midnight. They will take you someplace safe. They will move you town to town by car, no public transportation. No trace. You can start fresh, and not even I will know where you are." Her voice quavers on that last sentence, and I see that it is costing her to give me up. Her calm face is so sad.

Perhaps this is justice, for her to give me up now, just when she has finally filled that gaping wound of a room she keeps upstairs. Her shrine has held its proper saint, and when I'm gone, it will be only a hole again. That is the word on the fourth card I laid out, the word written in curlicue letters below the gypsy-haired lady in the lace blindfold, clutching her sword and scales. Her word is "Justice."

"But what if Thom comes here?" I say. "He will find you and kill you, like he killed Daddy." We are back in my room again, and she presses one hand firmly on my shoulder, pushing me down to sit on the bed.

"No, he won't," she says. She sits beside me. Pats my hand. "Stop worrying, Rose. I am fixing this, I told you. Once you are safe away, I'll call the police. The ones in Fruiton, and in Amarillo, and here. I'll call the FBI and anyone else I can think of. I'll tell them about what your husband did to Eugene. At the very least, Thom will be questioned. I'll make sure he knows that I called, that you were already here, and are gone now. He won't be able to hurt me, because it will prove everything I've said. He'll probably get away with killing your daddy, but he won't be able to come after me."

I nod, my head aching. I say, "You called Saint Cecilia for me."

"Yes," she says. "Tough it out until midnight tomorrow, and Rose Mae Lolley will truly be gone. You will never have to worry about him finding you. You can live. You can live, and be made into someone new."

That sounds so beautiful to me. I want that. I want just that, so badly.

I let her put her arm around me. I am weak and suddenly so tired. I let her pull my head down on her shoulder and hold me. I am clay in her hands, ready to do whatever she says, to smash into whatever shape she makes of me.

CHAPTER

❧

17

IT'S PAST LUNCHTIME when I finally wake up. My gut is churning with anxiety, but the house feels empty. It is so quiet, I wonder if my mother has gone out again. Her bedroom door is firmly closed.

In the kitchen I find coffee prepped and a note that says, "I have a migraine. Canceled readings for today. Do not turn the sign on. Your ride comes tonight—Stay inside."

She's underlined the last two words. I nod as if she is present and expecting an answer. Under twelve hours, and I'll be out of Thom's reach. It feels like a race, but one in which I am my mother's passenger. It is a race that she is winning. Sherlock Holmes himself could not take make and model, maybe even a license plate, on a car that's parked legally all the way across the country and find me in three days. Especially since Daddy would have pointed Thom toward Vegas, where he believes his Claire is "playing cards."

I shy away from that path of thought. I do not want to think about the circumstances under which my father would have given Thom this information. I do not want to think about my part in it. I can't right now. I have to get through the next twelve hours, and at midnight everything will change. I don't know enough about what will happen to even imagine it. All I know is, I won't be here, I won't be me, and in almost every way, I'm fine with that.

In the front room, I hear Gret's one-footed scraping at the front door, asking to go out. I open it for her. Parker's dogs are out, too, but I call her firmly back to me as soon as she has done her business. I can't have her running the yard, perfectly visible, a three-legged beacon announcing to Thom that his Ro is in this house. As she swishes past my legs and comes inside, I see Parker opening the gate. His dogs surround him as he enters, leaping and wagging, so happy to see him. If Parker had been gone only five minutes, his three would still be palm fronding him through the front gate like he was Christ entering Jerusalem. Dogs are like that.

Miss Moogle puts her dirty feet right in the center of his belly, leaving muddy paw prints on his shirt. "Moogle! Be a lady," he says, but he's grinning at her and the hands that push her down are firm but gentle. He's one of the almosts, mucking up my every way.

Based on the clothes—khakis and a rumpled blazer—he's coming home from teaching an early morning class. His hair is out of its tail. It hangs to his shoulders, thick and dark, thin sunlight catching the red. I like how it looks around his bony Irish face.

I'm wearing flannel pajamas, and I'm barefoot with bed head and no makeup on, but even so I keep the door cracked open and smile at him.

Parker comes up onto the porch, bypassing his own door to walk toward mine. "Day six?" he says.

"Yep. Can't come out yet. But there's no rule that says you can't come in," I say. I am absurdly pleased that I brushed my teeth before I came downstairs.

He pauses, then says, "That's so."

I swing the door wide for him, saying, "There's coffee running."

"I'm more of a tea guy." I close the door behind him. He walks to the center of the room and pauses there, looking around. "Where's Mirabelle?"

"Out, I guess," I say, more for my benefit than his. I want to remember the feel of being alone in a house with a man like this. Maybe even with this man.

"Out?" he says. He sounds incredulous as he turns back around to face me. He is near the love seat, but he makes no move to sit down. No indication that he plans to stay for longer than a minute, but I want to keep him here. He's speeding time up with his very presence.

"I guess. Or upstairs in her room."

"Has to be," he says. "Have you ever actually seen Mirabelle go out?"

Last night, I think. I remember how she stood on the threshold, balanced with her toes even with the doorjamb, every molecule of her inside. Then she tilted forward and tipped herself out onto the porch like she was stepping off a cliff.

"Of course I have. I met her at an airport," I point out.

"Yeah." Parker nods, thoughtful. "She still leaves town a couple, three times a year. But she eats enough Ativan to soothe a whole pack of wild horses before she can get in the cab."

"She goes to the library," I say.

Parker shakes his head. "Not anymore. Has to be more than three years since she's gone there. There's this girl who works down at the branch who comes by a couple times a week and swaps out books for Mirabelle. Their book club even meets here."

"Groceries?" I say.

"Delivered. Last year I started bringing her mail in because she stopped crossing the lawn to go get it. The box kept overflowing."

I shrug. I find I am not terribly interested in my mother's possible agoraphobia. I don't want to talk about her at all. I have put my future squarely in her hands, and it disturbs me to realize how angry I still am with her under the numbness.

"Well, I guess I better . . ." Parker trails off, then he takes a step toward the door. I move to intercept him.

When we prayed together, me on my roof, him fighting nothing on his backyard lawn, it felt to me like a date. I think he felt it that way, too, but we never said good night. It's not like he could walk me to my window. Moreover, there will not be another chance. Tomorrow I'll be gone.

I've blocked him, and now I come in way too close for friendly morning conversation. He looks older at this distance; I can see the fine creases in the skin around his eyes. He is a little closer to thirty-five than thirty. I lift my hands up to touch his face. He holds still and lets me. I pull him down, rising up on tiptoe, and I kiss him.

He stands absolutely still for this, too, only his mouth moving with mine, as a yes. It's strange and static; it hardly feels like kissing. I'd never been with a man before who wasn't ready in some black underneath part to hurt me. A kiss with a dangerous fella makes its own fever, black and sweet. It is the goodest kind of dirty.

This, kissing Parker, is as edge-free and white as an egg. He smells like Ivory soap, and he tastes like mint toothpaste and cool water. It's a lot like drinking water, actually. Pleasant and quenching, nothing more.

I pull back and I look at him, and he looks back. His eyes are a very pale blue. His gaze is so calm that he seems almost placid, like now that this is out of the way, he might wander off and find himself a tasty cud to chew.

"That was nice," I say, stepping back. "I'm glad we did that." It's true; now I will regret him less.

He smiles at me, a strange smile I can't read. He says, "You're welcome."

"I'm welcome?" I say, quizzical, not sure how he means it. Maybe he means I'm welcome to kiss him again? Not likely. But this cryptic echo of my mother in the airport irks me. She told me I was welcome, and I hadn't thanked her, either.

"Yeah," he says. "You're welcome." His strange smile widens, and now I *can* read it: He's ticked.

"That was kindness? Charity work?" I say, ticked right back. "You're saying I should thank you?"

For a second, he seems mad enough to actually be considering my questions, but then he eases and says, "I don't mean that you should thank me. But, yeah, that was pretty much just for you." Now I'm on the verge of angry, and he isn't anymore. I'm not sure what he is. Not angry, not placid. "This is for me," he says.

He steps in close, moving slow so I have time to hit him or wheel away or say no, but I don't do any of these things. I like kissing when I'm angry. I let him tip my chin up, bend to me, and this time his arm wraps my waist and pulls my body in, bringing me close enough to feel his body's heat, even through his clothes. This time, I am not kissing Shaggy-Doo.

Again, it is utterly not dangerous, but even so, I lose a little breath. I have had wilder rides, but I begin to understand that I've been thirsty. I have been thirsty for so long, living in a dry and barren place, crawling along. He pulls me closer, up against him. I feel his body rising to me, and in response, a coiled feeling starts low in my hips. His hands slip down, cupping my ass and lifting me into him, and suddenly nothing is as sweet as this. When you've been in a desert, nothing is more basic and more necessary, nothing is better, than water.

I think this, and then the kiss gets slippery and really good, and I am not thinking at all. I tangle one hand in his thick hair. It's longer than mine. I slide my other hand between us to cup him and he is ready for me, hard and too long for my palm.

"No," he says into my mouth, and he steps back, three steps fast, until the backs of his legs meet the love seat and he sits down, fast and surprised. I am left standing there with my mouth open and one hand cupping the air where his not-at-all-impotent cock used to be, the other lifted high. Three strands of his hair have caught and pulled out, hanging from my raised fingers.

I drop my arms and find I am already so flushed that my embarrassment cannot redden me further.

"We're grown-ups, Parker," I say. This could have been a helluva send-off.

He points at me and says, "Married grown-up." He blows air out in a *whew* sound, then leans forward, his forearms resting on his knees. "This is not what I want from you. I'm sorry."

When he looks up at me, his eyes have gone so sad that it is difficult to stay angry or even feel ashamed. My mother, who apparently does not share my troubles with lying to women, told me he was impotent. She said that to make me leave him be when I would not believe that he was celibate. But it must be so; Parker has been celibate since his wife died. I feel like I've invaded some sacred space he's made. And what does it matter to me, really, if my mother's landlord has me on her reading table or kung fu dances the rest of his life away, his hands moving slowly through the air to touch nothing, like a monk? I won't be here, either way.

I say, as kindly as I can, "Do I remind you of her? Your wife?"

"Ginny? God, no. Not at all." I'm a little insulted, and it must show on my face, because he adds, "That's a good thing. I used to see a woman, and if she had two eyes, I would think, Ginny had two eyes."

"I understand," I say. "We don't have to talk about it. I apologize. I just want you to know, I think it would have been really good for me."

"Good for you. Yeah," he says. "Like a salad."

I laugh, startled. I come and sit down by him on the love seat. I leave a good ten safe inches of air in between us. "I didn't mean like a salad."

"Yeah, you did." He is chuckling, too, but I hear something serious behind his lightened tone. He turns to look at me before he says, "I don't want to be a salad again, Ivy."

That word *again* catches my attention. "You've been salad before?"

"Sure. You know how many girls—women—Mirabelle has filtered through that room? More than thirty since she started. Twenty-two since Ginny died. You're not the first neighbor lady to make a move on me."

"Oh, they all must have," I say in arch tones. "You're pretty irresistible."

"Don't be mean," he says, grinning. "More like five, maybe six, depending on what you'd call a pass. Two of them while my wife was still alive, which was . . . awkward. Ginny was really sweet about it. She felt sorry for them, and she knew I was her guy. The others happened long after Ginny. I wasn't thinking about dating. But I was missing the company of women, as they say."

And now I have to ask, "So why did you say no? To them, not me."

"Oh, I slept with them," he says. My eyebrows rise, and now I am thinking my mother is really quite a fine liar. He thinks I am reacting to him, because he's slightly on the defensive as he says, "Not all of 'em."

"How many?" I demand.

"Two. The first one, I wasn't attracted to her, and she was a wreck. Wanted to hurt her husband, I think, more than be with someone." He waves it away with one hand. "But then this blond girl, freckles, long legs. Funny and pretty and really, really crazy. It'd been more than two years. Hell, I'm not a saint. We were together for a week or so. Then she went back to her husband. I thought, I'm not doing that again."

"But you did," I say.

"Yeah," he says, rueful. "Have you looked at Lilah? It'd be hard to find a single man who wouldn't."

"Lilah," I say, but I'm not surprised. She was lovely, even weeping with half her face smashed in. It *would* take a saint to resist her if she came in close and said "please" with her thick black lashes all damp and matted up.

Parker says, "Just once. I think she wanted to see what it was like with a nice guy. Any nice guy. On my end, it felt like a sneeze. It only made me sad. It only made me miss my wife."

There could be something here, but after tonight, it will never be safe to cross my own old paths again. The best I can hope for is that kissing him has set my mouth for something sweeter down the line, even though it didn't work for Lilah. "Let's leave it," I say. "You're welcome and I'm welcome and we're both thanked."

I start to stand up, but he catches my hand and pulls me back down. The gap between us has closed by a couple of inches. "I'm not done. You want to test-drive a nice guy? Get divorced and then go find one. Decide if you like nice guys in general, but don't come kiss me unless you like me in particular.

"I'm lonely, Ivy. I like how you look, and I like how you do things I don't expect. If your marriage is over—when it's over, I'd like to sit up on the roof with you sometime. I don't want to start like this, with you in hiding, still married. I don't want to be your salad."

I nod at him, because it sounds nice, these things he is saying, like something I might want, too. It is time to stop talking about it. No sense in making leaving harder. No sense in making leaving hard in any way.

"It was a pretty good kiss, though, huh?" I say.

He grins. "It was a helluva good kiss."

"Pax," I say, and I stand up. This time he lets me.

"Pax," he answers back. He gets up, too, and walks to the door with Gret on his heels, gazing up at him all adoring, like a groupie.

He opens the door, and I say, "Bye, Parker." Gret and I watch him leave. It's a nice view.

After that, the day drags. Gretel smells my restlessness and asks to go out a hundred times. She doesn't understand why I keep calling her back in, and she follows so close on my pacing heels, whining and worried, that I finally shut her up in my room.

My mother does not appear. I suspect she does not want to say good-bye to me, and that suits me fine. When Saint Cecilia comes, I want my mother to open the door in silence and hand me over like a parcel. Nothing moist. No hugs.

I am repacked, all my clothes now neatly folded, my blue cloth bag by my bedroom door. About six, I make myself eat some toast and an orange. I hear my mother stirring in her room, so I go to mine. Gretel squirts out past me as I enter and trots downstairs. I go in and shut my door to spend my last hours curled in the reading chair finishing *The Bean Trees*. I can hear Gret and my mother rattling around downstairs.

She comes up at eleven-thirty. Gretel is following her, tags jingling. That's unprecedented.

She taps on the door as a courtesy before pushing it open. Her eyes are circled in brown shadows. She's carrying a mug of something hot. I can see steam rising. Gret stays beside her, her nose pointing at my mother's pocket. Also unprecedented.

My mother sees my raised eyebrows and says, "We've made friends."

"Really?" I ask, skeptical.

"No. But I put cheese in my pocket, and to a dog that's almost the same thing." She pulls out a cube of cheddar, and Gret takes it delicately from her fingers. I am smiling in spite of myself at this concession. It's the kind of good-bye gesture I can stomach.

"Did you eat?" she asks, and I nod. "Good, that'll help. How are your sea legs?"

"My what?" I ask.

"I think you're going up or down the coast on someone's boat," she says. "The Saint Cecilia didn't tell me that, of course, but she suggested you take Dramamine." She comes over and hands me the mug. It smells like chamomile and honey. She pulls a white bottle of drugstore motion sickness pills out of her cheese pocket and shakes two into her palm.

I nod and uncurl from the chair. I sit up straight to take the pills, washing them down with a sip of the hot tea. Even with the honey, I don't care for it. I set the mug beside me on the table.

"May I wait with you?" she asks in formal tones. I nod, and she sits on the bed. She must be out of cheese, because Gretel does not join her. Instead she goes and lies down on the area rug in front of the dresser.

The minutes tick past in uneasy silence. Finally I say, "Want me to strip the bed?"

"Why?" she asks.

"Fresh linens," I say. "For the next girl."

"Heh," she says. I am not sure if the noise is a snort or a laugh, but either way, it is a no. "Do you really think, Rose Mae, that there will ever be a next girl?"

I don't know how to answer that.

"I can't stay," I say. She says nothing, and I say with more emphasis, "You're the one who told me all along that he is coming. I have to go."

"We've covered this," she says, her tone brisk, almost bored. But she has such haunted, awful eyes. They seem to have grown two sizes larger in her face.

I think, *This is the only parent I have left alive now*, and it makes me sick and dizzy to think that, so I stop. I want to ask her to leave, but it is right for her to be here, for her to give me away. If we'd had a good family, the kind I've read about in novels, she would have given me away eventually. I would have had a sober daddy to stand beside her in a chapel and hand me to a better man than Thom Grandee. When the priest asked, "Who gives this woman?" he would have said, "Her mother and I."

We were never them. But she's called Saint Cecilia for me. She has given my dog a cube of cheese. She seems to understand I will not stand for any sort of tearstained, loving parting, so she made me tea.

I pick it up and drink it, as a gift to her, the best I have to give back. It is too hot to be swallowed this quickly. It scalds my throat, and I remember Thom Grandee on the night we met, drinking hot chocolate and my spittle, taking me in. My throat closes and I stop. I set down the mostly empty mug.

My mother and I sit in our separate spots. I feel the tick of each second like a heartbeat. I am listening for the doorbell. I still feel a little dizzy. I should have eaten more. My mother stands abruptly, dizzying me further. I hear the clock in her room, chiming midnight for the glass animals. Saint Cecilia is late.

"Are you all right, Rose Mae?" my mother asks. Her voice sounds very distant.

"I don't know," I say.

"I think you might be having an allergic reaction," she says. "Have you ever taken Dramamine before?"

I shake my head and the room swims slightly, like it is full of water that needs to slosh the furniture around to catch up to my head shakes.

"You'd better have some Benadryl," she says. She comes to me, and now she holds out a pink pill. I take it with the last inch of the cooling tea. The dregs are bitter. I drink them anyway.

My mother takes the mug from my heavy fingers. She sits on the bed, and a minute passes, or maybe it is longer. Time has changed. I can't tell how long I've sat since the pink pill. Now I am looking at my dog. My dog is rosy. My dog glows with holy goodness. Her goodness is a light in her that outbrights the lamp.

"You are a good dog," I say, and I hear how my voice slurs and catches on the vowels. My bright dog stays snoring heavily on the rug. "Gret," I call. Nothing. "Gretel? Good dog? Big fat? Dogly?" I say. She snores on, though all of her names have now been called.

My eyes are made of lead. I can feel them sinking backwards down into my skull as I turn them on my mother.

She watches me with dead-eyed, clinical interest.

I stand up, too, and the floor tilts under me like the floor of a boat, but I know now there is no boat.

I call, "Momma," as if she is very far away. She teleports to stand beside me, holding me up, and the skin of her on my skin is cool and smooth.

"You gave my dog cheese," I accuse her. I try to say, "Unprecedented," but it is too many syllables, and my tongue gets tangled up in them. The doorbell is silent, and I say, "You didn't call in Saint Cecilia."

"Of course not, baby," my mother says.

She lowers me down onto my back on the wood floor. It feels as slick and cool as her inhuman flesh. I stick to it. I can't get up.

"Gret," I call, but Gret snores on.

I should have realized. I should have understood. I was close to realizing today. I try to say, "Parker's dick works fine, and you are a fantastic liar." I'm not sure how much of that she understands. It's like a long slur of mumbled vowels.

"Sleep now, baby. You know that I can't let you leave."

My mother looms down and puts her glass hands on me. She is bending me. I am folded on my side into an S-shape on the hard-wood floor, and she lies down by me and slips her shoes off. She turns her feet to me. I am so waterlogged and heavy that I cannot move away from her feet.

The feet push at me, moving me along the floor, toward the bed. I slide along the slick wood. The world turns sideways for me as I move, so now I feel that I am sliding down a wall. The crack under the bed opens below me. It is a hole in the world, and she will bury me there and trap me so I can never leave. I must stay like a plug and fill this hole of a room. Her feet push me down. The room is a pit trap, just as Saint Sebastian showed me, but it is not Thom Grandee sitting at the lip of it, closing me in. It is my mother.

The crack of light shining from the top is blocked then. My mother's inexorable feet are pushing my drugged dog down into the pit on top of me, like a hairy lid.

Gretel eclipses the lamplight. It is so dark that I do not know if my eyes are closed or open. I don't know anything at all.

A long gray time later, I come to understand that I am not in any hole. I am five years old. I am under a bed, my bed. My spine presses against the wall. I smell hound and hear a doggish rumbled breathing. Leroy has crept down under with me. We are hiding. I hear my daddy, and he is very, very angry. He has a voice like a big storm.

Under his voice, I hear my mother. Her voice is angry, a hiss, goading him. I wait for the sounds that will come, although I do not want to hear them. That thunderous boom of his voice will stop, and when it does his hands will talk for him, talk to her flesh in hard tones while I hide here. In the morning she will move very, very slowly as she makes my eggs. He might take her face away again, leave her with a monster face, purple-black and almost eyeless. Then we won't go out. He'll bring home groceries to say sorry, and she will creep slow around the kitchen to make the groceries into dinner.

"Ivy," Saint Cecilia calls.

"Shhh," I tell her. I am five, and we must be very quiet now. My mother is a fantastic liar, and Saint Cecilia doesn't know my true name. Saint Cecilia will not bring me to a boat.

"Rose Mae," Saint Sebastian calls. It is harder to ignore him. He made me win the race. I wrap my arms around myself. I can feel the softness of my own breasts, full for my small frame; my spine may be against the wall, but Saint Sebastian and my breasts do not believe that I am five. I have not been five for a long time.

"Rose Mae," he says again, and my name reminds me who I am. I do not hide under beds with dogs and cry and hope someone will come and make it stop. I am all grown now, and I will make my daddy stop. It is only fair that he should stop now that he is dead.

I push with weak hands at my dog, and I can't move her. My Gretel is a fat, wide wall.

"This way . . ." Sebastian's voice sounds somewhere near the top of my head. I crane my neck back and see there is a crack of gray light at the bed's foot. It is the light of a foggy morning. I creep longwise, leaving Gret where she snores, until I am out from under the bed's end by the door. I stand up, but the floor is so tilty that I have to lean on the wall. Now the silver morning air seems blinding bright, and the air is full of prisms.

Downstairs, Daddy is so angry, and how he can be angry when the light is this pretty is a mystery. I creep along the wall like a

clever little creepy thing, trying to walk soft in Ivy's clompy boots.
I will make him stop before he hits her. I have left my gun in Mrs.
Fancy's shoebox, but I can tell him no, because I am Daddy's favorite. My mother told me so, and I think this may be true, though
God and Saint Sebastian know my mother is an excellent liar. Even
so, I will stop him with my giant head that is hard and weighs a
thousand pounds. I tote it like a great and wobbling weapon on my
Silly Putty neck. I grab the banister and hand-crawl myself down
the steps, stair by slippy stair. At the bottom, the closed front door
ripples in its wriggling frame.

I come down full of mighty, like I came down when there were
bad sailors. At the bottom, I grab the banister post to turn myself
away from the front door to look at the back of the room where my
mother is standing. Her smile is smug and goady as she leans with
her butt against the edge of her reading table. He is loomed up over
her, taller than I ever remember him being.

His hair is bright and yellow like wheat.

This is not my daddy.

This is not the sailor.

I hold myself up with the banister post. I know this man. My
mother sees me, and her smug face changes to despairing, and her
mouth is shaping words—"No! God, no!"—and the man who is
not sailors or my daddy turns, and he is Thom and his dead eyes
kindle to see me there. He is Thom come to kill me, and he smiles
his wide bright monster smile with his teeth so white, and he says,
"There's my girl!"

He puts one big palm on my mother's chest without turning
and he pushes her, hard, so that she falls and flips back over the
table and disappears. I am alone with him. He is walking toward
me, his big hands empty and flexing at his sides. I spin around,
and the room keeps spinning as I open the front door and stumble
through it, out onto the porch, which is tipping and tilting like a
fun-house floor.

The sunlight slaps my eyes. Lilah stands by the gate, hands

kneading the fence top. When she sees me, her wide mouth stretches to make an O.

"Run," I say to her. The word is a roaring in my head, but it comes out barely a whisper. She stands still, making her O mouth, and I can't run, either.

I tumble straight off the porch and fall into a loamy flower bed, crushing the dahlias. I crawl away as fast as I can. It is early morning, and Lilah has a host of fresh new bruises and wide eyes, round to match her mouth, and I know she must see Thom behind me.

I flip onto my back to see how close he is. He is standing at the edge of the porch, fifty times taller than he has ever been before. I crab backwards.

"She called you," I say to him. "My got-damn mother told you where I was."

He nods. He is done yelling. His face is restful now and set because here I am in front of him, too weak to do more than keep creeping backwards. My head hits the fence and I am far down from the gate and I can't make my legs stand up and take me through it anyway.

"Both your parents have been very helpful," he says, smiling his dead smile. His big hands flex, and he jumps lightly down onto the ruined flowers I tore up with my crawling. He says, "Let's finish this, hey, Ro?"

"I am calling the police!" screams Lilah, standing phoneless and unmoving behind me at the fence. He doesn't even glance at her. She does not matter. Nothing matters to him but that I am here in front of him, and his big hands fold and unfold and he steps out of the flower bed and crosses half the small space in between us in only two big steps.

A great calm takes me. I see that this is finished now. We are about to be finished. Only seconds stand between us. There is only one thing that I need to know.

"The card," I say, and he pauses, as if he wants to hear the last words I will say to him. "The one that fell faceup in the airport. I guessed right, didn't I? It was Justice."

"I don't even know what that means, babe," Thom says, stepping toward me once again. His open hands come toward my throat, but I wasn't asking him.

I was asking my mother, standing behind him with Pawpy's .45 pointing right up at the base of his skull.

"Yes," my mother says, and pulls the trigger.

I see Thom's face go away, his forehead, that Roman nose I always liked, the whole top of his face folds open like a bright flower. I am washed in red before my eyes can close, before I even hear the boom, before Lilah begins her long, unceasing screams.

I crawl sideways, three feet away, before I dare look. He has landed mercifully, mercifully, on his belly. The hole in the wheat-bright back of his head is small, almost tidy. Lilah is still screaming, loud and strident, and now her scream is words, and the words are, "No, Mirabelle! No, Mirabelle, no!" Her face is speckled in bright crimson, and under her cries I hear the rising sound of sirens coming.

The porch fills up with nervous dogs, all milling. Cesar adds in barking, so the yard is a cacophony of ugly sounds. I lean forward, crawl a few feet to get my mouth closer to Thom's ear.

"Baby?" I say. "Baby?"

There is no answer. There is no Thom.

"Shut up, Lilah," my mother says, and then more harshly, "Shut up, dog!" Lilah obeys, but there is no stopping Cesar. I look at my mother because it's better than looking at Thom. A thousand times better. My mother says to me, over Cesar's noise, "I couldn't have you leaving, Rose Mae."

"Now you'll have to leave," I say.

"Oh, that's all right, then," she says. "I'm used to that."

Sirens and running feet and the endless yap of Cesar are breaking the air. Neighbors are appearing in their bathrobes, coming to stand in shocked clusters in the street.

I hear running feet behind me, and a man and then a woman come to the gate and yell words. The man says, "Put it down." And the woman says, to me, I think, "Ma'am? . . . Ma'am? Are you shot?"

My mother has Pawpy's old gun pointed down between her feet, threatening only the flower bed I've ruined. I see one of Thom's big boot prints in the center of the churned earth.

"It's fine," my mother says to the police behind me. "I'm finished."

She sets Pawpy's gun down carefully on the porch edge, and the man cop comes running through the gate to grab her and turn her and chain her bad hands.

The woman kneels beside me. "Is any of this your blood?" she asks. She is searching my body.

"I need to go to the hospital," I say.

She says, more frantically, "Is this your blood?"

"I think my mother roofied me," I say.

The woman cop grabs my shoulders, says insistently, "Is any of this blood yours?"

I lift my hand to touch my face in wonder, and it comes away smeared in red.

"No," I tell her. "I think I lived."

Nobody is more surprised than me.

EPILOGUE

✐

I STEP OFF THE BART train and hear the doors swish shut behind me. I've come to understand the train system here, very quickly. It's easier to take them than to risk losing the parking place I finally scored for the Bug on Belgria Street. I walk back toward my mother's house in the fading Cali sunshine. The salt air is getting chilly on my bare arms and my toes. Ivy's boots have been taken away. They are in separate plastic bags in an evidence locker somewhere downtown. I've bought myself a pair of walking sandals.

I see the "bull daggahhh!" shouter coming down the road toward me, his wild braids sticking up in a haggle from his head wrap. He is a local fixture, and I have come to feel a strange affection for him.

"Hey, Walter," I call to him. He grunts, but he has no message for me today. As I pass, he stops and unzips, turning to pee in Mrs. Delgado's rosebushes. I don't so much as blink. The Berkeley attitude seems to be that everyone has to pee somewhere, and I am going native.

Perhaps he is leaving a message for Gretel in the only language she can read. Later I'll come out walking with her, and I'll pack a soft lunch—peanut-butter sandwich, some fudge, a ripe banana—in case he is still around.

I reach the fence around my mother's house. All along the outside edge of it there are bunches of flowers, six or seven of them, in various states of decay. It's like a shrine where someone died, but I don't think they are for Thom. I find them there a couple of mornings a week. I leave them be until they are unquestionably dead, then clear them to make room for the new ones.

Parker is sitting on the porch steps, swamped in dogs. He waves as I come in the gate, and all four come galloping to greet me, my own Gret leading the charge. I wade through them, patting heads and scratching ears. Even Cesar has decided to be glad to see me. I ease myself down and sit on the other side of the stairs. The dogs station themselves between us, like a herd of furry chaperones.

When I was in the hospital, Parker was my first and only visitor. I fell asleep in the ambulance, my mother's potent antianxiety and sleeping meds still in my system, but he was by my bed with field daisies and a worried face when I woke up.

"So it's Rose," he said. "Not Ivy, huh?"

"They're both plants," I told him, yawning. "But I'm a flower, as it turns out. Next time, you should bring me candy."

He grinned at me, an easy upturn of his lips, and I smiled back at him and thought, *Not now. Not even soon. But there is going to be a next time.* I was glad to learn he'd missed seeing the carnage in his yard. By the time he got home from his job, it was down to yellow tape, some stains, and a tech in a jumpsuit who told him what had happened and where to find me.

"How is she?" he asks me now.

"Good," I say. "Jail is not a bad place for an agoraphobic. Where's she gonna go, right?"

It took a long time, almost a week, before they'd let me come sit in a plastic chair and see my mother through a wall of glass. She told her lawyer not to bother asking for bail.

"Did you tell her I'm going to come see her on Wednesday?"

I nod. "We met with her lawyer. He's still hammering out details with the DA, but he told us where he thinks they'll end up. She'll take the deal."

"Second degree," he says, and whistles out between his teeth. "That's a lot of years."

I shrug. My mother has left me again, but we are both fine with it. She seems to think that we are even. Me, I have a different take.

I tell Parker, "She doesn't care about the time, if the DA will agree to send her to a jail that's close enough for her friends and me to visit. Neither side wants to go to trial. A case like this, when the deceased is . . . not the world's best citizen, the jury could spook and let her go. On our side, we don't want them to put first degree on the menu. Juries are crazy."

"I don't think they could get first," Parker says.

I shake my head, less certain. They found me on the lawn, after all, newly baptized in my husband's blood. Three neighbors saw my mother gun him down execution style, putting one through the back of the head. More came running when they heard the shot. Only Lilah, that loyal little liar-pants, was close enough to see he was an imminent threat, and she oversold it. The Thom she invented was screaming that he'd come to kill me, slashing at the air with a mysterious vanishing knife.

My medical records have helped, my mother's lawyer told me. My old nemesis, that yogurt-breathed nurse from the Amarillo ER, was beyond delighted to give a statement. But Thom was unarmed and only walking slowly toward me, according to the neighbors. My mother did not call a warning or ask him to stop. Not even Lilah thought to invent that.

Most damning of all, some vigorous cop or another checked phone records. He found the late-night call to Thom's home made from the West Branch Berkeley library's outside pay phone. There was a quarter in the change case with my mother's perfect thumbprint on it. The DA seems to think that proves premeditation, and a jury might believe it. It's not a risk her lawyer cares to take. Not in a death penalty state.

The DA does not know that it was never my mother's plan to

kill Thom Grandee. Her own lawyer doesn't know it. Her silence on the subject tells me she believes that I don't know it, either.

But I've seen through her. If my mother planned to kill him, Thom Grandee would have died before I ever heard them fighting. My mother called 911 with the cordless phone. She had the connection open, the phone hidden on the chair seat under the reading table, before he even walked into her house.

My mother planned a murder all right, but not my husband's. Killing Thom was useless to her. If he was dead, there was still no guarantee that I would stay. The only murder my mother ever planned was her own.

Her lawyer played the 911 tape for me. It's pretty clear to me that she is goading him. She's telling him I'm being hidden by the Saint Cecilias, saying in loud, smug tones that they took me away on a private boat and he'll never find me. She is careful to clearly state his whole name for the 911 operator several times, even once calling him "Thom Grandee of Amarillo, Texas." She's identifying her killer, right before the fact, in case he leaves before the police arrive to catch him with her body. The 911 tape ends as I come down the stairs. She landed on the phone and accidentally broke the connection when Thom shoved her over the table.

Her plan is clear to me, though: Thom goes to jail forever. I am free to walk. She is free to never see me leaving.

Her only mistake was in underestimating his travel time. She should have given me more Ativan. I woke up and interrupted before he had time to kill her.

Parker waves his hand in front of my face, saying, "Where'd you go?"

I blink and shake my head. "I was just thinking," I say. "I want to put a lemon tree in the backyard."

He laughs. "You can try. But I doubt it will survive the amount of dog pee it is sure to be subjected to."

My mother's lawyer finds it strange that I am still living here in this apartment, after what I witnessed. He doesn't understand that I've shared space with living violence for most of my years on this earth. I sleep just fine with the ghost of it in the yard. Besides, this is the least I can give her, a mental picture of me living in her house, filling up that empty hole of a room.

Really, though, I've moved over into hers. It's bigger and it has a ceiling fan, and she won't be needing it for years and years and years. Next week, I plan to cover the furniture and paint the walls a thick, rich butter color. I'll stay, but I'm done with all her blue.

As long as she can think I'm tucked into the twin bed she placed just so to hold me, she will sleep perfectly fine in prison. It's a gift I am giving her in secret, because I do not think now that we are even. I think the scales the blindfolded gypsy holds have tilted. I may owe her a little something.

"Want to go get some dinner?" Parker asks.

"Tomorrow?" I say. "I have something to do tonight."

"Okay," Parker says. "I should grade papers anyway." He starts to get up.

"Do me a favor?" I ask.

"Sure," he says.

"Leave the porch light off?" He gives me a long, level stare. "And maybe lock the dog door once your crew is in?"

"Sure," he says again.

I sit out on the porch, and it gets cooler and darker. When I go in to get a jacket, I bring Gretel inside for the night. I want the yard dog-free for when Lilah comes to bring the flowers.

Parker steps back out onto the porch a couple of hours into my vigil, bearing a flat bowl of brown rice and shrimp and stir-fried vegetables. He sits down beside me and says, "Can I wait with you?"

"I'd like that." He's figured out my mission. I hope he doesn't mind it. I ask him, straight up, "Are you okay with this? It is your house, and considering the history . . ."

"I think it's great," he says, and hands me the bowl. He's put chopsticks in, the optimist. The man's still in denial that I'm from

Ala-got-damn-bama. I pass them to him with an arched brow, and he pulls an emergency backup fork out of his jacket pocket. I find myself gobbling—the man can cook—then set the bowl aside. We wait quietly together. We're getting good at it. It's a comfortable thing, all the waiting we've been doing. I feel a good, expectant happiness moving up behind it. It won't go on much longer, I don't think.

It's after midnight when we finally hear her creeping down the street. Parker stays still, but I stand and step silently across the yard to meet her at the gate.

Lilah steps into the light from one of Belgria's bright street-lamps. She stands at the fence like Moses gazing into the Promised Land. Her left arm is in a sling. Her right arm is full of tulips.

She hears me coming out of the dark yard when I am a few feet away. We have not seen each other since the shooting.

"Hi," I say. I am on my side of the fence, but the streetlamp spills enough light into the yard for her to see me.

She looks flushed, embarrassed.

"You're her daughter, they told me," she says. "Her real one."

"Yeah," I say. "They tell me that, too."

Lilah nods. "I shoulda known. You look like her around the mouth." She leans down to set her tulips by the fence.

"I told her about the flowers, Lilah. Tulips are one of her favorites." I have no idea if that's true, but the information seems to please her, and I'm pleased, too. I'm learning how to lie to women. Or girls, anyway. She can't be more than twenty-three or -four. Her jawline still has a baby softness to it. "It's chilly out, and your house is not a good place to be living. You should come inside."

Her gaze flicks back to me, her eyes impassive. "I'm not allowed back in."

"Mirabelle's not home," I say. "She's not coming home. Not anytime soon."

"I know." Lilah's eyes fill up with tears. "She made me soup. No one has ever been nice to me like she was. I blew my chance, but she was so nice to me that I never thought she wouldn't give me another."

I nod. "Yes, you blew it. With her. You haven't blown it with me." I can't read her expression. "You need to leave your husband, Lilah, and your room is standing empty." Still, she says nothing. "I can try to be nice. I know how to make soup." She doesn't crack a smile. I walk down the fence a few feet, open the gate. "Okay. Maybe not today. I'll leave it empty, you understand? As long as it takes. I'm not Mirabelle, looking for a herd of lost sheep. I'm saying that the room belongs to you. It will always be ready for you. Clean sheets and empty drawers for your pajamas. Just yours."

She looks away, a shy gesture, as if she is not sure what the right answer is. I walk away, across the yard. Parker has gone inside. I am not even back to the porch steps when I hear the gate closing. I turn around, and Lilah is inside it. I grin at her and wait at the steps. We go inside together.

"I'm real tired," she says.

"Go on up, then," I say. "My stuff is in Mirabelle's old room, if you want to borrow a nightie. Borrow anything you like. Tomorrow, we'll start making plans."

She hesitates, but only for a moment, and then she goes on up the stairs. I wonder if it will bother her to find I've moved all the furniture in her room around.

I stand in what is still my mother's downstairs. I've taken her palm reader's sign down, but I still need to clear out her store. I'll pack away the inventory or maybe have a mystical garage sale. This very week, I will put in a full-size sofa, paint the kitchen red, and buy a television and a radio to break the over-Zenned silence. Then it will be my apartment, and that's as far as I have gotten. There will be time for plans tomorrow, like I said to Lilah, and more time the day after that.

I go upstairs and undress, pulling on a clean T-shirt. It is strange to sleep alone in a queen-size bed after years of marriage. My mother has a puffy duvet, very snuggly, and I call Gret up from the foot and let her under. I feel like a little girl, tucked into my mother's bedding with an illicit dog. Her rule was always that Leroy could sleep with me, but not under the covers.

Down the hall, Lilah is tucked safe into a child's bed. For now, anyway. For tonight.

I wonder who we'll both grow up to be.

READING GROUP GUIDE

Rose Mae Rambles

I always said that I would never write a sequel. My feeling is, if you are a character who arrives whole at the end of one of my novels, you have earned the right for me to leave you alone. My characters shoot each other and whang each other in the head with tequila bottles and blow up whole, small towns. While I do not always have perfectly happy endings, I strive for hopeful ones, and I don't want to break whatever peace I have crafted by going back into these characters' lives and setting them on fire all over again. Sequels require turmoil; no one wants to read a sequel about happy people who pet the cat and plant a garden and smile at each other over a nice baked chicken supper. A good life and a good book are not the same thing.

In 1996, I wrote a short story called "Little Dead Uglies" that was published in *TriQuarterly* magazine; you can find it on my website. Arlene Fleet, the narrator of *gods in Alabama*, appears very briefly. She's set dressing at a family reunion presided over by her racist grampa, and she's brought her black boyfriend. The natural assumption is that she brought him so she could stick him right up her grampa's nose.

But her body language is wrong for that. She is nervous and huddled in on herself, chain smoking. I realized that she must love him, and she knows he is not going to go over well with a family that she loves, too, no matter how abhorrent she might find their world view. I also thought she might be carrying a whopping great secret, and I wondered if she was nervous because the lies she'd told her boyfriend and her family wouldn't match. Maybe if her boyfriend and her family did miraculously come to get along, the truth would get out?

Whenever I had one martini too many—and I was in my twenties so let's calculate this as "frequently" and say no more about it—I would pontificate about this girl in "Little Dead Uglies." When I got down to the olives, I would tell anyone who would listen, "If I ever figure out that girl, I'm gonna write about her. Wait and see." It would take years for that girl and her secret to grow into my debut novel. I was genuinely surprised when it all came together in my head and I started writing it instead of just drinking and talking about it.

I had never had that experience before: a character from one story feeling as loud, if not louder than the main character. And I never did again, until I started writing Rose Mae Lolley.

Rose began in *gods in Alabama* as a nameless, faceless plot device I thought of as "Jim Beverly's girlfriend." I didn't write a word about her until I was drafting chapter eight. But within three pages, she had taken the whole chapter over. Arlene mirrored my obsession for her, and began following her all over Fruiton High School, trying to figure out the slow-floating, beautiful, unreadable, and untouchable cipher that was Rose. At one point, Rose Mae hid between some lockers and popped out, ambushing her stalker. Arlene says, "She hissed at me, letting her breath out between her teeth like a cat, and looked me up and down. She said, in a fierce whisper, 'Quit following me, you little freak.' Then she pinched me as hard as she could with her dry, baby fingers, turned her back on me, and stalked off. I had a purple and yellow bruise on my arm for days, shaped and colored like a pansy."

Writing that moment, I realized Rose Mae had a secret, too, and she didn't want Arlene following her and figuring it out.

That meeting also spawned of all kinds of late-book mayhem,

almost without Rose being aware of it. Trouble seemed to love her, and I suspected that under her drifty, boy-magnet exterior, Rose loved trouble right back. That was when I knew I had to rewrite the opening of *gods in Alabama*. If trouble is what makes a novel interesting, then Rose needed to be present in chapter one. I let her show up there, and sure enough, she upped the stakes immediately, sending Arlene careening out of her comfortable life and back to all the secrets she thought she'd left safely buried in the kudzu.

After *gods* came out, it was readers who kept Rose alive for me. I got a ton of mail asking about her, and she was always a hot topic when I spoke at libraries and bookstores. Most of the questions were about Rose Mae's relationship with her father and with Jim. My standard answer was that since *gods in Alabama* is written in first person, I can't know anything that Arlene doesn't know. Arlene only knows what she sees, from the outside of Rose's life, so I wasn't sure. I told everyone who asked that they could decide for themselves and left it at that.

One night, I had a conference call with a book club, and as was often the case, they wanted to talk about Rose Mae. One woman phrased her question in a way that I had never heard before. She didn't ask about Rose's complicated relationships with men or even her relationship with Arlene. She simply asked if I thought Rose Mae was telling the truth.

That night, I woke up in the small hours of the morning and couldn't get back to sleep. That question was ringing in my head. When Rose shows up, she tells Arlene she is looking for Jim Beverly because he is the only man who has ever treated her right. I had always assumed that she *was* telling the truth, but looking at her past and her present, examining the girl she was and the woman she becomes, I suddenly understood: Rose Mae was an exceptional liar. Good enough to fool even me, the person who had made her up.

I shook my husband awake. "Scott!" I said, "Scott, guess what! Everything Rose Mae says to Arlene in *gods in Alabama* is a big fat lie. And I just realized—I know why she is really looking for Jim Beverly! It's all there!"

He cocked one eyebrow at me and said, "Hi, honey! It's three in the morning."

I let him go back to sleep, but I got up and started writing. Not a sequel, I knew immediately. It would be Rose Mae's own story, running parallel to Arlene's and using the same time line.

Counting back, I wrote *gods in Alabama* seven years after "Little Dead Uglies," and then it took about seven years more for Rose Mae to get so loud in my head that I had to write about her. It makes me wonder if this chain will keep on going. Maybe, in 2017 or so, I'll be getting ready for the launch of a book about Allswan, the braless Berkeley librarian with her chain of bird tattoos. Or perhaps a reader will ask in exactly the right way what happened to Lilah after she stops mooning on the fence, and it will make me want to know, too. I hope so, anyway.

Rose Mae's Reading List

I have always been an avid reader, and my written vocabulary was always much wider than my speaking one. Growing up in the rural South, I knew how to use words like "epitome," but I had no idea how to pronounce them. I went around saying "eppy-tome" until I heard a professor read the word aloud, at which point I promptly died of embarrassment, thinking of how many times I said that word incorrectly over the last decade . . .

Rose Mae Lolley has a wide vocabulary for a girl who dropped out of high school, and this is entirely due to her love of reading. Here is a partial list of the books Rose reads, mentions, or runs across in her journey. Her favorites are—of course!—mine as well; I love sneaking in references to the books and authors who made me want to be a writer.

A Good Man is Hard to Find and Other Stories by Flannery O'Connor

O'Connor is probably my favorite writer, and indeed, Rose is Catholic partly as an homage to her. When I began drafting the book, I wanted Rose Mae to grow up isolated, so I made her mother an agnostic. In rural Alabama, the church is the social center and almost everyone is either a Baptist or a Methodist. Being unchurched gave Rose Mae a lonely childhood and left her open to Jim Beverly's strange friendship. But early in the novel, Rose Mae quoted a piece of The Misfit's dialog from the title story in this collection. I realized Rose had to be Catholic, just as Flannery O'Connor was. Still isolated, Rose became both haunted and protected by Saints, while her mother's Catholicism devolved in into Mirabelle's hoodoo-influenced spiritualism.

A Prayer for Owen Meany by John Irving

Easily my favorite of the great John Irving's many brilliant works, I thought it was a perfect choice for a conservative Baptist book club who might read the first line and be tricked into picking it. It reads, "I am doomed to remember a boy with a wrecked voice—not because of his voice, or because he was the smallest person I ever knew, or even because he was the instrument of my mother's death, but because he is the reason I believe in God; I am a Christian because of Owen Meany." I agree wholeheartedly with Mrs. Fancy's assessment: "That book has a lot of God in it, but it was quite dirty." I too cannot help but remember that boy with the ruined voice, and he makes Irving's earthy mediations on fate and will endlessly fascinating.

The Bean Trees by Barbara Kingsolver

This was the first Kingsolver I ever read. I was a freshman in college, and I was browsing around in my local mall's Walden Books when the cover caught my eye. I picked it up and read that great opening sentence about the narrator's fear of exploding tires. I immediately took it to the register and bought it, and I've been an avid fan of hers ever since. This book and *Owen Meany* are the reasons I spend so many hours noodling around with my opening lines; they both have immediately compelling voices and a kind of instant narrative drive that I aspire to capture in my first sentences.

Watership Down by Richard Adams

I first read this book when I was nine, the same year I read *To Kill a Mockingbird*, and I have reread these two novels more times in my life than any other. It purports to be an adventure story about rabbits trying to find a new home, but it speaks to the human condition in huge, loud ways. It has never failed to bring me to tears, and it's also entertaining as all get-out. I especially admire the way Adams created and incorporated a rabbit pantheon and mythology. This book also appears (and indeed, plays a significant role) in my third novel, *The Girl Who Stopped Swimming*.

Persuasion and *Sense and Sensibility* by Jane Austen

I reread all of Austen, including *Lady Susan* and her partial manuscripts, about every three or four years. *Persuasion* is probably my favorite Austen novel, and *Sense and Sensibility* was the first Austen I ever read. As I child, I thought they were sugary, delicious love stories. As an adult, I reread them mainly for the black-hearted, chewy humor and adroit social commentary. But yeah, I still like the love story parts, too.

The Eyes of the Dragon by Stephen King

Mirabelle's airport book is a longtime favorite of mine from a writer I have admired since my brother hooked me up with *Salem's Lot* when I was about ten. "Don't tell Mom and Dad I gave you this," he said, so I read it on the sly, flashlight-under-the-comforter style. I blame both my continuing love of King and my lifelong battle with insomnia on this experience. In middle school, I bought blank books and filled them up with truly deplorable knock-off King-style horror novels, such as *Don't Go Into the Woods*. In that book, cheerleader after cheerleader goes into the woods after specifically and exhaustively being told not to go. There they find a magical silvery dome filled with whatever they fear most—including mummies, giant squids, and carnivorous sentient designer jeans that work like fashionable Venus Flytraps—all with one thing in common: an insatiable hunger for busty blonde dinners, hold the pompons.

Just So Stories for Little Children by Rudyard Kipling

My mother used to read some of these stories aloud to me when I was little, and I imagine Rose Mae's mother did the same. I forgot about them until grad school, when I ran across them in the school library. I read them for myself for the first time, shocked to find out how many my mother had skipped or expurgated to avoid feeding me the racism inherent in many of these tales from 1902. Kipling addresses these stories to his Best Beloveds; I have stolen that term and apply it to the regulars who hang out on my author blog, Faster Than Kudzu.

The Tale of Mrs. Tiggy-Winkle by Beatrix Potter and
The Complete Grimm's Fairy Tales by The Brothers Grimm

Two more books Rose Mae's mother read to her. My mother read all of Beatrix Potter to me, as well, but I had to find the Grimm Brothers on my own. Rose has a twisty inner landscape, so I wanted her to remember all the details of the Grimm's tale she paraphrases, down to the exact words of the poem Rose Red and Snow White chant to the bear prince. Meanwhile, she gets the cheery Mrs. Tiggy Winkle's name wrong. I am not sure more than three readers will notice this, but it pleases me inordinately.

Discussion Questions

1. In the first chapter of the book, Ro says about Rose Mae that she was "a girl I buried years ago." How distinct are these two facets of Ro's persona? Is it helpful or harmful for her to try to keep her two—and later, three—"identities" separate?

2. Rose Mae's mother has been flying to Amarillo and stalking Rose for years before Rose finally catches her at it in the airport. Do you think Claire allows herself to be seen, or is it an accident?

3. Ro feels she is complicit in the violence Thom subjects her to. Is this possible? What role do you think her father's actions against her—and her mother—play in her current marital situation?

4. Think about Rose Mae's houses throughout the book: Thom Grandee's house in Texas, Gene Lolley's house in Alabama, her mother's house in California. Does Rose consider any of these places *home*? What would it take for Rose to be truly at home, and do you think she finds one, or ever will?

5. Ro discovers her mother has changed her name just as she herself has. What does a name change really do to each woman's identity? What does Mirabelle's refusal to call her daughter

Ivy mean? Are their intentions in shedding their old identities the same, and are either successful in accomplishing this? What do you think Jackson is saying about names and identities in this book?

6. What is the significance of the "backseat saints"? How do you explain or discount their existence here?

7. What does it say about Mirabelle that she reads people's futures for a living? Why do you think she chose this line of work? How does she reconcile this talent for foretelling with her past? Does Rose believe in the tarot cards? Do you? Why or why not?

8. When Rose Mae comes up with the idea that Jim Beverly will save her, do you believe that he can? Do you think she could have left Thom without the potential of Jim's saving her? What do you think the inability to find Jim did to alter her perspective?

9. A haircut is a powerful tool for change—what did it signify for Rose? Does an external change often bring about internal change? Have you ever wished for—or had—such a transformation? What were the effects?

10. Mrs. Fancy and Ro have a unique bond that deepens as they find out more about each others' lives. Do you think Mrs. Fancy was drawn to Ro as a way to make up for her daughter's troubles? Do you think Ro was actively seeking a mother figure in Mrs. Fancy? How has their relationship helped and hindered each woman?

11. One of the novel's central themes is forgiveness. Who has the most difficulty forgiving, and is this legitimate? Who in this book most deserves forgiveness, in your opinion, and why?

12. Rose Mae brings only her trusted dog, Gretel, with her from Texas on her travels. She also meets and befriends Parker's dogs in California. What is the significance of the company of animals here? What role do Parker's dogs have in allowing her to trust their owner?

13. When Rose is first interested in Parker, she reverts to the only mode of male interaction she knows—flirtation. Why is this such a dangerous instinct for her? Do you think she is able to break herself of this habit in the end?

14. Many characters in this book are overly attached to, or "stuck" in, the past. Consider Rose Mae's unchanged childhood room in Gene's second house, and in her mother's house in California, for example. What do you think this says about the Lolley family, or about Southern culture? Of what in your life have you had difficulty letting go?

15. What do you think of the manner in which Mirabelle went about saving Rose Mae? Do you think she had a choice in killing Thom? Was she wrong or right to do so, and why? Is her punishment justified?

More sparkling dialogue, unpredictable plot twists—
and the first appearance of Rose Mae Lolley—
from *New York Times* bestselling author
Joshilyn Jackson.

Turn this page for the first chapter of

gods in Alabama,

the debut novel of this "enormously gifted writer."*

*Anne Rivers Siddons

gods in Alabama

❧

CHAPTER I

There are gods in Alabama: Jack Daniel's, high school quarterbacks, trucks, big tits, and also Jesus. I left one back there myself, back in Possett. I kicked it under the kudzu and left it to the roaches.

I made a deal with God two years before I left there. At the time, I thought He made out pretty well. I offered Him a three-for-one-deal: All He had to do was perform a miracle. He fulfilled His end of the bargain, so I kept my three promises faithfully, no matter what the cost. I held our deal as sacred for twelve solid years. But that was before God let Rose Mae Lolley show up on my doorstep, dragging my ghosts and her own considerable baggage with her.

It was the week before summer vacation began, and my uncle Bruster was getting ready to retire. He'd been schlepping the mail up and down Route 19 for thirty years and now, finally, he was going to get a gold watch, a shitty pension, and the federal government's official permission to die. His retirement party was looming, and my aunt Florence was using it as the catalyst for her latest campaign to get me home. She launched these crusades three or four times a year, usually prompted by major holidays or family events.

I had already explained multiple times to Mama that I wasn't coming. I shouldn't have had to explain it at all. I had not gone back to Possett since I graduated from high school in '87. I had stayed in Chicago for nine Christmas vacations, had not come home for nine spring breaks, had faithfully signed up to take or teach classes every summer quarter for ten years. I had avoided weekend fly-downs for the births, graduation ceremonies, and weddings of various cousins and second cousins. I had even claimed exemption from attending the funerals of my asshole grampa and his wife, Saint Granny.

At this point, I figured I had firmly established that I would not be coming home, even if all of Chicago was scheduled to be consumed by the holy flames of a vengeful Old Testament–style Lord. "Thanks for the invite, Mama," I would say, "but I have plans to be burned up in a fire that weekend." Mama, however, could wipe a conversation out of her mind an infinite number of times and come back to the topic fresh as a daisy the next time we spoke.

Burr had his feet propped up on my battered coffee table and was reading a legal thriller he had picked up at the grocery store. In between an early movie and a late supper, we had dropped by my place to intercept Florence's eight o'clock call. Missing it was not an option. I called Aunt Florence every Sunday after church, and every Wednesday night, Flo parked my mother by the phone and dialed my number. I wouldn't put it past Florence to hire a team of redneck ninjas to fly up to Chicago and take me down if she ever got my answering machine.

Florence had not yet mentioned my uncle's retirement to me directly, although she had prepped Mama to ask me if I was coming home for it through six weeks' worth of calls now. With only ten days left before the party, it was time for Aunt Florence to personally enter the fray. Mama was so malleable she was practically an invertebrate, but Florence had giant man hands on the ends of her bony wrists, and she could squeeze me with them till I couldn't get any breath to say no. Even over the phone she could do it.

Burr watched me over the top of his book as I paced the room. I was too nervous about my upcoming martyrdom on the stainless-steel cross of Florence to sit down with him. He was sunk hip deep into my sofa. My apartment was decorated in garage-sale chic, the default decorating choice for every graduate student. The sofa had curlicues of moss-colored velvet running all over its sage-green hide, and it was so deflated and aslant that Burr swore he only ever kissed me the first time because of it. We sat down on it at the same time, and it sucked us down and pressed us up against each other in its sagging middle. He had to kiss me, he claimed, to be polite.

"About how long do you think this is going to take?" Burr asked now. "I'm starving."

I shrugged. "Just the usual Wednesday-night conversation with Mama."

"Okay," said Burr.

"And then I have to have a fight with Aunt Florence about whether or not I'm going down for Uncle Bruster's party."

"In that case," said Burr, and he levered himself out of the depths of the sofa and walked the five steps to my kitchenette. He opened the cabinet and started rummaging around for something to tide himself over.

"It's not going to take that long," I said.

"Sure, baby," he said, and took a pack of peanut-butter crackers back over to the sofa. He sat down with his book but didn't open it for a moment. "Try to keep it under four hours," he said. "I need to talk to you about something at dinner."

I stopped pacing around. "Is it bad?" I asked, nervous because he'd said it in such a serious tone of voice. He could mean he wanted to break up again or he could mean he was going to propose to me. We'd broken up last year over Christmas and both hated it so much that we'd found ourselves drifting back together casually, without even really talking about it. We'd been coasting along easy for a few months now, but Burr would not coast forever. We had to be going somewhere, and if he thought we weren't, then that would be it for him.

I said, "You know I hate that. You have to give me a hint."

Burr grinned at me, and his brown eyes were warm. "Don't panic."

"Okay," I said. I felt something flutter down low in my stomach, excitement or fear, I wasn't sure which, and then the phone rang.

"Dammit," I said. The phone was on a crate full of books at the other end of the ugly sofa. I sat down next to Burr and picked it up. "Hello?"

"Arlene, honey! You remember Clarice?"

Clarice was my first cousin, and we were raised in the same house, practically as sisters. Mama was possibly the only person on earth who could have asked this question sans sarcasm to a daughter who had not been home in almost a decade. Aunt Florence would have gotten a lot of miles out of it, and in fact I couldn't help but wonder if Aunt Florence hadn't somehow planted the question in the fertile minefields of my mother's mind.

It was not unlike the Christmas card Mama had sent me for the last five years. It had a red phone on it, and it said, in bright red curling text, "Daughter! Do you remember that man I introduced you to the day you were born? Why don't you give him a call? I know he never hears from you, and today's his birthday." Open it up and there, in giant candy-striped letters, was a one-word explanation for the terminally stupid: "Jesus," it said. Three exclamation points.

Mama got those abominations from the Baptist Women's League for Plaguing Your Own Children to Death in the Name of the Lord or whatever her service club was called. My aunt Florence was, of course, the president. And my aunt Florence, of course, bought Mama's cards for her, held them out for her to sign, licked the envelopes, got stamps from Uncle Bruster, and mailed them for her. In Florence's eyes, I was on the high road to apostasy because my church was American Baptist, not Southern Baptist.

But all I said was "Obviously I know Clarice, Mama."

"Well, Clarice wants to know if you can drive over to the home and pick up your great-great-aunt Mag on Friday next. Mag needs someone to carry her over to the Quincy's for your uncle Bruster's party."

I said, "Are you seriously telling me that Clarice wants to know if I'll drive fourteen hours down from Chicago, and then go another hour to Vinegar Park, where by the way Clarice lives, and pick up Aunt Mag, who will no doubt piss in my rental car, and then backtrack forty-five minutes to Quincy's?"

"Yes, but please don't say 'piss,' it isn't nice," my mother said, deadly earnest. "Also, Clarice and Bud moved on in to Fruiton. So it's a good forty minutes for her to go get Mag now."

"Oh, well then. Why don't you tell Aunt Florence—I mean Clarice—that I will be sure to go pick up Mag. Right after Aunt Flo drops by hell and picks up the devil."

Burr was jammed deep into the sofa with his book open, but his eyes had stopped moving over the text. He was too busy trying to laugh silently without choking to death on his peanut-butter cracker.

"Arlene, I am not repeating blasphemy," said my mother mildly. "Florence can ask Fat Agnes to get Mag, and you can drive me."

Oh, Aunt Florence was crafty. Asking my mother to have this conversation with me was tantamount to taping a hair-trigger pistol to a kitten's paw. The kitten, quite naturally, shakes its fluffy leg, and bullets go flying everywhere; a few are bound to hit something. I was, after all, talking with my mama about whether or not I would pick up Mag, not whether or not I was coming. A cheap trap worthy of Burr's legal thriller, and I had bounced right into it.

"I can't drive you, Mama," I said gently. Why shoot the messenger? "I won't be there."

"Oh, Arleney," my mother said, sounding vaguely sad. "Aren't you ever coming home for a visit?"

"Not this time, Mama," I said.

Mama made a pensive little noise and then said, in a cheerier voice, "Oh well, I will just look double forward to Christmas, then!" That I hadn't been home for the last nine Christmases was not a factor in Mama's fogbound equations. Before I could even try a quick "Love you, bye" and escape, I heard Aunt Florence's voice barking in the background, and then Mama said, "Here's Aunt Flo's turn!"

I heard the rustle of the phone changing hands, and then Aunt Florence's muffled voice asking Mama to please go check the Bundt cake. There was a brief pause where my mother presumably wafted out of the room, and then Aunt Florence took her hand off the mouthpiece and said in a disarmingly affectionate tone, "Hello, serpent."

"Hi, Aunt Florence," I said.

"Do you know why I am calling you 'serpent,' serpent?"

"I couldn't begin to guess, Aunt Florence," I said.

"I am referencing a Bible verse. Do they have the Bible at that American Baptist church?"

"I believe I may have seen one there once," I said. "No doubt it fled the moment it realized where it was. As I recall, it had a lot of serpents in it, and I am sure I could justly be called many of them."

Burr was still amused. I busted him looking at me, and I gestured at his book. He stifled his grin and turned his eyes virtuously back to the pages.

Aunt Florence, adopting a low and holy voice, intoned, "How like a serpent you have nestled to your bosom is a thankless child."

"That's not the Bible, Aunt Florence. You're misquoting *King Lear*."

"Do you realize that the women in our service group at church all sit around nattering like biddy hens about what horrors your poor mama—and me—must have inflicted on your head to make her only girl-child flee the state, never to return? Do you realize the vicious things those biddies say about your poor, poor mama? And me?"

"No, Aunt Florence, I didn't realize," I said, but Aunt Florence wasn't listening. She barked on and on into my ear, etc. etc. you-a culpa with breast beating and a side of guilt. Who did I think had put bread in my mouth? Uncle Bruster and his mail route. And now all he wanted was for his family to gather and eat buffet dinner at the Quincy's in his honor. I countered by asking Florence to please pass Bruster the phone so I could tell him how proud of him I was right this second.

Florence wasn't about to give up the phone, not even to her husband. She shifted gears abruptly, dropping her voice to a reverent whisper as she segued into the "Your mama will probably be dead by next year" theme, asking sorrowfully how I would feel if I missed this last chance to see her. I pointed out that she'd used that argument for nine years running and Mama hadn't died yet.

Burr set his book down and reached across me to grab the pad and pencil I kept on the crate by the phone. He scrawled something down on the top page and then tore it off and passed it to me. The note said "Say yes to the trip and let's go eat."

I crumpled it up and bounced it off his chest, sticking my tongue out at him.

"You don't know how bad off she is, Arlene," Florence said. "She's failing bad. She looks like the walking dead. She's been to the hospital to stay twice this year."

"The real hospital?" I said. "Or the place in Deer Park?"

"It's a real hospital," said Florence defensively.

"Real hospitals don't have padded walls in the card room," I countered. Burr uncrumpled the piece of paper and held it up like a sign, pointing to the words one at a time, in order. I shook my head at him and then dropped my head forward to hide behind my long dark hair. "It isn't just that I am not coming. I can't come. I don't have the money to make the trip down right this second."

I peeked up at Burr. He narrowed his eyes at me and touched two fingers to his chin. This was code, lifted from his mock-trial days back in law school. It meant "I am in possession of two contradictory facts." I knew what he was referencing. Fact one: Burr knew that as of last week I had almost three thousand in savings. Fact two: Burr knew I didn't tell lies. Ever. I pointed at him, then touched my chin with one finger, signaling that there was no paradox; one of his facts was off.

Aunt Florence talked about wire transfers and loans and me getting off my butt and taking a part-time job while Burr thought it through. After a moment a light dawned, and he got up and walked towards my front door, looking at me with his eyebrows raised. I braced the phone against my shoulder and clutched my arms around my middle, pantomiming that I was freezing. I realized there was silence on the other end of the line, and I hurried to fill it.

"Aunt Florence, you know I won't take your money—"

"Oh no, just the food off my table and a bed in my house your whole childhood."

Burr reversed direction and went to my kitchenette. I pretended I was even colder, wrapping an imaginary blanket around myself.

"The school pays me a stipend and a housing allowance, plus my tuition," I said into the phone. "It's not like I'm on welfare."

Burr walked the four steps past my kitchenette, back to the doorway into the walk-in closet my Yankee landlord called a bedroom. I mopped imaginary sweat from my brow and threw the invisible blanket off, then fanned myself. He disappeared through the doorway, and I could hear him rummaging around, feet padding on the scuffed hardwood as he searched.

"No," I said into the phone, "I don't think this rates a special collection at church."

But maybe it did. Florence was getting to me a little. She always could. I thought of my uncle Bruster, with his wispy blond tufts combed over his bald spot, his big belly, his broad sloping shoulders. Bruster looked like what would happen if the bear got over on the mountain and they had a baby. He had the Lukey blue eyes, large and powder blue and a little moist-looking, and when I was eleven, he had been my date to the Possett First Baptist Father-Daughter Pancake Brunch. Clarice had been on his other arm, but he had pulled out my chair for me and called me Little Lady all morning.

I heard my closet door squeak open, and then a pause that Florence filled with alternating sentiment and invective. The closet door shut, and Burr came back in the room toting the Computer City bag with my new laptop in it. He pantomimed a whistle, looking impressed, but I didn't believe it. Something else was going on in his head as he stared down at the laptop in its bag. I couldn't tell what he was thinking.

Burr was a good lawyer and an even better poker player. He and I used to play a card game we made up called Five-Card Minor Sexual Favor Stud, but I quit for two reasons. One, it led us too far down a path that could only end in frustration and a whomping great fight. And two, he almost always won.

Burr sat back down and put the bag on the coffee table. He picked up his book again, but he wasn't reading, and he wouldn't meet my eyes.

Eventually, against all odds, Aunt Florence got to the part where she told me she would be praying to God, asking Him to help me not be such a selfish little turd. Then she let me get off the phone. I gave her a vague promise about taking a hard look at my summer course schedule and seeing if I could squeeze in a trip home sometime before fall. Aunt Florence's final skeptical snort was still ringing in my ears as I hung up.

"That's a speedy machine," Burr said casually, indicating the bag. "You really are broke."

"Yup," I said. I had cleaned myself out to buy it. In fact, I bought it to clean myself out.

"Lucky I'm not," said Burr.

"Very lucky, since you're taking me to dinner," I said. I got up, but Burr stayed wedged down in the sofa.

"That's not what I meant," he said. "Lena, remember I said I wanted to talk to you about something at dinner?"

"Yes?" I said, and all at once the flutter was back. I was standing up, already looking down at him. I was wondering if there was room between the sofa and the coffee table for him to slide down onto one knee, or if I should move out from behind the coffee table to give him space.

"I think I better ask you now," he said, and his dark eyes were very serious. Burr had nice eyes, but they were small and square. I never noticed how sweet they were until I got close enough to kiss him. His face wasn't about his eyes. It was about his cheekbones and his sharply narrow jaw, severe enough to contrast with his wide, soft mouth, with the gorgeous teeth his mama paid eight thousand dollars to straighten. "I'm a little nervous."

"You don't have to be nervous," I said, but I was nervous as all hell.

"Take your aunt Florence out of the equation, and your mama. Take everything out of the equation but you and me. If I said it was important to me, would you take the trip down to Alabama for this party next week?" Burr asked.

I sat down again abruptly. "What?" I said.

"I can pay for the trip."

"I can't let you pay for me to go down and see my family," I said.

"I wouldn't be," he said. "I would be paying for both of us to make the trip."

"I can't let you do that, either," I said.

"Can't or won't?" he said. He was smiling, but I could read him now, and underneath the smile he was angry.

"Won't," I agreed. There is a big, fat downside to never telling a lie.

"Don't worry," Burr said, gesturing at the laptop, still smiling his beautiful, angry smile. "Computer City has a ten-day no-questions return policy." He stood up and stalked around the coffee table away from me. "Because obviously you have no intention of keeping this thing."

"No, of course not," I agreed. And immediately the words "There are gods in Alabama" rolled through my head so powerfully that I thought I was going to say them aloud, but Burr stopped them by speaking again.

"Lena, if you won't take me down and introduce me to your family, we're coming to a dead end."

"But I love you," I said. It came out flat and wrong, though I was remembering how it was with us when we made out on the sofa in the late nights when Burr came over after I'd studied myself sick. I was thinking of how we were together when his huge hands were on me, and we both knew the rules.

His hands were so big, Burr could practically span my waist with them. And he had a jet-rocket metabolism, so his skin was always liquid hot to the touch. His big hands would slide over my body, slipping up or down into forbidden zones. As he touched me, I could see in my mind the flex of the muscles, how the dim light would reflect on the shifting planes of his hands as they moved on me. And I could take my hand and push that big hand away, down off my breasts, onto my waist. Guide it so slowly out from between my legs onto my thigh. His hands always went where mine told them to go, immediately, no matter what. The power of that, the ability or maybe the permission to move something so much stronger than me, left me light-headed and feeling something I couldn't name, but it was close kin to longing. Eventually I would have to shove him away, push him out the door with hasty little kisses, both of us dying of wanting to and not, both of us laughing.

Burr said, "You say that a lot." He was standing by the front door, looking at a point somewhere just over my left shoulder. He sometimes did that when he was ticked off, carry on a fight while peering moodily off at the horizon, as brooding and ugly-beautiful as Heathcliff thinking, "Oh! The moors! The moors!"

I said, "If I didn't love you, I wouldn't say it at all. You know I don't lie."

"There are a lot of things you say you don't do, Lena," he answered. "You don't lie, and you don't fuck, and you don't take your boyfriend home to meet your family. You say you love me, but you have a hundred ways to avoid the truth without ever lying." He pointed at the laptop on the table. "Case in point. Today you tell your aunt that you're broke, and tomorrow you return that and get your money back. And that's what you call telling the truth."

"No, it's what I call not lying. There is a difference, you know. I am not under any obligation to tell anyone everything. I just don't lie, which is more than ninety percent of the freakin' world can say, and anyway, why are we having this fight? Why did you this minute decide I need to take you to my uncle's retirement party? That's not what I thought you were going to ask me."

Burr said, "Maybe it's not what I planned to ask you, either. But Lena, I watched you work your aunt over, and I found myself wondering—not for the first time—how often you work me, to keep me out of the middle of your life."

"First of all, Possett, Alabama, is not the middle of my life. It is not my home. It's the fourth rack of hell. I don't go there myself, let alone want to take you—"

"Look at your phone bill," Burr said.

"And second of all," I went on as if he had not spoken, "I don't see the connection between not having sex with you and taking you to Alabama."

"It's what women do when they fall in love with a man," Burr said. "They have sex with him, or they take him home to meet their family. In point of fact, Lena, most women do both."

"But my family is insane," I said in what I hoped was a reasonable tone. "Why would you want to meet them?"

"Because they're yours," he said matter-of-factly, one hand reaching for the doorknob. "I thought you were mine."

I was instantly furious. It was too good a line, a movie line. People don't get to say smashing things and then walk out in real life. Burr could say crap like that more often than most because of his low-slung basso profundo voice. He could say hyper-dramatic lines that, if I said them, would have whole crowds rolling on the floor, shrieking with laughter and telling me to get over myself. But Burr? He could say "Luke, I am your father," and get away with it.

But not with me.

"Don't you dare try to Rhett Butler your way out the door in the middle of a fight," I said, getting up and coming around the coffee table after him.

He let go of the doorknob and said, "You've never so much as mentioned my name to your folks, but you spend half your free time at my mama's house. You won't be my lover, but you can't keep your hands off me until I'm clinically insane. I'm a twenty-nine-year-old man, Lena. Not some fifteen-year-old kid who says he loves you in the hopes of seeing his first tit."

I said, "It isn't that I don't love you. But I swear before God, you don't want to make this trip. It would be like stepping into a soap opera, except no one is beautiful or rich or interesting. If we went down there, you have to know what it would be like. I mean, come on, Burr, what do you see when you look at us?"

Burr said, "I always saw the best couple going. The question is, what do you see?"

"Same thing," I said. "But that is not what they are going to see down in Possett, Alabama. They'll look at me and see that weird Arlene Fleet who was never any better than she should be, and when they look at you, they'll see that nigger she's fucking."

Burr smiled a little and said, "But I'm not fucking you."

"Well, we could maybe get you a T-shirt that says you aren't, but they wouldn't believe it, because why else would I be with you? It can't be that you're smart, or handsome, or interesting, or successful, because you can't be any of those things when you're in Possett, Alabama. You will be much too busy being black. When you're with my family, being black is such a big job, it takes up your entire definition. You don't get to be anything else.

"If I show up home, wanting to bring my black boyfriend to my uncle Bruster's good-ol'-boy retirement party, they're going to take that as personal. Like I got a black boyfriend specifically to use as spit for their soup.

"And maybe then you'll get it in your thick man head that I picked you because you're black and that's a button I can push. I mean, a girl doesn't go home for ten years, you have to guess she has some issues with her family. But that's not why at all. I picked you because you're you, and you're perfect for me, and because I'm so in love with you."

Burr said, "I love you, too, Lena. But I'm done being played."

I said, "What does that mean? You're giving me an ultimatum? 'Fuck me or lose me'? Because that sucks, Burr."

"Don't misunderstand me," he said, his voice rising. "Don't make this about me trying to get over on you. I've never pressured you that way. And yeah, obviously I want to have sex with you, but that's not what I'm saying here. I'm asking you to introduce me to your family. That's all. I'm asking for a commitment, Lena. We've been together two years now."

"On and off," I said.

"Mostly on."

He reached for the doorknob again, and I said, "Don't you dare walk out on me in the middle of a fight." I was so angry, I was practically screaming. "I mean it, don't you do it." He paused for a second, but then he flipped the dead bolt.

The door seemed to catch in the frame, so he gave it an angry shove. It swung open, knocking back a girl who was standing on the other side. She was so close she must have had her ear pressed up against the wood, and the force of Burr's exit spilled her all the way backwards onto her bottom.

"What the—" said Burr, and he stepped over the threshold towards her, already reaching down to help her up. She went scuttling backwards like a panicked crab. He stopped moving, and she bounced back to her feet, scrabbling frantically in her huge macramé purse. She was dressed like one of my students, in tight jeans and a peasant blouse, but I didn't recognize her. Her hand came out of her purse and up, holding a tiny spray can aimed at Burr's face.

"I heard you yelling," she said to me. She was breathing hard, but once on her feet, she seemed more exhilarated than frightened, taking a theatrical *Charlie's Angels* pose with the spray can.

"Whoa," Burr said. He put his hands up. "Calm down."

She didn't take her eyes off him, but she was talking to me. "You go for the soft parts," she said. "And then we run while he's down."

I realized I had put my hands up, too, instinctively. I dropped them and walked over beside Burr. "Are you all right?" I said to her. "It was an accident. We didn't know you were there. What on earth were you doing?"

"Lena, is this one of your students?" said Burr. He angled himself, trying to stay between me and the Mace, which was easy since she had it pointed aggressively at his face. She had her legs apart in a fighter's stance, and both her arms were fully extended, aiming the can like a gun.

"I don't think she's after me, Burr," I said, and because I was so angry, I couldn't help but be amused, watching this tiny girl hold him at bay. "Her problem's with you, looks like."

"I was just leaving," said Burr.

"Bet your ass you are," the girl said.

"He was only trying to help you up," I said to her, but she ignored me and kept the can trained on Burr.

Burr dropped his hands slowly and walked past her, and she turned in a circle, keeping him covered.

"We're not done with this conversation," I called after him.

"I am," he said and went on down the stairs.

I started after him, but the girl turned sideways and then stepped to block me. She whipped her head back and forth, trying to keep an eye on both of us.

"Excuse me," I said, but she ignored me. Burr turned the corner, and the moment he was out of sight, she faced me and dropped her arms, grinning triumphantly. "They're almost all sonsabitches."

At second glance, she was too old to be one of my students. I put her at about thirty. She was my size or maybe even a little shorter. I doubted she could claim five-one in bare feet. Her thick dark hair was cut in an aggressive bob, shorter in the back and angling down into two razor-sharp points on either side of her fiercely pretty face.

"We were only arguing," I said. "Excuse me, I need to catch him." I started after Burr, but she moved into my path, blocking me again. She still clutched the spray can.

She said, "If I had a dime for every time I said those words!"

"Put the Mace away," I said.

"Oh, right." She dropped it into her bag. "What timing, huh? I heard you yelling in there, and I was about to bust this door down and come in after you."

She said the word "you" as if it had a W on the end. It was pure Alabama. I forgot about going after Burr and stared at her, taking in her pointy face and the huge violet-blue eyes gazing out from between the sharp wings of her hair.

"Rose?" I said, but it simply couldn't be. The last time I'd seen Rose Mae Lolley, she'd had waist-length hair and had moved with the slow grace of an underwater ballerina on opium. The Rose Mae I knew and loathed years ago, back in Alabama, would never go leaping around wielding Mace in a Yankee stairwell. And she certainly wouldn't lower herself to speak to me.

But she was nodding and saying, "Can you believe it? I look different, huh? You don't. Not much, anyway. I mean, older, sure. But I knew in a glance I'd found Arlene Fleet. May I come in?"

"I don't think so," I said. I thought for one absurd moment that she had to be here on a mission from Aunt Flo, a tactical maneuver in the perpetual war to bring me home. Before I could stop myself, I found myself asking, "Who sent you? Was it Florence?"

Rose looked puzzled and said, "Florence? Oh! Mrs. Lukey? Clarice's mom? Lord, no, I haven't seen her in a dog's age. How is she doing?"

I boggled at her. "This isn't some sort of old-home week, Rose. I haven't seen you in ten years. I didn't even know if you were alive or dead, and quite frankly, I didn't much care. And now you are standing out in my stairwell, apparently eavesdropping on me and my boyfriend? It's none of your business how my family is. If Aunt Florence didn't send you as some form of torture, then how the hell did you even find me? What are you doing here? What do you want from me?"

She briefly looked nonplussed, but then she plastered a smile on her face and said, "Okay, Arlene. I guess you never were one for social graces. That's fine. It's kind of a long story, but if you want the short, standing-in-a-stairwell version, I can do that. I got in a fight with my therapist, and now I'm on a spiritual journey. Congratulations, you're my next stop."

I looked at her skeptically. "Is this about the retirement party?"

"No, I don't even know what that means. Surprisingly, everything in the world isn't all about you, Arlene. This is about me. I told you, I am trying to follow a path I've devised for my own spiritual development—"

I held up my hand to stop her talking and said, "If this is some sort of twelve-step thing, making amends or whatever, fine. I forgive you. Now I need to go catch Burr."

"Forgive me for what?" said Rose. We did a little three-step dance in the hallway as I tried to get around her, and she bounced back and forth from foot to foot, hair swinging, to stop me. "Wait, Arlene, one minute. I'm sorry I sounded snippy. I really do need your help. I'm only doing what you're trying to do. Going after the one that got away."

I stopped trying to get around her and eyed her warily. You can take the girl out of Alabama, but how do you stop Alabama from following you over a thousand miles to lay siege to your doorstep? I felt the beginnings of an old anger stirring; God was not supposed to let this happen. It was an unspoken part of the deal. I took a step back towards my open apartment door. "Whatever this is, it can't have anything to do with me," I said.

"But it does, indirectly. See, my therapist said I get crappy men because I go looking for them, not because men are mostly crappy." I took another step back, and she started talking faster, trying to make me hear her out. "She thinks I choose assholes because that's what I think I deserve, blah blah, masochism, blah blah, low self-esteem. You know how shrinks talk."

"No," I said pointedly. "I don't."

Rose looked skeptical. "With your mother? Come on. Anyway, she's wrong. I've been thinking through my romantic history, looking for a guy I picked who wasn't an asshole. If I can find just one, then my shrink is wrong and it isn't me, it's the men. And there is one, I know it. I remember. But I need you to help me find him."

"Find him?" I said. While she was talking, I continued to edge backwards. Rose followed me, step for step but with a longer stride, so she was now much too close to me. I could smell fruit gum on her breath, and her eyes held the fervid light of a convert.

"Yes. I have to find Jim Beverly," she said.

The last syllable had not cleared her lips before I was leaping wildly into my apartment. I slammed the door in her face and then shot the bolt and put the chain on. I couldn't breathe. I had not heard his name spoken aloud in ten years.

Outside, Rose Mae Lolley gave my door three sharp raps. "Arlene?" she called.

I bolted across the room to the boom box that was sitting by the sofa. I dug around in the box of jumbled CDs next to it, looking for something, anything, loud. I came up with the Clash. I had not noticed until I tried to get the CD out of the jewel box and load it into the player how violently my hands were shaking. All of me was shaking. My teeth were banging together as if I were freezing.

"Arlene? This is ridiculous. I need maybe five minutes of your time," Rose Mae Lolley called, kicking my door once for emphasis. At last I got the CD tray to slide home. I pumped the volume up to about six.

Rose gave the door a good pounding I could hear over "London Calling," so I upped the dial to eight, neighbors be damned. Then I sat on the floor with my arms at my sides, pressing my palms down against the cool hardwood while the first song played out. I wanted to go and look through the peephole, but I was afraid I would see her giant lavender eyeball peering in at me.

I cast about for something to distract myself. I had a stack of freshman world literature papers I needed to grade, but I wasn't in any shape to face the grammar. I also had three books I was reading in tandem, research for my dissertation, but my heart was pounding and I doubted I could concentrate. I felt like going to bed, or maybe crawling under it and never coming back out.

I noticed Burr had left his book behind, facedown on the arm of the sofa. The old cushion had a sinkhole in it where Burr had been. I wedged myself into his warmth and read, forcing myself to concentrate on the words, and not on whatever Alabama drama might be playing itself out in my hallway, or Aunt Florence's demands, or the fact that my boyfriend had just walked out on me, maybe for good this time.

It might have been easier if Burr had left a better book. He liked courtroom dramas, and he was the fastest reader I had ever seen. He ate text like pudding, no chewing, but he still managed to digest it. And these lawyer thrillers, he devoured two or three a weekend. In real life he was a tax attorney who wouldn't touch criminal law, but he loved the books. They ran the gamut from literature to penny dreadfuls. Burr didn't care about the quality. He ate them in bulk. If it had a lawyer protagonist, plot twists, and someone with big tits in jeopardy, he was all for it.

This was one of the bad ones. The prologue alone had a body count of seven. The bad guy had killed five of them. Because he was bad, his reaction was to laugh gleefully and dance in the mayhem. The young DA, backed into a corner and in the wrong place at the wrong time, whacked two people. Self-defense, of course. Because he was good, his reaction was to vomit and think deep thoughts along the lines of "Oh the humanity." Complete crap.

I've personally committed only one murder, but the truth is, it's not that simple. You can't tell whether you're the good guy or the bad guy based on whether you laugh or throw up. The truth is, I did both.

I read for as long as I could stand it before I reached down beside me and hit the pause button on the boom box. My ears rang in the sudden silence. I did not hear anything from the hallway. I threw Burr's book across the room. It smacked into the front door and bounced off to the floor. No reaction. Rose Mae Lolley was gone, for the moment.

I was still shaking. I wanted to pray, but I was too angry with God to concentrate. Ten years, ten years I had been faithful, and now God was breaking the deal.

Before I left Possett, I had promised God I would stop fucking every boy who crossed my path. (Although when actively involved in prayer I used the word "fornicating," as if this would spare God's delicate ears.) Now I was losing Burr over it. The truth was, I had worried that I was losing him for months, but still I had stayed faithful.

I had promised God I would never tell another lie, and I hadn't. Even when lying would make everything easy with Aunt Florence and my family, I had never let a word of untruth cross my lips.

Lastly, I had promised that if He would get me out safe, I would never go back to Possett, Alabama. Not for anything. I wouldn't even look back, lest I turn to salt.

And now God had allowed Possett, Alabama, to show up on my doorstep.

As far as I was concerned, all bets were off.